WHEN YOU ARE NEAR

Books by Tracie Peterson

*with Judith Miller **with Kimberley Woodhouse

For a complete list of titles, please visit www.traciepeterson.com

WHEN YOU ARE NEAR

TRACIE PETERSON

BETHANYHOUSE

a division of Baker Publishing Group
Minneapolis, Minnesota

Published by Bethany House Publishers
11400 Hampshire Avenue South
Bloomington, Minnesota 55438
www.bethanyhouse.com

Bethany House Publishers is a division of
Baker Publishing Group, Grand Rapids, Michigan

Printed in the United States of America

Library of Congress Cataloging-in-Publication Data

Names: Peterson, Tracie, author.
Title: When you are near / Tracie Peterson.
Description: Minneapolis, Minnesota : Bethany House Publishers, a division of
    Baker Publishing Group, [2019] | Series: Brookstone brides ; 1
Identifiers: LCCN 2018034300| ISBN 9780764219023 (trade paper) | ISBN
    9780764232879 (cloth) | ISBN 9780764232886 (large print) | ISBN
    9781493417223 (e-book)
Subjects: | GSAFD: Christian fiction. | Mystery fiction.
Classification: LCC PS3566.E7717 W48 2019 | DDC 813/.54—dc23
LC record available at https://lccn.loc.gov/2018034300

Scripture quotations are from the King James Version of the Bible.

Cover design by Jennifer Parker
Cover photography by Mike Habermann Photography, LLC

19 20 21 22 23 24 25   7 6 5 4 3 2 1

With thanks to Karen Vold and Linda Scholtz for your amazing insight and help with trick riding. It was so much fun to see the history you both have in trick riding and rodeo. Attending your clinic was so much fun and gave me a much better understanding and love for what you do.

Thanks too, to Amber Miller— another amazing trick rider who has answered my questions faithfully. I appreciate your patience and help.

"Come one, come all to the Brookstone Wild West Extravaganza—the only wild west show to give you all-female performers of extraordinary bravery and beauty! Women whose talent and proficiency will amaze and delight people of every age!"

⇥≒ ONE ≒⇤

Lizzy Brookstone sat atop her perfectly groomed horse, Long-fellow, and waited for her cue. The sleek Morgan-Quarter horse crossbreed was a dazzling buckskin with sooty dappling. Named for one of Lizzy's favorite poets, Longfellow was one of two buckskins she used for the wild west show her father and uncle had started back in 1893.

The horse did a nervous side step, and Lizzy gave him a pat. "Easy, boy. I'm just as anxious as you are, but you know the routine."

She glanced down at her prim English riding costume. The outfit had been created to break away easily, and under it was her basic performing costume—a comfortable split skirt tucked into knee-high boots to allow her a full range of motion. Under the restrictive lady's jacket, she wore a specially designed blouse that easily accommodated her acrobatics. But at first glance she looked like nothing less than a refined lady of society out for an afternoon ride. She even wore riding gloves and a proper top hat with a netted veil.

The crowds cheered as her uncle Oliver continued to build

up their anticipation for the show. He was the perfect master of ceremonies, and the audience always loved him. He announced every event and explained each of the three main acts.

"And so without further ado, I proudly present my darling niece, Elizabeth Brookstone—the most accomplished horse-woman in the world today!"

The crowds roared with approval.

Lizzy straightened in the saddle. "That's our cue, Longfellow." She drew a deep breath and urged him forward.

The cheers were thunderous as she entered the arena. Lizzy put Longfellow into a trot and gave a ladylike wave with her gloved hand as they circled. This was her chance to assess the audience. The stands were packed to full capacity, just as all Brookstone events were. Souvenir banners were waved by those who had purchased them, while others waved handkerchiefs or simply clapped. Lizzy had ridden with the show since her father and uncle created it, and had never known anything but sold-out shows and crowds such as these. The Brookstone show was known far and wide to be of the utmost quality and satisfaction.

"Isn't she lovely, ladies and gentlemen?" Oliver Brookstone asked through his megaphone. The audience roared even louder.

Lizzy set Longfellow into his paces. She signaled him to rear, causing the crowd to gasp. Longfellow began to prance and rear as if agitated and out of control. Lizzy let her top hat fall to the ground. Her chestnut brown hair tumbled down her back. She gave every pretense of being in peril as she signaled Longfellow to gallop.

As the gelding picked up speed, Lizzy pretended to be in trouble. She threw herself across the saddle first one way and then the other in order to rip away the special skirt and jacket. The audience that only moments earlier had been cheering now fell silent except for an occasional woman's startled cry. This was how the audience always reacted. Lizzy saw one of the other trick riders racing out to pick up her discarded articles of clothing. Freed of impediments, Lizzy slipped her foot into one of the special straps on her custom-made saddle and went into a layover, looking as if she would fall headfirst off the saddle. From this point on, she didn't hear the crowd or pay them any attention. Her act required her full attention.

Since she was a little girl, Lizzy had performed tricks on horseback. Her father and uncle had been part of Buffalo Bill Cody's Wild West show. They'd joined up in 1883, when their friend William Cody had decided to put together his famous show. Lizzy's mother had been needed to help with cooking for the crew, and naturally that meant bringing Lizzy along. Lizzy had grown to adulthood under the show's influence, performing her first tricks with the help of her father when she was just twelve. Every winter they'd gone home to Grandfather Brookstone's ranch in Montana to rest and plan new tricks. It was an unusual life to be certain, but one Lizzy enjoyed—probably because her father loved it so.

"You are the very heart of me, Lizzy," her father had often told her. *"You and your mother. Without either one of you, I'm not sure I could go on."*

But he had never considered how they might go on without him. Earlier that year, Mark Brookstone had suffered a heart attack. He had lingered for several hours after the initial onset, and during that time, he had made his wishes known before dying in the arms of his beloved wife.

Lizzy's body shifted in the wrong direction. *Focus on what you're doing or you'll get yourself killed.*

She pushed the memory aside. Focus was key to not getting hurt. She went into a trick that put her upside down along the horse's neck. The gelding didn't even seem to notice and continued to gallop around the arena. The audience applauded, now understanding that Lizzy's situation was quite under control.

Lizzy swung back into the saddle and gave a wave. The crowds went wild with cheers and the fluttering of the colorful Brookstone Wild West Extravaganza pennants they'd purchased.

She performed various moves for nearly twenty minutes, wowing the crowds with layovers, saddle spins, and shoulder stands, then ending with a death-defying drag that put her upside down, her hair and hand sweeping the floor of the arena. The people loved it. They were on their feet, cheering and whistling. The applause was thunderous as she reclaimed her seat and rode out of the arena.

The other nine performers for the show were waiting on horseback. Lizzy's was the final performance, but now the entire troupe would go out to take their bows. Lizzy positioned Longfellow while the others made their way out to the cheers of the audience. They lined up the horses, and each rider raised her hand high as the horses bowed.

An old man rushed to Lizzy's side, holding up a flag. With quick action, she secured straps over her feet and took the unfurled cloth. She returned to the arena, standing in the saddle and hoisting an American flag as she circled the ring. It was hard to imagine possible, but the cheers grew even louder.

Lizzy smiled and waved the symbol of America back and forth just as her father had taught her.

"People love a good finish, Lizzy. Give them a surprise and something to cheer, and they'll never forget you."

Longfellow headed out of the arena once again with the other riders following close behind. The audience continued to cheer and clap. As usual, no matter how much the performers gave, the audience wanted more.

Lizzy pulled off to the side, and the same older man who had given her the flag now retrieved it.

"Thanks, Zeb. I'm sure glad that's over." Lizzy had pushed herself nearly beyond endurance, having given a private performance for the president and his friends earlier in the day. She was tired and sore and relieved that her obligations were concluded. She could feel in Longfellow's gait that he was too.

"Wonderful performance, Lizzy," August Reichert declared, taking hold of Longfellow's bridle. "You were amazing."

"Thanks." She smiled at the sandy-haired head wrangler, who was the brother of her dear friend Mary. He had once tried to pay her court, but Lizzy kept everything professional. She had no interest in losing her heart to anyone in the show or anywhere else. Falling in love was even more dangerous than the act she'd just performed.

She slid from the saddle. Longfellow gave a soft nicker, knowing they'd both done well. "That's my boy." Lizzy kissed the horse's velvety nose. "You were wonderful. You always are." The horse was puffing and sweating but bobbed his head as if agreeing with her. "I'll bring you some treats later tonight." She gave him one last stroke as August loosened the cinch. "Take good care of him, August. He needs to walk awhile." She knew she didn't need to tell August his job, but it was a force of habit.

"I'll see to it, Lizzy." August led the horse away.

She made her way to the small room where her mother was waiting. Rebecca Brookstone was a fine-looking woman with a slender figure. Just shy of fifty years old, she and Lizzy shared many features. Both had chestnut brown hair, although Rebecca's bore gray as well. They had dark brown eyes—a trait passed down from Rebecca's mother's side of the family—and a brilliant smile. Although Mother smiled less these days. Losing her husband had clearly left Rebecca Brookstone with a broken heart.

"I'm so glad you're safe," Mother said. "Were there any problems?"

"No. None." Lizzy gave her mother a kiss on the cheek. "Are you ready to go?"

The black-clad widow nodded. "I am. I'll be glad to be back on the train."

"Me too." Lizzy picked up the one remaining bag her mother motioned toward and offered Mother her arm. "Let's get out of here before anyone spies us."

Her mother happily complied, and they made their way to their home on wheels. Usually there would be a carriage or wagon to drive them, but the train station was only six blocks away, and Lizzy and her mother had walked it more than once that day. The walk helped Lizzy clear her head, and on this particularly warm night, it was pleasant just to stroll and let the evening breeze cool them.

"The capital is a fascinating city, isn't it?" Mother stated more than asked.

Lizzy nodded. "It is, but given the upcoming election, it seems to almost be running amok."

"I suppose that's to be expected. Still, it was a lovely visit at the White House. I thought Mrs. McKinley such an amiable hostess."

"I remember the first time we met her." Lizzy paused at a busy street corner to wait until the traffic cleared. The other pedestrians around them seemed less inclined and dodged in and out of the traffic, much to the annoyance of the drivers. When they were once again on their way, Lizzy continued. "Do you suppose the president will be reelected?"

"I think so," Mother said, nodding. "The country has returned to prosperity, and industry is progressing. I believe most people will see the president as having a part in that."

They reached the train depot and made their way to the area where the Brookstone railcars awaited. There were eight bright red cars in total, artistically painted with performance scenes. Each bore the lettering, *THE BROOKSTONE WILD WEST EXTRAVAGANZA*, and all were customized to their personal needs. Half were dedicated to the animals' welfare and equipment, while the other four were set up for sleeping and living on the rails.

Lizzy made her way to the family car and helped her mother up onto the temporary wooden platform. Once they were inside, both women heaved a sigh in unison.

Mother smiled, but it didn't quite reach her eyes. "We're a sorry pair."

"We're tired. It's always hard when we get to the end of the season. I'm just thankful that you don't have to furnish the evening refreshments. Mrs. McKinley was so kind to send over all that food from the White House."

"She was indeed. I don't think I would have had the energy to lay out a table this evening. I'm glad there won't be too many more meals to arrange for this tour."

"Maybe we should hire someone to assist you next year."

Mother shook her head. "No, this is my last tour."

Lizzy wasn't all that surprised to hear this declaration. Since Father had died, neither of them had much passion for the show. They would have quit immediately had he not begged them to continue.

"The show must go on," he had said in barely audible words. *"Promise me you'll finish out the tour."*

They had promised, although neither had the heart to continue.

"I think it shall be my last as well," Lizzy said, plopping down on the comfortable sofa. "After all, I'm twenty-eight. I'm getting a little long in the tooth to be doing this." She rubbed her abdomen. "I get sorer with each performance, it seems."

"Besides, you should consider settling down, getting married and having a family. I would find it a great comfort to have grandchildren." Her mother took off her black veiled hat and set it aside.

Lizzy shook her head. "I'm sorry that I've disappointed in that area, but I'm not sure it's ever going to happen." She couldn't say that seeing her mother's pain from Father's death had made her look at romance and marriage in a completely different way.

"There's always Wes," Mother said. "He's free now. We both know he married Clarissa out of pity, but he's always cared about you."

This was not the conversation Lizzy wanted to be having. She had watched her mother go through the overwhelming grief of losing the man she loved. It had made Lizzy rethink her dreamy notions of marriage. She had loved Wes since she was a child, but he had never cared about her in the same way, and maybe that was for the best.

"There are other things in life besides marrying and having a family. Wes has his own life, and I have mine. Besides, he thinks of me as his sister," Lizzy said, shaking her head. "Nothing more than a pesky sibling."

"But that could change," Mother countered.

Thinking about Wesley DeShazer, their ranch foreman, always made Lizzy's heart ache. She had first met him when Wes was just eighteen and she was eleven. Her adoration of the young ranch worker had been overwhelming. She followed Wes around like a puppy for days, asking him questions and showing off her tricks. Wes had been kind and fun. He had treated her with tenderness. He was never condescending toward her, which only served to endear him to her all the more. It had been hard to leave him behind each spring when they returned to the wild west show. Lizzy would count the days until they returned, and when they did, she had rejoiced to find him still working at the ranch and more handsome than she'd remembered. As he grew into a man and took on more and more ranch responsibilities, Lizzy had determined he was the man she intended to marry.

"Lizzy?"

She glanced up to find her mother watching her. Lizzy smiled. "Sorry, I'm tired. What were you saying?"

Mother sat down beside her. "I was speaking of Wes."

"Ah, yes."

"Clarissa's been gone two years now."

"True, but during those two years, Wes has avoided me whenever we've been home. I don't think there's any future with him. If we were meant to be together, he wouldn't have married Clarissa."

"You were just a child when he married."

Lizzy frowned. "I was eighteen. Hardly a child." She yawned. "I'm sorry. I'm too tired to talk about this. I think I'll get ready for bed."

Mother took her hand. "Darling girl, you mustn't give up on true love. If Wesley is the man God has for you, then it will come about."

"And if he's not?" Lizzy already knew the answer but voiced the question anyway.

"Then you wouldn't want him for a husband. We need to rest in God's will for our lives, Lizzy. You know that. To seek our own would only result in a world of hurt and problems."

"Seems we have that anyway."

Her mother's eyes filled with tears. "I know. It's been so hard without your father." Tears trailed down her cheeks. "I don't know why God took him from us. He was so loved."

Lizzy hated seeing her mother cry. She put her arm around her mother's shoulders and hugged her close. "I don't know either. I do my best to trust God for the future, but losing Father makes the future seem grim."

Her mother sobbed into her hands. Lizzy couldn't count the number of times her mother had broken down like this, which was exactly the reason she couldn't be honest with her mother about her own feelings. "Come on, Mother. We're both done in and will soon be lost in our tears. Let me help you get to bed." She helped her mother to her feet and led her to one of the four private sleeping rooms in the family car.

The space wasn't all that large, but there was a small built-in dresser and a rod to hang clothes on beside a double bed, which was also built in with a nice ledge at the side of the headboard. One of the cleaning girls had opened the window and lit the kerosene lamp, which was affixed to the wall above the bed. Lizzy wished they could spare the extra money to electrify the car. It would be much safer, less smelly, and far easier to manage an electric switch.

Still pondering that matter, Lizzy helped her mother undress. She hung up the discarded clothes while her mother donned her nightgown.

"Would you like me to help with your hair?"

"No, I'm fine. You go ahead and get to bed yourself. I know you're tired."

Lizzy smiled. "I'll fetch you a glass of milk. I know you enjoy that before bed."

"No. Don't bother." Her mother sat down on the edge of the bed. "I just want to read my Bible for a while." Her tears returned, and Lizzy knew it was better to just go.

She slipped from the room and pulled the door shut behind her. Her own sleeping quarters were next to her mother's. Close enough to hear her sobs well into the night. Lizzy prayed God would give her mother comfort.

Maybe it was best not to marry. She couldn't imagine the pain her mother was bearing. Losing a father was misery enough, but losing a lifelong companion had to be like losing part of yourself. An amputation of the very worst kind.

Lizzy went into her small room, sat on the bed, and began unlacing her boots. She spied the pitcher of water, steam rising from the open top. The cleaning girl was no doubt responsible. Once she was rid of her boots, Lizzy poured some of the water into the bowl and washed her face, then began discarding her clothes.

Just as she'd anticipated, her mother's sobs could be heard through the thin wall. How Lizzy wished she could comfort her mother, but as Uncle Oliver had told her, this was a burden a wife or husband must bear alone. No one else understood the pain of a marriage severed. Especially when it involved a couple who had loved each other as deeply as Mark and Rebecca Brookstone had loved.

Lizzy looked at her reflection in the mirror on the wall. *Why would I ever want to experience that sorrow and pain? Loving Wes and being rejected was painful enough. I can't imagine how hard it would be to share his love and then have him die.* No, the best way to avoid widowhood was to avoid love.

She quickly finished washing up, then readied herself for bed. With her hair braided and nightgown in place, she extinguished the lamp before crawling beneath the covers. Her window was still open, and she heard Uncle Oliver conversing with someone as they drew near the car. No doubt he was settling last-minute problems before their railcars were hooked up to the next westbound locomotive. It was a strange life, living on the rails. Sometime in the next hour they'd feel the gentle—or not-so-gentle—bump of the cars being coupled, and then they'd begin to move as they were transported to their next stop. At each city where they performed, their eight cars were moved onto a siding, and there they would live until the performances were complete. It was an exciting life—seeing America, meeting new people. Lizzy had even met three presidents: Grover Cleveland, Benjamin Harrison, and William McKinley.

When Lizzy was younger, her mother had always seen to it that they visited places of historic importance at each stop. Lizzy had learned so much along the way. The trips had always been something she looked forward to. Now, however, there was no joy. She was ready to be done with it all.

"But then what?" Her voice was a barely audible whisper.

The ranch in Montana was home, but without Father, it wouldn't seem that way. Then there was Wesley. If she quit the show and stayed on the ranch with her mother, could they find a way to just be friends?

"Can *I* find a way?" Lizzy gazed at the top of her berth, then closed her eyes.

Her mind whirred with questions, but by the time the train car began to move, she was starting to fade off to sleep. Sadly, without any hope of answers.

TWO

izzy and her mother sat at the table, reading the local paper and eating a hot breakfast brought to them from their current stop. While the railroad men handled their routine business, Uncle Oliver had left the car to make certain the rest of Brookstone's workforce had what they needed before the train started up again.

"It says here that the Galveston hurricane last month may have killed as many as twelve thousand people," Mother said, lowering the paper. "Can you imagine? Oliver told me there are only about two hundred thousand people in all of Montana."

"I can't imagine it," Lizzy admitted. "To think of that many people suddenly killed is beyond me. Those hurricanes must be terrible storms to endure. I hope we never encounter one."

"It says the loss of livestock and crops was unimaginable." Mother shook her head. "Seems the newspaper is full of such sad things these days."

A knock sounded on the car door, but before Lizzy could get to her feet, it opened and her uncle peered inside.

"Oh good, you're both awake and ready to receive," Uncle Oliver declared. "I want you to meet someone."

Lizzy stood and smiled as her uncle stepped into the car. The

WHEN YOU ARE NEAR

young man who followed him was expensively clothed and nearly a head taller than Uncle Oliver. He carried himself like a man who had been brought up in privilege. He glanced around their accommodations, seeming to assess the situation. Lizzy wondered if he thought their little home on wheels quaint or appalling. Finally, his gaze settled on Lizzy and then Mother. He offered them a wide smile that seemed sincere enough and took off his hat.

Uncle Oliver did likewise and offered an introduction. "This is Jason Adler. He joined us last night, but you ladies had already gone to bed."

Mother and Lizzy exchanged a look. Lizzy knew that Henry Adler was responsible for her father and uncle having the money to start their own wild west show back in the day, but she had no idea who Jason was. Better still, what was his purpose here?

As if reading her thoughts, Uncle Oliver added clarity. "He's the son of Henry Adler. Jason, this is my brother's widow, Mrs. Rebecca Brookstone, and her daughter, Elizabeth."

Mother spoke first. "I'm pleased to meet you, Mr. Adler. My husband spoke so highly of your father."

"And my father spoke highly of your husband. He sends his deepest regrets, Mrs. Brookstone." Jason Adler gave a slight bow. He looked at Lizzy. "We are sorry for your loss as well, Miss Brookstone."

"Call her Lizzy," Uncle Oliver declared. "Everyone does."

Lizzy wasn't sure what Jason Adler was doing here, but she couldn't deny that he was quite the dashing gentleman. He looked about her age, maybe a little older, and his accent clearly revealed his English heritage.

"Jason has come on board to help me," Uncle Oliver continued. "He has all sorts of ideas for benefiting the show."

"Won't you join us?" Mother said. "There's hot coffee and extra pastries, though I'm afraid if you want something hot to eat, we'll have to send someone out."

"We've had our breakfast, Rebecca, but a cup of coffee would suit me right down to my boots. How about it, Jason? Coffee?"

Jason Adler smiled. "I'd be happy to share coffee with two such lovely ladies."

The men put their hats aside and took the empty chairs at the small table for four. Lizzy retrieved extra cups and brought them to the table. She didn't understand Jason's purpose. Uncle Oliver said the Englishman had all sorts of ideas, but Lizzy couldn't see any reason they needed his or his father's thoughts on the show.

Once Mother had poured the coffee and Uncle Oliver had made small talk about the weather, Lizzy decided to press the matter.

"I'm afraid I don't understand the reason for having Mr. Adler join the show. You mentioned he has ideas for us, but I wasn't aware that we needed . . . ideas."

She glanced at Mr. Adler to judge whether or not he'd taken offense. He seemed completely at ease, however, and merely sipped his black coffee. He met her gaze over the rim of his cup, and it looked to Lizzy as if there was a twinkle in his blue eyes. He seemed amused.

Uncle Oliver, on the other hand, looked a bit sheepish. "Well . . . you see . . . a while back, I sold part of the show to Henry Adler."

"What?" the women questioned in unison.

Jason Adler slowly lowered his cup while Uncle Oliver held up his hands. "It's a long story, but the show has been struggling to make a profit. I thought some fresh ideas might benefit us. Mr. Adler has proven very helpful in the past."

"Still, you should have discussed it with Mother, at least. She speaks in place of my father now," Lizzy replied. She knew her tone revealed her outrage.

To his credit, Jason Adler said nothing.

21

"I think in time you'll see how good this will be for us. Jason's ideas are good ones—things I know your father would have approved."

What could she say to that? If Lizzy even thought to argue, it would no doubt bring on another round of tears from her mother. No opinion was worth causing her mother pain.

For several minutes and another cup of coffee, her uncle explained that the Adlers were devoted to the best interests of the Brookstone family.

Finally, Jason spoke up. "My father—in fact, my entire family—is eternally grateful for what your father and uncle did for us. He often speaks of the hunting trip in the Rockies that your father and uncle guided him on. The fact that they saved his life will never be forgotten. Now, if there is a way for us to help you save the show, then we want to do whatever we can."

"Save the show?" Lizzy asked, looking to her uncle. "What is he talking about?"

Again, her uncle looked uncomfortable. "The fact is, we can't go on like this. There isn't enough money to go around. We're barely able to make our payroll."

"But we're always sold out." Lizzy knew there was a great deal of pride in her voice, but she couldn't help herself. "We have more towns asking for performances than we can say yes to."

"Indeed," Jason said. "It's more a matter of management. There are ways to save money and economize. Your father and uncle were not . . . well . . ."

"We weren't schooled for such things, Lizzy," Uncle Oliver said. "We've managed as best we could, but Jason here is educated. He and his father both attended college, and they've run all sorts of businesses and know how to manage money better than I do."

A knock at the door interrupted their conversation. Lizzy got up to answer it, and Jason stood quickly to help her from her chair. She didn't feel very hospitable toward him but forced herself to be polite. "Thank you."

She opened the door to find Agnes, the show's head seam-stress. "Mrs. Brookstone," she called from the platform, "I wonder if you could come to the costume room when you have time."

Mother started to rise, and again Jason was there to lend a hand. She gave him a warm smile, much more sincere than the one Lizzy had offered him. "I'll come right now." She looked to the men. "If you'll excuse me. Oliver, I trust you to manage the matter. You've always had our best interests at heart."

"August asked me to tell Mr. Brookstone that he needed to consult him on a matter related to the horses," Agnes added. "He said he needed to speak to you before we pulled out of the station."

Uncle Oliver got to his feet. "Jason, perhaps you could stay and explain some of your ideas to Lizzy. I want you two to become good friends."

Lizzy didn't want to contradict her uncle even though sitting and talking with Jason was the last thing she wanted to do. She walked back to the table and found Jason waiting to help her with her chair. She certainly couldn't fault his manners.

Once she was seated and the others had departed, Lizzy looked at Jason. Previously he had been seated beside her, but now he took the seat opposite her, where Mother had been sitting. His expression was concerned. "I suppose this is a rather uncomfortable situation for you."

"*Uncomfortable* isn't the word I would choose." She shrugged. "I'm confused and concerned, but not uncomfortable."

"I'm glad to hear it." His blue eyes sparkled, and his expression relaxed. "I wouldn't like you to feel uncomfortable in my presence. Like your uncle, I very much want us to be friends."

Lizzy tried to put aside her suspicion. "Why don't you explain your money-saving ideas? Then perhaps I'll be less concerned and confused."

"I'd be happy to." He tugged absentmindedly at the cuffs of his shirt. "As you know, a show such as yours is hardly guaranteed an income. There are all sorts of overhead costs and unexpected problems."

"Isn't that true of all industries?"

"Quite right. However, a performance-based industry such as yours has many variables that other businesses might never have to concern themselves with. Your business is in constant motion. You take it on the road, and for most of the year you go from place to place. The wear and tear takes its toll. The business is also dependent on living, breathing beings, both human and animal, for its success. That only serves to increase the risk and expense."

"But all industry and business requires living, breathing beings." Lizzy didn't know why she felt so at odds with Jason. He was only trying to help, she supposed, but he wasn't family, and the fact that he would be allowed to help make decisions in their business irritated her sense of balance.

He shifted in his seat and gave a hint of a shrug. "It's true that any business is only as good as the individuals running and working it. However, Brookstone's adds an additional element to that. In other industries, when a worker is injured or falls ill, there are many others who can step in to manage their position. The same is true for industries reliant upon horses. However, in your situation, that isn't the case."

Lizzy had to concede he was right. "I understand what you're saying. It wouldn't be possible to suddenly procure animals as well-trained as my horses, should something happen to them."

"Exactly so." He smiled. "Even harder to replace the rider." His right brow rose, as if daring her to contradict him.

Lizzy remained silent but gave a nod.

"The most important thing is to assure quality housing and care for yourselves as well as your stock. I'd like to see the railcars inspected and repairs made. There are new, safer ways to transport horses, for instance. I can show you some of the designs I have with me. Perhaps later, when we're actually on our way."

"Yes, I'd like to see what you have in mind."

"The key is to keep both performers and livestock at their optimum health and ability. After all, venues will hardly pay if there is no performance."

"I imagine our contracts allow for some sort of compensation."

Jason shook his head. "The contracts created by your father and uncle were hardly more than handshakes and letters. In the twentieth century, attention to detail is required. My father had our solicitor put together some sample contracts that we might use. We can discuss this when the time is right."

She felt her anger building. "I see. So our problem is that my uncle and father mismanaged the show?"

"Not entirely. They did what had been done in the past. What they learned from the show in which they had once performed. I'm not here to point out fault, but to help. I hope you won't always be hostile toward me."

"If someone came into your home, started suggesting changes, and told you that your father hadn't sense enough to know how to manage his affairs, wouldn't you feel a tad hostile?" She fixed him with a stern gaze.

"If my father had asked someone to help him figure out how he might better his home and family," Jason replied calmly, "I would hope that the remaining members of the household wouldn't treat that person as the enemy."

Lizzy forced herself to calm down. He was right. He wasn't here to be her enemy. "So what do you suggest, besides improving the railcars and new contracts?"

"It will be necessary to look at the operation and see where money can be saved. Perhaps we can start by eliminating some of the men who work with the stock and equipment. I've noticed quite a few are well into their years and able to do very little. It seems the younger men could handle their responsibilities along with their own, thus saving money in wages."

"Those older men are friends of my family. They were given jobs with the show because they aren't able to work full-time on our ranch. They've been with us for a long time, and although broken and aged, they still provide good help."

"I know it's hard to imagine letting them go, but no one will earn a wage if there is no longer a show."

Lizzy hadn't realized things were so dire. She wanted to ask Jason about the details, but at the same time, she didn't want anything to do with him. Apparently he noted this dilemma as well.

"Over time, we can go over the ledgers and review where costs might be saved. For now, however, just let me say that I think the show is amazing. I know the crowds love it and will continue to do so. I want your help to figure out how we can keep it alive."

His change of direction made Lizzy remember her own thoughts from the night before. "My mother doesn't plan to continue with the show. It's been so hard on her since my father's death."

"I can't begin to imagine. Why didn't she return to the ranch with . . . your father?"

"She wanted to." Lizzy felt her anger fade. "She would have, had she not promised him to stay with the show. Father was a firm believer in honoring his commitments, and he didn't want to disappoint the people who were looking forward to our performances. He made Mother and I promise we'd stay on until the end of the tour this year." She shook her head. "I think he also knew that Mother would be lost in her grief if she didn't have something to do."

"And now she'll return to the ranch?"

"Yes." Lizzy met his sympathetic expression. "I may remain with her."

He frowned. "But why? You're the main attraction."

"I am only one of several, if you'll recall. I'm also twenty-eight. It's getting harder to perform those tricks. Besides, without my father, I've lost the heart of it all."

"But your fans can surely help reinstate that passion. They're devoted to you. You may not realize this, but some people actually follow you from show to show—at least within a certain radius of their homes. If you leave the show, I believe it will fail. Like it or not, you are the main attraction and the reason the show continues to garner large audiences."

"I wouldn't go without training a replacement. The other girls who trick ride are quite good. With some practice, they could take over my tricks—even mimic my costumes and styles. No one will ever know the difference. They come for the Brookstone all-female wild west show. Not for Elizabeth Brookstone."

"I don't think you realize your importance." Jason shook his head. "People know exactly who you are. You receive fan letters, don't you?"

"Yes, but so do the others."

He leaned forward. "Miss Brookstone, would you please at least delay making your final decision until the end of the tour? I'd like to convince you to stay on for at least one more year. The changes I'm going to suggest will upset things enough, but if you leave, then I can guarantee the show will fall apart."

Lizzy sighed. She didn't want to be the reason the show failed. In some ways it would be like losing her father all over again, and it would break her uncle's heart. Uncle Oliver would never give up the show. He loved it too much. The show was his entire life, although since her father had died, Oliver had taken to drinking a bit too much, and she wasn't sure how much life he had left in him.

Jason leaned forward. "Just give me some time, Miss Brookstone. Think about staying on for one more year. Please."

His pleading tone stirred something deep within her. Lizzy knew what it felt like to desperately want something to work out. She also knew how it felt when the one key person refused to do their part.

"I'll pray on it, Mr. Adler." She met his gaze. "That's the best I can give you."

He smiled. "It's enough. For now."

⊰⊱ THREE ⊰⊱

Their next show was in four days and would take place in
St. Louis, Missouri. It was the second to last show for the
season, and Lizzy found herself counting down the days.
She longed to return to the family ranch in Montana, where
the show would spend the winter. She had memorized every
inch of their large house, and there was nowhere she could
go in the ten-bedroom, two-story house without remembering
something pleasant or humorous. It was a haven—a sanctuary
of love. It was there she had grown up, and hopefully it was
there she might one day raise a family.

Lizzy gazed out the train window at the Kentucky country-
side gently rolling past. Before the show in St. Louis, they had
a stop to make.

Jason Adler loomed in the open doorway of the railcar. "I
hope you don't mind the interruption."

Uncle Oliver had told them Jason was to be treated like
family, so Lizzy welcomed him into their car and pushed aside
thoughts of her father. "Not at all. We'll arrive at the station
soon, and then the railroad will move us to a siding and we'll
head to Fleming Farm." She shrugged. "But I'm sure you know
all of that."

"Yes." He took a seat on a ladder-backed wooden chair near her spot on the sofa. "You look quite lovely."

Lizzy glanced down at her simple mauve promenade suit. It wasn't the most current style, but was one of her better outfits. "Thank you. It may not be fashionable, but it is very comfortable."

"You make it look quite fashionable. I especially like the way you've done up your hair."

She flushed and looked at her folded hands. "That would be Mother. I'm used to braids and tight little buns. However, since we're visiting the Flemings, it's important to look our best. They're very splendid and proper."

"Ah, yes. The Flemings. Your uncle explained the arrangement. I understand their horses are important for the show."

"Yes, after a fashion." Lizzy was glad the focus had moved away from her appearance. "We've always used Morgan-Quarter horse mixes. We have a very fine older quarter horse stallion at the ranch, but we lost one of our mares, and the others are getting up in years. We need a couple of new breeders. Mother and Father were both of a mind to expand the ranch to breed horses."

"I see. And this mix of bloodlines is what they hoped to promote?"

She could hear the doubt in his voice. "I suppose it's difficult for you to understand, not having grown up around a ranch and wild west show."

"I did, however, grow up—at least part of the time—on our country estate, and we had a fine stable of animals. I know the value of a good brood mare."

"I'm glad to hear it. I'm sure it's difficult enough to comprehend why we do what we do." She tried not to sound sarcastic.

His expression grew serious. "Then tell me. Start with the ranch in Montana. Did you always live there?"

Lizzy knew they still had time before reaching the station. "The ranch belonged to my granddad, father, and uncle jointly. Granddad inherited some money and had always wanted to move west. My uncle and father were both like-minded. They sold everything, and we relocated to some land several miles outside of Miles City, Montana. I was ten years old when we moved. I saw the move as a grand adventure, but my aunts— Granddad's daughters with his second wife—cried and whined all the way."

"Perhaps they were leaving suitors?"

"Yes, I'm sure that didn't help. There were five of them, but the elder two were already married. The other three were certainly of marriageable age, although I don't recall if they were serious about anyone at the time of the move. I do recall that my mother and grandmother were the only women in our party who were in favor of the move."

Jason chuckled and crossed his legs. "Please go on."

"When we arrived, we found there wasn't much to this ranch Granddad had purchased, but thanks to his inheritance, that wasn't an issue. He knew the tiny house already in place would never work for us and had logs and finished lumber brought in to make a colossal two-story house. Granddad had visions of his sons having large families to fill it and stay on with him and Grandmother. There are ten bedrooms in the house, which I suppose sounds terribly overdone, but Granddad was always a big dreamer."

"It sounds charming," Jason said.

Lizzy remembered then that he came from a wealthy family— a father who was an English lord and well-propertied. "I suppose I sound silly. I'm sure you must have a much larger estate and a great deal of finery."

"Our country estate is quite large, but our London house is smaller. I'll tell you all about it sometime, but right now I'd like to know more about your upbringing. Did you enjoy living out there in the wilds? As I understood it from my father, there aren't many cities or people."

She nodded. "That much is true. There still isn't all that much, but yes, I love it. I wouldn't live anywhere else."

"Perhaps you only say that because you haven't yet seen a better place." His smooth voice was compelling.

"Perhaps." Lizzy shrugged. "But I've toured all over this country."

"Maybe," he said, his voice lowering, "it isn't in this country."

Lizzy felt her cheeks grow warm. "Well, anyway, by 1885 my aunts had married, and of course my father and uncle had decided to take up the offer from their friend Bill Cody to join the wild west show he was putting together."

"And you and your mother went along?"

"Yes. Mr. Cody wanted Mother to cook for him, and they figured I might as well come along. Mother and Father both agreed it would be a grand education. And it was. I learned a great deal and saw so many places of historical relevance."

"So why did your father and uncle quit the show?"

Lizzy remembered it as if it were yesterday. "We were home for our winter break when Grandmother fell ill. She never recovered and died in the spring of 1886. We were all devastated. Even though she wasn't my father and uncle's natural mother, she was the only mother they could remember, and she had been so good to them. She was dear to all of us." The words seemed to back up in her throat, choking her. Lizzy coughed.

"How old were you?" Jason asked. His gaze was sympathetic.

"I was fourteen." She thought of her sadness and how much she had cried. "Grandmother was an incredible woman. To know her was to love her. My father was home from the wild west show, recovering from an injury. He and Uncle knew that Granddad could never bear it if we left, so they resigned from the show, and we stayed on the ranch." Lizzy drew a deep breath and let it go. "The summer that followed was hot and dry, and then winter came early and hard. By January, things went from bad to worse. Are you familiar with the winter of 1886 and 1887?"

He shook his head. "I don't believe I am."

"Most of the ranchers hadn't put up feed for the winter. When the snow came early and deep, the cattle were already underweight because of the drought that summer. In January, there came a warming that melted some of the snow. We thought maybe the worst was over, but of course it wasn't. The temperatures dropped, and the melted snow formed a thick ice crust that the cattle couldn't break through. Then more snow came. By spring, the loss was nearly total for all ranchers. We were no exception. I think Granddad lost the will to live after Grandmother died, but if not then, he certainly did when he found his entire herd dead. He and my father and uncle worked day and night to dispose of the carcasses, and Granddad caught pneumonia. He was dead within a week." She felt her chest tighten. She didn't want to remember those days.

"That must have been truly difficult for someone with such a tender heart."

The train slowed and brought Lizzy back to the present. She glanced out the window to see they were still some distance from town. The Fleming horse farm was not far from Louisville, and they planned to stop there for two days. The year before, Lizzy's father had made arrangements to buy twin four-year-old mares. He'd watched the fillies almost since birth—checking on them each year. After the second year, he told Fleming he wanted the pair, but Fleming had thought to keep them for himself. Finally, after some bartering back and forth, Fleming gave in and sold them. Father had been proud of that accomplishment. The mares were buckskin, a favorite of the Brookstone family. Just before he'd died, Father had talked with such excitement about bringing the horses home.

Jason seemed to read her mind. "If I might change the subject, tell me why you prefer the Morgan-Quarter horse mix. Your uncle said that most of the performing horses are of this cross."

Lizzy appreciated the chance to focus on something else. "They're marvelous. Spirited and easily trained."

"But so too are Thoroughbreds."

Lizzy nodded. "But they're too tall and their backs are much too long. In order to do tricks, you must have just the right-sized animal. Of course, that is totally dependent on the rider's size. We do have one horse that's a Thoroughbred-Morgan, but I still find the back too long, which makes it difficult to perform some tricks. One of the other girls, however, loves him."

"And what of other breeds?" He leaned back and crossed his legs in a casual manner.

"Well, with the American Saddlebred the neck isn't quite right. It's too difficult to do stands and vaults. Morgans by themselves are too stocky, and Arabians can't manage the shifting of weight that's required." She considered other breeds for a moment. "The Standardbred is better suited to harness racing."

"I quite agree," Jason said. "And I presume that while Barbs would be small enough, their gait is too unpredictable for trick riding. They're more suited to racing."

Lizzy could see he was knowledgeable on the topic of horses. It gave her a bit of respect for him. "Yes. Over the years we've just found the quarter horse and Morgan make the best horse for trick riding. I'm sure you've seen my horses, Longfellow and Thoreau."

"Beautiful buckskins. I particularly like the dappling on Longfellow. I also appreciate the names. Are you a fan of Longfellow's and Thoreau's writings?"

"I am. I enjoy a great many writers, but particularly poets. We also have horses at the ranch named Blake, Burns, and Byron."

Jason grew thoughtful and closed his eyes. "'She walks in beauty, like the night of cloudless climes and starry skies; and all that's best of dark and bright meet in her aspect and her eyes: thus mellowed to that tender light which heaven to gaudy day denies.'" He opened his eyes and gazed at her with such intensity that Lizzy found herself unable to look away.

"Umm, yes. Exactly," she said when he finished.

"I'm a fan of Byron's work. He always captured a depth of emotion that appealed to my spirit."

Lizzy had no desire to discuss Jason Adler's spirit. "I recall Mother saying something about you having American relatives." The train was now nearing the station and barely crept along. The braking made for a jerky ride.

"Yes. There are a great many Americans on my mother's side. She is, you see, American herself."

"Oh." Lizzy gave a closed-mouth smile.

He laughed. "I thought perhaps you already knew. Her family is quite wealthy, which was no doubt one of the many reasons my father married her."

"I hope he also married for love."

Jason shrugged. "If not, love is surely the reason they remain together. Father adores her and her family. Her people are industrialists from New York."

The door opened at the end of the car, and Uncle Oliver strolled in as if he were making his way through the park. "Lovely day. Just perfectly lovely, Lizzy. Is your mother awake?"

Lizzy shrugged as the train continued to jerk as it slowed down. The whine of metal wheels on metal rails was enough to wake the dead. "I'm sure she is now. I'll go see if she needs help dressing." She glanced at Jason and gave a little nod. "If you'll excuse me."

He jumped to his feet and helped her up. "I enjoyed our conversation. I hope it will be the first of many."

His thumb rubbed the back of her knuckles. When he didn't let go, Lizzy pulled her hand away. "I must go." Her tone was curt, perhaps edging on harsh. But it was necessary.

The last thing she wanted or needed was for Jason Adler to try to woo her.

·→≡ FOUR ≡←·

Your home is just as lovely as I remember it," Mrs. Brookstone said, patting Beatrix Fleming's hand.

Ella Fleming watched her mother graciously welcome the Brookstones to their estate. She smiled when her gaze met Elizabeth Brookstone's. She liked Lizzy very much. Ella had in fact found a kindred spirit in her, even though Lizzy was eight years her senior.

"It's so good to see you again, Ella," Lizzy said, coming forward. "Did you have a good journey?"

Lizzy glanced around the room as if familiarizing herself with the house again. It had been over a year since she'd been here, after all. "It was the same as always." She looked at Ella. "I just love how bright this foyer is. You've done something different, haven't you?"

"We did. Mother thought it much too dull, and we repapered it in this lovely gold stripe. We also added a few mirrors to reflect the light."

"I like it very much. Perhaps we can do something like this at home to brighten the interior."

"I'm so glad you've come. I so enjoy our visits." Ella lowered her voice. "Father rarely allows me to entertain."

"What are you girls whispering about?" Ella's mother asked.

Ella put her arm around Lizzy's waist. "We're hoping to have a chance to ride together."

"There's no reason you shouldn't," Mother replied. "The weather has been lovely." She returned her attention to Lizzy's mother.

"Forgive me," Ella whispered. "I'll explain everything later."

Lizzy looked concerned, but she said nothing.

Ella saw her father and Mr. Brookstone speaking with a tall, handsome stranger. She lowered voice and leaned closer to Lizzy. "Who is that?"

Lizzy glanced over her shoulder. "That's Mr. Jason Adler. He's from England and apparently will be with our show for a time."

Ella returned her attention to Lizzy. "Doing what? I thought it was all female performers."

"He'll be helping Uncle Oliver. You did hear that my father passed away earlier this year, didn't you?"

Ella felt the blood drain from her face. How unfeeling she'd been not to mention it first thing. "I apologize. How thoughtless of me. I'm so sorry for your loss. We received your uncle's telegram and were devastated for you."

Lizzy was all graciousness. "Don't feel bad. My father was an amazing man, and he will be missed, but he was also very practical. In fact, he insisted that the show had to continue— that it was his legacy and the only memorial he wanted. He begged Mother and me to continue with the performances. I suppose he knew that by keeping us busy, we would have less time to be swallowed up in sadness."

"I liked your father. He was always so pleasant—even humorous. So unlike my father." Ella fell silent, knowing she'd said too much. "I'm sure you must be tired. There's time to rest before supper. Why don't I show you upstairs, where you can take a nap or at least freshen up? I'm sure the servants have already taken up the bags."

"Well, I wouldn't want to desert my mother," Lizzy replied, "but I would like to be able to talk to you without everyone else listening in."

Ella took her hand. "Mama will see to your mother's needs. Come along."

"Thank you."

Taking the grand staircase in the deliberately slow manner she'd been taught, Ella glanced back down at the guests still speaking in the foyer. "Mr. Adler is quite handsome."

"I suppose he is." Lizzy sounded distant.

"Is something wrong?" Ella hoped she hadn't offended.

"No, not really. I suppose I'm still wondering what role he'll play in our show. Apparently there has been some concern about how we're managing the business and, well . . . everything related to it."

They reached the top of the stairs, and Ella stopped. "I know we're not all that close, although I consider you my dearest friend."

"I feel the same and must contradict you. We're very close," Lizzy said, smiling. "I don't confide in many people as I do with you."

Ella glanced down the hall where a black woman stood dusting one of the tables. She lowered her voice even more. "We need each other, then."

She hurried to pull Lizzy down the hall and past the uniformed woman. When they reached the final door on the right, Ella opened it and all but dragged Lizzy inside.

"I'm sorry to seem so rude, but there is always someone listening in on conversations around here." Ella let go of Lizzy and glanced around the room. There was no sign of Lizzy's suitcase.

"They'll bring your things up soon, but in the meantime, let me open a window. It's rather stuffy."

Ella could feel Lizzy's gaze on her. She had been hoping they might have a chance to talk about Ella's situation. It was unseemly to involve an outsider in family matters, but Ella was starting to feel nervous. Still, it would be best to wait until they could be away from the house. Perhaps on their ride tomorrow.

"You seem upset." Lizzy's voice was soothing and kind.

Ella grew a deep breath and turned back to face her. It was silly to pretend nothing was wrong. "There is . . . a problem. But I can't speak of it just now."

As if to stress the point, a knock sounded on the bedroom door.

"Come in," Ella called.

"I has Miz Brookstone's things," the young man declared. He brought in the bags and set them at the foot of the bed. "Mara say she be in by and by to put 'em away."

"Thank you, Elijah. You may go."

He gave a bit of a bow, then hurried from the room.

Lizzy looked at Ella. "We could go for a walk. I'm really not all that tired."

Ella shook her head. "No. It will keep. I probably shouldn't bother you with it at all." She bit her lower lip. Had she already said too much? "Get some rest. Dinner will be served promptly at seven. Tell Mara what you intend to wear. She'll have it pressed and ready for you."

Lizzy nodded. The look of worry on her face left Ella feeling guiltier than before.

"Everything is just fine," Ella said, forcing a smile. But it wasn't fine. Nothing in her life was fine.

When they came down to supper that evening, things went from bad to worse. Jefferson was there. Jefferson Spiby was the basest form of man. He was also Ella's fiancé, thanks to her father's business arrangements. They had been engaged since she was fifteen, and the only reason they hadn't married yet was that Mother insisted Ella was too young. But now that she was twenty, that excuse no longer applied. The wedding was planned for Christmas.

Jefferson spotted Ella and smiled in that suggestive way of his. It was embarrassing and terrifying at the same time and always left her feeling like she wanted a bath, even if she'd just come from one.

She had very nearly convinced herself that she should say nothing to Lizzy Brookstone, but seeing Jefferson here and knowing what he planned for her, Ella couldn't remain silent. She had been making plans for weeks, ever since learning that Lizzy was coming to the farm. If she didn't see them through, her fate with Jefferson would be sealed.

"Ella darling, your intended could not stay away," her father declared as she and Lizzy joined the family in the large parlor.

Jefferson watched her like a cat eyeing its prey. He made his way to her, sleek and calculating in his moves. When he finally stood before her and Lizzy, he smiled and took Ella's hand.

"My dear, you are deliciously beautiful." His words were barely whispered, and no wonder. Ella knew her father would never allow such talk. He kissed her hand, rather than hover over it respectfully, and touched his tongue to her knuckles, leaving Ella nauseated.

"Lizzy, this is Jefferson Spiby," she said. "Jefferson, this is Miss Brookstone. Her father and uncle are the owners of the Brookstone Wild West Extravaganza."

He straightened and let go of Ella. Turning to Lizzy, he smiled and extended his hand to take hers. He lowered his head until his lips nearly touched her knuckles, but then quickly straightened. "Miss Brookstone, I am charmed."

Lizzy's expression was guarded. She looked at Jefferson as if she were assessing the truth of his statement. Ella should have warned her that he couldn't be trusted, but that would have required further explanation.

"I understand you are a trick rider, Miss Brookstone," Jefferson said.

"I am," Lizzy replied.

His smile turned to something more like a leer. "You must get into some very . . . interesting positions."

Ella was mortified at his suggestive tone and glanced around quickly to make certain no one else had overheard. Everyone seemed otherwise occupied in conversation, however. She looked back just as Lizzy replied.

"You have me at a disadvantage, Mr. Spiby. You know my relationship to Ella and the Flemings, but I know nothing of why you're here."

Ella wanted to laugh out loud at the look on Jefferson's face. He wasn't used to women standing up to him. He regained his control quickly, however, and looked at Ella. "Why, I'm our dear Ella's fiancé. We're to be married very soon. Christmas, in fact."

A servant appeared at the entryway. "Dinner is served."

"Ah, thank goodness," Mr. Fleming declared. "I'm positively famished. He extended his arm to Lizzy's mother. "Might I escort you to dinner, my dear? I'll trust your brother-in-law and Mr. Adler to bring my wife."

"And I'll bring along Ella and Miss Brookstone," Jefferson announced. "That will leave Robert to bring up the rear."

Ella glanced at her brother Robert, who stood gazing into the eyes of his wife, Virginia. They had been married for five years and had two little boys, but they were still very much in love. Robert put his arm around his wife's waist and smiled. "I'd be delighted," he said.

They made their way into the dining room and, once everyone was seated, began to enjoy the delectable dishes Cook had created. Ella tried to keep her mind on the meal and polite conversation, but Jefferson made it nearly impossible. Not only had he broken with protocol to position himself at her side, but he insisted Lizzy sit at his side as well. Ella had hoped she might have Lizzy to herself.

The table was set with Mother's finest Royal Worcester china in the Pompadour pattern. The cream-colored china was artistically exquisite, with gold-painted leaves, flowers, laurels, and other delicate designs. Created prior to her mother's family coming to America, the set was their very best. Everything on the table was of the finest quality, from the crystal to the silver. This dinner was staged to impress. Something her father loved to do.

The evening passed surprisingly enough in easy conversation. Oliver Brookstone was full of stories and entertained them all. Ella had very nearly forgotten about Jefferson and her own troubles when one of the serving girls tripped and spilled orange sauce on the sleeve of Lizzy's gown.

"Oh, I'm sorry. I'm so sorry," the poor woman said, looking frantically for a napkin.

"You stupid girl," Jefferson declared, jumping to his feet. "You should be whipped."

Lizzy only smiled and shook her head. "It's not a problem, I assure you." She had her own napkin in hand and waved the girl away. "It wouldn't be the first time I spilled something or had something spilled on me. Please, don't worry about it."

Ella tried to hide her horror. She glanced toward her father. He looked livid. She knew he wouldn't make a scene here, but later he would punish the girl for her clumsiness, maybe even fire her. He could be so cruel at times.

Jefferson muttered something and reclaimed his seat. The lighthearted atmosphere faded quickly, and from that point on, everything seemed to be on edge. Gone were the entertaining stories of the wild west show and soft laughter.

When supper was finally concluded, Ella's father rose. "Rather than take our brandy and cigars in the library, I suggest we make our way to the stables. I know you're anxious, Mr. Brookstone, to have a look at your horses, and we can enjoy our cigars while considering their merits. Then we can have a brandy before retiring."

Ella hoped the men might spend a good long time there and give her a chance to speak to Lizzy about her trouble, but it wasn't to be.

"If we're going to look at the horses," Oliver Brookstone declared, "then I want Lizzy to accompany us. She knows more about horseflesh than anyone in our family save my brother, and in his absence, I'll trust her to know that the animals are fit for our needs."

It felt as if a hand had tightened around Ella's throat. No one challenged her father, and no one ever suggested that a woman was qualified to pass judgment on Fleming horses. She couldn't even bear to look at him for fear of what she might see in his expression. The entire room went silent, and even the servants went rigid, awaiting the coming storm.

"Well then," her father finally said after a lengthy silence, "I suppose we can forgo the cigars. After all, I wouldn't want to offend a lady's delicate constitution."

Lizzy had the audacity to smile. "I assure you, Mr. Fleming, my constitution can bear up under most anything."

Ella would have groaned aloud had she not feared the repercussions. Here was yet another challenge to her father's authority.

He motioned for one of the footmen. "Have the groom bring the Brookstone mares to the sale room. I wouldn't want Miss Brookstone getting her lovely gown dirty by traipsing all over the grounds."

Thankfully Lizzy didn't comment further. Ella knew that

would have been more than her father's temper could have tolerated.

"If the rest of you ladies would excuse us—" He paused, then without warning called Ella's name. "Why don't you join us? Ella also knows horses, and it might be nice for Lizzy to have her friend along. Certainly more appropriate." He didn't give anyone a chance to speak but turned and led the way.

There would be a price to pay for all of this later, but for now, Ella took up her shawl and kept very close to Lizzy Brookstone.

Lizzy could see that Mr. Fleming was unhappy with the turn of events. She had learned long ago that men of his breeding were often reluctant to believe a woman held any value outside of keeping a house and bearing children. She hadn't meant to comment on his remark, but the words were out of her mouth before she could hold them in check.

"You can see for yourself they are a handsome pair," Mr. Fleming announced as a uniformed groom lead the mares into the showroom. "I'm still disappointed in myself for agreeing to part with them."

The four-year-old Morgans were finer than any Lizzy had seen. Their large brown eyes seemed to watch her with concentrated care. They were nervous at the new attention, but Lizzy could see their quality and the remarkable strength of character, even in this brief encounter. Her father had told her about the horses long before she'd ever seen them, and his instincts about them had been right.

"They are very fine." She moved slightly to the right to better see them.

"Samson," Mr. Fleming called, "walk them around the room."

The man quickly followed the command. He led the mares together, one on either side of him. He walked them the full length of the showroom and back.

They were superb. Their buckskin coats glistened in the lamplight. They bore all the Morgan qualities Lizzy loved. Delicate, fine-chiseled features marked their heads. Their elegant necks were draped with black manes, and their tails bore the same ebony hue. Lizzy could only imagine the beautiful foals they would bear.

"They are handsome," Uncle Oliver declared. "My brother never failed to find the best. That's why he preferred your farm to any other."

Mr. Fleming smiled for the first time since the trouble at dinner. "I'm glad to be appreciated."

Lizzy looked at Ella, who stood between her father and fiancé. Spiby held on to her in a possessive manner, and Ella looked miserable. They were completely mismatched. Ella was petite and childlike, while Spiby was at least twice her age and stood a head and a half taller. It was appalling to imagine her having to marry the much older man.

A cat skittered through the room and spooked the mares. The one on the right started to rear, which upset her twin. Neither horse would easily calm. Lizzy watched as Jefferson Spiby stepped forward and yanked down on the rope that held the mare on the left.

"You must show them who has control," he said even as the horse backed away from him and shook its head. He reached up and twisted hard on the mare's ear. The horse on the right became even more agitated.

Lizzy started to say something, but Uncle Oliver put his hand on her arm. The look he gave her urged restraint.

"For pity's sake, Samson, control those animals," Mr. Fleming demanded. He turned back to Lizzy and her uncle. "As you can see, they're high-spirited, but with the right trainer, they will perform in whatever manner you choose."

Spiby finally had his horse under control and looked back at them with a broad smile. "Rather like a good woman."

Lizzy stiffened and considered throwing back a sarcastic comment, but one glance at Ella changed her mind. Spiby wasn't worth it, especially if it only served to cause her friend more pain.

Thankfully, August Reichert, the Brookstones' head wrangler, took that moment to appear and try to get the attention of Lizzy's uncle. Lizzy could see the other men were already deep in conversation about something, so she went to August, curious at the look of perplexity upon his face.

"Good evening, August. Do you need something from Uncle Oliver?"

"Since he's busy, maybe we could have a word in private, you and me?"

She smiled. "Of course." She glanced back at Ella. "If you'll excuse me."

Lizzy followed August from the showroom, and once they were well away, he stopped to look back at the building. "They're a touchy lot around here. I'll be glad when we leave."

"Why do you say that?"

They were far enough from the lanterns that lit the path from the house that Lizzy could barely make out the frown on August's face. "I turned our horses out in the field as I was instructed, but when I came back to the stables, lookin' for some liniment to rub on Betty's black, I was all but strong-armed out by Fleming's men and accused of snooping. I tried to explain what I needed and that I wasn't trying to cause a ruckus, but they wouldn't hear me out."

Lizzy considered this. Mr. Fleming had allowed them to graze the Brookstones' horses in his pastureland, but apparently his generosity only went so far. "I admit that Mr. Fleming and Mr. Spiby are hardly the sort I like doing business with. Father never spoke much about them except to say they produced excellent stock."

"Well, I just want to let you know that I'll be riding back to the train to get some of our own liniment and salve. I didn't want anyone wonderin' where I'd gotten off to, and the other boys are in town for a night of fun."

"That's fine, August. Since the horses are in the pasture, I don't foresee any problems. I'll let my uncle know when he's finished with Mr. Fleming." She gave a slight shrug. "Perhaps I'll even mention what happened in front of Mr. Fleming so that it doesn't happen again. There's nothing quite like embarrassing a man in front of his guests to bring about better behavior."

August shook his head. "Or worse."

☆≈ FIVE ≈☆

Wesley DeShazer sorted through the stack of bills. He had taken a chance and bought extra feed and hay. The old-timers felt certain it was going to be a bad winter. Maybe not as bad at '86–'87, but sure to be rough. Eastern Montana wasn't known to be kind when the months turned bitter.

He leaned back in the well-worn leather chair and stretched his arms over his head. The show folks would soon return to the ranch, and that would mean extra work and animals. Extra men to help with the herd as well.

It also meant Elizabeth Brookstone would be in residence. He tried not to think about her, but once in a while her memory snuck in like a fox to the henhouse.

He'd first met Lizzy when she was no more than a scrawny tomboy yet already an accomplished equestrian. He had marveled at how she could crawl all over the body of her mount at a full gallop. He could still see her standing on the back of her horse, her dark brown hair flying out behind her and her arms raised heavenward, as if she might be able to touch the sky.

As a child, Lizzy had been carefree and inquisitive. She'd taken to Wes immediately and hung around him like a faithful puppy. He pretended to be annoyed, but they both knew he didn't mind. He was barely a man doing his first real job and so homesick that having a little sister around, chattering about whatever popped into her head, made life away from home bearable.

It wasn't long before he met Clarissa Strong in Miles City—or Milestown, as some of the old-timers called it. She was the only daughter to a sickly mother and an abusive father. Her father was a good-for-nothing drunk who seemed to take special delight in tormenting his wife and child. Mrs. Strong worked at taking in laundry and mending, and Mr. Strong worked occasionally helping the blacksmith. His real job, however, seemed to be drinking up whatever earnings they made. It got to be so bad that Clarissa had to leave school and get a job at the local bakery in order to keep a roof over their heads.

They barely scraped by, and Wes had always felt sorry for them. Clarissa in particular. Her father thought nothing of hitting her for the most minor offense. It wasn't at all unusual to see her with a black eye, or hobbling because her father had kicked her repeatedly. Wes had wanted to confront the old man, but Clarissa told him it would only make matters worse.

When her mother died, things took a truly grim turn. Her father's anger surged, and it wasn't long before he wasn't even allowed in the local drinking halls. No one wanted to deal with his violent temper. Clarissa had barely turned eighteen when her father got himself killed in a fight. After that, Clarissa had few choices. She could marry one of the local cowboys or find a job that paid enough to support her in the tiny shack her father had leased. Bakery work certainly couldn't pay enough, and Clarissa hadn't the skills to earn more. Wesley had felt obligated to help her and proposed marriage.

They'd both known it wasn't a love match. Wes was fond of Clarissa, but more than anything, he wanted to save her from a plight worse than death. Clarissa had known her prospects were limited and eagerly accepted his offer. Plenty of men wanted her, but most were like her father, and the decent ones were just as bad off financially as she was. Wesley was the better choice. He had a good job—a foreman at a ranch—with his own little cabin to live in.

When Wes returned to the ranch with a wife in tow, the Brookstone family had been congratulatory and generous. Mrs. Brookstone went to work immediately to dress up his bachelor cabin. Not only that, but she'd taken Clarissa under her wing and helped her learn all she needed to know about ranch life.

Lizzy, however, hadn't taken the news well at all. He hadn't registered it then, but she and Clarissa were the same age, or nearly so. Lizzy had declared herself in love with him, but he'd figured it was just the silly notion of a little girl that would pass soon enough. Instead, Lizzy had been truly hurt by his marriage.

For weeks he hadn't understood her attitude toward him. It took her father's comment one day to open Wesley's eyes to the truth.

"It'll take time for her to get used to you having another woman in your life," Mark Brookstone had told him after Lizzy snubbed Wes during branding. *"But her heart will mend in time."*

Wes banged his fist on the desk. Thinking about the past wasn't going to get his work done. The Brookstones would soon be home, and he needed to be able to account for the year to Oliver rather than to his brother Mark. Wes was sad that Lizzy's father was gone. He had been good to work for, and he'd always known how to coax Wes to talk about what troubled him and then given great advice. But now he was dead. The ranch wouldn't be the same without him.

Without warning, Wes's office door opened. Matt, one of the hands, gave a nod toward something behind him. "Fella here says he needs to see you. Says he's your brother."

Wesley's eyes narrowed. Phillip? Here? "Send him in."

Wes gathered his papers and ledger and stuffed them into the top drawer. He got to his feet just as his brother strolled into the room, acting as if they had seen each other only the day before.

Phillip grinned. "I guess you're surprised to see me."

The reply stuck in Wes's throat. He hadn't seen his kid brother since their father's funeral. Wes had been a bridegroom only a few months when word came that their father had been killed. He'd seen Phillip at the funeral, but not again—until now, over ten years later.

But it *was* Phillip, as sure as they lived and breathed. He was taller, but not by much, and still scrawny, although as Phillip pulled off his coat, Wes could see he'd muscled up over the years.

"I know I've given you a shock, but you could at least say something," Phillip declared.

"I guess I'm not sure what to say." Wes sat back down and just stared.

"Well, maybe you could say you're glad to see me. Or maybe, 'How are you doin'?'"

"Or how about 'Where have you been?' Or 'Why didn't you bother to show up when our mother died?'" Wes asked in a snide tone. Anger was beginning to replace his surprise.

Phillip held out his hands. "That wasn't my fault. I didn't hear about it until the day of the funeral, and I wasn't able to leave." He grinned. "I was a guest of the city jail in Cheyenne." He pulled up a chair and turned it around backwards before plopping down. He leaned his arms across the back. "I would have come if I could. Ma knew how I felt. I'm sure she forgave me."

Wes clenched his teeth. He didn't want to fight with his brother—not when it was the first time they'd seen each other in a decade. "Where have you been?"

"Everywhere. Mostly Wyoming." Phillip gave a shrug. "Been workin' wherever I could get hired on. I'm good with horses, like you. There ain't a mount I can't break."

"Is that a fact?" Wes crossed his arms. He really was glad to see Phillip. He'd feared his brother was running with outlaws or dead.

Phillip laughed. "You know I always liked to do whatever my big brother could do . . . only better."

"I reckon I do."

"Well, I heard you were still up this way and figured it was about time I checked up on you. Thought you might be glad to see me."

Wesley nodded. "I am. I would have been glad to see you nine years ago or even five at Ma's funeral. I would have been glad just to get a letter. Do you have any idea how worried we were about you?"

"Ma always said worry was a sin." Phillip straightened and gave another of his good-natured smiles. "Besides, I wrote Ma twice."

Wes shook his head. "Twice in how many years?"

Phillip smacked the back of the chair. "That's all in the past. I can't make up for it now. I thought maybe we could just put it behind us."

"Funny how people who've done wrong are always the first to want everyone to forget about it."

"Well, we were always told that good Christians were supposed to forgive and forget. Ma would have wanted that."

For all that Phillip was twenty-six years old, Wesley couldn't help seeing him as a little boy. There had been times when their father had taken Phillip to task for one offense or another, and Phillip had sat before him with the same look on his face. He was so willing to receive correction, but just as willing to turn around and repeat the wrongdoing. Their folks were hard-pressed to get mad, however. Phillip was just too sweet, and his joyful countenance made it impossible to stay mad at him.

But Wesley wasn't sure he felt that way anymore. His brother had broken their mother's heart by disappearing after Pa's funeral. With each week that passed without word, she'd grown more concerned that Phillip might have fallen on hard times, gotten sick, or maybe even died. She refused to move to the ranch where Wes could take care of her for fear that Phillip would come home and not know where to find her. Then a letter would finally come, and all of Ma's worries were forgotten.

Until another stretch of time passed without word.

Yes, there had been two letters. She'd read both until the writing was faded and barely legible. She'd held on to the hope that there would be more letters and that Phillip would one day return to her, but that day never came. How was Wesley supposed to forgive and forget that?

"You mustn't hold it against him," Ma had said just before succumbing to her sickness. *"He doesn't know what he's done—how he's hurt us. He never meant to hurt anyone. That was never his way. Forgive him, Wes."*

The memory of his mother's words haunted him. She would have welcomed Phillip with open arms and never questioned the missing years. But Wes wasn't his mother, and he didn't know if he could forgive.

"What do you want, Phillip?" Wes finally asked, unable to find any peace in his heart.

Phillip's grin reappeared. "Why, that's simple. A job."

———

"Now can you tell me what's wrong?" Lizzy asked as she and Ella began their ride across the large open pasture the next day.

"I'll try, but you must swear to say nothing." Ella rode beside Lizzy on her favorite gelding. She called him Pepper because of his black coat. "If word ever got back to my father . . . well, it wouldn't be pleasant. You saw how angry he was last night when you mentioned what happened to your wrangler."

"I was surprised by how enraged he became. It was terrible when he promised to whip the grooms involved. I've never heard of such things in this day and age. So don't worry, I promise your father and the others will hear nothing of it from me," Lizzy assured.

"As you know, I'm supposed to marry in December."

"Yes, but I get the feeling it isn't what you want." Lizzy looked over at Ella with unwavering concern. "And frankly I can't fault you for that."

"I don't want to marry him. Jefferson is old enough to be my father. Well, nearly so. He is Father's dearest friend and confidant. They have many business dealings between them, and I happen to be one of them."

Lizzy looked away, as if contemplating the landscape. "It's 1900. Arranged marriages went out of fashion long ago."

"Not here. Proper young ladies only marry with their father's approval, and often that approval is only given in arranged marriages." Ella glanced over her shoulder, still not completely comfortable discussing the matter aloud. "But I am afraid I can't be a proper young lady. Not if it means marrying Jefferson. He's cruel and lewd. I've heard horrible rumors about him. They say he has not one, but three mistresses."

"Good grief!" Lizzy turned to her with a look of stunned disbelief. "Three?"

Ella nodded. "He has a reputation for being with women of all kinds, and he gambles and deceives. Whenever he's here and we're alone, he tries to take liberties."

"Have you mentioned it to your father? Surely he doesn't approve."

"I tried to talk to Father. He told me Jefferson is just overcome with love for me and anxious for us to wed. I mentioned the other women, but Father told me that men of power have needs that go beyond the home. He said that I need to concern myself only with being a wife and mother and that I'm not to listen to any of the rumors. But how can I not? And how can I bear a life with that man?"

"Why can't you just refuse to marry him?"

Ella's shoulders slumped. "Father said he would force me if I refused."

"But surely a minister would insist on your being willing."

"Father has powerful people on his side. He told me he would have one of his judge friends sign all the papers and declare us married, even without my permission. Almost every man in the county owes my father for something."

Lizzy considered that for a moment, then spoke. "But wouldn't that be an embarrassment to the family? I know reputations down here are important. If the community knew that he'd forced you to marry against your will, wouldn't that bring shame upon him?"

"He wouldn't allow me to say anything of the kind. I'm sure I'd be whisked away and locked in a room with Jefferson until I agreed to cooperate. I heard Father tell Jefferson that he'd be wise to get me with child as soon as possible." She shook her head. "Like I'm a brood mare and nothing more. Certainly not a cherished daughter." Tears formed in her eyes. "I don't know what I'm going to do."

"Why don't you leave? Didn't you tell me you have a sister in Chicago? Surely you could go live with her."

"They won't allow it. I'm virtually a prisoner. If I showed up in town to purchase a train ticket, my father would hear about it and drag me back home. Either him or Jefferson."

They rode on in silence for some time. It was clear there was no easy solution, but Ella couldn't help hoping that Lizzy might have an idea. God knew, Ella was out of ideas herself. She'd tried praying for direction, but God seemed strangely silent.

"What about your friends?" Lizzy asked after some time. "Isn't there someone nearby who could help you get away?"

"My girlhood friends are all married with families of their own. I've lived a very secluded life the last two years. Once my betrothal was formally announced, Father and Jefferson sought to keep me away from my friends. They always make excuses for why I'm not at various parties. I attend church with Mother and Father, and of course Jefferson, but I'm not allowed to be alone or say much to anyone."

"And no one thinks this strange?" Lizzy asked. Her tone was astonished. "What's wrong with the people around here?"

"They are in my father's debt, for one thing. His or Jefferson's. No one questions their actions or deeds. Those who benefit from them are more than happy to keep the truth from being known, and those who would protest or condemn are quickly silenced or ruined."

The sun was rapidly sliding toward the horizon, and Ella knew they'd soon have to return to the house and dress for supper. "I'm sorry for involving you in this, Lizzy. You don't deserve having to listen to all of this."

"I'm the one who's sorry. I had no idea anything like this was happening . . . or could happen." Lizzy looked around. "How were you allowed to come out alone with me?"

Ella tried to appear nonchalant. "I didn't tell them. Father was busy with your uncle and Mr. Adler, and Jefferson wasn't here. I'm sure once they figure it out, Father will send someone to find us."

"I'm so sorry, Ella. I don't know what to do. We'll be gone so soon."

Ella could hear the sincerity in Lizzy's voice. A thought came to her, sparked by her friend's words. "I don't know how we might pull it off, but perhaps I could . . . sneak away with the show."

"What?" Lizzy pulled back on the reins. A smile broke across her face. "Why, that's a brilliant idea. No one would ever expect that."

Ella felt hope wash over her. "I know it would be a risk, but I think if I could just get out of town and far enough from here, I could catch a train to Chicago, where my sister lives."

She could see that Lizzy was pondering how to make it work. "We're heading back to town around noon tomorrow. Mother has some shopping to see to, and I promised I'd help. Then there are the other performers' needs to take care of. Our horses won't be rounded up until evening, however."

Ella nodded, remembering that the Brookstones' horses had been given one of the Flemings' pastures. "I could feign a headache and retire early, then sneak out and ride in."

"But how would you get to the train? That's several miles from here. And you'd be in town, so someone might see you."

"I'll get Mara to help me. She can get Elijah to take my horse out to the edge of the trees. When it's good and dark and Father is busy with seeing your horses returned, I can ride into town through the woods. None of our people will accompany the horses back to town, just yours."

"If you can manage to meet August down the road, I can get him to put your horse in with the others. He's our head wrangler and loyal to a fault. He'll keep our secret. Do you think Mara could help you to dress like one of the wranglers?"

Ella brightened. "You want me to look like a boy . . . a man."

"Yes. When you reach town, you'll appear to be one of the Brookstone workers. August can board your horse with the others and then show you which car is mine. You'll stay with me and Mother. Once the horses are loaded, we'll leave with the late train bound for St. Louis."

"It sounds like it could work." Ella could feel her burden lighten.

Lizzy nodded. "I'm positive it can work. You'll see. We'll get you out of here and then figure out how to get you to your sister's place."

———◆◆◆◆———

"August, could I bother you for a moment?" Lizzy asked as she came upon him tending to Betty's horse. "Is he better?"

The wrangler released the gelding's leg and nodded. "He's doing just fine. This rest has done the trick. Couldn't have come at a better time."

"I'm glad to hear it. I've enjoyed the rest myself."

August gave the black a pat. "He's a good animal." He pushed back his hat. "Just let me get him back in the field, and you can have my full attention."

"I'll walk with you. I'd rather no one overhear us."

August frowned. "Secrets?"

Lizzy nodded and tried her best to look perfectly at ease. "Yes. A rather delicate one."

They said nothing more as they walked Betty's horse back to the white-fenced field where the rest of the Brookstones' horses were grazing. Lizzy opened the gate for August and waited for him to release the horse. She didn't like involving him in the situation, but it couldn't be helped. She pitied Ella more than any woman she'd ever known, and Lizzy knew she couldn't stand by and do nothing.

August joined her, wrapping the lead around his arm and grinning. "What can I do for you?"

"I need your word that you'll say nothing about this to anyone. It's very important—very nearly a matter of life and death."

That wiped the smile from his face. "I promise."

Lizzy nodded. "Miss Fleming needs our help. She must get away from here, or she'll be forced to marry that awful Mr. Spiby. I've told her that if she can disguise herself enough to get away and join you when you bring our horses back to the train tomorrow night, we'll hide her and take her with the show."

"But won't her people think of that first thing?" He leaned back against the fence and shook his head. "I can't help but think they'll come to us looking for her."

"I've thought of that as well. That's why no one but you and me will know anything about it. Ella will get to the woods and then join you in the dark. After that, you'll come to the train. I'll be waiting, so just have her hide somewhere if it doesn't look possible to get her to my family's train car unseen. After that, I'll take care of her. She has a sister she can go to in time, but for now we're her only hope."

"All right. I'll do it, because I've got a bad feeling about this place and don't blame her one bit for wanting to leave. Did you know that Fleming whipped his men for what they did to me?"

"I heard. I don't like it any more than you do. It was never my intention that anyone come to harm."

"Nor mine. I'm sorry I ever said anything about it."

"Don't be. Whatever the reason for the way the men acted, whatever Fleming's issues, I won't have our people treated badly." She could see her uncle and Mr. Fleming making their way from the stables. Uncle Oliver waved to her. "I think I'm wanted. Please remember: Don't breathe a word of this to anyone. I'm counting on you."

August grinned. "Miss Lizzy, you know there's nothing I wouldn't do for you."

She smiled. "I do know that, August, which is exactly why I came to you in the first place."

⬥━◦✕◦━⬥

The next day Ella felt as though she were floating on air. She listened patiently as her father finalized plans with the Brookstones, then bid Lizzy good-bye without hesitation. She had arranged for Mara to bring boy's clothes to her room. Given Ella's tiny frame and short stature, there was no hope of being able to wear the clothes of a full-grown man. It was a pity Robert's boys were so young, or she might have snuck into the nursery to borrow some of their things.

The only problem came when Jefferson made an unannounced appearance in the late afternoon. Ella had been about to take an afternoon ride, and rather than deal with her fiancé, she hurried down the servants' stairs and slipped out to the stables unnoticed. She hurried one of the stableboys through saddling Pepper and was out and away from the house before anyone could stop her. Hopefully her exit that night would be just as easy.

Unfortunately, when she returned from her ride, she heard her father's unmistakable voice in the stable. He was angry, shouting and ranting about something. Her blood chilled as Jefferson replied.

"I'll take care of it. That man won't cause us any trouble, because he won't be allowed to speak about what he's seen."

"You'll have to act quickly," Father replied. "If he talks about what he's witnessed, we'll be ruined."

"Hardly that. Who would believe him?"

"I can't take the chance," Ella's father answered. "Neither can you."

Ella froze in place, afraid to advance farther into the stable. What were they talking about? What man? What had he seen?

"I said I would handle it, and I will," Jefferson said. "After today, it will no longer be a concern."

SIX

The day dragged by for Lizzy. She and Mother handled the shopping with the help of Zeb and Thomas, two of the oldest of their show's crew. The men had worked a great many years for the Brookstones, having been hired by Lizzy's grandfather. Now they were nearing the end of their days, and their options for earning a living were extremely limited. What were old cowboys supposed to do when they could no longer handle the physical strain of the job? They had no family to take care of them, no money saved with which to support themselves in their final years. She thought of Jason's desire to eliminate their positions in order to save money. Where would these old men go then? Who would take care of them? She couldn't bear the idea of them being turned out.

But on top of her worries over them and what Jason would suggest or even demand be done, Lizzy couldn't stop thinking about Ella's situation. She was glad to be able to help, but the problem would not disappear just because Ella managed to leave her father's farm. Men like Mr. Fleming and that Mr. Spiby would never give up. They would hunt Ella down, and they had the money to do whatever was necessary to find her.

Am I just putting my family in danger by helping her?

Several times Lizzy had thought about telling her mother about Ella, but the time was never right. She worried that someone might overhear and word would get back to the Flemings, and then all would be lost and whatever small effort Lizzy might have managed would be for naught. No. It would be better to wait until Ella was on the train and they were safely on their way to St. Louis.

"Look, there's Agnes. She must have finished sooner than she expected," Mother announced. "I still need to go to the market to pick up some things for our supper tonight. Time's getting away from us, and if I'm going to have it ready on time, I'll need to get right to work."

Lizzy glanced down the street to the bakery they'd passed earlier. "Why don't we keep supper simple? I could go to the bakery and buy bread and perhaps a cake. Then we could get some ham and cheese for sandwiches. I'm sure everyone would get their fill, and that way you wouldn't have to work so hard."

"I suppose we could," Mother said. "Mrs. Fleming sent a wagon full of homemade canned goods as well as jams and jellies. They were made from her own garden and orchards."

Lizzy was relieved. "See, we'll have plenty to eat."

Mother smiled. "I suppose that would make it easy on everyone."

They finished the shopping and made their way back to the train. Lizzy found a certain comfort in being on board. It wasn't that she hadn't enjoyed their time at Fleming Farm, but the train car reminded her of her father. His influence and choices were everywhere, as he had designed the car to be set up just as it was. He had made much of the furniture and found smart ways to secure things in place.

How she missed him.

"Would you help me change my clothes?" Mother asked as she pulled the pin from her hat. "I feel too overdressed for preparing a meal. Even wearing black."

Lizzy felt the same way. "I don't mind getting dressed up from time to time, but I much prefer my riding clothes and costumes." She smiled and gave a shrug. "If you were hoping for a frilly and fancy daughter, I'm afraid I must disappoint."

Mother reached out and touched Lizzy's cheek. "I am never disappointed in you, Lizzy. You've always been good about just being yourself. No one can fault you for that."

"Oh, some can and do." The words slipped out before she could hold them in check.

Mother looked at her. "Who would fault you?"

Lizzy shook her head. "It isn't important. Frankly, I had no one particular in mind." Although now that she was contemplating it, she easily recalled more than once when Wesley had chided her for her tomboyish ways.

Mother touched her cheek again. There were tears in her eyes. "You are a beautiful young woman. Just remember that your love for God would make you that way even if you weren't otherwise pleasing." She sniffed. "Your father always said he could see the love of Jesus shining through your eyes."

Lizzy's throat tightened, but she would not allow herself to cry. She patted her mother's hand. "He said the same of you. I'm so glad we have the Lord to guide us and help us through our sorrows. Now, come on. You undo my back buttons, and I'll undo yours." Lizzy forced a smile. "Then I'll help you with supper."

The troupe shared their evening meals in what was called the entertainment car. One train car was set up to be a gathering place for all the performers and crew who weren't needed in the livestock or tack cars. At one end was the show's office, and at the other Agnes's sewing room. When en route, it was here that the crew passed the hours reading, playing cards, writing letters, or even singing. More than once, the ladies had come together as a choir to entertain the others.

Lizzy usually spent her time on the rails in the family car, however. Especially now that her father was gone. She didn't feel much like socializing. She was still open and willing to discuss whatever was necessary with her fellow performers, but she preferred the quiet of her own space. She supposed that was another reason she didn't particularly want to have to treat Jason Adler as family. He seemed to always seek her out and want to talk. Tonight was no exception. Three times now he'd tried to corner her, and all she wanted was to be left alone to keep watch for Ella.

Finally, as the hour grew late, Uncle Oliver became her savior.

"Jason, why don't you come with me and the boys?" Uncle Oliver announced. "The horses will be arriving soon, and I'd like you to see how we handle the loading."

"I'd be glad to," Jason said, casting a glance at Lizzy. "Perhaps we could speak later?"

Lizzy shook her head. "No, I plan to go to bed early. Maybe tomorrow."

She hurried back to the family car before he could speak. She didn't want him trying to change her mind.

"I don't need you courting me, Jason Adler."

Ella paced her room frantically, hoping and praying the time would pass quickly. Each time she stopped in front of the fireplace, she glanced at the beautiful ceramic clock. Was it even working? She was certain the hands hadn't moved in hours.

She still had to get through supper without giving herself away. That wouldn't be easy. Her father seemed to note her every mood. Still, she could easily excuse her silence and reflective manner by explaining that she was sorry to see Lizzy go. He'd believe her. He had no reason not to. He was the one, along with Jefferson, who had made her a virtual prisoner at the farm. He was the one who saw to it that she received very few guests.

She would perhaps emphasize her sadness and remind him that she had no friends.

She shook her head. "It would serve no purpose. He doesn't care, and I'll soon be gone."

Mara appeared to help Ella dress for dinner. The maid knew about her plan to escape and had even offered to go with her. Poor Mara. She had been at the receiving end of Father's anger more than once.

"Elijah say he'll have Pepper waitin' for you just over the bridge and in the trees," Mara whispered as she did up the buttons on the back of Ella's silk dress. The gown was a new creation her mother had ordered from Paris. It was lush and beautiful, exactly the kind of dress any young woman would love. Ella had to admit she would miss the finery her father's money could buy. But her sister Margaret was by no means poor. She'd married well enough. Her husband, Isaac, was in business with his father and brother, and together they owned Knox Saddlery. Their saddles were sought out far and wide. Margaret and Isaac lived quite well on a beautiful estate outside of Chicago, but they weren't as rich as Father.

"I'll come back after supper—early, if need be," Ella said in a hushed voice. "Did you get the clothes?"

"Yes'm. I gots 'em, and I'll have 'em ready." The black woman led Ella to the vanity chair in order to arrange her hair. "I also packed you some other things you be needin'. Elijah gonna bring them with your horse."

Ella had figured she'd have to go with nothing but the clothes on her back. "Truly? That's wonderful. Would it include a change of clothes?"

"Yes'm. It's all in your small travel bag. He'll be havin' it for you, never you fear."

Ella sighed. "I'm going to miss you, Mara." She looked up at the dark-skinned woman. She and Mara had been raised together.

Mara's mother, Lucille, had cared for Ella throughout her child-hood. Lucille had taught Ella not only to embroider, but to actu-ally sew. Mother would have had a fit had she seen her daughter on the floor with the servants, cutting apart clothes and making patterns from each piece. Of course, Mother and Father both would have had a fit if they'd known Ella had learned to Roman ride and do other stunts on horseback. Her brother and one of the servant boys had taught her when she'd been barely old enough to ride alone. It was just one more reason she felt a close bond with Lizzy Brookstone. She longed for the same freedom Lizzy enjoyed.

"I'll be missin' you too, Miss Ella." Mara's eyes were damp with tears, but she held on to her emotions and continued to arrange Ella's blond hair into an acceptable fashion. When she was done, Mara stepped back. "I be finished."

Ella stood and nodded. "I'll be back as soon as I can without arousing suspicion."

She made her way downstairs and found her brother and sister-in-law in the family parlor. Virginia smiled as Ella came into the room, but it was Robert who spoke.

"My, but don't you look pretty. Jefferson is sure to press for an earlier wedding day."

"That's hardly my goal." Ella looked around. "Is he here again?"

"Of course, little sister. He's not going to let you get far from sight. Frankly, I'm surprised he hasn't taken a room here." Her brother chuckled.

"Don't say as much to Father, or he'll no doubt extend the invitation." Ella went to the window and pulled back the sheers to look outside.

Robert joined her at the window. "You could do much worse than Jefferson Spiby. You'll always have a life of comfort and ease married to him."

"Especially if he spends more time in town visiting his mis-tresses than with me at home."

Her brother frowned. "He isn't the man I would have chosen for you, but you'll have a good life. Jefferson would never allow his wife to lift a finger. And not only that, but you'll always be close to home—no fear of him taking you off away from the family."

"But what if I want to lift a finger? What if I want to move far away?" Ella looked up at him. "You know as well as anyone that I'm kept here against my will. I'm never allowed to go to town unless Mother and Father are at my side, and usually Jefferson as well."

"They're only looking out for your well-being. You know there have been difficulties in town. Some of the women have complained about not feeling safe," Virginia said, joining them. "I, for one, am always glad to have Robert along."

He nodded and put his arm around his wife's shoulders. "It's far better to be overprotected than abused."

Ella sighed. "I have no desire to marry Jefferson. You both know his reputation."

"You're nearly twenty-one," Virginia protested. "People would already be talking about you if not for your engagement."

"Jefferson is more than double my age. I don't want to marry an old man."

Virginia took her hand. "If you feel so adamant about it, perhaps you should speak to your father again."

"He won't hear me on the matter. He's told me quite firmly that I am never to bring it up. He doesn't care that Jefferson is a bully, nor about his reputation as a womanizer. He only tells me to keep my thoughts to myself and be a good girl who allows the men in her life to speak for her."

Virginia frowned and looked up at Robert. "Well . . . I have heard that Mr. Spiby doesn't always conduct himself in a good Christian manner."

"As have I, but Father is right. Ella just needs to be silent and let him direct her. Father would never want anything bad for you, Ella." He smiled down at her. "Just trust him. He'll see that Jefferson does right by you."

Nothing more was said, because her mother stepped into the room. "Goodness, why are you all gathered at the window? Is there something interesting to see?"

Robert laughed and led Virginia across the room. He bent to kiss Beatrix Fleming's cheek. "Good evening, Mother. How lovely you look."

Their mother smiled. "Thank you, Robert. You're quite dashing yourself." She smiled at Virginia. "And you are lovely, my dear. I told you that butternut color was perfect for your complexion."

"You did, and I'm very pleased with the results," Virginia said, running her hand down the side of her pigeon-breasted, lace-embellished gown.

Father chose that moment to enter. Jefferson was at his side, as usual, and the two had their heads close together in low conversation. They looked up and separated quickly, however, at the sight of the others. Both looked quite grim.

"What is it, George?" Mother asked.

"I'm afraid there's been an accident."

Mother put a hand to her mouth.

"What kind of accident?" Ella asked, coming to her mother's side.

"The Brookstones' wrangler has been killed."

Everyone gasped, and the color drained from Mother's face.

"What happened?" Robert asked as Ella led her mother to a chair.

"Horse trampled him," Jefferson answered before Ella's father could speak.

"That's awful," Virginia murmured. "Poor man."

"One of the risks of the job. We've sent word to the train. Our men will take the horses in and . . . the body."

Ella felt her stomach knot. This was terrible. Not only because of the loss of the poor man, but her plans were now in jeopardy. What could she do? She could hardly go along with the Fleming Farm workers. They'd know who she was, even in boy's clothes.

"We'll have them move out as soon as the sheriff arrives," Father said. "He'll have to ask his questions before the body can be moved."

"Oh, dear. I'm afraid I don't feel very well," Mother said. "I must go lie down."

Father nodded. "I think it would wise for all of you ladies to take supper in your rooms tonight. This is a terrible affair, and we will need to explain the situation to the sheriff."

Ella nodded. "I'll see that Mother gets to her room." She tried to think past the moment. How could she use this terrible situation to her advantage?

Once upstairs, Ella summoned her mother's maid. "Serena, Mother has had a shock. Please see she gets to bed. I'll have some food sent up." The maid took Ella's mother in hand and led her away to the bedroom.

Ella quickly returned to her own room, and it wasn't long before Mara appeared. She had already heard the news and wondered if Ella's plans had changed.

"No, I still want to go. Only now I figure I'll have to leave when the sheriff arrives. Everyone will be too busy to notice. Please have Elijah take my horse now. They won't go into the family stables—at least I presume they won't. I figure the accident must have happened on the west end, where they'd gathered the Brookstones' horses. After you instruct Elijah, please hurry back here to help me with my clothes."

"Yes'm." Mara raced from the room while Ella began to do what she could to undress.

She heard the arrival of the sheriff, since her bedroom faced the front of the house. He'd come with several other men, including the doctor. She couldn't see well enough to tell who the other men were. Everyone raced toward the far west stables, just as Ella had figured.

She went to her jewelry box and opened the lid. She had several pieces that had been given to her by her parents. None of them were family heirlooms, so Ella stuffed them into a little drawstring bag. She would sell them in St. Louis to get money for her new start. She started to turn away but noticed the bracelet Jefferson had given her. She wanted nothing to remind her of him, but it was sterling and jade. Perhaps it would bring her a few extra dollars. She took it as well.

Mara returned and helped Ella change. They had never managed so quickly. Mara was perspiring profusely. No doubt she was just as scared as Ella. Until this moment, it hadn't dawned on Ella that Mara might be punished.

"Look, no matter what," Ella said, stopping to take Mara's hand, "I don't want you to get in trouble. When they ask you where I am, tell them I went to bed, sickened by all that's happened, and said I didn't want to be disturbed."

Ella went to her vanity and picked up her room key. "Lock the door, then hide the key. Throw it away, even. Whatever you do, don't take it back to your room, because they're sure to look there when they start to suspect you might know where I went. In the morning, make a fuss. Come down crying or upset and tell Mother that I won't open my door. That way it will be clear that you still think I'm in my room."

Mara nodded. "Yes'm. I'll do just that."

Ella gave her a hug. "I love you, Mara. You're like a sister to me." This would be the first time they'd ever been separated.

"I be prayin' for you, Miss Ella. Prayin' real hard," Mara said as Ella pulled away.

"I know you will. I'll be praying for you as well. If all goes well, Father won't find me until after I turn twenty-one. That's just until January, and then maybe I can send for you." She doubted her father would ever allow Mara to join Ella, but it comforted her to say as much.

Glancing once more out the window, Ella could see lanterns and all sorts of activity at the far end of the stables. "I must go. It's now or never." She pulled an old hat down over her blond hair. "Do I look passable?"

"In the dark, nobody'll know." Mara went to the door and opened it. She looked out, then nodded.

Ella slipped quietly down the back stairs. She stopped often to listen and make sure no one was nearby. She had to reach the trees, and it wouldn't be easy to cross the long, open lawns without someone seeing her. Hopefully anyone who did see her would presume she was just one of the boys searching for something.

She'd nearly reached the kitchen when she stopped cold at the sound of Jefferson and her father. They were speaking in hushed, quick statements.

"There was no other way."

"But now we've got this to deal with," her father said.

"He'd seen and heard too much."

"I know." It sounded like they were moving toward the back door. "I just don't like that you had to kill him."

Ella thought her heart might stop. She pressed hard against the wall of the stairs.

Jefferson actually laughed. "It wasn't my first killing, nor will it be my last. Now, you do your part and manage the explaining." His tone turned sarcastic. "I shouldn't have to do everything."

She heard them leave the room, and only after the screen door slammed shut did she feel she could continue. But Jefferson so casually admitting murder kept her frozen in place. He was the reason August Reichert was dead. The wrangler had seen too much.

But what in the world had he seen that merited death?

⋄⊱ SEVEN ⊰⋄

Wes looked around for his brother. It was nearly eight o'clock, and most of the men were headed to bed, if not already asleep. They were getting up at three in the morning to take calves to market, and every man there knew it would be a long day.

Wes left the bunkhouse and went to the barn. If Phillip's horse was gone, then he'd know the day of hard work hadn't agreed with his brother and he'd left. Probably for good. If that were the case, Wes figured it would be for the best. He was still uncertain about hiring his brother, but he'd promised their mother he would watch out for Phillip if he ever came around again.

The barn door was open, which gave him hope that Phillip might be there. Maybe he was just grooming his horse or taking care of his gear.

"Phillip?" Wes asked as he entered the barn. "Are you in here?"

"'Course . . . I am." Phillip staggered toward him. "Whaddaya . . . want?"

Wes frowned. "You're drunk."

Phillip stopped, pulled his chin back, and struggled to keep from swaying. "Wha'. . . if I am?"

"Brookstone cowboys aren't allowed to drink on the job. You aren't allowed to have liquor in the bunkhouse. Where'd you get it?"

Phillip laughed and shook his head. "I've always got a bottle. Not havin' a drink is . . . well . . ." He swayed again and caught hold of a stall gate just before falling. "Fella's gotta have a drink at the . . . the end of the day."

"Not here, they don't. And you've clearly had more than a drink." Wes shook his head. "Get rid of it. Any liquor you brought with you I want gone. Get rid of it immediately."

"Now wait jes a . . . jes a minute." Phillip's words were slurred, but he offered a grin as usual. "I finished it, but . . . why can't I have it?"

Wes closed the distance between them in two long strides. He took hold of Phillip's shoulders and gave him a fierce shake. "You can't have it because I need my men sober. If that's not possible for you, then you need to pack your gear and leave. We don't allow liquor on the Brookstone ranch."

Phillip's eyes widened. If possible, Wesley's words had sobered him. "You'd throw me out?" He blinked several times, as if the shaking had loosened something in his head.

"I'd throw you out, same as I'd throw any of the rest of them out. We have firm rules around here. I told them to you when I hired you on. If I can't depend on you to abide by them, you have to go. Even if you are my brother."

"Don't the res'. . . . res'. . . ." He smiled. "Don't the res' of the men drink?"

"If they do, they do it in town on their time and not mine." Wes pulled Phillip with him toward the door. "I'm going to put you to bed, and we'll discuss this in the morning. It's senseless to argue with a man who won't remember anything come daylight."

He'd no sooner gotten Phillip in bed and his boots off than the younger man was asleep. He hardly looked like more than a boy. With all the hard living and fights he'd no doubt been in over the years, Wes had figured it would change his appearance, but it hadn't. There was still something almost angelic in Phillip's expression. Their mother used to comment on it at times just like this. She'd sit beside her sleeping son and smile.

"For all his orneriness, there's really a good boy deep inside," Wes could almost hear her say.

Wes sat on the edge of the bed and pushed back the sandy brown hair that had fallen over one of Phillip's eyes. Where had he been all these years? Why had he forsaken his family? Wes knew there were issues in the past—things Phillip wouldn't even talk about. Their mother had tried and tried to get him to open up, but Phillip had always laughed it off or simply avoided the discussion. Maybe that was why he'd left. It definitely hadn't been for a lack of love, because no one had ever been as cherished and loved by their mother as Phillip had been. Wes couldn't even fault her for her favoritism, because he felt the same way. There was just something so loveable about Phillip that it was impossible to stay mad at him for long.

"Don't be angry with him. Pray for him instead." His mother's words echoed in Wesley's head.

Heaving a heavy sigh, Wes got to his feet. He pulled the blanket from the end of the bed and covered Phillip. He wanted to pray, but he wasn't sure God was even listening to him these days. It always seemed, when he tried to seek God in prayer, that the words just bounced back off the ceiling. He knew God existed—he truly believed that God did answer prayers. So why couldn't Wes shake the feeling that God was listening to everyone else but him?

As a part of her routine, Lizzy went to visit her horses every night before retiring. Longfellow and Thoreau had come to expect this, as well as the treats she brought. Zeb had put together a rope pen on land owned by the railroad. It wasn't much, but it was better than keeping the animals on the train.

Smiling, Lizzy offered carrots, apples, and her love to her beloved horses. "How are you boys doing?"

Neither paused in their munching. The treats were far too compelling. Lizzy stroked their manes and continued to talk as if they might join in at any moment.

"I'm glad we brought you two back early, but I'm sorry you don't have a better place to rest. The others will be here soon. Uncle Oliver said August would have them back by nine, but as you can see, that time has come and gone."

She frowned. August should have been here hours ago. Ella too. What had happened to delay everyone? Lizzy gave each of the horses one last piece of apple and then headed toward the train to find her uncle. She hadn't gone two steps, however, when someone called her name in a whisper.

"Lizzy?" Ella appeared from the shadows. She led her black horse and glanced around like a thief avoiding capture.

"Hurry. Bring him this way." Lizzy led the way to the railcar where the horses were kept. She startled at the sight of Rupert, one of the wranglers.

"Hey, Miss Lizzy." Rupert limped toward her. He'd been severely injured years earlier, and the leg had never healed properly. "What are you doing out here at this hour?"

"Rupert, I need your help and your silence." Lizzy motioned over her shoulder, then looked all around them, fearing they'd be seen. "We need to hide Miss Fleming's horse with our own. She's leaving the farm, and it'll spell trouble for everyone if she's found."

He frowned. "No problem, Miss Lizzy. I'll see that he's in

with the other blacks. He's enough like Miss Betty's horse that no one will ever notice."

Lizzy nodded. "Say nothing. I plan to tell Mother and Uncle Oliver after we're on our way."

"Yeah, I thought we'd be long gone by now. If August doesn't get here soon, we'll miss the midnight train."

"I know." Lizzy frowned and turned to Ella, who looked terrified. Lizzy felt bad for her. She was leaving the comfort of all she'd ever known, but not only that, if anyone found out before they got her safely out of town, it could cause no end of problems. "Come on, Ella. Rupert will see to your horse. I need to get you hidden away."

Ella nodded and fetched a bag from where it hung on the horn of her saddle. Rupert took the reins and led the horse down to another car before leading it up the boarding ramp.

"I'm going to hide you in the family car." Lizzy led Ella to the other end of the train. She hoped her mother was still busy with Agnes. She hurried to open the door and peer inside, then motioned Ella to join her.

Once inside, Ella paused to take a deep breath and steady her nerves. "It's such a dark night. I think I got a bit spooked. I thought I'd never get here. I had to ride out by myself for fear of being found out."

"Why? Where are August and the horses? They should have been here by now."

Ella's face paled, and her expression filled with fear. "I . . . uh . . . don't know exactly. There was some sort of trouble. I think it was with one of the horses. My father and Jefferson were both involved, and since they were both busy, I came on my own."

"That must be what has slowed August's return. Come with me." Lizzy crossed the car to the far side and opened a door. "This will be your room for now. There's a bunked berth. You can hide on top under the covers. Scoot clear to the back. No one will see you there, given the way it's positioned."

Ella pulled off the old felt hat she'd been wearing. Her hair was slightly mussed but styled as if for a party.

Lizzy couldn't help but smile. "Your hair is pretty, but it doesn't fit the rest of your ensemble."

The petite blonde looked down at her costume. "Mara found this outfit for me." She bit her lower lip.

Lizzy could see her friend was exhausted and scared. "You're safe now, Ella. Come on, let's get you settled."

Once Lizzy had seen to Ella, she made her way outside just as the horses arrived. She smiled and started over to where the riders were halting the string of animals. August was nowhere to be found, but the sheriff was prominently leading the herd.

Uncle Oliver and Jason Adler welcomed the sheriff as he climbed down from his bay. Some of the other wranglers came out and began to converse with the Fleming men. Lizzy moved to her uncle's side.

"What are you saying, Sheriff? He's dead?" Oliver said, his voice pinched with shock.

Lizzy stiffened. Who was dead?

"I'm surely sorry, Mr. Brookstone, but it appears the poor man was kicked in the head and then trampled to death. Mr. Fleming and Mr. Spiby are following behind with the wagon and the body."

Uncle Oliver turned to her. "August is dead."

"August?" Lizzy looked at the sheriff.

The sheriff tipped his hat. "I'm mighty sorry, miss. Fleming sent his men to bring your horses back. He should be here directly to explain what happened."

By now most of the Brookstone troupe had gathered. Mother took Lizzy's arm as Uncle Oliver and the sheriff continued to discuss the tragedy. The Brookstone wranglers took the horses from the Fleming Farm men and began loading them on the train. Jason remained with Lizzy and her mother.

"If there's anything I can do," Jason began.

"What happened?" Mother asked. "Someone said August is dead."

"That's all I know, except they said he was kicked in the head and then trampled to death." Lizzy could hardly believe it.

"With horses there is always a danger," Jason declared. "I've been kicked myself. Very nearly broke my leg."

"Yes, I'm sure anyone who's around a horse for long is going to experience some sort of injury, but August handled horses in such a way that he rarely had any trouble." Lizzy shook her head. "In fact, some say August had a divine touch."

Jason looked doubtful. "Things happen to even the best of men."

"He was so young and such a dear man," Mother said, shaking her head. "How will we manage without him?"

"I'm sure the other men can handle the horses," Jason said. "You've got a great team of people working for you."

"At least for the time being," Lizzy muttered.

Within a matter of minutes, Mr. Fleming and Mr. Spiby arrived in an old wagon. They had somehow arranged for a coffin. The wooden box no doubt contained the body of August Reichert. It seemed a foreboding sign, and Lizzy knew many in their troupe were superstitious.

Mr. Fleming was first off the wagon. He came to Mother and Lizzy and took off his hat. "Mrs. Brookstone, I'm so very sorry. We've brought your man back. My people did what they could to clean him up, but there wasn't much that could be done to make him presentable. I'm afraid the horses were brutal."

Mother shook her head. "How did it happen?"

The stocky man lowered his head. "We have a couple of green broke colts, and I'm afraid they got the better of Mr. Reichert."

81

"I've never seen a horse that August couldn't handle," Lizzy declared. The thought of August being killed by horses didn't make sense to her.

"He *was* talented," Mr. Spiby said, joining them. "I even offered to hire him away from you, although I'm ashamed to admit it now." He smiled, then gave his mustache a stroke with his index finger. "But accidents happen, and no one is immune to danger."

"That's true enough," Mother said, clinging to Lizzy's arm. "I appreciate that you've cared for him so completely." She turned to Lizzy. "Make sure Uncle Oliver pays them for the coffin and . . . anything else."

"Nonsense, Mrs. Brookstone," Fleming declared, raising his gaze. "It was my privilege to do this for the young man. I won't accept money, given the accident happened on my farm."

"Well, thank you so much for your kindness." Mother's words caught in her throat. "He . . . he was such a good man."

"Come on, Mother," Lizzy encouraged. "Let's go inside. We can't do anything more here."

"She's right," Jefferson Spiby said with a great deal of smugness. "You ladies shouldn't have to bother with such matters. You just leave it to us, and we'll see to everything."

Lizzy wanted to say something—anything—to show Spiby what she thought of his attitude, but she held her tongue. Leading Mother inside, a dozen questions raced through her head. Green broke colts were dangerous, that much was certain, but so too was it certain that August Reichert knew this and would have handled them carefully. Besides, what was he even doing with them? He was there to manage the new mares and the Brookstone stock. Why would he have been handling Fleming's colts?

"I can't believe the sorrows we've had on this tour," Mother said, sinking into the sofa.

Lizzy leaned against the wall. Her mother looked so fragile. There were lines in her face that hadn't been there this time last year. "Mother, I don't mean to add to our troubles, but there is something I need to tell you. I hope you'll understand."

"What is it?"

Lizzy knelt beside her. "You can't say anything to anyone about this."

"Is there anything I can do for you ladies?" Jason Adler asked from the doorway.

"No." Lizzy huffed and went to the door, blocking his entry. "We just need some privacy for the moment."

Jason looked apologetic and shook his head. "I'm sorry to have disturbed you."

Lizzy immediately regretted her harsh tone. "No, I'm sorry for snapping at you. It's just a lot to take in."

"I completely understand. If you have no need of my services, I'll go see how I might help your uncle. I believe we're arranging for the funeral home to manage the body and ship it back to his family."

Lizzy thought of Mary Reichert. She was August's sister and until this year had been Brookstone's sharpshooter. She would be devastated. She had quit the show in order to marry her childhood sweetheart, and their wedding was in less than a month. August's death would probably postpone it.

"Thank you for your help, Jason, but we'll be just fine." Lizzy waited until he'd gone, then closed the door.

"What's going on?" Mother asked, eyeing Lizzy suspiciously. "What do you need to tell me?"

Lizzy sat down beside her mother. "Ella Fleming has run away from home. She's hiding in the spare room." She pointed toward the tiny cabin.

"But why?"

"You saw Jefferson Spiby and the way he acted. He's even

worse when no one is around. Ella is being forced to marry him—some sort of financial arrangement. She's begged her father to release her from the agreement, but he won't hear of it. He plans for them to marry at Christmas, because Ella turns twenty-one in January and can speak for herself then."

"But interfering in a family matter isn't wise, Lizzy."

Lizzy looked at her mother's weary expression. Perhaps she should have waited to tell her. No doubt the news about August was only serving to bring back the pain of losing Father.

"I know it's not, Mother, but I felt strongly about this. I believe God would have us help her. She was in danger—I can't say exactly what might happen to her if she marries Mr. Spiby, but she's terrified. She planned to do whatever she had to in order to avoid marrying him."

"But where will she go now?"

"Eventually she wants to go to Chicago to live with her sister. But for now, I thought she could stay with us. We'll keep her hidden until it's time to take everyone back to Montana. I figure she can stay in our car, and I can bring her what she needs. We'll just have to keep everyone else out of here. At least until after our show in Kansas City."

Mother glanced at the door to the small sleeping room. "Very well. Since you feel so strongly about this, I'll trust that it is the right thing to do. I've never known you to act in a rash manner. Should I go speak with her?"

Lizzy smiled. "That might reassure her."

Mother nodded and got to her feet. "Does she know about August's death or her father being here?"

"I don't think so. She knew something was going on at the farm, which was why she set out by herself to get here. I'm sure she'll be very sorry to hear about August."

✧═ EIGHT ═✧

The St. Louis showground was packed to overflowing, as most of the Brookstone performances were. Lizzy led Longfellow through his paces as usual. The crowd was completely aghast at her maneuvers aback a galloping horse. Several women in the audience fainted, which wasn't unusual. It happened with such regularity during their tour that Uncle Oliver always gave a warning before the show. It only served to further excite the audience.

It seemed silly that anyone should faint doing nothing more than watching. It was different if they were asked to participate in the show. She remembered once last year when Mary Reichert was still shooting for the show. She had asked for a volunteer, and a giant, burly fellow quickly accepted. He came to the arena floor, and Mary made him stand with an apple on his head. She aimed her rifle and put a bullet straight through the center of the apple. The crowds went wild, and the man passed out. Lizzy could understand why the stress of that situation might cause someone to faint, although the man quickly recovered and promptly asked Mary to marry him. She declined.

Lizzy brought Longfellow to the far end of the arena, quickly adjusted some straps on her saddle, then put him back into a full gallop. With Longfellow in motion, Lizzy did a rump spin and then a backward somersault onto the horse's neck. In one fluid motion, she whirled back around, slipped her feet into the straps, and stood. The audience went wild with applause and cheers.

Longfellow reached the end of the run, and Lizzy slid back into the saddle and maneuvered the horse back to their starting position. She slipped her right foot through the drag loop and gave the gelding a couple of pats on the neck. There was just one more trick, perhaps the deadliest. She urged Longfellow forward while giving the crowd a wave. Without pausing, she appeared to fall backward and slip over the left side of the horse, bringing her left leg straight up in the air as she did. With her right foot securely anchored in the strap's hold, she raised her hands over her head to complete what some called a Cossack drag. It all happened at once, so the audience couldn't be sure that it was intended. There were gasps, more fainting no doubt, and then silence as Lizzy rode upside down, her head hanging right beside Longfellow's front legs.

With her long hair nearly dragging the dirt, Lizzy gave a wave, and the crowd jumped to their feet in raucous applause. She smiled to herself, caught the horn, and pulled back up onto Longfellow's neck. She freed her foot and did a simple saddle spin, ending in a shoulder stand.

"Isn't she amazing?" Uncle Oliver called out from behind his megaphone. "Let's hear it for Elizabeth Brookstone and her valiant steed, Longfellow!" The crowds went wild.

Lizzy righted herself and led Longfellow out of sight of the audience. She positioned her feet for the final stand and flag wave. There had been a couple of minor accidents with earlier performances, but overall the show had gone very well. She breathed a sigh of relief, remembering this was the next to last show of the season.

The other performers were taking their final bows. The sharpshooting girls raced around the arena on horseback, shooting their guns in the air to further stir up the audience. As if they needed any encouragement.

Next, the girls who did Roman riding circled the arena side by side. Each of the three girls had two horses apiece and stood astride their team. After they made one full circle, they joined two teams together, and the two performers stood astride the center horses, one in front of the other. For their final move, the third team joined them, and while one of the girls managed all six horses, the other two climbed onto either side of her. With a firm grip on a harness that ran under her jacket, each of the side performers stuck out their free arm and leg to create a star pattern. The cheers were deafening.

Brookstone's other trick riders preceded Lizzy into the arena, doing vaults and twists as they circled and waved to the audience. Finally, Lizzy rode out standing and waving the American flag. The small band provided by the arena broke into "The Star-Spangled Banner," and everyone began to sing. It was the perfect end to the evening.

Lizzy rode her horse from the arena. Zeb took the flag and offered them both praise while Lizzy slid off the buckskin.

"Longfellow, you were amazing! Such a good boy." She gave him a hug. "You're all done for the year."

Rupert took the reins from her. "They loved you tonight."

Lizzy laughed. "Indeed they did." She gave the horse one more rub of affection. "I'll use Thoreau for the last show," she told Rupert. "Longfellow's earned his rest, although I know he won't see it that way." She made her way over to the costume seamstress. "I managed to tear my blouse, Agnes." She pointed out the ripped shoulder seam.

"No problem, dearie. I'll have the girls pick it up for washing and then mend it on our way to Kansas City. It'll be ready for the performance."

"Thanks, you're the best."

Lizzy made the rounds, thanking everyone for helping with the show. It was something her father used to do, and Lizzy didn't even think about what she was doing until she was half-way through the performers and crew. It felt right to offer the others praise. Her father had always been so encouraging, and Lizzy knew it had always blessed everyone.

"You did a mighty fine job out there, Miss Lizzy," Thomas, the oldest of their wranglers, told her.

"Couldn't have done it without you, Thomas. No one person is responsible for our success, as you well know. You boys are the very heart of this show."

The old man beamed with pride, just as Lizzy knew he would.

"Praising someone for a job well done costs you nothing, Lizzy, but the returns are tremendous. People need to know they're appreciated," Father had often told her.

Oh, Father, why did you have to leave us?

Exhausted, Lizzy made her way to the bright red Brookstone train. The men would soon be loading the animals for the next leg of the trip. Mother and Agnes would see to all the other girls, and with them busy, Lizzy wanted to check on Ella before going to Uncle Oliver's office to count the ticket sales.

"Did everything go all right?" Ella asked when Lizzy opened her door.

"It went very well, although I ripped my blouse."

"I'm a good seamstress," Ella said, perking up. "I could repair it for you."

"Thanks, but I've already mentioned it to Agnes. She handles all the costumes." Lizzy began unbuttoning her blouse. "I have to change my clothes and then do some bookwork. I'll be back soon. Mother or I will bring you something to eat, however. We always have a snack—well, it's more like a full meal—after the show."

Ella smiled. "I really appreciate all the help you and your mother have given me. I don't know what I would have done without you. I've been afraid, but you've both been so kind. I'm especially blessed by the way your mother prays with me."

Lizzy felt a momentary sense of guilt for not having done the same. Sometimes prayer just skipped her mind.

"I'm just glad we've seen nothing of your father or fiancé. It seems he hasn't considered you might have come with us. Especially given he saw the train off."

"I'm praying it won't even occur to him. Hopefully, he'll just think I've gone to Margaret's. She knows nothing about what I've done, so even if he goes to her, she can't tell him a thing."

Lizzy considered the future for a moment. "After the last show in Kansas City, we'll dismiss the performers and head home for a brief break. I think you should stay with us. Our ranch house is large, and you could stay there until you think it's safe to go to your sister."

"When is the performance?" Ella asked.

"Three days from today." Lizzy shook her head, and her brow furrowed. "Why do you ask?"

"Well, I'm anxious to be far from my home. There's still a chance it might occur to Father that I snuck off with the show. I won't rest until we're a long way away."

"Your concerns are exactly why I want you to come home with us."

"I'd hate to put your family in any more danger than I already have. I doubt Father would ever go all that way to find me, but he might hire someone." Ella bit her lower lip.

Lizzy patted her arm. "It'll be all right. If he comes to Montana, he'll be on Brookstone land—with Brookstone people. They won't allow him to take you."

Ella looked up, her face betraying her anxiety. "What if he comes to Kansas City?"

"Well, we've managed to keep you hidden from everyone else. No one in the show knows about you except Rupert and Mother. I would trust either of them with my life and know they'll keep your secret. We'll be just fine. You'll see."

Lizzy left her and quickly changed out of her performance clothes and into a simple wool skirt of brown plaid paired with an old white blouse. She combed through her long brown hair and knotted it into a bun at the back of her neck before making her way to the entertaining car, where Agnes's sewing room was at one end and Uncle Oliver's office at the other.

Mother was adding finishing touches to a buffet of treats. She smiled when Lizzy came into the car. "You did such an amazing job tonight. I tell you, I still feel my heart skip a beat when you go into that death drag."

Lizzy crossed the room and kissed her mother's cheek before snagging a couple of cookies from the platter she held. "I learned from the best."

Mother nodded. "Your father made it look so easy. Oh, how I miss him." Her eyes dampened.

"I do too. Especially after the shows." Lizzy pushed aside her grief, just as she had every day since her father's passing. "I'm going into the office to work on the receipts."

"Jason's already hard at it. Uncle Oliver sent him to get started."

Lizzy frowned. "He's letting him handle the money?"

"I suppose he feels Jason is trustworthy. He does have an interest in seeing the show succeed," Mother reminded her.

Sighing, Lizzy grabbed another cookie, then headed for the office. If Jason was going to be in charge of the books, then she wasn't going to stick around.

"Mother told me you were managing the show receipts," Lizzy said, looking in on Jason, who sat at her uncle's desk.

"Come in," Jason said, jumping to his feet. "Two sets of eyes are always better than one. I've started counting the coins. I've put them in stacks of ten dollars. Why don't you double-check them?"

Lizzy took a seat despite wanting to turn around and leave. "Very well." She started on the stack of nickels nearest her.

"I saw part of your act tonight. I was completely terrified for you." He grinned.

She couldn't help laughing. "You needn't be. It's all controlled chaos. My father was good at using each act for maximum effect."

"Yes, he was, but it's your talent and skill that makes the show. That's why we can't lose you. You have to see that they come to watch you."

"They come for the show in full. I'm only one small part of it. I don't make an entire show by myself."

"Perhaps not, but you are the star performer. I've been reading through the mail. Most of the letters are for you." He lowered his voice. "There were at least three dozen proposals of marriage in the last batch alone."

"Yes, I get that a lot," Lizzy admitted. She finished with the first stack of nickels and moved to the second. "I have no idea why a man would propose to a total stranger. He has no idea who I am or what I want out of life."

"It would be nice to know those things," Jason said. He looked up from the table and met Lizzy's gaze. He smiled.

She had to admit he was a handsome man. His eyes were the color of sapphires and seemed to sparkle as much as the gems themselves. His face reminded her of chiseled marble sculptures she'd seen in museums.

"I would very much like to know who you are and what you want out of life," he said.

Lizzy grew uncomfortable. "I can't give you those answers, Mr. Adler."

"Can't or won't?" His smile never wavered.

"I can't." She shifted and pushed the stack of nickels aside. "I don't know the answer myself."

"It might be fun to explore the answers together," he said, jotting down some figures.

"Why are you here?" She hadn't meant to be so blunt, but now that the question was out, she was glad she'd asked it.

Jason leaned back in his chair. "Because I'm thirty years old and need to decide what I want for my future."

Lizzy shook her head. "And you plan to do that working around a wild west show?"

He shrugged and picked up a stack of dollar bills. "I had to start somewhere, and this pleased my father. I've been working for him in some capacity since I graduated from university. He's allowed me to take part in any and all of his businesses to see if something strikes my fancy." He put the money back down and leaned forward. "Now that I've answered your question, perhaps you'd be so good as to answer one of mine."

"I'll try." Lizzy had no idea what he might ask but figured it was only fair.

"What do you want for your future?"

"We already discussed that. I don't have an answer for you."

"But you have decided you don't want to stay with the show, so you know at least that much." He cocked his head slightly. "If you left the show, what would you do?"

"Pick up with my life at the ranch."

"And you like living on a ranch in the middle of nowhere?"

Lizzy laughed. "Who says it's in the middle of nowhere?"

"Your father, for one. Your uncle, for another."

"You knew my father?"

"Of course. He and your uncle visited my parents at their New York house several times. When they did, I was also there." He chuckled. "Your father said the ranch was perfectly situated in the middle of absolutely nothing."

Lizzy smiled. "I remember him saying that."

"Well, given where you grew up, I would think you'd enjoy experiencing some different places before you settle down to one."

"I've experienced a great many places with the show. We've been to every corner of the United States and most every state in between."

"But that's just in passing. You should try staying for a time—living in one of the larger cities like London or even New York before deciding to lock yourself away on a ranch in Montana."

"I suppose it could be interesting to try, but my heart is in Montana."

"Is there someone special there who holds it?"

Lizzy grew uncomfortable at his prying. She got to her feet. "I'm afraid, Mr. Adler, that I'm more worn out than I realized. If you'll excuse me."

She left without waiting for his response. He was so refined and well-mannered that she knew he'd never demand she stay.

Many of the performers were starting to arrive for the evening meal, and Lizzy had no desire for company. Mother caught her attention and held up a plate. Whether it was for Lizzy or Ella, she didn't know, but Lizzy nodded and walked over to her.

"I thought you might want to take this with you back to our car," Mother said without hesitation. "I knew you would be much too tired to stay here."

"Thank you. I'm exhausted."

"Oh, I nearly forgot. One of the local businesses brought us root beers. I put several in the icebox in our car."

The idea of a cold root beer appealed very much to Lizzy. "Thank you. I think that will make my night complete." She took the plate and headed to the door that connected to the family car.

Jason stood just outside Uncle Oliver's office, watching her. "I'm sorry if I offended you."

Lizzy shook her head and tightened her grip on the plate. "You didn't. I'm just overly tired. Good night."

He opened the door for her, but Lizzy didn't acknowledge the gesture. She had to get away from him. She had to get away from all of them and sort through her thoughts.

She passed between the cars, carefully managing the door to the family's private refuge. Once she was inside, Lizzy let out her breath. She hadn't even realized she'd been holding it.

Why had Jason's questions bothered her so much? The last thing she wanted was to explain herself or the past to him. Perhaps that was all it was. Then again, perhaps it was because his questions were the very ones for which she had no answers. Hearing them aloud only served to drive home the point that she was completely uncertain about her future.

She glanced down at the plate in her hands and thought of Ella. She went to her tiny cabin and knocked before opening the door a crack. "I have some food."

"Come in."

Lizzy left the door open to allow the light inside. Ella had to be careful about even lighting a candle for fear someone might see the light glowing under her door or from her shaded window.

"We always have food after a performance, and it's always delicious. Mother has been cooking up a storm. There's a tidy little kitchen at one end of the female performers' sleeping car, and she makes some of the most amazing things." Lizzy sat on the edge of the berth and set the plate on the mattress between them. "There are all sorts of cookies and melted cheese toasts and little biscuits baked with sausages in them. Oh, and there's cold root beer in our icebox."

"Yes, she told me about that and brought me one." Ella held up the bottle. "I was supposed to tell you in case she forgot."

"I'm going to have one myself," Lizzy said, then sighed.

"What's wrong?"

"Nothing, really." Lizzy shook her head and smiled. "Mr. Adler was just asking me a lot of questions. Personal questions that I had no answers for."

"I think he likes you very much," Ella said. "Perhaps he wants to court you."

"I'm afraid you may be right."

"Is that such a terrible thing? He seems nice and he's very pleasant to look at. Falling in love might be a nice change of pace."

"True enough, but I'm not interested in falling in love."

"Have you ever been in love?"

The question was asked innocently enough, but it felt as if Ella had punched Lizzy in the stomach. Why did everyone want to know the intimate details of her heart? Why did people she barely knew feel they were entitled to ask such questions, much less receive an answer?

The look on Lizzy's face must have revealed her feelings. "Please forgive me," Ella began. "I didn't mean to pry. It's far too personal a question, and I meant no disrespect."

"I know that, but . . ." She let the words trail off as she considered Ella. There was no harm in confiding in her. Ella had, after all, confided in Lizzy. So much so that her very freedom depended on being able to trust Lizzy. Lizzy picked up a piece of toast. "I have been in love. Unfortunately, I think I still am."

"Why unfortunately?" Ella clapped a hand over her mouth.

"It's all right. I don't mind talking to you. There's this guy back home. He's the ranch foreman, so you'll meet him."

Ella lowered her hand. "And you love him?"

Lizzy toyed with the toast. "I do. I've loved him since I was just a girl and he was a young cowboy working for my grandfather. He's always just seen me as his little sister, though."

"Well, what have you done to help him see you otherwise?"

Lizzy considered that for a moment. "I told him I loved him, but he married another woman."

"Oh, how awful. Especially since you still love him."

Lizzy shook her head. "When he married, I was determined to never think of him again. I did pretty well at it. I focused on the show and avoided him as best I could. I thought I was getting over him, but then his wife died a couple years back, and I realized I'd never stopped loving him. I know that sounds awful. I would never have done anything to interfere in his marriage. And I swear I didn't covet him while he was wed to another."

"I believe you," Ella replied.

"I begged God to take away my feelings for him."

"But now he's single again, and you still love him." Ella looked at Lizzy. "What are you going to do about it?"

Lizzy got to her feet and shrugged. "Nothing. I have no desire to marry him or anyone else."

Ella tossed and turned in her sleep. She dreamed she was running through a thick forest of trees. It was dark and cold, and she couldn't see. She didn't know what she was running to or from, but the sense of dread and overwhelming danger hung all around her.

She thought she saw a light just ahead and rushed from the trees toward what would hopefully be sanctuary. An old but pleasant-looking house appeared, and from it spilled welcoming light. Her legs felt like lead as she moved toward the refuge. But when she was within a few feet of safety, Jefferson appeared from the shadows.

"Where are you going, my dear?"

Ella stopped and backed away. Her legs were just as heavy in retreat as they had been in her desperation to reach the house. "Stay away from me."

Jefferson laughed. "You're my wife, Ella. You should know better than to try to leave me."

"You killed the wrangler," she accused.

He laughed all the more. "He saw too much."

"What? What did he see?" She glanced over her shoulder and found herself on the edge of a cliff. Below was nothing but blackness. In front of her, Jefferson continued his advance.

"It doesn't matter what he saw. He's dead. You don't want to join him, do you?"

She looked once again at the abyss. "If it means you can never touch me or hurt me, then yes."

She turned and stepped off the edge, feeling herself falling and falling. Jefferson's laughter echoed all around her.

Ella awoke with a start. Darkness engulfed the room, and for a moment she couldn't remember where she was. Then she felt the rocking movement. The Brookstone train car. She was running away, with no idea where she would end up.

She really had stepped into the abyss.

✦⊰ NINE ⊱✦

Things in Kansas City were bad from the beginning. The show was well attended, as it was a side entertainment to the large American Royal show given each year. Lizzy generally enjoyed getting to be around other horse and cattle people, but the large show tent had issues with their electricity, and several surges caused bulbs to explode, startling the horses and performers. Not only that, but tent performances always required altering the tricks in order to avoid ropes and stakes and tent poles.

Uncle Oliver was also not himself. Lizzy smelled alcohol on his breath prior to the first act. Mother had mentioned that he'd taken to drinking quite heavily at night before bed. After Father's death, he'd moved out of the family car and set up with the other men in the men's sleeping car. Mother felt certain he had not done it out of propriety, as he stated, but rather so that he might be able to drink without being observed by the womenfolk. They both figured it was his way of dealing with his grief over the loss of his brother. However, he'd never before compromised the show in such a way.

Thankfully, the performances were awe-inspiring enough that the people didn't seem to mind the emcee slurring his words and weaving a bit on his feet. But Lizzy was gravely concerned, and that took her focus away from the act, and she banged her face against her saddle during one of her maneuvers. She had momentarily seen stars and wasn't sure that it hadn't loosened a molar or two. But the show had to go on, and she pushed through the pain and finished her trick.

Thoreau seemed annoyed by the problems and people. It was as if he sensed Lizzy's anxiety, and their timing and responses to each other were just not what they needed to be. To add further frustration to an already trying evening, a fall thunderstorm came up during the last quarter of the show, setting everyone's nerves on edge. Thankfully it was short-lived and not much more than a brief rainstorm with sporadic lightning and thunder. Nevertheless, it made the horses fretful.

"I'm so glad this night is done. And glad this tour is done," Lizzy said, handing Thoreau over to Thomas. She stroked Throeau's head. He was still pretty worked up. "You did a good job, boy. It wasn't your fault that I was out of step." She hugged the animal's neck, then turned to Thomas. "You might need to walk him extra, Thomas."

"I'll take the long way down to the big pen. It's quieter there, and he'll calm down soon enough."

"Looks like it rained enough to make things muddy," Lizzy commented as she caught sight of some water puddles.

"Yeah, we had a gulley washer there for a few minutes, but the storm moved through so fast, there wasn't much time to worry about it. Even though it's muddy, I think the animals have been glad for the freedom of the pen rather than bein' cooped up in their stalls."

"I'm sure you're right." She gave Thoreau one more stroke. "I'll be down later with their treats."

It had been arranged to corral the animals in a large pen well away from the performance tent. The entire area was surrounded by stockyards, and a multitude of pens and people were everywhere. The stockyards in Kansas City moved millions of animals through the city each year, rivaled only by those in Chicago. This, coupled with the annual horse show, gave everything the feel of a three-ringed circus.

Even so, Lizzy knew it would do their animals good to have a couple of days out of the confines of their train stalls. Especially given that they would be headed to Montana afterward, and the trip would take several days, possibly longer if there were problems on the line. And it seemed there always were problems of some sort. Lizzy never liked to have the horses on the train for long hours, and when they planned the tour, they always scheduled stops along the way, like Fleming Farm, where they could take a day or two for the horses to rest and feed off natural pasture. Of course, here they would only have hay, but at least they wouldn't be tightly confined.

"Miss Brookstone, I must say you performed exceptionally well," Jason Adler said, coming to join her.

Lizzy rubbed her cheek. It was starting to throb. "Thank you."

"Your uncle has called a meeting in the entertainment car. I told him I would make sure you knew about it and escort you there."

A sigh escaped her lips. "Very well. I need some ice first."

"Ice? Are you hurt?" He stood back, and his gaze traveled the full length of her body before coming back to rest on her face.

Lizzy placed a hand over her right cheek. "I hit it kind of hard, and it's starting to hurt. I'm sure it's just bruised, but I want some ice to stave off swelling."

"I'll arrange for it after I get you to the car. Are you certain you aren't injured anywhere else?"

"No, I'm fine. I just—"

"Miss Brookstone!" A man with a derby hat and three-piece

suit jumped in front of Lizzy. "I've never seen anyone like you. I was completely overwhelmed by your beauty and your talent. I've written you a poem." He waved a piece of paper. "I'm dying of love for you!" Lizzy forgot about all about her cheek as the man fell to one knee, hat in hand. "Please say you'll marry me. I can provide well for you. I have my own home—it's small, but we'll sell it and buy another. We'll buy however big a house you want."

"My good man, you will contain your enthusiasm and refrain from further embarrassment to yourself. Miss Brookstone is soon to be my wife," Jason declared.

The man looked as though Jason had punched him in the face. For a moment, Lizzy wasn't even sure he could breathe. He looked at her with a forlorn expression, then slowly got to his feet and put on his hat.

"I should have known someone as wonderful as you would already be promised." He looked at Jason. "In another time, I might have called you out for a duel." He shook his head and let his gaze travel back to Lizzy. "I shall live the rest of my life in the memory of this night and what might have been." He folded the piece of paper and put it in his pocket. Lizzy wondered if he might use it on another ladylove at another time.

"Be off with you, sir, or I shall dispose of you myself." Jason possessively took hold of Lizzy's arm, and the man gave her one last look, then turned and walked away. By the slump of his shoulders, she felt certain he was completely heartbroken. She knew very well how that felt.

Jason led her toward their train cars. The stockyards in Kansas City had multiple rail lines, and their cars had been positioned at one of the farthest points. Lizzy was actually glad for Jason's help navigating the yards, especially given there were a great many people—mostly men—milling about.

"Thank you for your help back there," she murmured. She

didn't want to encourage him and intended to set him straight. "Although I can't advocate lying."

Jason chuckled. "Lying? Whatever are you talking about?"

"You know very well what I'm talking about. That part about me soon being your wife." Lizzy stopped, forcing Jason to stop as well. "I'm not trying to play games with you, Mr. Adler. I'm not looking to marry anyone, and I don't want you to have the wrong impression of me. I just lost my father, and my mother needs me at this time. I want to return to the ranch and heal from my loss. I hope you understand."

She saw a look of regret cross his face. He nodded. "I apologize, Miss Brookstone. I was thoughtless and hope you will forgive me."

Lizzy nodded. "Of course."

"Friends?" he asked.

"Yes. I'm happy to be your friend." She paused a moment, then looked up at him. "I wonder if you might be willing to do me a service?"

"Anything." He smiled. "And I assure you there will be no strings attached to my response."

"Thank you. It's just that I'm worried about my uncle. He's drinking—that much was obvious tonight. Mother says it's due to his grief over Father. Since you're working with him closely and in the same car with him at night, I wonder if you might try to keep him . . . from the alcohol."

"It won't be easy. Despite his own rules about the workers drinking, your uncle seems to have no trouble sneaking alcohol aboard. I will do whatever I can."

"I know it's not my business to tell my uncle what he can and can't do, but I'm very worried about him. Mother is too. When he was younger, Uncle Oliver drank a lot. My father encouraged him to give it up, and he did. But now, with Father's . . . well, it's apparently more than he can stand."

"I'll try to be available to him, but I can hardly dictate rules to him."

"Thank you. I appreciate it and know it will add comfort to his days."

"Your father's loss is no doubt deeply felt by all of you." His words were sincere and his expression sympathetic. "I know it has to be very hard for you."

Lizzy stiffened. "I get by. I have fond memories of my time with him, and I must go on for the sake of my mother. She needs me, and I want to be a comfort to her."

"Ah, Lizzy Brookstone, but who will be a comfort to you?"

"I appreciate what everyone has done this year," Uncle Oliver began. "We've had a very successful season, even with the misfortune that has seemed to follow us."

He had sobered up a bit, and Lizzy breathed a sigh of relief. She glanced across the room to where her mother sat. Their eyes met, and Mother gave her a smile. It would seem all was well.

"Here you are," Jason whispered, handing Lizzy a cloth-wrapped piece of ice.

She pressed it against her cheek. "Thank you."

All around the car, the performers and crew sat listening to Uncle Oliver's closing address. Every year her father and uncle spoke to their people and praised them for a job well done. They would tell them about the plans for next year and when they should arrive at the Brookstone ranch in Montana to begin training for the show.

"All of you have performed exceptionally well, and I am proud of each and every one of you. I know my brother would be too." He paused a moment, and Lizzy could see his eyes well with tears. "Mark will be missed, but he was determined that the show go on, and so next year we hope to be even bigger and better. Mr. Adler has plans to make the Brookstone Wild West Extravaganza the most sought-after show in America—possibly the world."

Everyone clapped and looked toward Jason. He gave a little nod of acknowledgment before Uncle Oliver continued.

"The performers and crew will head home tomorrow. Mrs. Brookstone will accompany those of you going back to our ranch." He looked Mother's way and smiled. "After I'm done talkin', you'll each get your salary and travel money for your train tickets. Those heading back to Montana for the winter will depart at seven o'clock tomorrow evening. Feel free to enjoy a night on the town, but make sure you're back here by five tomorrow for loading the horses."

Uncle Oliver grew serious. "As you know, we lost not only my brother, but also our head wrangler, August Reichert. Lizzy and I will go to Topeka tomorrow to visit with the Reicherts before we head back home."

This was the first Lizzy had heard about this, but she was glad Uncle Oliver had thought of it. She had wondered if they should do something more than just ship the body back. She knew her mother had sent a lengthy telegram, but even that seemed too inadequate. August and his family were good friends of the Brookstones, and it seemed only right that they offer their condolences in person, even if it was too late to attend the funeral.

"Mr. Adler will also accompany us, and he has decided he will winter with us in Montana so that he might understand every aspect of the show. He will be with us next year as well."

Several of the female performers beamed at Jason. They were clearly pleased to know he'd be around. Lizzy wondered if her earlier comments would make Jason change his mind. She sincerely hoped he hadn't planned to come to Montana for the winter in order to woo her.

"Now, I'm going to let you all get to the party you're antici-
pating. Mrs. Brookstone has prepared us a feast." He motioned
over his shoulder at the table. It was covered to capacity with
plates of food. "I've been informed that some of the local ven-
dors have provided us with barbecue, and I, for one, am looking
forward to that."

Most of crew cheered at this comment, then grew silent,
as they knew their boss would pray a blessing on the bounty.

"Let's offer thanks." Uncle Oliver bowed his head. "Father,
we thank You again for Your protection this evening and Your
loving-kindness to us throughout the year. We don't understand
why we lost Mark and August, but we trust that You know best.
We thank You now for this food and pray a blessing on each
person as they travel to their various locations. Abide with us
as we abide in You. In Jesus' name, amen."

There was no hesitation or waiting to be invited to chow
down. Everyone was on their feet and heading to the buffet before Uncle Oliver could even wave them forward. Lizzy
wasn't surprised when the youngest of their female performers,
Debbie and Jessie, came to Jason and encouraged him to sit
at their table. Lizzy let him be dragged away without protest,
although he threw her a look that suggested he wished she
would intercede. She was tired and had no desire to pretend
to be jealous or otherwise desirous of his company. Instead,
she put together a large plate of food and quietly slipped back
to the family car.

"Ella?"

"I'm here," the young woman said, peeking out the door of
her room. She had dark half-moons under her eyes. No doubt
she wasn't sleeping well. Lizzy wasn't sure she would sleep well
either, if the roles were reversed.

"We've had a development in our plans that will affect you,
and I think we have to explain to my uncle and Mr. Adler about

your situation," Lizzy said, placing the food on the tiny bedroom dresser.

"What's happened?" Ella's eyes were wide with fear.

"I don't think it'll be a problem, so please don't be upset." Lizzy sat on the edge of the berth and motioned for Ella to do the same. "Uncle Oliver feels we should pay our condolences to the Reichert family, and I think it's the right thing to do. They live on a farm outside of Topeka, so tomorrow we'll take the train there."

"What about me?"

"Well, I've been thinking about that. Mother is heading back to the ranch, but I think it's best if you stay with me. In fact, it might work to our advantage. If your father decides to check out whether you've gone to Montana with the show, he won't find you there. I'll speak to Mother later tonight, but for now, I figure Uncle Oliver will have the family car unhooked from the rest of the cars and then send everyone and everything else to Montana. It'll be easiest that way, and we can follow from Topeka in this car. Jason Adler plans to come with us, so it'll be the four of us, and since there are four small bedrooms in this car, it will suit us well enough. Although I could bunk with you if it made you feel safer."

"Are you sure they won't mind? I don't want to be any trouble. I could make my way from here to Chicago . . . if you helped me. I'll just need you to sell some jewelry for me."

"No. Not unless that's truly what you want to do. I'm sure by now your father has contacted your sister. I truly think you'll be safer to stay with us."

"Then, if your mother and uncle approve, I will do that. I just don't want to put anyone out on my account."

Lizzy shook her head. "It's not a problem. In fact, I want to talk to you about your own riding experience and whether you might like to join the show."

"What? Join as a performer?" Ella sounded completely stunned.

Laughing, Lizzy got to her feet. "You've ridden all of your life and have your own mount. You told me you and your brother used to play around with Roman riding and various tricks. I think you could probably learn to do what I do with relative ease. If you're of a mind to."

"It would be wonderful to learn your tricks, Lizzy. I so admire what you do." Ella's voice was animated. "It would be so exciting to perform for an audience. Do you really think your uncle would let me be part of the show?"

"I think he might, especially once he realizes that I intend for you to replace me."

Ella found sleep impossible that night. She tossed and turned, and with every creak or outside noise, she sat straight up, clutching her covers to her chin. Would it always be like this? Would she spend the rest of her life in fear of being hunted down and forced back to Kentucky? Was there never to be any peace?

She thought of the fact that her father was party to a murder, and it soured her stomach. Did her mother know? Did Robert? Jefferson had said it wasn't his first killing. Ella shuddered. How could he speak so casually about life and death? She'd known his reputation for cruelty but realized that she'd assumed it was exaggerated.

"Lord, I'm so afraid."

She forced herself to lie back down, but she couldn't bring herself to close her eyes. Maybe she should have made her presence known when Father and Jefferson came to the train with August Reichert's coffin. The sheriff had been there, and all the Brookstone people. Maybe she should have declared the truth she'd overheard.

Shaking her head, Ella knew it would have made no difference. No one would have believed her.

"God, I feel so alone. Please help me," she whispered. "Please give my spirit rest and show me what to do."

She hated knowing that August had been murdered and wished she'd never overheard her father and Jefferson. She didn't want to know the truth. Knowing it meant keeping it hidden from Lizzy, who had done nothing but offer friendship and help from the start. Would Lizzy still want to help if she knew what Ella was keeping from her?

TEN

"Well, I must say this is a big surprise," Mr. Brookstone said, looking at Ella. "I didn't say anything to Lizzy before, but your father sent a man to us in St. Louis. He was asking if you had somehow managed to slip away with us. I assured him you hadn't, but now I see otherwise."

"I didn't want you to know for exactly that reason," Lizzy explained. "I didn't want you to have to lie."

"And I certainly didn't want to cause problems for you with my father." Ella looked from Oliver Brookstone to Jason Adler.

"I don't know what the legal implications might be." Lizzy's uncle looked to Jason. "She's nearly of age and certainly isn't a child."

"True." Jason nodded. "I don't see why it should be a problem. You didn't know until now about her being here, so as Lizzy said, you didn't lie."

Ella knew they were risking a great deal, going up against her father and Jefferson. "I never thought about any legal implications. If you think it best, I'll leave."

"No!" Lizzy was adamant. "We all know what will happen if they find you. You'll be forced to marry that abominable man. We must keep Ella safe."

"Of course," Mr. Adler assured them. "I cannot abide the idea of a woman being forced to marry against her will. We'll deal with any trouble when it comes."

Lizzy's uncle nodded as well. "Given the situation, I'm happy to do my part. Although I suppose it will burn our bridges with your father and his horses."

"We've got two good mares now," Lizzy interjected. "We can breed them to Morgans if we want a pure line. Besides, there are other Morgan farms."

Her uncle nodded. "I'm sure we'll get by just fine." He smiled at Ella. "I appreciate you both being frank with us and telling the truth of the situation."

Ella grimaced. She hadn't told them the half of it. She still hadn't admitted to Lizzy that she knew Jefferson Spiby was responsible for the death of August Reichert. And now she'd have to face August's family on top of everything else. The nightmare, it seemed, had no end in sight.

"Thank you so much," she said. "I promise to do whatever I can to earn my keep. I'm a capable seamstress and happy to lend a hand."

"Agnes will be glad of that," Mr. Brookstone said, nodding. "Although she won't be with us in Montana until late January."

"I plan to teach Ella my tricks," Lizzy interjected. "She's spent her entire life around horses and knows them as well as I do. She's even done Roman riding and a few tricks of her own. I think she'll be the perfect person to replace me."

"Replace you?" Lizzy's uncle looked appalled.

Lizzy pushed back her long, dark hair. "Yes. I think it's about time, don't you?"

Mr. Brookstone shook his head. "I don't think we'd have much of a show without you, Lizzy."

"Then we need to build the show around Ella and the others."

"You have yet to even see her perform," Jason Adler said, sounding skeptical.

Ella didn't want any of them to worry. "Mr. Adler, I understand your concern, but I assure you that I'm capable and willing to learn. You should be able to tell my value or lack thereof by the time the show sets off again in late February."

"She's right." Lizzy pulled back the drapes covering the train window. "Oh, look. I believe we've arrived in Topeka."

Ella could feel that the train was slowing. She wished Lizzy had told her uncle and Mr. Adler everything the night before, but Lizzy had assured her it was better to do it today, just before they reached Topeka.

"Mother gave Ella her mourning veil," Lizzy said. "She thought it might provide some privacy. If Ella wears my black cape and the veil, no one will be able to tell who she is. Then, if you escort her, Uncle Oliver, just as you would have Mother, nothing will appear out of order."

"That makes sense." Oliver Brookstone nodded. "Your mother always was a smart one."

"Then Mr. Adler and I will follow behind," Lizzy finished.

Ella appreciated all the extra effort they were going to. She was touched that they cared so much about her plight. She only wished their support would allow her stomach to stop churning.

She hoped the men could be trusted not to ask her too many questions. The last thing she wanted was to explain what she knew about August's death. She felt selfish in her silence, but her desperation to escape a hopeless future seemed more important than a murderer going to trial. Besides, most of the men in their county, including the law officials, were obliged to her father. Even if she had *seen* Jefferson kill August, her father and Jefferson had enough friends to keep the matter from ever coming to light. The Flemings could do no wrong. Even if it involved murder.

Mary Reichert's pale expression and reddened eyes told Lizzy what she already knew would be true. Her friend was devastated by the loss of her only brother.

"Lizzy, I can hardly believe he's gone," Mary murmured. The man beside her put his arm around her as she continued to speak. "As for the suggestion that he was killed by those colts . . . well, I simply don't believe it."

"Neither do I, Mary," Lizzy admitted, looking across the room at her uncle. "None of us do."

"She's right," Uncle Oliver declared. "But I can't imagine what really did happen, and Fleming's people seemed to know nothing. They said they simply found him that way."

All gazes turned to Ella. The poor young woman shook her head and looked as if she might burst into tears at any moment. "I'm so sorry."

Mary's grandfather, Oscar Reichert, spoke up in his thick German accent. "Our August vas a superior horseman. He vould not be trample."

"He vould not," his wife, Hannah, agreed.

Lizzy had known this family most of her life. Mary's father had once worked with Uncle Oliver and Lizzy's father in Buffalo Bill's Wild West show. Though all three men were superior in their horsemanship, Wilhelm Reichert was also a master marksman. A talent he passed down to his daughter. It was said that the only woman better at shooting than Mary was the famous Annie Oakley.

"Our Vilhelm, he died performing," Mr. Reichert said, shaking his head. "He broke his neck ven he fell from de horse."

Lizzy remembered the accident that had claimed the life of Wilhelm Reichert and injured her father. They had been working together with a team of four horses. Lizzy's father held the reins while straddling the center two. Mary's father would make a flying vault to join him. The trick started out just fine, and Mr. Reichert made it to an upright stance atop the horse. But he'd no sooner gotten there than the animal stumbled and hit the horse beside him. This in turn upset the rest of the team, and the horses began to rear and fight Lizzy's father for control. The men were thrown beneath a tangle of hooves. Mr. Reichert died instantly from a broken neck, while Lizzy's father suffered a back injury bad enough that he had to return to the ranch to recuperate.

"Horses are a danger," Uncle Oliver said, shaking his head. "Anyone who works with them knows as much. Still, I find it hard to believe August would put himself in such a position that he couldn't escape trouble."

Everyone nodded, then fell silent.

"Ve're mighty sorry for your loss too," Hannah Reichert finally said. She took her husband's hand and turned to Lizzy. "I'm sure it's hard for your mama to lose her husband, and you, your vater."

"Thank you." Lizzy straightened and gave a nod. "It hasn't been easy for Mother, which is why she didn't feel up to coming with us. I think she knew how sad you would be and didn't want to add to it."

"So much sorrow," Mary said, wiping a tear from her eye with the back of her hand. "At the funeral yesterday, I thought I would cry myself out, but it seems I have a never-ending supply of tears."

The man beside Mary was her fiancé, Owen Douglas. He quickly pulled a handkerchief from his pocket and pressed it into her hand.

"Thank you, Owen." Mary dabbed her eyes. "I won't rest until I know what happened to August and who's to blame."

Lizzy knew Mary and Owen had been promised to each other almost since childhood. Owen's family owned the farm next to the Reicherts', and Mary and Owen had grown up the best of friends. After a time, it was just assumed that the two would marry.

Mary and her brother had grown up on this Kansas farm. When their mother died in 1879 giving birth to her third and final child, Katerina, Wilhelm had taken his grief and hit the road, leaving his three children to be raised by his parents. Eventually his ability with horses and guns put him in good standing with Buffalo Bill Cody, and Wilhelm was hired to perform in the same wild west show that employed Lizzy's father and uncle. The influence of Lizzy's godly parents helped Wilhelm deal with his grief, and eventually he returned to his family for visits. That was when Lizzy and Mary had first met.

Hannah Reichert got to her feet. "Our dinner vill be ready shortly. You must excuse me. Mary—you go bring in de clothes, ja?"

Mary nodded. "I'll get them now."

"I'll help," Owen said, getting to his feet.

Mrs. Reichert nodded and headed for the kitchen.

"Let me help with the food," Lizzy said, standing. Mrs. Reichert stopped and turned.

Ella stood. "Me too."

"No. No. You are our guests," Mrs. Reichert said, gesturing for them to sit back down. "Our Kate vill be here soon, and she can help."

Lizzy crossed the room and took the old woman's arm. "But guests can help too. Please show us what we can do."

Lizzy followed Mrs. Reichert to the kitchen. The old farmhouse was pretty much unchanged from the first time she'd come here. It was nothing elaborate—a square, boxy house with two stories. The living room constituted the first third of the house with the dining area in the center room along with the stairs that led up to the bedrooms. The kitchen was located in the back third, with a curtained-off area that could be used for bathing.

The kitchen table was laden with food. It dawned on Lizzy that most of this must have been for the funeral. She saw various desserts—cakes, cookies, and a few pies. There were a couple of casseroles as well, which Mrs. Reichert uncovered.

"Ve have lots to eat. It's good you came. Ve cannot eat it all ourselves." She went to the oven and opened the door.

The aroma of Mrs. Reichert's German cooking made Lizzy's mouth water. Her own mother was handy in the kitchen, but this was a special treat that Lizzy experienced only occasionally.

"With all this food, you're still cooking something special?"

"*Wir haben Krautspaetzle*," Mrs. Reichert announced, then shook her head. "I mean, ve are having . . ." She paused with a frown, not certain of her next words. She shrugged. "Krautspaetzle. Sauerkraut, noodles, and sausages. Mr. Reichert asked me to make it. He doesn't like some of de food our neighbors bring."

"It smells heavenly. I can hardly wait, Mrs. Reichert. You make the best German food I've ever had. Ella, you're in for a treat."

Mrs. Reichert smiled. "Danke. You are kind to say so."

"Well, I mean it."

Mrs. Reichert laughed. "If you two vant to help, I vill let you set de table. Lizzy, you know vhere to find de dishes. Dey are der—same as last time." She pointed across the kitchen. "I'll varm up de casseroles."

Lizzy went to the cupboard and began pulling out dinner plates and handing them to Ella. It seemed little ever changed on the Reichert farm.

Mrs. Reichert had just managed to squeeze the two casserole dishes into the oven when the back door opened in a gust of wind and in blew Katerina—Kate, to her family. She was dressed in a dark gray suit with only a hint of white blouse peeking out from beneath the fully buttoned jacket.

"Oma," she declared and went to kiss her grandmother on the cheek. They conversed momentarily in German before Kate noticed Lizzy and Ella. She smiled and switched to English. "There's a storm coming from the west. I'll let Opa know." She went to Lizzy. "I didn't know you'd be here."

"We wanted to give our condolences in person." The two women embraced. Lizzy pulled back to get a better looked at Mary's younger sister. "It's so good to see you again. I feared it might be a long time before we came to the farm again, since Mary quit the show."

Kate smiled. "It's wonderful to see you too." She looked past Lizzy to where Ella stood.

"This is Ella," Lizzy said. "She's a friend." She thought it best to keep explanations to a minimum.

"It's nice to meet you." Kate turned back to Lizzy. "Will you be with us several days?"

"No. Just a few hours. We have to get back home," Lizzy explained. "Mother went on ahead with the crew, but there's a lot of work that needs our attention when we get back, so we can't stay."

Kate frowned. "Well, I suppose we should make the best of our time together." She pulled off her gloves, then reached up to take the pin from her hat. "Let me go change, and I'll help get dinner on the table." She hurried from the kitchen.

Mrs. Reichert went back to tending the food. "Our Kate, she verks at de school in Topeka. She's a good teacher and de children like her."

Lizzy hadn't heard that Kate was actually teaching. The last letter she'd received from Mary had come just before they'd headed out on tour. At that point, Kate had just received her teaching certificate from a college in Emporia.

118

"And what of Mary?" Lizzy asked. "Is she working too?" She could hardly wait to see Mary in private. She wanted to talk to her about August.

"No. Owen, he doesn't vant his vife to verk." Mrs. Reichert wiped her hands on her apron. "It's not good for de vife to go off to a job vith other people. She needs to keep her home."

Lizzy smiled. "I'm sure Mary will be good at keeping a house. She's a very hard worker."

"Ja, she is."

Kate soon returned, and the trio made short work of getting dinner on the table. By the time they sat to eat, Lizzy could hardly contain her excitement. She found herself chattering to Jason about the meal. "You have to try the red cabbage—it's pickled. Oh, and the ham-wrapped figs. They're so good."

Jason gave her a bemused look. "Uh, I've traveled extensively and enjoyed German food . . . at its source."

Lizzy shook her head. "I doubt any of it was as good as what Mrs. Reichert makes."

Everyone laughed at this.

She dug into the meal, determined to forget her frustrations and concerns about the show and their troubles. She didn't want to think about their financial woes or the loss of her father or Mary's brother. She just wanted to relax and enjoy the company of good friends and good food. But unfortunately, watching Owen's attention to Mary served as a reminder of Wesley.

Was he still at the ranch? There was no reason to believe he wasn't, but one never knew. He might have decided to move on. People did. She felt sad at the thought that he might not be there waiting for her. Missing her as much as she missed him. One thing was certain—she was determined they were going to talk. He was going to tell her once and for all what she had done wrong—why he had put up a wall between them. He owed her that much.

No, he doesn't. He doesn't owe me anything.

She glanced around, almost afraid her thoughts had been heard. No one else seemed the slightest bit concerned. They were too busy eating and talking. Amazingly enough, Jason was praising Mrs. Reichert for her impressive food.

Lizzy forced thoughts of the past and future from her mind and enjoyed the meal. Rumbles of thunder brought up conversations about the weather, which in turn led to the farm. Crops had been good that year, and Mr. Reichert was ahead of schedule readying the place for winter. It was inevitable that they should discuss Mary and Owen's wedding. Lizzy knew that the celebration was set for November.

"We have to have the farms in order before we get married," Owen said.

Mary frowned and ducked her head. Only Lizzy seemed to notice. It had to be hard to continue planning for a wedding when you had just buried your brother.

"De verk is never done," Mr. Reichert said, shaking his head. "But ve try."

Owen continued to talk about his plans for the farm after he and Mary were wed. His parents had been gone for several years, and it would be nice to have someone in the house again, he said.

"Hopefully before long, there will be children," he added, grinning.

"May you have a dozen!" Uncle Oliver said, raising his glass of apple cider. Thunder rumbled again, this time a little closer.

"I'd be happy with a dozen," Owen declared.

"Lots of help for de farm verk," Mary's grandfather added.

The more they talked about the wedding and the family the young couple might have, the more uncomfortable Mary grew. When the meal finally concluded, Lizzy pulled her friend aside.

"Can we go somewhere and talk?"

"I'd like that very much." Mary looked at her grandmother. "Oma, I'll clean everything up, but first, if you don't mind, Lizzy would like to speak to me privately."

"Of course. You girls go ahead. Kate and I can gather de dishes."

"I'll help too," Ella offered.

"Dat storm is blowin' up fast," Mr. Reichert announced as he stepped away from the window. "This autumn ve been havin' quite a few thunderstorms lately. Some years are like dat." He grabbed his hat. "Ve best put your hired carriage in de barn in case it comes a-hailing."

"I would imagine you're right," Uncle Oliver said, giving Jason a glance.

Jason got to his feet. "Allow me."

Owen rose too and went to retrieve his hat while the old man opened the front door. "Ve'll be right back, ladies," Mr. Reichert called.

Mary took Lizzy's arm. "Come to my room." She all but dragged Lizzy up the stairs.

Once they were safely away from everyone else, Mary made her announcement. "I can't marry him."

"I wondered about that." Lizzy gave her a sympathetic smile. "Is it because of August?"

"In part, but that's only a very small part." Mary plopped onto her bed and patted the thick feather tick. "Sit and I'll explain."

Lizzy sat beside her friend. "Go on."

"I don't know where to begin. I suppose I could start with the problem and work my way back." She frowned. "I'm supposed to marry Owen in just a few weeks, but the closer the wedding gets, the more I realize I can't. Owen and I have always been the best of friends, and I know he cares for me. But, Lizzy, I don't think either of us is in love."

"Maybe you're just confused because of all that's happened."

121

"No, I've felt this way for, well, years." Mary got up and began to pace the small room. "I'm twenty-four and old enough to know my own mind, and I know that I don't want to be Owen's wife. He's like a brother to me. A brother . . ." Her face contorted, and tears came to her eyes. "Oh, my poor brother. Lizzy, I'm sure there's more to this than a simple accident. Perhaps someone spooked those colts, and August was caught in the middle."

"That could be. It's a puzzle why August was anywhere near the Fleming colts in the first place. He should have been readying our horses to bring them back to the train."

"That's why this doesn't make any sense. August knows it would never be acceptable to handle another man's horses. Something happened, and the people who know about it aren't talking."

"I doubt they ever will. But whatever the cause or reason, our knowing won't bring August back."

"But my brother wasn't foolish, and I can't help but think someone else had a hand in this."

Lizzy thought back to August's confrontation with the Fleming grooms. The Fleming men had been severely punished for the incident. Would they have sought revenge? "August did tell me about an incident our first night there. He wanted some liniment for one of our horses, but the Fleming grooms got rather heavy-handed about the matter and made August leave the stable. The employees were later whipped. Quite severely, as I understand it."

Mary's eyes widened. "That's it, then. Someone wanted revenge."

"And forced August into a dangerous situation with green colts? That doesn't make sense. Who would do such a thing, Mary? The whipped men were hardly in any condition to force August to do anything."

"I don't know," Mary said, shaking her head slowly. Tears

streamed down her cheeks. "But someone does. Someone knows more than they're saying, and I intend to find out who that someone is and learn the truth."

"But how?" Lizzy had already been thinking about the situation herself, and she could think of nothing.

"I'm going back to Montana with you. I'm going to rejoin the show. Your father and uncle told me I'd be welcome back anytime. Maybe one of the men who worked with August has some idea what happened. One of them might have even been responsible." She stopped and shook her head. "Oh, I don't know why I said that. I'm so sorry. Those men are all good men."

"It's all right." It wasn't anything Lizzy hadn't already considered. They'd picked up a couple of new men to help after Father died. They really didn't know all that much about them, and maybe they were no good. Of course, they hadn't acted out of line—at least not that Lizzy knew.

"Maybe Ella Fleming will think of something that might help me, since it happened at her farm." Mary shrugged and wiped her tears with the hem of her gown. "I don't know. But what I do know is that I can't sit here and do nothing. I have to try. I owe August that much."

"But what about Owen?"

Mary drew a deep breath. "I have to tell him the truth. If he's honest with himself, he'll know calling off the wedding is the right thing to do." Thunder sounded, making Mary shiver. She went to her window and looked out. "I hate storms. Why can't we just have some peace and quiet?"

"Owen does care deeply for you, that much is evident."

"He does care, and we'll go on caring about each other. But not as man and wife. I can't do that to him. It wouldn't be right." Mary came back to where Lizzy sat. "Look, I'll go and—"

A knock sounded on the bedroom door.

"Who is it?" Mary called.

"It's Kate."

Mary looked at Lizzy. "Say nothing."

"Don't worry."

Mary smoothed her gingham dress and squared her shoulders. "Come in."

Kate opened the door. She wore a worried expression. "Owen is looking for you."

A sigh escaped Mary's lips. She looked at Lizzy as if for affirmation. Lizzy nodded. Mary turned back to Kate. "Tell him I'll be right there."

Kate looked suspicious of her sister's attitude but turned and left without another word. Lizzy got to her feet as Kate disappeared.

"You're doing the right thing. I'll let Uncle Oliver know you plan to rejoin the show. He'll be thrilled. You truly were a cornerstone of the Extravaganza."

"Well, if I was one, then you were the other three." She smiled and gave Lizzy an unexpected hug. "I'm so happy at the thought of returning. If only August were still alive. Everything would be perfect then. We would all be together again."

Lizzy hesitated. "Actually, I'm thinking of leaving the show."

"Please don't." Mary's eyes searched Lizzy's face. "Please. I need you to help me."

"I don't know. Mother needs me too."

"But she'll have others at the ranch to help her through. Oh, I know how selfish that sounds. Please just stay with the show long enough to help me. We must get justice for August."

Lizzy could see Mary's distress. "I'll help get justice for him. I'll do whatever I have to in order to help you find the truth."

"Thank you, Lizzy. Thank you so much!" Mary hugged her again as the thunder grew louder. "I need to find Owen and tell him. Pray for me."

Lizzy smiled as Mary headed for the door. "Always."

ELEVEN

Ella wanted nothing more than to run from the Reichert farm and not look back. She'd hardly been able to bear Mary's tears, nor the sorrowful expressions of her grandparents. Her father and fiancé had ended the life of their beloved August. Ella knew this for a fact yet couldn't bring herself to be honest about it.

What good would it do? She went to the window and stared out, seeing nothing. *How could my speaking up change anything? August would still be dead, and there would still be little chance of Jefferson ever standing trial for what he's done.*

"You seem reflective," Jason Adler said, coming to stand beside her. "Are you regretting your decision? Perhaps missing your family?"

Ella stiffened and crossed her arms. "I do miss my mother, but I'm more worried than anything else."

"Worried?"

She met his sympathetic gaze. "My father and fiancé don't easily give up. I never meant to put Lizzy and her family in harm's way, and I certainly never considered that there might be legal issues. I only wanted to get away from the farm and make my way to my sister's house. Lizzy doesn't think that's wise, however."

"Given what you've told us, I don't think it is either." He gave her a smile. "I come from a land where arranged marriages have been the way of things since the beginning of time. I've never agreed with such arrangements—at least not without complete cooperation from both the bride and groom."

Ella found comfort in his words. Perhaps she had a friend in Jason Adler. "Thank you for being willing to keep my secret. I'll turn twenty-one in January, and then legally I'll have the right to speak for myself. Meanwhile, I need to make my way as best I can."

"And after that, you intend to trick ride in the show."

This made Ella smile. "The very thought thrills me to the core. I know you might think that's silly, but I love the idea. I know I'll be able to learn the tricks and do them well."

His smile broadened. "I say, you have the brave nature it will require."

Ella looked back out the window. She didn't know about having a brave nature. She didn't feel there was a courageous bone in her body right now. If there were, she wouldn't be suffering such horrible dreams and fears.

"I suppose only time will tell," she muttered under her breath.

<hr>

Mary Reichert had always been one to speak her mind. She supposed that was what bothered her so much about Owen. She'd never tried to hide the truth from him. She had always answered his questions honestly and tried to share her heart and dreams for the future without altering them to spare his feelings. But in the last year she'd done little but avoid the truth.

She'd tried so hard to fall in love with him. She'd spent time planning for their wedding and talking about their plans for the future, but she could never find any joy in the idea of either one.

She saw Owen waiting in the front room with the others and knew she couldn't avoid the conversation any longer.

She motioned to the door, and he nodded. Together they slipped out onto the porch as a light rain began to fall. In the west the dark clouds of the thunderstorm grew ever closer, making the air seem heavy.

"I think it's going to the north, if you're worried," Owen said.

"I'm not worried about the storm."

He pushed his hand through his black hair. "Then what, Mary? I know you're grieving, but it's something more. You've been this way for weeks, even before August."

Mary looked at him and nodded. "I've really tried, Owen. You know that. You know that I love you—but not like a wife should."

His shoulders slumped. His expression emptied of emotion. "Yeah. I know."

"There is no other man, save my brother and grandfather, who I've ever loved as much as you. But . . . we're like brother and sister. You have to admit you feel the same way. I've seen it in your eyes after a kiss."

He leaned back against the porch rail and nodded. "I just figured love would grow."

Mary moved closer to him. "But we already have bushels of love between us. It's just not a romantic love. It never has been."

"Maybe it's better that it's not." He looked up, and Mary gazed into his green eyes. "Maybe folks put too much stock in romantic love."

"I don't think so. I think God intends for husbands and wives to feel romantic toward each other." She smiled. "I think if you're honest with yourself, you'll admit you want that kind of love—that passion."

For several long moments, Owen said nothing. Mary watched

him turn and look out at the storm. A flash of lightning cut across the sky, and thunder followed within seconds. The wind picked up, and the rain fell a little harder.

"I guess the storm is coming our way after all," he murmured.

She touched his arm. "Owen, we will always be friends, but I don't think that would be true if we married."

"No. I don't suppose it would be. I just hate being alone. Since my folks passed on, that farm feels so empty. I thought a wife and family would make it feel like home again."

She forced him to turn and face her. "It will be home again. You'll find someone—probably sooner rather than later." She smiled. "You're a very handsome man, you know."

He gave her a sad smile. "Just not handsome enough to win you."

"That's hardly fair, Owen. Should I say I'm not pretty enough to win you?"

He shook his head. "No, Mary. You're right, and I know it. I know we're better off this way, but I still can't help feeling like someone has knocked me off the fence. I've been planning to marry you for well over twenty years. Probably longer, if I'm honest with myself."

"Well, now you have to make a different plan. Good thing the crops are in, huh?" Her smile widened, and she breathed a sigh of relief when he smiled as well.

"I suppose you'll rejoin the wild west show."

"Yes. That's what I plan to do. Like I told you, I don't believe August's death was an accident. I think someone intentionally put him at risk from those colts. Lizzy said some Fleming employees have reason to be angry with my brother. Maybe angry enough to want him dead. I intend to find out who they are."

"And how do you suppose to do that?" Lightning flashed again, followed by thunder, but it was evident the heart of the storm was moving to the north just as Owen had predicted.

"Ella will know who they were, but after that, I don't know how to go about proving one of them had a part in it," Mary admitted. "And it's possible that they had nothing to do with it. It could have been someone else who had it in for August."

"And it could have just been an accident."

She shook her head. "I don't believe that. It doesn't add up. August knew better, and he wouldn't have put himself in harm's way. Not unless there was a very good reason, and I need to know that reason."

"And you think someone will just up and tell you the truth?" Owen shook his head. "That's not likely."

"I figure if I'm part of the show again, I'll have a better time of it than on my own. I'm going to Montana with the Brookstones. That way I can ask my questions and listen in on conversations without seeming overly pushy for answers. Then there's that Fleming woman. August was killed at her place. I don't know what her story is, but she might have some idea what happened or who I can ask for more information. If nothing else, she can give me the address for her family, and I can write and ask my questions."

"And you really think they'll just provide them? I mean, if they were the ones to blame for his death, they're hardly going to admit that."

"No, I don't suppose they will." Mary crossed her arms. "But I have to try. August didn't deserve to die that way, and I feel obligated to dig for the truth."

"What if you never learn the truth?"

She met his gaze. "At least I'll have tried."

He nodded, and for several long moments silence hung between them. Finally, Owen rubbed his jaw. "Looks like things are calming down. I think I'll head on home." He touched her shoulder. "We're still friends, right?"

"Always." She put her hand over his. "I will always be your friend, Owen."

"And you'll let your grandparents know?"

She smiled and nodded. "Yes. Will you tell the pastor, since I'll be heading out with Lizzy and the others?"

"Of course. I'm sure word will get around quick enough."

He studied her face for a moment, then without another word headed down the steps and off to the barn. It was still raining, but he didn't even seem to notice.

Mary heard the door open behind her and turned. It was Kate. Her sister frowned as she saw Owen's retreating figure.

"Where's he going?"

"Home."

"But why?" Kate asked. "It's not that late, and it's still raining."

"It'll stop soon enough." Mary hugged her arms to her body. There was a distinct chill to the wet autumn air.

"Did you two have a fight?" Kate asked.

"Not exactly." Mary met Kate's curious gaze. "We just finally admitted that we can't marry each other."

"What?" Kate was clearly shocked.

"I can't marry my brother, and that's all I feel toward Owen. And he was finally honest enough to admit he lacks the same passion for me." Mary let her arms relax. "I love him, but only as a brother and a friend. I just can't marry him with nothing more to offer."

For several minutes they stood in silence. When the barn door opened and Owen led out his saddled horse, Mary gave a wave.

"Hopefully I'll see you next year!" she called.

"I'll be here," he said, then climbed into the saddle and headed for the road.

"What do you mean, you'll see him next year?" Kate asked.

Mary felt as though a tremendous weight had been lifted from her shoulders. "I'm rejoining the show. I'm leaving with Lizzy and the others tonight."

"What?" Kate took hold of her. "Do Oma and Opa know?"

"No, but I intend to go inside and make my announcement. I figure I might as well break the news about everything at once."

Kate still held fast to Mary's arm. "I can't believe you're just going to leave. We only just lost August, and now you."

"I'm sorry, Kate. I miss the show, and frankly, if it's possible, I want to find out what really happened to August. Surely you can't begrudge me that."

"I don't begrudge you anything." Kate let go and stepped back. "But I'll miss you. It was lonely around here without you."

Mary smiled. "You'll find plenty of things to keep busy with now that you're teaching. Who knows, you might even end up moving to Topeka."

"No. I don't want to live in the city." Kate bit her lip and looked away for a moment. "Mary?"

"What?" She'd never seen her sister act this way. It was almost as if she were embarrassed.

"I wonder . . . that is, if you wouldn't be offended . . ." She couldn't seem to spit out the words.

"What are you talking about? If I wouldn't be offended by what?" Mary could see the hesitation on her sister's face. "Just ask me."

"I know it may be in bad taste, but I wondered if you mind if I . . . well, I'd like to seek out Owen . . . for myself."

Mary couldn't help a giggle. "Wait. You're sweet on Owen?"

Kate seemed to relax as she nodded. "I've been in love with him for ages. I just didn't let anybody know because I knew he was your intended."

Mary took Kate in her arms and hugged her. "Oh, that would be an absolute answer to prayer, little sister. Owen won't have to go far to look for love, and I won't have to worry about losing you to some city slicker."

"Do you mean it?" Kate asked, pushing away. "You really won't be offended or feel awkward? I mean . . . what if we married?"

"It would be wonderful. Even better if you could persuade him to fall in love immediately and take our wedding date and save him from a lonely winter."

Kate blushed. "That would be pushing things rather quickly, don't you think?"

Mary shrugged. "Maybe. But I have a feeling that once you set out to win his heart, things are going to move fast."

Wes waved to the engineer as the train pulled away, leaving the Brookstone Wild West Extravaganza's red railcars behind. They had a special arrangement with the railroad at Miles City, and the cars would be left on a siding there for the winter so repairs and repainting could be done.

It was good to see the show's work crew again. Most of the men were longtime ranch workers, and Wes was good friends with them. He noted a couple of strangers, but old Thomas made short work of introductions.

"Wes, this is Judd and Richard. We picked them up shortly after Mr. Brookstone passed away."

Wes extended his hand. "Good to meet you men."

"They worked cleanup and helped with the equipment. They're good healthy boys and not afraid of hard work," Thomas said.

"Well, we have plenty of that." Wes made a quick assessment of the men. They were both muscular but definitely looked like city boys. "You two have any ranch experience?"

"No, sir," they replied in unison.

"I grew up in the city, but I love horses," Judd offered.

"Me too," Richard admitted. "I did help at a dairy once. I know how to milk and shovel manure."

Wes smiled. "We've got a couple of milk cows and plenty

of manure. For the most part it's horses and cattle that you'll be working with. I can use good hands, but the hours are long and dark in the winter. Cold too. Either of you afraid of that?"

The two men exchanged a look, then returned their attention to Wes. "No, sir." Again, the reply came in unison.

"Good. The cows will start calving in January, and we'll need everyone out there helping. Thomas and the others can show you around once we get back to the ranch. Right now we've got to get these cars unloaded, and that means everything. We strip 'em and leave only what's nailed down."

"I'll put them to work, boss," Thomas said.

Wesley smiled. He was at least half Thomas's age, but the old man had called him "boss" since the day Wes took the foreman position after old Gus died.

Before the men left to start unloading, Phillip joined them.

"Oh, I have someone I want you fellas to meet as well." Wes put his hand on Phillip's shoulder. "This is my brother, Phillip. He joined us a little while back."

Thomas shook the younger man's hand while the other two sized up Phillip. They weren't that far apart in age.

"Good to meet you, son," Thomas declared. "I've been friends with your brother for a long time now. He's a good man."

Wes felt as if Thomas were questioning whether Phillip was the same. Phillip only grinned and nodded, then looked at the younger two men.

"Wes!" Mrs. Brookstone called from the family car. She waved, then allowed one of the men to help her down the steps.

His heart caught in his throat at the sight of her black gown. She was in mourning. He'd thought many times about how different the winter would be without Mark to advise him. He'd even thought about how the ranch would be run, but he hadn't thought much about Mark's widow. She looked so small and pale in black.

Wes frowned. "Phillip, you go on with Thomas, and he'll put you to work. I need to tend to some things before we can head back to the ranch."

"Sure thing, Wes."

Wesley watched the group of men head off as he walked to where Rebecca Brookstone stood waiting. Thomas was already talking to the trio of younger men about their duties. Phillip seemed to be listening intently—or at least Wesley hoped he was. He'd been good at tending to his assigned duties these last days, but he never volunteered to do anything more than what was expected. Wes had talked to him about how people—especially those in charge—liked to see their employees go the extra mile.

"It never hurts to offer to do more than what's expected of you," Wesley had told him. "There's always extra work to do."

"Then why not just ask someone to do it?" Phillip had replied. It made no sense to him that people would just wait around to see if he might volunteer to do more. He was there to work a job and do what he was told. After that, he expected his time to be his own.

Phillip was twelve years Wesley's junior and was born after his mother had lost half a dozen other babies. Because of that, he was spoiled and doted on. He'd always been such a sweet-natured child, however, that even Wesley didn't mind the extra attention Phillip had received.

"You seem mighty deep in thought, Wesley."

He noted Mrs. Brookstone's kind but tired expression. "My thoughts are all over the place these days." He smiled. "Did you see that man who headed off with Thomas and the others?"

"I did. New hand?"

"My brother."

"Phillip, right?" she asked, her gaze following his toward the group of men.

"Yes." He was surprised she remembered. Wes continued watching his brother. "I haven't heard from him in years, and one day he just showed up. I hired him on, but I don't know if it'll work out or not."

"We have to give folks a chance to prove themselves. Sometimes they just don't realize what they're good at."

He turned to face her and smiled. "Mr. Brookstone was always telling me that. I can't tell you how sorry I am that he's gone." There, the subject was now open.

She lowered her gaze and nodded. "I miss him so much. Life won't be the same without him."

"I've thought a lot about that and about the ranch. I hope you know I'll do whatever I can to make sure things run smoothly."

She smiled, but it was a sad sort of effort. "I know you will."

"Wes," a voice called out. He turned to find Rupert limping toward him.

Rebecca Brookstone put her hand on Wes's arm. "You've got a lot to do. Come have supper with me tomorrow night. I want to talk to you about several things." She headed off before Wes could respond.

Rupert tipped his hat at Mrs. Brookstone as she passed him. "Well, you look fit as a fiddle," Rupert said to Wes, grinning. He thrust out a stack of papers. "Oliver wanted me to give you these. It's the inventory list of what we started out with."

Wes looked through the papers quickly. This was the routine when the show returned. "I'll have a better look tonight. Just make sure the boys put everything in the arena first so we can check it off the list."

"Will do, boss."

Wes folded the papers and tucked them inside his shirt. "How's the leg?"

"Hurts like the devil, but it's better up here where it's dry. That damp air just sets it to aching somethin' fierce."

"I don't doubt it."

Rupert frowned. "You heard about August, I suppose."

"Yes. Oliver sent me a telegram." It was hard to believe the young man was gone. August had been so good to work with, and Wesley had hoped he might be able to teach Phillip a thing or two.

"We could hardly believe it. Still not sure what to think. It wasn't likely for a horse to get the better of that boy." Rupert shook his head.

"No, you're right there. August was never lax when it came to horses. Even if he was handling the gentlest of animals, he knew better than to let his guard down." Wes didn't want to ask about Lizzy, but he couldn't help wondering. "Uh . . . how'd the rest of the troupe take the news?"

Rupert shrugged. "It was hard on everyone. Especially since we'd already lost Mark."

"I'm sure his loss was terribly hard on everyone, especially Mrs. Brookstone and Lizzy."

"She's a tough one, though," Rupert said, nodding and scratching his bearded chin. "Ain't never seen a woman quite like her."

Wes smiled. "Mrs. Brookstone has always been the epitome of strength."

"That she has, but I was talking about our Lizzy. She stepped into her father's shoes as best as anyone could. She never even stopped to shed a tear or miss a show. She's quite a gal."

Wesley could imagine Lizzy shouldering her father's responsibilities. She would want to protect her mother. She was always trying to bear burdens that didn't belong to her.

"I've got a feeling a lot of things will be changin' now that Mark's gone. I know Mrs. Brookstone plans to quit the show."

Wes wasn't surprised by this. "I'm sure it's been really hard on her. We expected her to return home with the coffin."

"She wanted to, but Mark made her promise she'd stay on. Made Lizzy promise too. They both put up a fuss, but he said it had to be that way. The show must go on."

Wesley nodded. "No doubt he was worried about the financial aspects." He wondered what Lizzy's plans were for the future. If her mother was quitting, perhaps she would as well.

"Oh," Rupert said, "Oliver said to tell you that, barring any railroad complication, they would only be a day or so behind us, but he didn't want you to wait here on his account. He said to leave horses and tack, and they'll ride out to the ranch."

"I'll arrange for his horse and Lizzy's."

"You'll need two more. One for Mr. Adler, and then Miss Fleming's horse." He looked around and pointed. "That black that's being unloaded over yonder belongs to Miss Ella Fleming."

Wes was puzzled by this new development. "I don't understand. Who is she?"

"She's a pretty little thing. Ran away from Fleming Farm. Nobody knew about it but me and Mrs. Brookstone and Lizzy, although I 'spect by now Oliver and Mr. Adler know about it well enough. So it'd be best not to say anything about the young lady. I think they're afeared her pa might try to hunt her down and force her back."

Wes couldn't imagine what kind of intrigue Lizzy had gotten herself caught up in this time. "All right, I'll make sure the black stays. And what of this Mr. Adler? You aren't talking about that old man the brothers saved on that hunting trip years ago, are you?"

Rupert shook his head and chuckled. "Nope. It's his son. He's supposed to learn all about the wild west show and help with the management."

This took Wesley completely by surprise. "Why in the world would Oliver need his help?"

"I don't rightly know," Rupert said with a shrug. "I heard some talk that Oliver sold Mr. Adler some shares in the show, but I couldn't say for sure that's true. It was just rumors and such."

"Well, I suppose that would make sense. If Adler has an interest in the show, he might feel the need to send his son to familiarize himself with the workings." Wes didn't like the sound of that. It was never good news when folks outside of a family business came in and had their say.

Rupert didn't look overly fond of the idea either. "Like I said, there's gonna be changes."

❖═ TWELVE ═❖

The next night, Wes sat across from Rebecca Brookstone at supper. He wondered what she wanted to discuss with him.

After he offered grace, she picked up the platter of chicken. "I'm glad you're here to run things, Wes. Mark put great store in you, and I know Oliver feels the same." She gave Wes several pieces of fried chicken, then put a single piece on her own plate. Next, she dished out mashed potatoes. She nodded to the gravy. "Help yourself. Biscuits will be out of the oven in a few minutes." She added potatoes to her plate, then put the bowl on the table. "What's the talk about winter?"

Wes poured gravy on his potatoes. "Some of the old-timers think there's going to be a lot of snow and cold temperatures. I laid in extra hay, since we didn't have but two cuttings."

"That was a good idea. Better get extra grain too."

"I'll see to it." He sampled the chicken. Mrs. Brookstone could fry up chicken better than anyone.

"Oh, the biscuits!" She hurried for the kitchen before Wes could even rise to help her.

When she returned, she held a plate of biscuits. They were golden brown, and the aroma was enough to make Wes groan.

"Don't tell Cookie, but I've missed your cooking, Mrs. Brookstone. More than just about anything or anyone."

She smiled and took a seat. "That's kind of you to say."

"It's true. Not even my mother made chicken this good."

She put her napkin on her lap. "I'm so glad you're enjoying it." She paused for a moment, then continued. "Wes, one of the reasons I wanted to talk to you in private is Lizzy. I'd like us to be frank."

Wes swallowed the lump in his throat and reached for a biscuit. "What would you like me to say?"

"It's more about what *I'd* like to say. I'm worried about her."

He relaxed a bit. "Worried about her? But why?"

"Wesley, she's not herself. She's trying so hard to be strong for me . . . for everyone."

"I can imagine that. She's always thought she had to be the nail that holds things together," he said, reaching for the butter. "You can't convince her she's not."

"No." Mrs. Brookstone smiled and chose a biscuit of her own. "You're right on that point. But . . . this is different. Lizzy has convinced herself that she needs no one. I saw it start when she lost her grandparents. Then, when you married Clarissa, she hardened herself a little more. When Mark had his heart attack, she was as worried as I was, and when the doctor told us he didn't hold out much hope for her father to recover . . . well, she was the stalwart support I needed. Even Oliver fell to pieces. Which brings me to another issue. He's drinking." She shook her head, and there were tears in her eyes. "We can discuss that later. I don't know what's going to become of either of them. Oliver is dealing with his grief by numbing the pain and Lizzy by ignoring it."

"What do you mean?"

"I mean she's carrying it all inside. She's always leaned toward that tendency, but this is worse." She eased back in her chair and fixed him with a motherly gaze. "She hasn't been herself since her father died. She never wants to talk about what happened, and she's never shed a single tear."

"Never?" Wes was surprised by this. He'd seen Lizzy cry bucketfuls when her grandparents died. She'd even broken down over the death of animals. She'd always been tender-hearted.

"Not once, not even when she's been alone at night and everyone has gone to bed." The older woman wore all her sorrow on her face. "I'm really worried about her, and I think you may be the only one who can help her."

"Me?" Wes shook his head. "Why would you suppose that?"

She wiped her eyes and picked up her fork. "Because she cares deeply about you and what you think. She always has. You know that." She stared down at her plate, moving her food around.

Wes felt that same strange tightness in his chest that came when he dwelled too long on Lizzy Brookstone. "But that was when she was a child."

Mrs. Brookstone raised her head and met his gaze. "She's not a child anymore."

<hr />

"I'm so glad we're on our way home." Lizzy sat on the train with Mary and Ella. Her uncle and Jason were sitting in the seats on the opposite side of the aisle. "I've missed the ranch more than I can say."

Mary giggled. "The ranch or the ranch foreman?"

Lizzy pretended to brush lint from her traveling jacket. "I'm not even going to acknowledge that question. It doesn't deserve an answer."

This only made Mary laugh all the more. She elbowed Ella Fleming. "Wesley DeShazer is the ranch foreman, and he's very handsome. If Lizzy isn't willing to own up to her feelings for him, then you might want to consider vying for his attention. He's one of the kindest souls you'll ever meet. Not at all rough and smelly like a lot of cattlemen."

"Stop it," Lizzy said, rolling her eyes. She caught sight of Jason Adler glancing her way and knew she needed to change the subject. "Ella knows some trick riding and Roman riding from when she was young. I think she's going to be easy to train to take my place."

Jason leaned across the aisle. "Don't forget, you've given us your word that you'll stay on for at least one more year."

"Lizzy's a woman of her word," Mary said in her defense, but she couldn't keep from smiling. "But Wes might have something to say about it . . . especially if you keep trying to woo Lizzy."

"Who is this Wes?" Jason asked.

"He's the ranch foreman," Uncle Oliver replied. "Lizzy's been sweet on him for years."

"Honestly, you are all impossible." Lizzy got to her feet. "Wesley is our foreman, and he married another, and she died," she said, looking at Jason. "When I was young I looked up to him. Now I'm just looking forward to some dinner." She stormed down the aisle toward the dining car, hoping they'd all leave her to eat in peace.

Of course, that wasn't to be.

"Please forgive me," Jason said, joining her in the dining car.

"Table for two?" the waiter asked.

Lizzy shook her head. "For one."

"For two," Jason insisted.

The man nodded and showed them to a table for two at the far end of the car. There was a partition between their table and the rest of the car due to the serving station. The waiter pulled out a chair for Lizzy and waited. She thought for a moment about leaving, but her stomach rumbled loudly enough that she was certain everyone could hear. Finally, she took her seat, and Jason did likewise.

They placed their orders and received water and bread before Jason leaned forward. "I'm sorry, but I had to speak to you. We are friends, after all."

Lizzy did not want to talk about Wes. Especially not to a man who so clearly wanted to court her himself.

"What is it you wish to discuss?" She placed her napkin on her lap. "If it's related to the show, you should probably speak with my uncle, and if it's personal—I don't want to talk about it." She picked up a piece of bread and began to butter it.

"It's your uncle."

Lizzy put aside her walls as a frown formed on her lips. "What is it?"

"He's somehow managed to procure several cases of liquor in Missouri. I didn't know about it, however, until last night. Apparently he arranged for them to be shipped back with the others but didn't tell them about it. He's having it held for him in Miles City."

Her stomach seemed to sour, and the bread she'd so eagerly buttered was no longer appealing. She put it on her plate and met Jason's gaze. "I don't want to know how you learned this. Just tell me what we should do about it."

"I have no idea. That's why I felt we should discuss it."

He looked as unhappy as Lizzy felt. She glanced out the window, but darkness obscured the world beyond the train. "When my uncle was much younger, he drank something fierce. My father got him to stop drinking, and we all hoped it would never again be a problem." She looked at Jason, whose expression was sympathetic.

"I'm sure the loss of your father—his brother—was deeply felt. Perhaps he will mourn for a time and then realize the futility of what he's doing."

"I'd like to think that's possible, but I don't know." Lizzy thought of her mother and how worried she was. "We've had a rule against alcohol on the ranch for years. It was my father's way of helping Uncle Oliver. Father always said that while he wasn't opposed to the occasional drink, we couldn't have the stuff around because it would be too great a temptation for my uncle. He used the entire matter as a Bible study, showing me Scripture about not being a stumbling block for others."

"Surely we needn't avoid having a drink or whatever pleasure we enjoy because someone else might have a problem with it," Jason replied. "Must their problem become ours?"

She nodded. "We must care for one another and do what we can to encourage each other, especially those who are weak." Lizzy picked up her bread and took a bite. Focusing on spiritual matters always calmed her, even when she was defending her beliefs.

"But God does not expect us to forgo our own happiness because of someone else's weakness, right? I can hardly keep someone from doing what they choose to do. If your uncle wants to drink, that is his business. He is an adult and, I presume, a partial, if not full owner of the ranch, so whether or not alcohol is allowed is surely up to him."

"In Matthew eighteen, Jesus tells us, 'Woe unto the world because of offences! for it must needs be that offences come; but woe to that man by whom the offence cometh!'" Lizzy straightened. "In other words, there are going to be obstacles that lead us astray, because that's just part of the world, but it's going to be really bad for the person who causes them. Worse still for someone who knows another person has a problem and puts temptation in their path anyway. I won't be that person if I can help it. I won't turn a blind eye when Uncle Oliver gives in to his sorrow and drinks. It's easy to walk away and pretend that it's not my business, but it is. If we are to care for one another

144

as the Bible tells us to do—if we are to love one another as Jesus loves us—then how can we turn away from a person in need?"

Jason seemed to consider her words as the waiter returned with their meals. Lizzy's senses filled with the tantalizing aroma of roast beef and vegetables. Her appetite was quickly returning.

"Am I to understand that you believe it necessary to avoid anything that might cause someone else to stumble?" Jason asked. "How can you possibly know what causes them to stumble? And how can you account for the entire world?"

She smiled. "I don't believe I have to account for the entire world. I'm not acquainted with the entire world. However, if someone comes into my life and I know that they have a problem, shouldn't I take care not to make that problem bigger? Even if I were not a Christian woman, would that not be the kind thing to do?"

"Shouldn't a person account for themselves? Am I not responsible for my own sin?"

"Of course, you are," Lizzy said. "But you are also responsible for loving others as Christ loved us."

"But He went to the cross and died a brutal death."

"Exactly so." Lizzy smiled and picked up her knife and fork. "So doing what I can to help Uncle Oliver not be stumbled by alcohol seems a terribly small effort, but a very useful one."

Jason was quiet for several minutes while he pondered her words, and Lizzy ate. She couldn't help but smile at the memory of her father's teaching. She had never expected to use it in such a manner, but she was always glad to share the Bible with those in need.

Still, there remained the issue of the alcohol. If Uncle Oliver had shipped it to the ranch, his drinking would only continue. Perhaps she'd talk to Wesley about it. He might have an idea of what they could do.

"I wonder if I might change the subject," Jason ventured.

Lizzy looked up and nodded. "What would you like to talk about?"

"Next year's show."

She considered reminding him that such matters should be discussed with Uncle Oliver, but then took pity on him. "What about it?"

"I think it would be a great success for us to take the show to Europe. London in particular. The queen is very fond of wild west shows and has inspired much of England to share her pleasure in them."

"You told me we needed to economize. How would this fit in with your plans to put old men out of jobs and cut back on other unnecessary expenses?" She knew her tone was sarcastic, but she was still put off by his attitude that the older men working for the show were excess baggage.

"It would be tremendously well received, and we could charge more per ticket there. We could also perform in one spot for several weeks rather than move about. The biggest expense would be transporting everyone to England, but after that, we could make up for it by pasturing your animals on my father's estate."

"I see. But what about the rest of us? We wouldn't have our train cars to live in."

He smiled. "No, you would be comfortably cared for in our home. The workers would stay in servants' quarters, but your family and the performers would be treated lavishly. So again, the cost would be minimal."

"To us perhaps, but what about your father?"

"He would benefit from the popularity of the show and the sales. After all, he is a stockholder." Jason cut into his fish. "I can show you better on paper, but the money is there, I assure you, and I believe it would be a tremendous boon to the show."

Lizzy could see that he was serious. Maybe he was right. Maybe the trip abroad would breathe new life into the show, and maybe under his managing techniques they would see the Brookstone Wild West Extravaganza once again solvent.

"I think it would be very interesting to see Europe." She smiled at the thought of castles and beautiful lands that she'd only ever read about.

"You would have a remarkable time. I would show you around all the sights. London is full of beauty and history. I know you would enjoy it."

"I'm sure I would." Lizzy put down her fork. "But why tell me all of this? I have little say in the future of the show. Uncle Oliver is now completely in charge, and though my mother has inherited my father's part, she doesn't want to be bothered with any of the decision-making."

"Understandable. However, I believe your uncle is concerned about many things right now, and that, added to his drinking, might make it difficult for him to see the potential of my idea." Jason dabbed a napkin to his lips, then smiled. "I think he would listen to you. If you told him how much you wanted to do this, I think he would quickly agree."

Lizzy wondered if the idea of something bold and adventurous would help Uncle Oliver put aside his grief and look toward the joy of life again.

"I'll pray about it," she finally said, meeting Jason's blue-eyed gaze. "You might do the same."

———◆◆◆———

"I wonder if you might answer some questions I have."

Ella looked at Mary and felt a rush of guilt. "Questions about what?" She already knew that Mary wanted answers about her brother's death, but Ella needed to stall for time and figure out what she would say. If only Lizzy's uncle hadn't gone off in search of Lizzy and Jason, she might have had an excuse to avoid the matter altogether.

"Lizzy said one of your father's employees had an encounter with August. It resulted in your father having the man whipped."

Ella breathed a sigh of relief. At least this was something she didn't have to lie about. "I don't know anything about that. Father never allowed me to know anything about his running of the farm. He said it wasn't appropriate."

The look of disappointment on Mary's face only added to Ella's feelings of guilt. "I had hoped . . . prayed that you might know something. Do you have any knowledge of the people your father had working there? I mean, you went riding a lot, from what Lizzy said. Surely you knew the groomsmen."

"Father had one particular groom . . . an elderly man . . . who generally helped me. My fiancé was the jealous sort and he didn't want any of the younger men near me. So no, I don't think I know the man you're talking about. I heard nothing of anyone being whipped . . . but then again . . . I wouldn't have."

Mary sighed and sank back in the seat and said nothing more. Ella watched her a few moments, then closed her eyes as if she were trying to sleep. She couldn't bear knowing how much pain Mary was in and not do something to help ease her concerns.

But I can't tell her the truth. I just can't. If I did, they'd all expect me to stand as witness—to confront my father and Jefferson.

She sighed and drew her lower lip between her teeth. How could she ever hope to make this right—to give Mary and the others the truth?

THIRTEEN

L izzy was happy when the train arrived in Miles City. Everything was just as she'd left it the previous February, but without snow. Stepping from the train, she smiled. The dry air and pleasantly cool temperature brought to mind hours of riding Longfellow across their property, drinking in the scenery and solitude. She would have a lengthy trip from town back to the ranch, but the others would be with her, and there would no doubt be plenty of chatter. It seemed the last few months had been nothing but noise and conflict. How she longed for hours of silence just to think and pray.

"I see our home away from home is waiting for us," Mary said, pointing to the Brookstone railcars.

Lizzy nodded. "They need to be repainted. I hope we can get the same artist as last time. He did such a good job."

"What a quaint little town," Ella said, coming to stand beside Lizzy and Mary.

"It's a wonderful town." Lizzy motioned down the street. "Let's do a little shopping while the menfolk get our things squared away." She went to Uncle Oliver and Jason. "The girls and I are going to pick up a few personal things at the store. Do you gentlemen need anything?"

Uncle Oliver shook his head. "I don't believe so. I arranged for a list in Missouri."

She thought of the liquor and wondered if that was what he was talking about. She forced a smile. "And you?" she asked Jason.

He returned her smile. "Thank you, but I managed to secure my needs in Topeka. Although given the wild look of this country, I wonder if I thought of everything."

Lizzy laughed. "It is rather wild, but we have our comforts too. Don't worry, if you've forgotten something . . . you'll learn to live without it." She turned back to her uncle. "Where shall we meet you?"

"Just come over to the livery. Jason and I will have the horses ready," Uncle Oliver replied. "Don't buy too much stuff, though. I didn't tell the boys to leave us a wagon, just horses."

Lizzy gave her uncle a kiss on the cheek. "We won't buy out the store, I promise."

She felt relieved that Uncle Oliver was acting more like his old self. She didn't bother to bring up the question of how he planned to get several crates of alcohol home. Knowing there wasn't a wagon to use made her hope the alcohol wouldn't make it to the ranch at all.

She walked back to where the girls were waiting for her. "So did Mr. Adler propose?" Mary asked with a grin.

Lizzy looked at her, unable to hide her horror. "Why would you even think that?"

"Well, it's obvious he's sweet on you."

"Look, like I said before, I have no interest in him or anyone else. If you're looking for a beau, then by all means pursue him."

Mary laughed. "I just got rid of one fiancé. I certainly am not looking for another."

"Then don't try to sell me one." Lizzy hiked her skirt and picked up her pace to avoid a grain wagon.

Ella and Mary quickly followed, and they made their way into the nearest mercantile.

Lizzy stopped to speak to Ella. "I know your circumstances prevented you from bringing much and that you are limited on funds. I don't want you to worry about that. We have an account here, so just get whatever you need, and we can worry about settling it later. The sewing room at the ranch is full of fabric and notions, so we can make you some skirts and blouses or dresses, if you prefer."

"I don't want to add to what you've already paid out," Ella said, glancing around at the shelves of goods. "And I do have my jewelry. We can sell it. I don't want to be a bother."

"You'll be a bother if you need something at the ranch and don't have it." Lizzy turned Ella and gave her a little push. "Now, hurry. Uncle Oliver doesn't want us to dally."

A young man stepped up to the register from the back room. "Miss Lizzy! I heard you were back."

She smiled. "How are you doing, Barney? How's the folks?"

"They're all doing well. Me too. I graduated high school this year."

Lizzy could see the pride in his face. "That's wonderful, Barney. Do you have plans for furthering your education?"

He shook his head. "No. Mr. Levine said I could work my way up here. Said I'd be making twenty-five dollars a month in a couple of years if I worked hard."

"That's impressive, to be sure. Next thing you know, you'll be married."

The young man blushed. "I already know who I plan to marry, Miss Lizzy. I haven't asked her yet, but I plan to next summer."

Lizzy smiled. "I'm sure she'll say yes." She glanced over her shoulder. "I'd better get my shopping done, or the others will be ready to go and I'll still be dawdling." She hurried toward the selection of books before Barney could even reply.

Lizzy thumbed through the books, but nothing interested her. She turned her attention to items she thought would be useful, including a couple pairs of boy's long underwear. She hadn't told Ella how cold the winter could get and knew these would be welcome when they were training outside. Lizzy grabbed wool stockings and socks as well.

When she put her things down on the counter, she spied a notice about collie puppies for sale.

"You want one, Miss Lizzy?" Barney asked.

Lizzy thought about Christmas. Her mother had always said that once she settled back on the ranch, she'd like to have a dog. A collie would be perfect.

"I do. I think I'd like to get one for my mother for Christmas. Who has them?"

He chuckled. "My folks do. I can have them save one for you. The pups are already weaned and ready to go, but I think for you, Miss Lizzy, we can hang on to one until Christmas. You want a male or a female?"

"A male. Mother won't want to worry about a female having puppies and such."

Barney nodded. "I know just the one I'll save for you. First-born and a real sturdy fellow. He'll be a good watchdog. I can even start training him to obey. You know, heel and sit and lie down. Those kinds of things."

"Thank you, that would be useful, I'm sure. I'm so glad you had the notice here." Lizzy hadn't given much thought to Christmas yet, but it would be on them before she knew it. "I suppose I should do some ordering for Christmas, but Uncle Oliver wants to get back to the ranch. We all do."

"That's all right. Did you have in mind what you wanted to purchase?" Barney looked eager to help. "Are you buying for a man or a woman?"

She frowned. They would have Mary and Ella at the ranch

as well as Jason Adler. But it was Wesley who concerned her most. "I've got quite a list, Barney."

He pulled a catalog from behind the counter. "Take this home with you. That way you can find whatever you want. Make a list and then get it back to me." He leaned forward. "The catalog too. We only have two."

Lizzy took the Sears, Roebuck catalog. "Thank you. This will definitely help."

"We might even have what you want on hand, but if not—I'll order it."

"How much time do you need if we have to order something?"

He straightened and puffed out his chest. "We're completely modern here, Miss Lizzy. If I send in the order, we can almost always have it in a month or so."

That didn't give her a lot of time, even if Miles City was completely modern. "Very well. I'll try to get back in a few days."

Ella came to the counter, her arms full of various items. She looked apologetic. "I promise I'll find a way to pay you back. You could always put me to work around the house. I could even sew for your mother."

Lizzy laughed and started helping her put the things on the counter. "Don't fret about it."

"This one of your new performers?" Barney asked.

Lizzy hadn't considered hiding Ella from the townsfolk. It had never even occurred to her, but now that the question had come up, she was hard-pressed to know what to do. The chances of Ella's father following her all the way to Montana were slim, but she couldn't help wishing she'd been more careful.

"Yes." Lizzy kept stacking the purchases on the counter. "Would you go ahead and tally these? Like I said, Uncle Oliver is in a hurry. Just put them on our account. Miss Reichert's things too." Mary had joined them at the counter with her meager selection.

153

"You don't have to do that," Mary said. "I brought the money I saved up. I can pay."

Lizzy was really starting to worry about Ella being seen and didn't want to argue about it. "We'll figure it out later."

Once things were settled at the store, Lizzy hurried the girls to the livery, where Uncle Oliver was just about to send Jason Adler to find them.

"If we don't get a move on, we'll lose the light. Sunset comes sooner this time of year." Her uncle handed her a saddlebag.

Lizzy stuffed some of Ella's packages inside it, while Ella and Mary split the rest of the load in saddlebags Mary had brought with her. That accomplished, Lizzy went to Longfellow and secured the bags. Without any help, she got into the saddle and looked down on her uncle with a grin.

"So what are you waiting for?"

Wes sat on the fence, watching his brother work with a new horse. Sandy Anderson, Wes's assistant foreman, had recently returned with a string of horses. They'd been purchased for using with the cattle, and most weren't saddle broke. Sandy was more than a little glad to learn that Wes had hired Phillip for such tasks so that the job didn't fall to him.

Phillip was delighted by the challenge. He lived to ride—wild or tame, it was all the same to him. He had been working long hours with each of the new horses, and though he'd taken minor injuries, nothing seemed to slow him down. He loved horses, that much was certain, and he was good with them. Wes had seen a lot of horsemen in his years, and most weren't concerned with breaking a horse in a gentle manner. They slapped the halter and bridle on, threw a saddle on their backs, and then rode them wild until they gave up the fight. Phillip, on the other hand, liked to take his time. He was that

154

way about most everything. Wes had decided not to hurry him along. They had a little time, and he wanted to see what Phillip could accomplish.

"Looks like your brother is nearly as good at this as you," Thomas said, coming to stand beside Wes.

"I heard that, and I'll have you know," Phillip called out, "I'm better!"

"Yeah, well, just remember, this horse was already broke, just hadn't been ridden much," Wes countered.

"Trouble is, he's a bully," Phillip said, "but I'm a bigger one."

The men continued to watch as the horse, a beautiful bay, settled down and began to surrender to Phillip's demands. It wasn't long before the horse was trotting a circle around the corral.

"You've got him now," Thomas declared.

"There was never any doubt I would." Phillip slowed the animal to a walk. "It gets a little easier each time, that's for sure. This big boy just about broke my back the first time I climbed on him."

Thomas and Wes laughed. Wes jumped down from the fence. "Did you just come out here to watch Phillip, or did you need me for something?" he asked Thomas.

"Mrs. Brookstone sent me to tell you that Oliver and the others should arrive today."

He knew the others would include Lizzy. For a minute that old tightness in his chest returned. He'd pretty much avoided her for the last couple of years, but now Mrs. Brookstone wanted his help in drawing her daughter out, helping Lizzy get past losing her father. It wasn't a job Wes wanted, but it was also not something he felt he could ignore. The Brookstones had been good to him, and he owed them.

The dinner bell rang, and Wes breathed a sigh, but it wasn't one of relief. "I suppose we'd better go get our grub." He started for the bunkhouse. "Cookie doesn't like to have the results of his talents go cold."

"I'm gonna miss Mrs. Brookstone's meals," Thomas said. "Cookie fries and boils the life out of everything."

Phillip slid off the horse. He praised the bay, stroking his neck. "Save me some," he said, leading the horse across the corral.

Thomas and Wes made their way to the bunkhouse dining room. "How's Phillip settlin' in?" Thomas asked.

"Pretty good. There's been a little grumbling and rough-housin'. I think some of the boys thought I'd give Phillip special privileges or not make him toe the line, but I think they're start-ing to see that isn't the case. I figure if all goes well, everybody will be settled in by Christmas. Those new fellas you took on during the show seem to be working out well. Judd and Rich-ard might be city boys, but they aren't afraid of hard work or getting dirty."

Thomas nodded. "Yeah, I didn't have any trouble with them on the circuit." He opened the door to the bunkhouse. "It's gonna be good to have everybody back home. Did you know Lizzy's thinking of quittin' the show?"

Wes shrugged. "It was bound to happen sooner or later."

"Well, after hittin' her head so hard in Kansas City, I think she got to figuring her time out there was gettin' shorter and shorter before something really bad happens."

"She hit her head?" Wes tried not to sound overly concerned. "How bad was it?"

"It made her see stars, that's all. She bruised a bit, but you know Lizzy. She used some of the theatrical makeup, and no one was the wiser—except for her ma and me. I told her she needs to get married and start a family. That's not nearly as dangerous." Thomas grinned. "Mr. Adler seems mighty interested in her, so who can tell what'll happen."

Wes tried not to feel worried by the old man's statement. He didn't like the idea of a man he didn't know getting close to Lizzy. If he was honest, he didn't like the idea of any man getting too close.

❖✕❖

That evening the family gathered in the living room. Wes was touched that Mrs. Brookstone had invited him to join them and have dessert. She had made a wonderful apple cobbler and served it hot with fresh cream. Wes devoured two large servings during the casual conversation. Seeing Lizzy again had stirred something inside that he wasn't sure he understood, especially after he'd all but ignored her the last two years. He'd put a wall between them, but now he felt it crumbling.

"So you see," Oliver said, "Jason is important to our situation. His father has a vested interest in the future of the show, and Jason is here to learn every possible angle. He's also hoping to save us some money."

"Well, we're all going to be busy, for certain," Mrs. Brookstone said, speaking up for the first time. "Since I won't be returning to the show, we need to figure out who's going to take my place and then teach them how to manage my jobs. Also, Agnes mentioned to me that she might not return after next year, so in light of eliminating extra crew and saving money, I suggest we find someone who can come to the ranch in February, and I'll teach them how to handle cooking for the crew and managing the costumes."

"I think that's an excellent idea," Jason said, nodding. "The more crew jobs that can be combined, the better. Thinning the numbers will certainly help in the long run, and I find that people can generally take on additional duties with proper management of their time. The other important thing is teaching another person or two on the crew how to manage your position in case of illness or, as in the case of Mr. Reichert's . . . death. We've found this system very beneficial in our industries."

"You mentioned that should include performers as well," Lizzy said.

Jason nodded. "I think it should . . . don't you?"

Lizzy considered the question for a moment. Wes studied her. She was all grown up, that much was unavoidably true, but there was still something of the innocent tomboy he'd first known in her face.

"I do see the sensibility of it," Lizzy said. "And I think it could be managed. Ella knows some trick riding as well as Roman, and Mary can definitely teach some of the trick riders to shoot. I suppose we might all be able to do each other's jobs to a certain point. Of course, none of us will ever match Mary's marksmanship."

"Perhaps not, but in a crisis, having people familiar with her part of the act might allow us to fill in during her absence. Just as teaching Ella and the others how to do some of your tricks would allow the show to continue should you be unable to go on. I wouldn't expect them to do all of your tricks or come anywhere near to doing them as well, but having performers at the ready to take over in desperate situations could save the show."

"I agree. In the past, if someone was ill or hurt, we simply shortened the act and doubled up in another area, but this makes sense."

"Good," Jason said, beaming at her. "I'll count on you to do your part in helping the others learn what they need to know. Perhaps you could oversee it all, Lizzy. Better still, you and I could work out the details together. It might take long hours, but I'm sure you're up to the challenge." He winked, and she laughed.

Wes didn't like the suggestion of Adler and Lizzy spending all their time together. Adler was far too familiar, and he was always smiling at her. Who knew what he might attempt if they were alone?

Mrs. Brookstone started gathering the empty bowls and spoons. "Well, I'm afraid Lizzy can't oversee it all, Mr. Adler. She will be needed to help with the ranch and, of course, to work on her own tricks for next season. Perhaps Mary could step in to take the job."

Jason's expression sobered, nearly making Wes laugh out loud. Good for Mrs. B.

"I'd be glad to help," Mary declared. "And once we figure out what we want each person to know, we can put together a training schedule."

"It's sure good to have you back with us, Mary." Oliver handed his bowl to his sister-in-law. "Since Teresa up and got married just before the last show, I was starting to fret about who our main shooter was going to be next year." He looked at Mary. "She was never as good as you, and the audiences were less than impressed. I had so many people asking me where you were and if you were ever returning."

"I'm glad to be back." Mary stretched. "But I have to admit that, at the moment, I'm completely done in. I hope you won't mind if I go on up to my room for the night. After I help with the cleanup."

"Nonsense," Mrs. Brookstone said. "I don't need your help tonight. You go ahead and rest."

Wes noticed that Adler was whispering something in Lizzy's ear. Didn't he realize how rude he was being? Unfortunately, Lizzy didn't seem to mind.

"I'll help you with the dishes." This came from Ella Fleming. Wesley wasn't sure what to make of the tiny girl. She was genteel and pretty—like one of those fancy china dolls. He knew from Rupert that she was on the run from her family, but he didn't really understand why the Brookstones would put themselves in the position of facing an angry Mr. Fleming. Especially when they had done so much business with him.

Ella and Mrs. Brookstone headed off toward the kitchen, and Mary made her way upstairs.

"Jason, I want to show you a few things in my office before you retire," Oliver said, getting to his feet.

Adler frowned. He didn't look at all happy about this but said nothing. He stood and looked back at Lizzy, giving her a slight bow. "Shall we try for that ride in the morning?"

Lizzy shook her head. "I'm afraid not. Mother has several things she wants me to tend to. Maybe later in the day. We'll have to see how things go."

Wesley gripped the arms of his rocker. He didn't like that man. Didn't like him at all. Adler was all smoothness and refinement, and while he might be generally trustworthy, Wes didn't think it wise to turn his back on him.

"Well, that just leaves us," Lizzy said, looking at Wes. "Unless you intend to run off and avoid me like usual."

He looked at her and saw an expression that dared him to contradict the truth of her statement. "I wasn't planning on going anywhere. At least not yet."

Lizzy got up and went to the fireplace. She put another log on the fire, then turned to face him. Wes couldn't help but admire her. She had her long brown hair loosely tied back and wore a skirt and blouse. It was simple but perfect. She was beautiful. Of course, he couldn't tell her that. Their relationship was too strained right now. Then there was all that stuff her mother had talked about. It was best to go slow.

"I heard you got hurt in Kansas City." It was the first thing he could think of to say that wasn't overly personal. He looked for a bruise.

"I got banged up a bit, but not really hurt. I have a bruise on this side." She touched her cheek, then walked over to take one of the chairs near him. "How have things been here at the ranch?"

"Good. We've got quite a few animals to take to market yet. Then we're expecting most of the cows to start dropping calves in January. We have a few older cows we'll butcher next month. It'll keep us in meat all winter, along with a couple of hogs your mother arranged for."

Lizzy nodded but kept her tone aloof. "Did you see the new mares?"

"I did. They look good. It's no wonder they were all your dad could talk about last winter."

"Yes." She looked back at the fire and said nothing more.

Wes went to stand beside her. She didn't seem to notice, so he touched her arm. She startled and looked up at him. He felt bad that he'd surprised her. "Sorry." He paused. "I'm sorry too about your dad. It was the hardest news I've had to hear since I lost my ma."

Lizzy nodded and got up. She moved closer to the fire and held out her hands. "And Clarissa?"

He looked down toward the flames, embarrassed that he hadn't thought to mention her. "Of course. But your pa was special."

"Yes, we all miss him." She turned her back to the heat and shrugged. "But everyone dies sooner or later. My concern is Mother. She's taken it very hard. Father was her whole world."

"Yes, I know. We had supper together last night."

"I don't know how it's going to be for her, being back here. Father was such a presence. I can almost see him." Lizzy's voice softened. "He's really just everywhere."

"I'm sure it's really hard for you. I know you'll miss him very much." Wes studied her face. It was like finely chiseled marble, cold and void of emotion.

Then Adler cleared his throat. Wes and Lizzy looked toward the sound at the same time.

"I hope I'm not interrupting anything." Adler smiled and fixed his gaze on Wes.

Lizzy moved away from the fire. "If you'll both excuse me, I'm going to see if Mother needs any more help, and if not, I'm going to bed." She left the room, with both men watching her.

When she was out of sight, Wes looked Adler over from top to bottom while Adler did the same. It was like assessing an obstacle and trying to figure out the best way to deal with it. Wesley didn't like that Adler would be staying in the house but knew it wasn't his place to speak against it.

Wes gave a slight nod. "Evenin', Mr. Adler."

The Englishman returned the gesture. "Good evening, Mr. DeShazer."

Wes headed out of the house, barely remembering to grab his hat on the way out the door. He didn't like Adler's smug attitude and familiar handling of Lizzy. He didn't like his plans for remaking the show and figuring out ways to manage it.

He just didn't like the man.

As he neared the bunkhouse and headed for his own cabin, Wes ran headlong into his brother.

"Whoa there, big brother. You het up for a fight?" Phillip asked, laughing. "You look like someone stole your prized saddle."

Wes pushed Phillip aside. "It's nothing. I'm tired and headin' for bed."

"Hope nothing isn't still bothering you in the morning." He stressed the word *nothing*.

Wes stopped and turned to face Phillip. He started to give him an earful, then released a heavy sigh. This wasn't Phillip's fault. "Good night."

⤜ FOURTEEN ⤛

For three days, Lizzy did very little. She offered to help around the house, but Cookie's wife, Irma, took care of most of the household duties and wouldn't hear of it. Lizzy read a little and went for a couple of rides but unfortunately had to take Jason Adler with her on most of them. Because she didn't want to ride out alone with him, she asked Mary and Ella to accompany them. She knew that didn't please Jason, but she'd made her feelings clear, and if he didn't like it, that was entirely too bad. The rest of the time she spent trying to familiarize Ella with the ranch and house.

Mother quickly lay claim to Mary and Ella. She taught Ella how to wash clothes and cook, and enticed Mary to bake some of her grandmother's favorite German recipes. The three women worked well together, and Lizzy found herself unneeded in the kitchen.

"You need to learn how to run the ranch," Mother told her more than once. "For all these years you've paid it little mind. Now, with your father gone, I need you to help me in this."

Lizzy knew it was just an excuse to put her and Wes together, but at the same time, she hoped to make this place her home after retiring from the show. She imagined a good life, just her and Mother—and Uncle Oliver when he was home from the show. It would serve her well to know the details of how the ranch operated. She had a working knowledge of the various duties that were performed throughout the year, but no firsthand experience. What little time she had been in residence, she was always training for the next show. And back then, Father had been alive and Uncle Oliver sober. There had been no need for her to know how the ranch operated.

Walking around the yard, Lizzy paused to look at the massive log house. It was nothing fancy, but she loved it. She had made so many memories here, and even now, in the early morning, she could hear voices from the past.

"I think we need a porch," Mother had said, standing arm in arm with Father.

"Whatever would we do with a porch?" he'd asked.

"We could hang a swing from it and then snuggle up on chilly evenings and talk about the future," Mother had replied.

But the show had taken up so much time, and the porch was never built. Maybe it could be now. Of course, that would cost money, and Jason would probably think the idea unreasonable. But Lizzy didn't, and while Jason might have something to say about the show, he didn't have any authority over the ranch. Maybe she'd talk to Wes about it.

That only served to remind her of her next duty.

"So what's planned for today?" Mary asked, coming to join her. "Another romantic ride?"

Lizzy grimaced. "No. I'm hoping Jason will be otherwise occupied. Uncle Oliver has taken to bed with a bad cold, but Mother said he still planned to meet with Jason about the show's schedule for next year. Meanwhile, I have to learn the business of running a ranch."

Mary looked at the house and nodded. "I suppose there's a lot to do before winter, and I suppose too that winter comes much earlier here than in Kansas."

"It does," Lizzy agreed. "I was just remembering how Mother always wanted a porch on the house. I thought maybe I could talk to Wesley about getting one put on. Of course, it might only make her sad." Lizzy frowned. "She wanted it so she could sit with my father and talk."

"Maybe you should ask her."

Lizzy considered the long, rectangular home for another moment. There were chimneys at either end of the house, and in back was enough chopped firewood to keep them warm throughout the snowy months to come. It seemed silly to consider a porch when winter was nearly upon them. "Maybe I will," she murmured.

"So what else is on today's agenda besides learning ranch business?" Mary asked.

Lizzy turned from the house and started across the yard. "I promised Ella a lesson at ten. That's why I'm wearing my performance skirt." She ran her hand down the side of the bloused leg. Her split skirts were specially designed to be banded just below the knee where they met the boot. The looseness of the leg gave her a lot of freedom without being roomy enough to cause any entanglements. "But before then, I must speak with Wesley."

"So you'll be thrown yet again into your father's footsteps, whether you like it or not."

"It's not a matter of not liking it. I just don't know that I'm qualified. I suppose I already know a good deal about the ranch. At least as far as the cow calendar, as Father used to call it." She smiled at the memory. "But as for the bookwork and other such details, I know nothing."

"And Wesley's the one you have to work with."

Lizzy glanced at Mary, who kept in step with her. "Yes."

Ella came from the house and gave them a wave. "Where are you two headed?"

Lizzy tried to sound less discouraged. "I'm off to see what I must learn to keep this ranch running smoothly."

"Who do you see for that?" Ella asked.

"Wesley." Lizzy frowned. "Wesley will have all the answers."

"Pity that," Mary teased, then took hold of Lizzy's arm. "Look, now that he's a widower, why don't you make him see how you feel about him?" Her expression was all innocence, yet she knew very well how Lizzy had loved Wes. Ella knew it too, given their conversations on the train.

"Just so you both know, it doesn't matter how I felt about Wesley before. Now it's just business. I don't plan to marry— ever." Lizzy buttoned her heavy work jacket as a sharp wind cut across them. She didn't know if her friends believed her. She wasn't yet convinced that she believed herself. What she did know was that she never wanted to go through what her mother was going through. If that meant closing off her heart, then she'd just have to find a way.

"But Clarissa died two years ago," Mary declared. She looked at Ella. "That was Wes's wife. She died after getting thrown from her horse. Just like my father . . . well, not exactly. She didn't break her neck, did she, Lizzy?"

Ella sucked in her lower lip. She looked like she might break into tears.

Lizzy knew Ella's emotions were delicate. No doubt leaving her family for the first time, and under such dire circumstances, weighed on her. "Let's not talk about such sad things."

"We're all dealing with our griefs," Mary replied. "They won't go away simply because we stop talking about them. I would think you'd have learned that by now."

"Yes," Lizzy agreed. "But I must put that from my mind and go learn the affairs of the Brookstone ranch. Sorrow and grief won't help me in this." She sighed and pulled up the collar on the coat. "If either of you need me, I'll be in the bunkhouse office. Mary, you might help Ella better understand about the show. Tell her about our routines and how we'll all come together in February to train and get everything lined up. Or even teach her how to shoot."

"Sure, I'd be happy to." Mary looked at Ella. "The more you learn, the more comfortable you'll be. For me, it's old hat."

Lizzy left them as Mary started to explain that she hadn't normally wintered at the ranch. Walking across the yard to the bunkhouse and barns, Lizzy did her best to stuff her feelings into all the proper places, where they couldn't get loose and cause her problems. She wanted to talk things out with Wes—wanted to know why he'd made it his job to keep out of sight the last two years—but at the same time she didn't want him to think she was trying to get too close.

She glanced across the open pasture as the wind picked up again. There was a taste of snow in the air. The skies were gray, and the wind had turned cold. No doubt they'd soon be facing bad weather.

"Bad weather and bad memories," she murmured.

She stopped about ten feet in front of the bunkhouse and prayed for strength. She had hoped when they returned to the ranch that she'd find she no longer had feelings for Wes. She'd played it all out in her mind. Wes would come into the house for their gathering, and she'd look at him and feel nothing more than brotherly love.

But that wasn't how it had been. In fact, when Mother had asked him in for dessert, Lizzy had thought she might be ill. Her stomach did all sorts of quivering maneuvers, and a sort of light-headedness overcame her. She'd carefully positioned herself between Mary and Ella and thought everything would be fine, but then Ella went to retrieve something, and Jason took her spot. From that point forward, Lizzy was keenly aware of both men. Jason, because he wouldn't stop talking to her, and Wesley, because he looked so angry.

Now she'd have to face him alone. Well, that was just the way it had to be. She squared her shoulders. She'd certainly faced bigger obstacles in her life.

She marched to the bunkhouse door and walked in, knowing that the men would be out working—preparing for the storm and doing their routine jobs.

"Wes?" she called. The bunkhouse was a long, rectangular building with a kitchen to the left and living quarters in the middle. To the back were the dorm-style sleeping quarters, and to her right was the bunkhouse office. The door was closed. She started to knock.

Cookie called out, "He'll be right back. Some unscheduled supplies came in from town, and he went to see them properly stowed."

Lizzy turned and wandered over to the kitchen. It was nice and toasty here by the large cookstove. The grizzled old cook smiled at her, revealing several holes where teeth had once been.

"Best place to be on a day like today," he said.

Lizzy nodded and held out her hands to warm them. "How are you doing, Cookie? I'm sorry I haven't been out to see you before now. I hope Irma gave you that hot water bottle I picked up for you."

This only caused his grin to broaden. "She did. I used it last night. Helped my lumbago, and I'm fit as I can be this morning."

She chuckled. "So should I expect you and Irma to be kickin' up your heels in town tonight?"

"Grief, no. It's comin' up a storm. Don't you feel it?"

"I do." Lizzy sighed. "I was hoping for a few more days of nice fall weather."

"Bah, you know how things are up here. It could snow a foot today and be gone tomorrow. Don't be gettin' all disappointed. Ain't winter yet."

The door to the bunkhouse swung open and Wesley walked

in. He seemed to fill the room, and Lizzy felt her breath catch. He caught sight of her and immediately stopped. A fierce wind blew in and froze Lizzy to the bone.

"Close the door, you fool!" Cookie yelled.

This seemed to shake Wes back into the moment. He did as Cookie ordered, then looked at Lizzy again. "I figured you'd come see me sooner or later. Your mother told me to expect you." He sounded matter-of-fact.

Lizzy had let her guard down talking to Cookie, and now just the sight of Wesley set her heart aflutter. Why did she have to love a man who clearly didn't love her? Why did she have to love at all?

"Yes," she said, trying her best to sound businesslike. "Mother wants me to be aware of all that's going on with the ranch. She said Uncle Oliver is bound to be much too busy, and since it was Father's interest anyway, the duties fall to me."

"Are you trying to step into your father's shoes?" Wes asked. His tone was even, and there wasn't a hint of what he was thinking in his expression.

Lizzy nodded. "As best I can. Someone has to."

Wes looked like he might say something, but then he just nodded. "Well, come on in." He opened the office door and stepped inside.

Lizzy hesitated. She glanced back at Cookie, who was coming toward her with a cloth-covered plate. "What's that?" she asked.

He pulled back the dish towel. "Buttermilk biscuits and jam. He didn't eat this morning, and I figure if you take this in there and have one, maybe he will too."

She took the plate. "I suppose I can try, but he never listens to me."

Lizzy followed Wesley into the office and found he was already sitting behind his desk. He watched her in that casual way of his—seemingly uninterested, while at the same time taking in every detail. She'd seen him deal with snakes the same way. She felt her cheeks flush and put the biscuits in the middle of the desk just to ensure his focus would be on something other than her face.

She reached for a biscuit. "I hope you don't mind, but I'm hungry." Without waiting for his approval, she plopped down in a chair and started munching.

"Thought you might like some coffee to wash down those biscuits," Cookie said, following her in with a couple of mugs.

Lizzy happily accepted and smiled at the coffee's milky hue. "Thank you for remembering that I like cream in my coffee."

"It's the other way around, isn't it?" Cookie teased. "You like a touch of coffee in your cream."

Lizzy smiled and nodded. "You know me too well."

"I should hope after all this time that I do." Cookie put Wesley's cup beside the plate of biscuits. "Now, you just holler if you want anything else."

"I didn't want this," Wes said sarcastically.

"Well, that's too bad," Cookie replied with a chortle, "'cause you've got it now, and I'll be offended if you don't eat and drink what I've served." He left and closed the door behind him.

For just a moment, Lizzy waited in silence, trying to figure out whether she should tease Wesley or just get down to business. She wished things could be lighthearted between them. It seemed so terrible that such a good friendship had to be compromised by the past.

"I'm glad we have you, Wesley. Father said you were by far the best foreman he'd ever had. He said he would have been proud to call you his son—that if God had blessed him with a son, he would have wanted him to be just like you." Lizzy put down her cup and placed the half-eaten biscuit beside it. "My mother also puts great stock in what you think. She has admired your abilities for years."

As she talked, Wesley watched her without attempting to comment. There was no hint of pride in his expression for the praise she offered, but when she spoke of her mother, she saw a softening in his face.

Lizzy continued talking, desperate to fill the silence. "Mother is very wounded over losing my father. He was her very best friend, and she will never be the same. However, I'm hopeful that with your help and mine, she will be able to find happiness here at the ranch again. I know she wanted to come home to be near his grave, but also to be in the place she thought him happiest."

"If he was happiest here, why stay with the show?" Wes asked, then looked surprised, as if he'd never meant to be caught up in the conversation.

Lizzy shrugged. "That's easy enough. He did it for Uncle Oliver. My uncle hates ranch life—always has. Uncle Oliver was born to perform. He loves to make pretty speeches and promote the show. If he hadn't been injured so many times, he'd still be out there, performing on horseback." She tried to look relaxed. "My father put Uncle Oliver's desires ahead of his own. He promised his mother they would always look after each other."

"Oliver was five years your father's senior. If anyone should have been looking out for anyone, it should have been the reverse."

"That's probably why Uncle Oliver is having such a difficult time with Father's passing. He's drinking again. Did you know he bought several crates of alcohol and brought it back here?"

Wes frowned. "No, I didn't know that. I knew your mother was concerned about him drinking."

"Well, whatever we can do to keep him from getting that liquor is going to be to the betterment of everyone. I heard an unexpected shipment came in today. Was it by any chance for Uncle Oliver?"

Wes nodded. "It was."

"I was afraid of that." She picked up the biscuit and nibbled at it. There had to be a way to keep Uncle Oliver from receiving the alcohol. She supposed she could just take it and dispose of it somewhere. But where, and how could she manage huge crates by herself?

"What do you want me to do about it?" Wes asked.

She glanced up to see him watching her. She swallowed. "I want you to help me take the crates away from here and get rid of them." She fully expected an argument, but instead he nodded.

"I can do that, but you don't need to be involved. I'll just load it up and drive it out of here."

"No. If you do it alone, he might get mad and try to fire you. If I do it, then he'll be angry, but he'll get over it."

"I'll take care of it," Wesley insisted. Then he gave a wry smile. "He's not going to fire me. Like you said, he hates ranch work."

Lizzy decided it wasn't worth the fight. "Thank you. I have to do whatever I can to help Uncle Oliver stay sober. It's bad enough that he even took another drink, but that he's been drunk several times is going to make this even worse."

"It's really not your responsibility. He'll most likely just find more liquor."

"That's true, but Mother hopes to convince him otherwise, especially now that he has a bad chest cold. He might listen to her. He respects her and loves her like a sister. She plans to sit down with him and talk about Father. Maybe if he talks about how much he misses his brother and how hard losing him has been, then he won't feel the need to drink."

"And what about you?" Wesley asked. "Are you willing to talk about how much you miss your father and how hard losing him has been on you?"

Lizzy hadn't expected that turn and nearly dropped the coffee she'd just picked up. "I'm not seeking alcohol to comfort myself, so I'm not sure why you ask that question. Of course I miss Father, and it's been very hard to lose him." It was her turn to speak matter-of-factly—with no emotion. She raised her chin and looked Wes square in the eye. "Not that I believe you are overly concerned about my feelings. No doubt Mother told you to be concerned, but you needn't be. I'm just fine."

"Yeah, I can see that. Stubborn and closed up. I guess that equals being fine to you."

"You're one to talk. You wouldn't even speak to me for the last two years. Would you like to tell me how much you miss Clarissa? How difficult it's been for you to lose her?" Lizzy regretted the words the minute she said them.

Wes stiffened, and something hardened in his expression. "No."

She nodded. "Then I suggest we discuss ranch business and leave it at that. I hoped we could at least be friends, but in lieu of that, I'll simply be my mother's envoy."

She was surprised to see him shake his head and frown. "I don't want that, Lizzy."

"No? Then what do you want?" For a moment she thought he might actually tell her.

But then he opened the desk drawer and took out two large ledgers. He tossed them on the desk. "For the books to balance."

Realizing he wasn't going to let the conversation get any more personal, she reached for the book on top. "Then let's get to it. I'm fairly good at math." *It's understanding a man's heart where I fail.*

They pored over the ledgers for the next two hours. Lizzy could see that Wes had been careful to keep track of every detail. He had noted every transaction. From what she could see, the ranch was in good order.

She was about to ask him about riding into town with her when a light knock sounded on his office door.

"Come in," Wes called.

Ella opened the door and peeked inside. She smiled at the sight of Lizzy. "You said you'd give me a lesson at ten, so I thought I'd come find you. I don't know much about the place yet, so I was hoping you'd show me where you want to work."

Lizzy got up. "We'll work in the enclosed arena. It looks to start snowing at any time." She looked back at Wesley. "I need to get to town soon—maybe once the threat of snow is past. I was thinking you could ride in with me."

Wes frowned and looked like he would refuse, but Ella piped up before he could answer. "I'll bet Mr. Adler would go with you." She smiled so sweetly that Lizzy wasn't sure if she was innocent of the suggestion or had done it purposefully to goad Wesley into agreeing.

"I can spare the time," Wes muttered.

FIFTEEN

Wesley didn't know why he'd just agreed to go to town with Lizzy. The last thing he wanted was more time alone with her. Thinking about her being alone with Adler, however, was more than he could bear to consider.

"I'm so excited to learn some new tricks," Ella said, stepping fully into the office. "Isn't it exciting that she's going to teach me, Mr. DeShazer?"

Wesley had been glad for the interruption, but at Ella Fleming's words, he felt a chill run up his spine. "Not particularly. It's dangerous."

Lizzy looked at him and narrowed her eyes, as she so often did when she was angry. If eyes could alight with flames, then Lizzy's would be blazing. Her feelings were evident, but maybe that was better than her pretense at having none at all.

"Ella is an experienced equestrian. She tried her hand at trick and Roman riding when she was younger. She wants to learn it again so she can perform and perhaps even take my place." Her words were clipped and hard.

"I like the idea of you quitting the show, but don't you think it's dangerous for someone like her to learn to do what you do? From what your mother said, Miss Fleming has been raised as a proper lady. Not just that, but in a refined Southern manner that would never allow for such things. A person needs a great deal of muscle and body control for what you do."

Ella responded before Lizzy could. "I appreciate your concern, Mr. DeShazer, but I know what I'm doing, and I didn't just do such things when I was a child. I'd try my hand at various tricks when I was out riding alone and knew I could get away with it. Lizzy has given me exercises to do in order to strengthen my muscles and gain additional balance. I practice them several times a day—faithfully. I want to learn all that I can. I'll need to be able to support myself, after all."

"I don't want to offend, but there are easier ways than this. It is, after all, 1900. A great many women work jobs, and the opportunities are far more numerous than ever before." He glanced at Lizzy for confirmation. The instant his gaze met hers, he regretted it. "I'm not trying to offend either of you."

"Well, for someone who's not trying," Lizzy said, taking Ella's arm, "you're doing a great job."

"Hey, Wes, do you have—" The voice fell silent as Phillip entered the room and nearly knocked Ella over. He reached out to steady her and grinned when she turned to face him. "I'm sure sorry for that. I wasn't lookin' where I was goin'."

Wes couldn't see Ella's expression, but his brother's left little doubt of his attraction to the pretty blonde. "Lizzy, Miss Fleming, this is my brother, Phillip. He's recently come to work for us."

Lizzy crossed her arms and looked at the ceiling. "Great, now there's two of you."

Ella smiled. "How nice to meet you, Mr. DeShazer," she said.

"Just call me Phillip. Everybody does, and I sure hope that the prettiest girl I've ever met would too."

"Phillip, you're in the presence of two very beautiful ladies. It's not polite to single one out, especially when the other is the ranch owner's daughter." He knew better than to point out Lizzy that way, but the words were said before he gave them thought.

Lizzy stepped up to Phillip. "That's quite all right, Phillip. I'm glad to meet you, and I believe people should be honest about the way they feel. I agree with you that Ella is very pretty, and I don't mind at all that you think her prettier than me."

Phillip went ten shades of red and shook his head. "But I didn't even see you, Miss Brookstone. I'm real sorry too, 'cause I think you're mighty pretty. But it's like dessert. I love cherry cobbler and I love chocolate cake. But I love them both for different reasons, and right now I'm really very fond of cherry cobbler." He grinned in his impish way.

Wes had seen that smile disarm even the angriest of opponents. Phillip was a sweet kid, and for the most part he could always talk his way out of trouble.

Lizzy laughed. Once again Phillip's charm seemed to work. "I'm very fond of cherry cobbler myself, so I completely understand. Please know that I am not offended in any way by anything you have said." She emphasized the word *you*, and Wes knew it was intentionally done to make sure he knew she was offended by him. As if concerned that he wouldn't pick up her subtle comment, she added, "I wish it could be so for everyone." She took hold of Ella's arm. "Sorry, but Ella and I have work to do."

"What are you going to do?" Phillip asked. "Is there anything I can do to help?"

"I don't think your brother would approve, and I learned long ago that when you step on his toes, there are repercussions." Lizzy looked at Wesley and raised a brow.

No one said a word for several long moments.

"Lizzy is going to teach me some riding maneuvers for the show," Ella interjected into the uncomfortable silence. "I'm going to trick ride."

Phillip grinned. "I break horses. I'm the best there is. You should come watch me sometime. I do my own trick riding."

Ella nodded. "Maybe I will, but for now I have a lot to learn, and I'm anxious to get started."

"No more anxious than I am to be out of here," Lizzy said and pulled Ella toward the door. "I definitely prefer the company of horses."

Once they'd gone, Phillip looked at Wesley with a grin. "She's an angel."

"She's a girl who left her home under bad terms. Stay away from her," Wesley said, sitting back down.

Phillip plopped down where Lizzy had just been sitting. He grabbed a biscuit and made a hole in the side, then spooned jam into the hole, mashing it down into the center. When that was done, he pushed the whole thing in his mouth.

"Have some manners." Wesley shook his head and moved the plate to the far side of his desk. "What are you even doing in here? Don't you have enough work to do? Do I need to assign you more?"

Phillip nodded and swallowed before speaking. At least that was an improvement. "I have a lot of work, but I just wanted to find out if you have any extra boots that might fit me. Mine are plumb worn out, and they're startin' to cause me trouble."

"I don't suppose you have any money, although you seemed to have enough to buy liquor the other day."

Phillip ate another biscuit before answering. "I didn't buy that whiskey—it was given to me. But no, I haven't got a cent until payday."

Wes shook his head, then pulled out his wallet. He threw down several bills of his own money. "Go to town and get another pair. Make sure they're good ones."

"I'll pay you back real soon," Phillip said, grabbing the money. "Thanks for helping me out. I won't let you down, I promise."

Wesley nodded. "You may have to hold off a day or two. We're due a snow, and I don't want you getting stuck in town."

"I'll take the new bay. He needs the exercise and a good, hard run. I'll be back faster than a whistle, snow or no snow."

"Phillip . . ."

For a moment Wes considered telling Phillip to take Lizzy with him, then thought better of it. He didn't know why, but even the idea of sending her off with his brother bothered Wes.

He shook his head. "Be quick about it, and no liquor!"

Phillip left, and Wesley tried to focus on his work, but Lizzy was all he could think about. He hadn't meant to upset her. He wasn't even sure how things had gotten so bad. Should he go apologize? His mother had once said that if that question came to mind, there was a good chance you already knew the answer.

"It's always good to practice first with the horse standing still and then with someone walking him around or leading him on horseback for control. Since Pepper is accustomed to you doing unusual maneuvers, he'll be easier to work with, but it's still a good idea to do some basic moves to start to remind him."

Lizzy looked the sleek black gelding over from nose to tail. "He's got a pretty long back. That makes it difficult for a lot of the tricks I do. We might do better to let you train on my horse and discuss what you want to do for the future. We have some other horses here that have been used for trick riding. I think in the long run, you'd be happier with one of them." She ran her hand over the black's rump. "I also have a smaller saddle that might be perfect for you. As you know, the saddles are very different. In fact, I've made quite a few personal changes and have pretty much created my own design. Come with me and I'll show you."

They left Pepper tethered to the gate and walked back to where several saddles were posted atop wooden stands.

"As you can see, these saddles are a little longer than the normal work saddle."

Ella nodded and ran her hand along the elongated horn. "This is longer too. I imagine that's a wonderful tool for tricks. I've had some rough moments and all because it was hard to get a grip on my horn. There were also times when I did tricks without a saddle, and sometimes I thought that was easier."

"I know what you mean. Sometimes I even perform a few tricks bareback. The crowds love it. But for the most part you'll use one of these saddles, so you should be familiar with them. If you decide you're serious about staying with the show, you'll want to have your own saddle made."

"My brother-in-law's family business is making saddles. He's part owner of Knox Saddlery. Maybe you've heard of them."

"Of course I have. Everyone knows Knox saddles. They're some of the finest."

Ella nodded. "That's how my sister and brother-in-law met. She was having a saddle made, and he came to our farm. It was all very romantic." She smiled and then sobered almost instantly. "I hope she's all right and that Father hasn't made it difficult for her. I never wanted to cause her pain."

Lizzy touched Ella's arm. "I know you didn't want to hurt her. That's why I suggested you come here. Maybe after Christmas or your birthday, you can send her a letter and let her know what's happened."

"I will. I've already started writing it." Ella paused and looked as if she were struggling to come up with the right words. "Lizzy . . . I really . . . that is, I hope you know how much I appreciate what you've done for me."

"I do. You're a friend, and you were in need. Goodness, given all that happened with August, I'd never have rested a wink if I'd known you needed to escape and I did nothing." Lizzy flipped her long braid back over her shoulder. "It's what friends do."

"I've never had that kind of friend. One who cared so deeply." Ella wiped away a tear. "I just want you to know how much it means. I sometimes lie awake at night and think of what must be going on back at home. I miss my poor mother. I know she must be beside herself."

"In time, you'll be able to write to her as well." Lizzy smiled. "Now, try to put it from your mind. We have a lot of work to do if you're going to perform in the spring." She knew that the best thing Ella could do for herself was concentrate on something else. "Come on, let me show you a few things about this saddle." She glanced at Ella. "Oh, I forgot to ask. How does that split skirt fit?"

"It's good. I had to take it in a little, but I think it'll be fine. It's a little longer than I need, but given it tucks into the boots, I don't think it'll be too loose. If I can get some material, I can make my own."

"Good. Mother has a whole sewing room full of materials and supplies. She even has one of the latest treadle sewing machines. Father bought it for her for Christmas last year." Lizzy sighed. She could still see the love that had shone in their eyes as her mother thanked Father with a kiss. How would she ever go on without him?

Lizzy shook the memory from her mind and hoisted the saddle. It weighed about sixty pounds, and she wondered if Ella was even able to lift something that heavy. No doubt Wes was right—Ella had lived a pampered life and probably never had to saddle her own animal. Well, they'd deal with that later.

She carried the saddle to where Thoreau awaited her. She placed it on the ground, then retrieved the saddle pad. She gave Thoreau a cursory rub on the nose.

"How are you today, Thoreau?" She let him nuzzle the pad. "You're such a good boy that I thought you might like to show off a bit for Ella."

Ella joined her, and Lizzy decided to start the lesson. "I presume you are familiar with all the components of saddling a horse."

"Yes, but I rarely saddled the horse myself."

That answered that question. Lizzy nodded. "Well, you'll be doing it for yourself here. If Jason has his way about cutting costs, we'll probably be doing a great many things for ourselves. You'll have to build some muscle before you can hoist these heavy saddles, but in time you'll do just fine. I was saddling my own horse when I was just a child, so I know it can be done."

"I'll do it," Ella assured. "You can count on me."

"Good." Lizzy put the pad on Thoreau's back. "I always let him see what I'm doing so he doesn't get spooked. And I always come from the left. We do that with all the horses." She lifted the saddle and brought it within Thoreau's line of sight. "You can see how I've secured the right-side stirrup and girth strap up and out of the way. This makes it easier to put the saddle on the horse's back." She placed the saddle. "I always shake it a bit back and forth to make sure it's in the right position. After a time, you'll get a feel for it."

She went on explaining, and after she'd seen to the cinches, she picked up a breast collar. "I use this for extra stability, but some of the girls don't." She fixed the collar in place, then stood back. "You can see there are a variety of extra straps and handholds. Most of these I've added as I've developed tricks where I found I needed a better grip or more security in one place or another. You'll learn as you train, and you'll be able to see what works best for you."

Ella was an attentive student, and Lizzy had no doubt she'd be able to master most anything, given her willing spirit.

Lizzy turned to the open arena. This had been a surprise gift from her father two years ago. It was a rectangular building with equipment and storage rooms at one end and an open area for training hour after hour without worry of the weather. There was a bank of large windows at either end to let in the light and overhead lanterns that could be lit if needed.

"We always keep the horses working in a long oval in the center. You don't want to get too close to the side for several reasons. If the tour locations are fenced, then you could risk getting snagged during the run. If it's open, as many of the performance areas are, you could come in conflict with the audience. Of course, we generally set up ropes to keep the audience from getting too close."

"That makes sense to me," Ella replied.

"To make the tricks look best, we have to prove to the audience the element of danger, yet not look afraid. And we definitely don't want to *be* afraid, or the horse will sense that, and then you'll really have trouble. It's all about balance and rhythm, and once you have that, you'll go far. The appearance of the act is the most critical thing. My father taught me that. We're entertaining people, just like actors on a stage, only our performance is much more physical."

Lizzy took up the reins. "I'll show you a few very basic tricks. Then you'll practice these over and over in the days to come." She climbed atop the horse and guided him to the center of the arena. "I don't know what you know and don't know, so we're going to start from scratch."

"That sounds wise," Ella said, moving a little closer.

Lizzy stroked Thoreau's neck, then looked back at Ella. "First are the spins. I usually tuck the reins beneath the bridle's headpiece or throat strap, like this." She doubled the reins, then slipped them partway under. "This way they're out of the way but easy to grab if something goes wrong." She shifted her weight slightly. "I'll show you this sitting still, but all tricks will be done in motion."

"I understand," Ella said, watching intently.

"The most important thing I can tell you is that you have to keep looking up. Fix your eyes on a mark well in front of you. Where your eyes go, your body follows, my father always said." Lizzy smiled. "He incorporated that into a spiritual lesson as well. If we put our focus on the things of this world, that's where we're likely to end up. So he always admonished me to fix my eyes on Jesus."

"That makes sense to me."

Lizzy gave Ella a nod. "Father generally made the best sense in every matter, and in this case, with trick riding, it's imperative. Your body follows your eyes. If you look down while trying to perform a trick, you'll go down." She put her hand on her left thigh. "We're going to spin counterclockwise. Take your feet out of the stirrups, tucking your leg up and back. At the same time throw your right leg over the horse's neck. Use the horn to shift your weight, like this." She made the backward turn. "Then tuck your left leg again and put your right leg forward across the saddle and turn again using the horn." She did the action as she spoke. "Now you're facing forward again. In time, you'll be able to spin just using the horn and your leg muscles, and your bottom won't even need to touch until you're back in the saddle. It's all about continuous motion, and practice will make it look smooth."

"I used to do that when I was little," Ella said, grinning. "I'm so glad I know at least something useful."

Lizzy laughed. "Well, just remember the placement of your hands, feet—well, really every part of your body is going to be critical to getting the tricks right. But I know you're going to take to this like a duck to water."

That night at supper, Wes watched Lizzy and Jason from across the table. He hadn't wanted to come to dinner with the others, but Rebecca Brookstone had insisted. She wanted to

184

talk to him about the crates that had been delivered and, it was discovered only recently, disappeared. Oliver was still in bed sick, but he'd been asking about them.

Wes knew he needed to apologize to Lizzy for his attitude earlier, but as the day wore on, more and more problems came to his desk to be dealt with. Before he knew it, it was supper-time, and the request from Rebecca came to share the meal with the family.

"I think that's marvelous, Lizzy. You have such a generous heart," Jason Adler declared.

Wes didn't know what he was praising Lizzy for, but just the fact that this stranger called her by her family's nickname irritated Wes more than he could say.

Mary shared a story about her brother. Something from the early days, when Wes had been working with August on the show. She looked at Wes. "Do you remember that? I think the two of you were up all night, trying to figure out what had happened to the saddles."

Everyone suddenly looked at him. Even Lizzy's expression suggested interest in his reply. He tried to put aside his frustrations with Adler. "I do. It was a nightmare, and little did we know it was a joke being played on us by Mr. Brookstone—Lizzy's father." He gave a slight smile.

"He's exactly right," Mary declared. "August was mortified because he was new and it was his job to see the saddles were put on the train. When he couldn't locate them, he thought for sure he'd be fired. But Wes was so kindhearted and took pity on him. He took responsibility for the entire thing and assured Mr. Brookstone that any fault was his. I think August was completely devoted to Wes after that. I know I was."

"Wes has always been such an important part of our lives," Mrs. Brookstone said. "Mark said he'd never met a man he trusted more, outside of family."

Wes was uncomfortable under the scrutiny and praise, but he forced himself to give her a smile before refocusing on his plate. Thankfully the conversation shifted again, and he was no longer the center of attention.

By the time the meal finally ended, Jason and Lizzy were agreeing with Mary and Ella to play a new card game that Jason intended to teach them.

"Why don't you come learn too, Wesley?" Mary asked.

"It's really just a game for four," Adler quickly said. "But of course, he could come and watch."

"No, I've seen quite enough," Wes muttered. His eyes met Adler's just long enough to convey his disapproval.

"Very well. Come, ladies. I think you'll enjoy this," Jason said, leading them away.

"We need to help Mother with the table and dishes, first," Lizzy said as she started to stack the plates nearest her.

"Never mind that." Mrs. Brookstone shooed them away. "Wes and I will manage it."

He hadn't expected to be volunteered but would have offered anyway. He got to his feet and started collecting plates even as laughter came from the opposite side of the house.

"You really should stake a claim on her," Mrs. Brookstone said as she took the plates from him.

"What?" He looked at her in surprise.

She chuckled. "You know you were her first love. In fact, as far as I know, her only love."

"You couldn't tell by the way she acted with me earlier. I think she has lost any and all love for me."

"Well, you did go and marry another. That hurt her deeply. Then when Clarissa died, you continued to avoid and ignore Lizzy."

Wes started collecting cups and saucers. He never wanted to talk about Clarissa or Lizzy, but something about having this conversation with Rebecca Brookstone put him at ease. It seemed natural to share his feelings with Lizzy's mother.

"Lizzy was a child, and besides that, I always saw her like a little sister." He shook his head. "If not that, then as a good friend."

"I don't think you still feel that way toward her, not if you're honest with yourself. And if you're being honest with yourself, then you should give some consideration as to what she means to your future."

He felt his face grow warm. "I . . . uh . . . I don't think Lizzy wants me in her future. I think she's well past her childhood dreams and thoughts of romance with me."

Rebecca chuckled again and shook her head. "I wouldn't be so sure about that. She may say and do one thing, but I know my daughter. She'll do whatever she can to keep from feeling the fool again. If you do have feelings for her, Wes—desires for a future with Lizzy—then you'd better not dally. Jason Adler has made his intentions quite clear."

"No doubt he has. Seems to me he's a pushy sort of fella."

The older woman smiled. "You might say that."

They deposited the dishes in the kitchen, but before Wes could leave, Rebecca took his arm. "What happened to the crates of alcohol my brother had delivered to the ranch?"

Wes shrugged. "Well, I figured it had to be a mistake since we don't allow alcohol on the premises, so I took it back to Miles City and sold it to one of the bars. I figured that made the most sense and wouldn't force any of us to lie. I'd be happy to go tell Oliver about it right now, if you like."

Rebecca smiled. "That was pure genius on your part. Now no one has to acknowledge that Oliver would do such a thing, and we can pretend it was a simple mix-up. Oliver will dry out, and the urge for liquor will ease. At least that is my prayer."

"It won't be easy."

"No, perhaps not," Mrs. Brookstone replied. "One doesn't cease being an alcoholic, I suppose."

"No." Wes shook his head. "I'm sure the desire remains. It was pure willpower and your husband's attentive care that got him off the bottle the first time around, as I hear it."

"Yes, that's true. Perhaps this time my attentive care will suffice to make him want to be sober." Her expression was tinged with sorrow. "But I know his pain, and it won't be easy."

"No, not for us or him. But God, on the other hand, will find this a simple matter." Wes tried to sound reassuring. "Like your husband used to tell me, 'Put it to prayer first and give God a chance. If He—'"

"'If He can't handle it, then you can give it a try,'" Rebecca interrupted. She smiled and nodded.

———— ◆◆◆ ————

Ella woke screaming. She clamped her hands over her mouth when she realized what she was doing, but it wasn't soon enough to keep from waking Mary, whose room was next door.

"Ella? Are you all right?" Mary came into the room without even knocking.

The darkness shrouded them, hiding Ella's pained expression. She fought back her fear and steadied her nerves. "I had a bad dream."

"I gathered that." Mary came through the dark to Ella's bedside and sat down beside her. "I've had my share of nightmares too. I think it's all the change and losing August. I'm certain it'll pass when you get used to being here."

Ella tried to ignore the rush of guilt that washed over her. "My father will be livid over what I've done. He'll never forgive me."

"Are you afraid he'll come here?" Mary's tone was surprised.

"I suppose I am. I know it's a long way, but you don't know

my father . . . or Jefferson Spiby. They aren't used to having their demands denied."

Mary patted Ella's arm. "You don't have to be afraid here. There are enough ranch hands to fight off an army."

Ella drew a deep breath. Mary was right. There were a great many people here who would keep her from being taken by her father or Jefferson. "I'm sorry I woke you."

"It's not a problem. I just wanted you to know you weren't alone. I'm your friend, Ella." Mary got up. "I'll always be here to talk . . . if you need me."

She left, and only after the door was closed and Ella was alone again did Mary's words truly register. Ella felt even worse. Mary was offering her friendship, and Ella was lying to her. Well, not exactly lying, but certainly not telling her the truth. How could they be friends if Ella wasn't willing to be honest?

"But how can we be friends if I am?"

SIXTEEN

Snow came and went, and just as Cookie had predicted, it didn't last long. The cooler temperatures did, however. The chill remained a silent reminder that winter was on its way.

Thanksgiving had always been a favorite of the Brookstone family, but this year there was a sense of bittersweetness for Lizzy. She had done well to be strong and not let her feelings get the best of her, but it hadn't been easy. Her father had cherished Thanksgiving. He loved to talk about all God had done and why he was thankful. He had taught Lizzy to be thankful, but this past year she had forgotten.

How she could possibly be thankful when Father was gone and Mother was so grieved? Nothing would ever be the same on the ranch or in the show. How could she have a thankful heart when there had been so much sorrow?

"Is God only worthy of our love when He's giving us good things, Lizzy?" her father had once asked her after her granddad died. This had come after Lizzy had told her father how angry she was that God had taken her grandparents.

That question sat heavy on her heart now.

This year her father's absence was clearly felt. Even with everyone gathered for the holiday meal, including Cookie, Irma, and all the cowboys, there was a sense of sadness. Lizzy listened to her Uncle Oliver lead them in prayer and then speak about what he was thankful for, hoping she might find something to be thankful for herself.

"It's hard not to remember that Thanksgiving was a day my brother relished. He was always good at reminding us of the blessings we have. He could see the good in almost any situation. I remember once, in fact, when we were surprised by a grizzly. We were trapped on the edge of a mountain with very few choices. The sun was just coming up, and this bear seemed uncertain as to what he should do with us. I thought for sure we weren't going to make it out unscathed. Then the sun came up over the horizon. Mark smiled and said, 'Isn't this just about the prettiest day you've seen in weeks?'"

Everyone laughed, although Mother had tears in her eyes.

Uncle Oliver's eyes dampened as well. "Then, just as if we weren't even there, that bear ambled off down the mountain, and we sat there thanking God for His rescue and the beautiful morning."

"I remember," one of the cowboys said, "when we were out rounding up cows. Couple of 'em got stuck down in a gully. We were havin' the devil of a time gettin' 'em out of there, and I was cursin' and stompin' around. After quite a spell of finaglin', Mr. Brookstone managed to make his way to them, and when he did . . . well, that was when we found that patch of coal. Turned out to be a thick vein, and it has served us well. Even then, Mr. Brookstone said, 'God's blessings are often at the end of places where we're stuck and can't see any good purpose in being.' He offered up thanks for the cows havin' got stuck down there and us findin' 'em and the coal. Kind of made me look at life different."

Others shared similar stories about Lizzy's father. They had learned thankfulness or gratitude through him for a wide variety of reasons. Lizzy feared the stories would only make her mother sad, but instead she was smiling and nodding, even offering her own comments. From time to time she wiped away tears, but Lizzy could see that the stories did her mother more good than harm.

I wish they'd do the same for me. But rather than offer Lizzy joy, they only served to put pressure on a heart already close to exploding. More than once during the dinner, she felt herself choke up close to tears. Only her fears kept her from giving in.

If I start crying, I might never stop.

She remembered when one of the newborn foals had died. She'd only been a little girl and had cried her heart out. Wesley had been upset at her tears, because he didn't know what to do. At least that was what she figured as the years passed. He had given her a bad time of it, telling her that life on a ranch was going to be full of death and she needed to be stronger or she'd spend all her time crying. But Father had put his arm around her and reminded her that death was just a season of life. He told her it was just fine to cry—that God collected our tears—that when our hearts were broken, He understood and would comfort us.

But I don't feel that comfort now.

She looked across the table at Wesley and wondered if he remembered the way he'd treated her. No doubt he thought he was helping her be strong, or maybe he was just embarrassed by a little girl's tears and didn't know how to deal with her. A year later, Mary's father died in the wild west show. Lizzy didn't know Mary then, and while it was sad that her father's friend had died, it wasn't as heartbreaking to her as the foal's death had been. But then her grandmother died, and her grandfather the year after that, and Lizzy had thought her broken heart might never mend. It hurt so much to lose someone she loved. Again the tears had flowed.

When she learned Wes had married, Lizzy's lessons in loss and pain were complete. Or so she'd thought. She had never hurt as much as she had then, and she spent every night sobbing quietly into her pillow. She couldn't understand the situation at all. She was in love with Wes and knew he cared about her. Why hadn't he fallen in love with her?

It was after weeks of tears that she had decided they were getting her nowhere. Tears were for the weak. She vowed one night that no matter what, she would survive her pain by hardening her heart. At least where romance was concerned.

After that, she forced back any rush of emotions. She was committed to dealing with life in such a manner that it couldn't hurt her. The price? It also diminished the pleasure she took in life. Lizzy found that she never had as much joy in simple things. Happy times were pleasant enough, but the extreme feeling of delight was sadly absent.

However, by handling her sorrow in that manner, Lizzy was better equipped to deal with her father's passing. His death was a hard blow to bear, but she handled it with the same stalwart manner she'd dealt with other sorrows. It had solidified her resolve to have nothing to do with romantic love and hold all other feelings of love in a carefully controlled manner.

If I don't feel anything too much—either good or bad—then I'm better off. I can still enjoy the good times, but the bad ones can't hurt me like they once did.

Was that such a terrible way to deal with pain and loss?

"I say, I very much enjoy this Thanksgiving dinner of yours. I've never eaten so much," Jason said after the dinner concluded and they were all trying to find room for dessert.

"Don't you celebrate Thanksgiving in England, Jason?" Mary asked.

"We have days of thanks that we celebrate from time to time, but nothing like this holiday of yours. After all, you are celebrating a group of people leaving England to start a new life in America. I doubt very much the English people would want to celebrate that."

"We're celebrating God's mercy and provision," Wesley corrected. "It isn't about those people leaving England. It's about how God kept them alive and provided for their needs and how we should celebrate our thanks for how He's done the same for us."

"Wesley's right," Mother added. "We're very grateful for all the blessings we've had this year. It hasn't come without loss and sorrowful moments, but we're thankful for God's provision and mercy. We are very blessed."

Murmurs of *amen* rounded the table, but Lizzy remained silent.

After dinner, Wes and his crew declared themselves in charge of cleanup, and the others were dismissed to enjoy themselves by the living room fire.

Lizzy collected some treats for her horses and slipped out of the house before anyone could notice and stop her. Snow was falling lightly in tiny flakes that were hardly noticeable. They fell straight down in a slow, lingering descent. Without wind to kick it all up, it was calming and restful.

She made her way to the pen where Longfellow and Thoreau were huddled with some of the other performing horses, as well as some of the horses they'd retired from the show. She offered encouragement to each of the mounts but gave special attention to her own.

"You are such good boys," she told them after giving them some carrots. She stroked their faces and scratched Longfellow behind the ears like he liked. "I am thankful for you. You work well with me and keep me safe. You also don't judge me or try to make me into someone I'm not. I'm definitely thankful for that."

"Aren't you cold out here?"

She grimaced. She was glad her back was to Jason Adler. She squared her shoulders and dropped her hold on the horses. "I wanted to give my boys some rewards." She turned and faced him. "What brings you out?"

"Why, you, of course. I didn't want you to be alone out here in the weather." He smiled in his pleasant way.

Lizzy shook her head. "Jason, I grew up here—as an only child, I might add. I often go off by myself. I like it that way."

"I am sorry." He looked rather worried. "I didn't mean to overstep."

Lizzy didn't want to offend him; she just wanted him to leave. "It's all right. I just enjoy some time alone."

"I can understand the need for reflection, but I hope you can learn to enjoy my company as well."

"I thought we decided you and I would be friends and nothing more."

"To start with." He stepped closer. "Lizzy, I don't want to make you uncomfortable. That has never been my desire. I've enjoyed our friendship, but surely you know I would like to see it become something more. From our first meeting, I knew there was something special about you . . . that I wanted you to be a part of my life, my future."

"We will share a mutual future, since I agreed to participate in next year's show. Isn't that enough?"

"I suppose for now it has to be," he agreed. "I won't lie to you. I want more. I'm so certain of what I feel that I would get down on one knee and propose right now if I thought I would get a positive reply."

Longfellow nudged her neck, and Lizzy dug out two more carrots and returned her attention to the horses. "I really don't want to discuss this. I'm not looking to be anything more to you than a friend."

He moved up behind her and stood so close that she was

penned between him and the fence. If she turned, she'd be in his arms. His familiarity made her angry, and for a moment she considered giving him a good shove. But her sense of propriety prevailed.

"Please step away. I don't appreciate you forcing yourself on me."

"That wasn't my intention."

He did as she asked, and when Lizzy turned, she could see he looked embarrassed. "Jason, we should maintain a good relationship because we will be working together. But otherwise I have much too much to concern my thoughts and heart. My mother is still mourning my father's death, and Christmas will soon be upon us. I have a lot of work to do between now and the next show, so fairy-tale romances are not on my schedule."

"But I'd love to be your knight in shining armor. I'd love to fight off your dragons and carry you safely to my castle on my beautiful white stallion." He grinned in a way that made him look like a lovesick schoolboy. "Although I'll have to purchase one first. All my horses are blacks or bays."

His entire face was aglow with what Lizzy could only suppose was adoration. Sad that she couldn't give him even a glimmer of hope that she might one day return his feelings, Lizzy shook her head. "I'm sorry, Jason. I'm all grown-up and no longer believe in fairy tales."

"And what of happily-ever-after?" he asked softly.

She shook her head again. "Only after we leave this life. Only when we're safely in heaven in the arms of Jesus. Not here. Not where we so easily lose the people we love."

His brow furrowed. She thought he might challenge her, but instead he gave her a slight bow and headed back to the house. She felt both relief and sadness. She was glad he'd left her alone but sorry that she'd obviously hurt him.

Turning back to the horses, Lizzy contemplated what had just happened and wondered if staying another year with the show was wise. Ella was far more accomplished than Lizzy had dared to hope. She was younger too. It wouldn't be long before she'd be able to handle anything Lizzy threw at her. Surely Ella could take on the starring role and do it as well, if not better, than Lizzy. Of course, she had promised Mary she would help her learn the truth about August. That was the biggest thing that had influenced Lizzy's decision.

But if I must worry about being pestered by Jason at every turn, I don't think I can endure another year.

"You got a couple of beauties there," Phillip DeShazer said as he joined her at the fence. "Probably the best in the lot."

"I think so," Lizzy said, giving him a smile. "By the way, I want to thank you for taking my list and that catalogue back to Barney in Miles City."

"It was no trouble. I like doing things for folks."

"How are you settling in?"

"I like it here. I can see why Wes has stayed on year after year. I always liked movin' around and meetin' new people. I never stayed long enough to get too bored. But I never met a family like yours either. Your ma is a real nice woman. Reminds me of our ma."

"She is first-rate, if I do say so."

Phillip was nothing like his brother. Phillip had a boyish charm and sense of innocence about him. She knew from things Wes had said in the past that Phillip was bound to have seen plenty of trouble in his life, but he didn't wear it in his expression or his attitude.

"You said you liked moving around. Where all did your travels take you?" she asked.

He shrugged. "Just about everywhere. Been to California and up the coast. Been to Texas and saw that coast too." He laughed. "I didn't go east of the Mississippi, though. I didn't figure they'd have as much use for my skills there as out here."

"You are amazing with the horses. I heard someone say that you've done exceptional work with that new string."

His expression grew thoughtful. "I've always felt a keen sense of understanding with horses. It doesn't mean they haven't tried to make me pay now and again. I've been thrown and kicked just like any other horse breaker. I guess I just feel I get along better with animals than humans."

Lizzy nodded. "I'm beginning to feel the same way. I don't seem to relate well to anyone anymore."

"Wes thinks a lot of you."

She met Phillip's dark brown eyes and shook her head. "Wesley thinks I'm a spoiled little girl sent to make his life a misery." She'd had enough of this discussion. She gave the horses one last kiss and turned to go. "It was nice talking with you, Phillip. If you ever need anything, just come find me."

"She said what?" Wes asked his brother.

Phillip grinned. "She said you think she's a spoiled little girl sent to make your life a misery."

Wesley knew he'd made mistakes where Lizzy was concerned, but he certainly never meant for her to think those things. Nobody was less spoiled than Lizzy. She was generous to a fault and never had to have the best of anything. He'd seen her give up her place at the table when company was overflowing the house. Give up her room and bed too. He'd seen her work with others in the show and put them in positions where they could outshine her. No, she wasn't spoiled. Nor did she make his life a misery.

He was able to do that all on his own.

"She's not spoiled, and I don't think that way about her."

Wesley bent to throw another long on the fire. Phillip had come to visit at his cabin for a bit before heading to the bunkhouse for the night. "You want some coffee?" Wes asked. "Cookie always leaves me half a pot in the afternoon. The stove's cold, but I could put it over the fire."

"Nah, I ate too much and drank too much already. I'm full up." Phillip pulled his chair closer and stretched out his legs. "It's sure nice here. Almost like being a family again."

"It is. The Brookstones have always treated me like family."

"That Oliver Brookstone is a cutup. He was in the bunkhouse a couple of nights back and had us all in stitches with some of his stories from the old days."

Wesley remembered what he'd heard about Oliver still drinking. "Phillip, you haven't been bringing whiskey back to the ranch, have you?"

"No, sir. I do my drinking in town just like you told me to."

"I didn't tell you to drink at all. I'd rather you didn't. You know it's not good for you. It serves no purpose other than to dull your senses."

Phillip sobered and nodded, but his gaze never left the flames. "That's a purpose."

Wes knew there were years of pain inside his brother, but he wouldn't talk about it, and any time Wes tried to get close enough to ferret out something of the truth, Phillip would push him away with a joke or a story about one of his humorous antics.

It seemed no one wanted to talk about anything . . . to anyone.

"Oliver, I think we need to have a talk now that you're feeling better," Rebecca Brookstone said, coming into her brother-in-law's office.

"You know I've always got time for you, Becca." He rose and placed a chair by his desk. "What's on your mind?"

"You are." She sat and gave him a smile. "I've been very worried about you since Mark's death."

Oliver stiffened. "And I've worried about you."

"I know you have." She waited until he reclaimed his seat to continue. "Oliver, I know that you suffer from losing your brother. Even though you say very little to me, it's evident."

"I don't want to burden you with my feelings, Becca. Your loss was much greater."

"I didn't know loss could be measured. You loved Mark just as I did. He was your brother, and the two of you were thick as thieves. I sometimes envied that." She put her hand atop Oliver's. "My loss was great, but yours was too, and I know that perhaps it was made all the worse because we had to keep the show going. We weren't allowed time to mourn or even give Mark a proper funeral."

"It didn't seem right."

"No," Rebecca agreed. "It didn't. But we did what Mark wanted, and that's what matters. And, in thinking on that, I have to say something else."

Oliver shifted his weight, and his jaw tightened. He shook his head and looked away. "I think I know what you want to say. You're upset with me about the drinking."

She squeezed his hand. "I'm not condemning you. You were hurting, and you sought comfort in the old ways."

"I drank so I wouldn't have to feel the pain. But it was always there."

"Made worse by guilt, I'm sure." Rebecca straightened, and Oliver looked at her and nodded.

"I didn't want to hurt you or the others. I just couldn't stand to think about Mark being dead—about everything falling on my shoulders. The more I let myself dwell on it, the worse I felt. The worse I felt, the more alcohol appealed."

Rebecca nodded. "But it doesn't have to be that way. You told me once that you have some ideas for the future, and I think we should talk about those now. It might help you continue on a sober path."

He drew a deep breath. "All right." He pulled open a drawer. "Let me tell you what I've done . . . and what I still want to do."

SEVENTEEN

I swear you'd think she'd never seen snow." Mary let go of the window sheer and turned back to Lizzy.

Lizzy had seen how animated Ella was when Phillip offered to teach her how to make a snowman. "I don't think it's the snow as much as the company."

Mary shrugged. "I suppose there's someone for everyone. Maybe one day I'll find mine."

"I don't think there's necessarily someone for everyone. God calls some people to be single. I'm beginning to think maybe that's His purpose for me."

"Hogwash." Mary came to where Lizzy was tightening the laces on her boots. "You and Wes were meant for each other. I knew that the first time I saw you together."

"Then someone forgot to tell Wes." Lizzy grabbed her jacket and made her way outside. The last thing she wanted to do was think about Wes. She and Ella were going to work on some of the more difficult tricks today, and it was important to maintain focus. "Ella, I'll be in the arena when you're ready."

"Just give us a couple more minutes, Miss Lizzy." Phillip bent to pick up a large snowball. "We're just about done. Got to put the head on and then find some things for his eyes and nose."

"And his mouth," Ella added.

"You could use coal." Lizzy motioned toward the bunkhouse. "The pail by the stove is usually full."

"Don't I know it," Phillip said, nodding. "I filled it. That's a good idea, though."

Lizzy smiled and watched as Phillip plopped the head atop the snowman's body. She could remember her father teaching her to make a snowman when they still lived in Illinois. Lizzy couldn't have been more than four or five. Father had been like Phillip. His nature had always been playful and infectious. Mother had even joined them, putting aside her normal chores to play. Lizzy smiled as she remembered the snowball fight her parents had gotten into. It had ended with Mother hitting Father in the head with a snowball. Father had fallen backward into a snowbank as if mortally wounded. It had frightened Lizzy and her mother. Both had run to see if he was still alive, and as they bent over him, Father had pulled them down into the snow with him. They had laughed until their sides ached.

"Lizzy?"

She looked up to see she was about to walk straight into Wes. She was still smiling, but that faded. "Morning, Wes."

"You getting ready to practice?" He pushed his Stetson back a bit.

"Yes. I promised Ella we'd work on some of the more difficult tricks today." She waited for his condemnation, but none came.

"Well, Cookie said you want to go into town to pick up some Christmas gifts. I'm planning to drive in to get supplies. I'm leaving in about ten minutes, and you're welcome to ride along."

She knew this was her best chance of getting to Miles City, but why did it have to be with Wes? She sighed and realized there was no way out of it. There was only another week until Christmas. The month of December had passed so quickly. If she didn't take the opportunity to go with Wes, she might not get another.

"Thank you. Just let me tell Ella."

Lizzy wasn't at all sure about this. She and Wes had worked together amiably enough on ranch business, but it had been hard to set her feelings aside. Try as she might not to love him, she couldn't help herself. Thankfully there was no chance of the feeling being returned, or she might have been in big trouble. With that thought as assurance that she'd be all right, Lizzy went back to explain things to Ella.

"I have to cancel our practice, but you and Mary can definitely work on some of her shooting tricks." Phillip was returning with coal from the bunkhouse. "I need to let Mother know what I'm doing. If you need anything from town, just let Wes know. He'll be out here with the wagon momentarily."

Ella nodded as she continued to pack snow to create a neck for the snowman.

Lizzy made her way back to the house. She found Mother in the kitchen, packing a basket of food.

"I'm going to ride to town with Wes. I have some things I want to pick up for Christmas."

Mother looked up and smiled. "I knew Wes was planning a trip in. I'm glad you can spare the time to go. It'll do you two good to have some time together."

"I don't know about that. I was thinking you could come with us." Lizzy spoke before thinking about how she'd ever be able to hide the puppy from her mother if she came.

"Goodness no. I've too much to do." Mother glanced toward the closed door to the dining room. "You probably shouldn't linger. Jason and your uncle are working at the table, and unless you want Jason going with you . . ." She let the words trail off.

"No, I would prefer not to be in the middle of things with him and Wes."

Mother handed Lizzy the basket of food. "I was going to send this with Wes so he'd have something to eat coming and going. There's plenty there, however, for you as well." She took her daughter's free arm and pulled her toward the back door. "Hurry along, now. You know how unpredictable the weather is this time of year."

"I do. Is there anything I can get for you in town?"

Mother shook her head. "I gave Wes a list for the kitchen, so I believe we're set." She kissed Lizzy's cheek. "See if you two can't clear up the past while you have nothing better to do. It's a long drive, and maybe God's giving you this opportunity where you'll be uninterrupted."

"I'm beginning to think you had something to do with all of this." Lizzy gave her mother a stern look.

Her mother just shrugged and waved her on. "You'd best go now."

Lizzy hesitated in the doorway. She didn't want to admit she was afraid of having so much time alone with Wes. They would have to talk about something, and there was no hope of walking away should things get heated.

By the time Lizzy left the house, Wes had the wagon pulled up and ready to go. Two strong Belgian geldings stood at the ready. Wes took the basket from Lizzy and put it in the back of the wagon under the tarp.

"Thanks for the grub, Mrs. Brookstone," he said, giving a wave.

Lizzy hadn't realized her mother had followed her outside. She gave Mother a wave, then climbed into the wagon without any help. Wes jumped up the opposite side and took the lines.

"It's clouding up, but if the weather holds, we should be back later this evening." He reached under the seat, pulled out a thick wool blanket, and handed it to Lizzy. "If it turns on us, we'll stay in Miles City." He released the brake, then snapped the lines. "Let's go, boys."

"Don't take any chances," Mother called after them.

Lizzy thought the entire trip alone with Wes was a big chance, but she did want to iron out the past so they could work together better. So many times she had made a comment about something from her childhood only to see Wes grow sullen. She wanted to understand why he had been so closed off with his feelings and thoughts these last few years. She understood why things had changed between them when Clarissa was alive, but why had he all but turned away from her these last two years? Was he afraid Lizzy would demand his love? Love that he could never give?

The first few miles of the trip were spent in silence. Lizzy had a dozen questions she wanted to ask, but sitting so near Wes made rational thinking impossible. She was still in love with him. She couldn't deny that—at least not to herself.

"Looks like some weather is moving in from the west," he murmured.

Lizzy looked out across the landscape. He was right. A dark bank of clouds lined the horizon, while overhead the skies were turning gray. They drove on in silence, but Lizzy was ever mindful of the weather. She remembered her father always admonishing her to be weather-minded.

"It's not like Illinois, Lizzy. The weather up here is different, and the distance to safety is farther. You always need to keep an eye on what's happening," he would tell her.

At the halfway mark, the wind picked up, and it began to snow. Grateful for the blanket, Lizzy wrapped it around her. She thought of offering to share it with Wes but knew there was at least one more blanket beneath the seat. If he was cold, he'd wrap up.

The snow came at first in tiny flakes. The wind blew it around them in a swirl of white, but it wasn't enough to stop their journey. It wasn't long, however, before it changed to a heavier assault with larger flakes. Lizzy hoped it would pass quickly and without any serious accumulation, but as the minutes passed, it was clear this wasn't the case. She knew they were in a dangerous situation when the visibility closed to no more than a few feet in front of the team. The blowing snow blinded them to any hint of the road.

"We're gonna have to take shelter and wait it out," Wes said. "Gus's Break is just ahead. We'll stop there."

Lizzy nodded. She had already thought of that place and figured it would be their best bet. Their old ranch foreman, Gus, had discovered the spot when he and Lizzy's uncle were making a better road to Miles City from the ranch. Positioned a short distance from the river, the hill and its rocky outcroppings made a nice place to stop if a person needed to rest or fix a wagon. The men hadn't built an actual shelter, but they had stored wood for fires and kept a variety of other useful tools on hand. It wasn't much, but it was better than trying to navigate in a blizzard.

"Take the lines." Wes handed them over. "I'm gonna lead them in."

Lizzy waited as he climbed down and took hold of the horse on the right. He pulled the team forward and then off the main road. The narrow trail wasn't too bad. Wes and the ranch hands had come this way when they took calves to market just two weeks earlier. They'd tramped down the path then, stopping at the resting place on their way back.

Wes led the horses in such a way as to bring the wagon close to the rocky outcropping where the best coverage could be had. "This is good." Lizzy barely heard his voice over the wind. "Set the brake," he said, coming back to the wagon.

Lizzy did so, then handed Wes the lines. She allowed him to help her down, given the icy buildup on the wheel and hub.

"I'll get the horses settled," he said with a nod. "You get a fire going."

She went to work without a second thought. The cowboys had left wood stacked under the rock ledge. She gathered several pieces and piled them close to the wagon. She found the wooden box where the men kept a number of helpful items and pulled a tinder box with matches and oily rags from it.

She looked around for the perfect place to make the fire and decided to clear the area where the tools were stored. There was the slightest rock shelf overhead, and it would give the fire a bit of protection. The wooden box was heavy, but Lizzy took her time scooting and rocking it along the ground. Next, she took the lid of the box and used it to shovel snow. Finally, she had a nice cleared spot and set the logs in place.

Despite the heavy snow, Lizzy soon had a decent fire going. Wes had positioned the wagon in just the right place, giving them protection from two sides, thanks to the way the hill was hollowed out. The wagon would block the wind from a third direction, and with the help of the tarp, they would do well enough.

While Wes finished with the horses, Lizzy went to the wagon and took out the basket of food. She placed it under the wagon not far from the fire. She returned to retrieve the blankets and a length of rope. Under the blankets was Wesley's rifle, so she brought that as well. It'd be good to have in case there was any trouble, although Lizzy couldn't imagine there would be. Not many folks were brave enough to endure the weather, and this road was only used to get from the ranch to the main road heading into town. She didn't anticipate anyone passing by.

Once she had gathered their provisions, Lizzy began to wonder what had happened to Wes. Icy snow stung her eyes, and she wiped her gloved hand over her face to clear her vision. She couldn't even see ten feet in front of her. The wind howled in her ears.

"Wes?" she called and pulled her hat down tighter.

Without warning, he appeared at her side. "Untie the tarp from the other side."

Lizzy did as he instructed despite her dislike of being ordered around. At a time like this, it would have been foolish to refuse. She unfastened the tarp ties and waited as Wes pulled the loosened edge over the wagon on the opposite side.

Seeing what he had in mind as he picked up some rocks, Lizzy quickly joined in without him having to say a word. They had to fight the wind, but eventually they managed a little lean-to tent. When it was complete, he crawled under and pushed out the snow as best he could. With that done, he spread one of the blankets on the ground under the tarp and motioned Lizzy inside.

"This should serve us pretty well," Wes said, stretching his legs just outside of the lean-to to knock the snow from his boots. "Fire looks good."

"I decided to move the box so I could make the fire there. It has a little more protection."

"Good thinking."

Lizzy was glad he was pleased. "I brought the basket. Oh, your rifle too." She motioned to where they sat just under the wagon.

"I'll get the coffeepot out of the box and melt some snow. Cookie told me he had the boys refill the coffee tin. You want some?"

"Yes, please." She was starting to shiver and wrapped the other blanket around her body.

Half an hour later, she sat nursing steaming coffee while the storm raged on. Until that moment, Wes had kept himself busy with one thing or another, but now he sat down with his own tin cup and gave her an awkward smile.

"Sure glad Gus and Oliver set this place up."

"It would have been even nicer if they had just built a range shack."

Wes chuckled and nodded. "That it would."

"Would you like something to eat? I've taken an inventory, and Mother has enough food here to feed an army."

"Food sounds good."

Lizzy pulled sandwiches from the basket. "They look like ham and cheese," she said, handing one to Wes. "There's more if you need it."

For some time they sat in silence, eating and drinking. Wes refilled their cups once, then accepted another sandwich and went back to concentrating on his food. Lizzy wondered how she could open the conversation between them, but she didn't have to wonder for long.

"Look, there's something I've been wanting to say for some time." Wes turned his cup in his gloved hands but didn't look up. "I've been kind of hard on you since you returned. I didn't set out to be that way, and I want to apologize. I've had a lot on my mind, what with Phillip showing up and all."

"He's a nice man. I know you've spent many years worrying about where he was. I'm glad he showed up." She was afraid to make too much of the apology and kept the focus on Phillip.

Wes glanced up. "Me too, but he's still full of trouble. He likes to drink."

She could see pain in Wesley's eyes and hear the regret in his voice. "He and Uncle Oliver have much in common, then. Mother says he's still sneaking drinks, although she's searched in vain for his supply."

Wes didn't speak, but neither did he look away. Lizzy wanted nothing more than to touch him but knew that was completely uncalled for. Another awkward silence fell between them. Why couldn't she just say what was on her heart?

"I'm glad you've decided to quit the show," Wes said.

The show had long been a bone of contention between them. Wes didn't like her risking her life to entertain. Lizzy, truth be told, was ready to leave it all behind—well, almost.

"I told them I'd stay for one more year." She sipped her coffee.

"I heard that, but I thought you were training Ella to be your replacement."

This time it was Lizzy's turn to avert her gaze. "I gave a promise."

"To Adler?" Wes's tone was full of sarcasm.

Lizzy met his questioning gaze. "Yes, to him and to Uncle Oliver. Mary too, if you must know. She wants to find out what happened to her brother."

"Maybe so, but it seems to me that Adler is the one trying to keep you close."

"Well, no one else wants my company." Her voice was taking on a shrewish edge, and Lizzy forced herself to calm down. "Why is it of any interest to you, anyway? You've made it perfectly clear that you don't care anything about me." Why had she said that? She didn't want him thinking she was looking to win his love. Even if she wanted exactly that.

"Don't care? Are you serious? That's why I don't want you to return to trick riding. I care very much about you. I've always cared, Lizzy."

"So much that you married the first woman who came along just to get away from me." Lizzy immediately regretted her words. She put the cup to her lips but silently wished the earth would open up and swallow her whole. This wasn't how she wanted to start a discussion about Clarissa.

"She was alone in the world," he countered. "Her folks were dead, and she had no one, Lizzy. She would have been thrown to the wolves. You know that as well as anyone. A woman all alone in the world doesn't have a lot of options."

Lizzy shook her head. "She wasn't your responsibility, Wes. Mother and Father would have helped her if you'd told them. You knew that. You also knew how I felt about you." She hesitated to use the word *love*, but she was certain he still remembered her declaration.

"You were the boss's daughter and just a kid."

"I was eighteen, and my father loved you like a son. He would have been happy to have you as one." She put down her empty cup, then pulled the blanket tight around her.

"I never meant to hurt you, Lizzy. I just didn't see things the same way." He turned and studied her for a moment. "By the time I realized . . ." He fell silent, as if he'd said too much.

"What happened to us, Wes? We were good friends—even after . . ." She hadn't meant to ask the question aloud, but now that she had, she knew it was the right thing to do. "I got past you marrying Clarissa, and I thought we had a good understanding. But you've hardly spoken to me since she died."

He sighed and poured himself another cup of coffee. He raised the pot in her direction, but Lizzy shook her head. She didn't want coffee. She wanted answers.

She felt awash in guilt. Guilt for something she didn't even understand. "What did I do wrong?"

His expression softened. "You didn't do anything. Although I did try to blame you."

She could see the regret in his expression. "Blame me for what?"

"Clarissa's death."

Her mouth dropped open. "You blamed me? But why? As I understand it, she punctured her lung when she fell from her horse. Complications set in, and she died several days later."

"Yes, that's how it happened." Wesley's expression turned grim. "But you were the reason she was on that horse and the reason she fell. At least that's what I let myself believe. In truth, she was desperately trying to get my attention. It was easier to blame you. At least then I wasn't . . . I wasn't . . ." He heaved a sigh.

Lizzy had never heard anything about this. "You said I was the reason she was on that horse and fell. How can you say that?"

For several minutes he said nothing. Lizzy wasn't sure he was going to answer her. She'd never in her life imagined that he blamed her for Clarissa's death. Did others?

"Lizzy, I don't know what to say. The truth is, I didn't love Clarissa as I should have. I married her because she was alone and needed someone to protect her and not go on abusing her like her drunk father always did. I felt sorry for her, and she knew it. She wasn't in love with me either, but we both thought we could find love once we were married. It just didn't work that way. She was jealous. All the time she was jealous . . . of you."

"Of me?" Lizzy thought of the pretty blond-haired woman. "But why?"

He rubbed his jaw and drew in a deep breath. "Because she knew how much I cared about you. For some reason, she thought it had to do with your trick riding. She figured if she started doing tricks on horseback that I'd care more about her than you."

"She tried trick riding?" Lizzy's eyes narrowed. "I never knew that."

"She convinced herself that my feelings for you were wrapped up in trick riding. That's why she fell from the horse. She was trying to do some sort of stunt. She lost her grip and slipped under the horse."

"I don't know what to say. No one ever told me."

"Because I didn't tell anyone what really happened. I figured it was better that way. I would have had a bad time trying to explain why my wife was performing stunts to impress me."

"I'm really sorry, Wes." Lizzy had never thought it possible that Clarissa had been jealous of her relationship with him. Lizzy had tried hard to bury her feelings for him after learning he was married. She respected the sanctity of marriage. God had joined them together, and while the truth of that devastated

Lizzy, she hadn't wanted to cause Clarissa any pain. Lizzy's own pain had been enough.

The wind died down, and everything suddenly seemed quiet. Lizzy tried to think of what she could say or do. She couldn't even imagine Clarissa trying to do stunts. She wasn't at all athletic and, in fact, had a rather weak constitution.

"Look, Lizzy, I'm sorry for the way I've acted. It was never your fault. I know that. I felt terrible that I couldn't make her happy. I tried. I really did. I offered to pack us up and leave, but she didn't want that either. I'm not sure anything I could have said or done would have made her happy."

"Maybe that's just it, Wes. She had to find happiness for herself. Nobody can create it for you."

"Just the same, when she died, I felt like it was my fault. I kept hearing her tell me over and over that one day I would love her as much as I did you, because she was going to do all the things you did. When she died, I guess my guilt made me keep you at arm's length. I figured it was the price I had to pay."

Lizzy startled at his words. Had he loved her then? Did he still? She couldn't ask him for fear of the answer. If he told her he didn't love her—could never love her again—it would be more than she could bear.

But you're determined not to love him or ever marry, she tried to reason with herself. *It shouldn't matter what he thinks or feels now. You know the dangers of caring too much. You know the pain that will inevitably come.*

But I can hardly go through life without friends.

Lizzy wrestled her thoughts in silence. The need for people to care about her argued with the part of her determined never again to feel the pain that came with loss.

After a long time, she gave up the fight. "Wes, can we start again? Can we go back to being friends?" The words seemed to echo around them.

He gave her a sad smile. "We've always been friends, Lizzy. Forgive me for letting my problems come between us."

She felt a weight taken from her. "Of course." Her voice barely sounded. "Forgive me for whatever part I had in all of this. Maybe I should have done more to make her feel a part of our friendship, done more to befriend her."

"It was never your fault, Lizzy. It was just easier to blame you than accept my role." He got to his feet. "I think the weather is clearing. We should push on and see if we can't get to town."

She crawled out from under the tarp and let the blanket drop. "I'll take care of all this. You get the horses."

For a moment he looked at her as if he might say something more. But then, without another word, he crawled out and was gone.

She watched him go, and for the first time she understood something about Wesley that she'd never known. He had sacrificed himself and his happiness for Clarissa's safety and well-being. At eighteen, Lizzy had been too worried about her own feelings to really understand. Wes had come home married, and it had devastated her. She couldn't believe anyone would marry for less than love, and it wasn't until years later that she'd overheard her mother and father speak of Wes's sad situation. She had never imagined people married without being madly in love. But this knowledge had only hurt Lizzy more. Mother had said he married Clarissa because she needed him. Well, Lizzy needed him too. If only she had understood then what she knew now. Wes had seen the need and given up everything to save Clarissa from a worse fate. The truth only made her love him more.

A warning went off in her head. *If you love him more, it will only serve to hurt you more.* She frowned. How could she rid herself of her feelings and protect her heart? It wasn't Wesley's fault that she felt as she did. For so long she'd been angry because he refused to return her feelings, but now . . .

"It would serve me right." She began gathering their things. How ironic it would be if Wes fell in love with her. Now that she was determined to love no one.

Wes nearly sighed in relief when they finally reached Miles City. The road hadn't been easy. Parts of it were drifted high with snow. The team was strong, however, and Wes had simply urged them on when the way was rough. The hardest part had been keeping to the road, since it and the land around them looked much the same.

The sun was nearly gone from the sky before they could see the town in the distance. Now, as they made their way down Main Street, most of the stores were closed, and the only places that showed signs of life were the saloons.

"Let's check with Clem and Eva Truman. I'm sure they'll let us stay at their place and save us the fee of a hotel," Wes said, guiding the horses in the direction of the older couple's house. The streets were in fairly good condition, making their journey to the other side of town easy.

"I haven't seen them in ages." Lizzy stretched. "I sure hope Mother won't worry about us."

"Can't be helped if she does. She knows that we're pretty capable." Wes looked at Lizzy and gave her a slight smile. "I'm sure she'll be fine. We'll head out first thing in the morning if the weather looks good."

He brought the team to a halt in front of a small clapboard house. The place was lit up, leaving little doubt that Clem and Eva were home. "Why don't you go talk to them, and I'll get the team put up."

Lizzy nodded and jumped down from the wagon. As she headed up the walkway, Wes moved the horses down the street and back toward the livery. He climbed down, feeling tired and frozen. He made arrangements for the horses, then grabbed the basket of food from the back of the wagon along with his rifle and headed back to the Trumans'.

Wes thought back on his conversation with Lizzy. He'd never been honest with anyone about Clarissa's death. He hadn't even allowed himself to think about it. He'd been unable to bear the guilt, and it had been easier to tell himself it was Lizzy's fault. Even though he'd never really believed that.

He walked on, grateful that it hadn't snowed as much here. Despite the cold, he wanted to take his time and sort through his thoughts. Lizzy had asked if they could go back to being friends, but Wes knew now that he wanted so much more. He loved Lizzy.

When had his feelings for her changed from that of a watchful big brother to one of romantic intentions? He thought back to when she'd first come back to the ranch after Clarissa's death. That was when it happened. He remembered seeing her standing in the barn, talking to one of the hands. In that moment, he had wanted nothing more than to take her in his arms and hold her. At the time, those feelings had only made him feel guiltier. He already knew that his friendship with Lizzy had made Clarissa feel the need to show off. Admitting his feelings for Lizzy was akin to having a hand in his wife's death.

Staring up at the Trumans' house, Wes felt a sense of sorrow as he remembered Clarissa just before she'd passed. He'd knelt at her bedside and held her hand.

"You need to fight, Clarissa. Fight to stay alive."

"There's no fight in me, Wes." She strained to breathe, and the sound of it caught in the back of her throat. The wheezy gasp chilled him to the bone. "There's never . . . been . . . any fight in me." She shook her head. "I'm so sorry, Wes. I did . . . you wrong."

"No," he tried to assure her. "We did what we had to in order to keep you safe."

"Not a good reason . . . to marry." She closed her eyes, and for a moment Wes thought she was gone. "You always belonged . . . with her. I knew that . . . but . . . didn't care."

Wes had never denied that he and Lizzy had a special connection, a relationship that went far beyond anything he had with Clarissa. But he never felt he belonged with Lizzy. She was just a carefree and adventurous child. She hadn't needed him like Clarissa had. Lizzy had a family who loved and protected her. Clarissa had endured beatings and starvation. She had no one. Wesley had truly believed that he was her savior.

He glanced heavenward. "Forgive me, Lord. You were the only Savior she needed, but I thought I could do the job." He heard Lizzy's laugh and looked at the house. His heart pounded harder at the full understanding that he wanted more than friendship with Lizzy. "I've wasted a lot of time, Lord, and I'm gonna need Your help if I'm ever gonna make this right."

❖⊱ EIGHTEEN ⊰❖

Lizzy opened her eyes and stretched. The intensity of the sun as it shone through the window actually made her feel hot. She pushed off the heavy quilts Eva Truman had given her the night before and stretched again. She might have stayed there for a long while if not for all they needed to do that morning. That, along with having spent the night in town when Mother expected them home, added a sense of urgency.

Lizzy dressed and made her way downstairs, where she found Wes reading the paper in front of the fire. She paused for a moment, just watching him—imagining they were married and this was their home.

"Finally decide to wake up?" he asked, shaking her from her thoughts.

Lizzy hid her embarrassment as best she could and shrugged. "I guess I was tired. Where's Eva?"

He put the paper aside. "She had to go to her sewing circle, and Clem is at work."

Lizzy looked around the room for a clock. "What time is it?"

"Nine thirty."

"I'm sorry. I haven't slept that long in years." She went to

221

the door to collect her boots. "We'd best hurry, or we won't get home at a decent hour."

"You can take the time to eat your breakfast. Eva kept it in the warmer on the stove."

She started to protest but realized she was starving. Her stomach even rumbled as if to remind her. "It won't take me but a minute."

After eating, Lizzy made her way to the store with Wes. They spent a minimal amount of time shopping, then went to retrieve the collie pup for Lizzy's mother.

"He's precious." Lizzy giggled like a little girl as the puppy squirmed in her arms and licked all over her face. He was all legs and nose, with the softest fur Lizzy had ever felt.

"I have a crate for you to put him in for the ride home," Mr. Daniels, Barney's father, said. "I'll put it in the back of your wagon."

"I'll give you a hand," Wes said, following him outside.

Lizzy looked at Mrs. Daniels and laughed. "I think he will cheer Mother considerably."

Barney's mother nodded. "We were sure sorry to hear about your pa's passing. Barney brought the news when the train arrived with the casket. It was a real surprise. Surprising too that you and your mother didn't come with it."

"We wanted to, but Father made us promise to finish out the show." Lizzy stroked the pup until he settled in her arms. She wanted to be angry at Mrs. Daniels's comment but knew it was a situation most people wouldn't understand.

"Will you have a funeral now that you're back?"

Lizzy frowned. She and Mother hadn't talked about it. "I honestly don't know. I suppose that will be up to Mother. We had a service with the show folk."

"Well, that's good. I know Wes arranged for the preacher to come out to the ranch when he was buried."

Lizzy hadn't known that, but then, she hadn't been willing to speak about her father and his death. She squared her shoulders and nodded.

"We're all ready to go," Wes announced as he and Mr. Daniels returned.

Lizzy handed Wes the puppy, which only excited the animal once again. "I have your five dollars." She reached into her pocket and retrieved the cash. "I believe that was the asking price for the puppy."

"I'd nearly forgotten," Mrs. Daniels said, taking the money. "Most of the others were sold off before Thanksgiving. Barney's enjoyed working with this little fella. Calls him Pup, but I know your mama will come up with another name."

"I'm sure she will, and I'm sure she'll appreciate all that Barney has taught him. This is going to make a wonderful surprise."

She and Wes made their way to the wagon. Wes held the puppy while Lizzy climbed up, then handed him over. Lizzy placed him in the crate. There was plenty of straw at the bottom so the puppy could snuggle down. Unfortunately, all he did was whine and bark in protest.

"That's going to be annoying," Wes muttered, taking up the lines. He gave them a snap. "Let's go home, boys."

They were on their way out of town when the sheriff flagged them down. Lizzy couldn't imagine what he wanted, but they had little choice but to hear him out.

"Wes, you got a few minutes?"

"Not many. We got stuck here overnight and need to get back to the ranch."

The sheriff frowned. "It won't take long. Just thought you could collect your brother."

"Phillip is here?"

"'Fraid so. He came riding in during the storm, lookin' for you two. Said Mrs. Brookstone sent him to make sure you weren't broke down in the weather."

"He must have ridden right past us." Lizzy could see by the way Wes clenched his jaw that he wasn't happy about this.

He set the brake and handed the lines to Lizzy. "I'll be right back."

She sat and waited. She wondered what had happened. What had Phillip done to get himself thrown in jail? Then she remembered what Wes had said about Phillip drinking. Had he gotten drunk and started brawling? A lot of men did.

Wes returned with Phillip behind him. Wes pointed toward the livery. "Your horse and gear are down there. Do you have any money left to pay them?"

"No." Phillip's head was down and his voice was barely audible.

Wesley dug into his pocket and handed Phillip some change. "Go pay the bill and collect your things. I'll come park out front. You can tie your horse to the wagon and ride in back."

Phillip took off without a word, and Wesley said nothing as he climbed aboard and snatched the lines from Lizzy. He released the brake and turned the wagon around to head back to the livery.

"I'm sorry, Wes. Whatever's going on, I'm really sorry."

Wes shook his head. "He was drunk and disorderly and got himself thrown in jail. Luckily just to sleep it off. No one pressed charges against him."

"Well, at least that's good."

"None of this is good." He turned to her. "None of it."

The ride home was long and silent except for the constant displeasure of the puppy. Lizzy finally took pity on him and took him from the crate. The collie settled down in her arms and went to sleep almost immediately.

Phillip also slept most of the way, and Wes was in no mood to discuss anything. Lizzy tried a couple of times to engage him in conversation, but he made it clear that he wanted no part of it. Finally, she stopped trying. When the wind picked up, she snuggled the pup inside her coat and wished there were somewhere she could hide away as well. She hated the silence and being stuck with only her thoughts to ponder.

When they finally reached the house, it was late afternoon. Mother was the first to greet them. Her expression was filled with relief.

"I'm so glad you're home safe. When it came up with such a howling wind and snow, I sent Phillip to find you and warn you that it was coming your way. I figured he could outrun it, since it was just starting up. I guess he found you all right." She nodded to Phillip, who was climbing off the back of the wagon.

"More like we found him," Wes muttered.

"What?" Mother asked.

Lizzy shook her head. "Never mind." The puppy squirmed inside her coat. "I have something for you. It's your Christmas present, but it can't wait."

Mother gave her a strange look. "What do you mean? We always wait for Christmas morning."

"I know, but I would have a hard time hiding this present." Lizzy opened her coat to reveal the puppy. A long nose came first and then the rest of his head. The collie gave a little yip to announce himself.

Mother's expression changed from confusion to absolute delight. "Oh, my!"

"You've talked about getting a dog once you were back on the ranch for good. I saw the advertisement in town when we came home. The Daniels family had a litter and held one for you so I could give it to you for Christmas." Lizzy handed the squirming pup down to her mother, then jumped off the wagon.

Mother laughed as the dog wiggled and began licking her face. "He's perfect. Thank you so much."

"What will you call him?" Lizzy asked. "Barney Daniels has

been working with him to obey a few commands. He's just been calling him Pup."

"I don't know what I'll call him." Mother released the puppy and let him explore the ground around them. He didn't seem to know what to think of the snow. "I guess I'll have to ponder that awhile and see what name fits him best."

Lizzy embraced her mother and planted a kiss on her cheek. "I hope he'll make you feel a little less lonely."

Mother nodded. "I'm sure he will." She hugged Lizzy close. "Thank you. I already know we'll be the best of friends."

Christmas morning was spent in the company of the entire staff and household guests. Mother had arranged gifts for everyone, even the newest ranch hands. She made certain that each man had a new pair of work gloves and two pairs of wool socks, as well as a bevy of baked goods that she and Ella and Mary had worked on while Lizzy was busy with ranch business.

Lizzy had gifted Mary and Ella with bottles of perfume and gave Jason and her uncle monogramed handkerchiefs. For Wesley, she had labored over the thought of a gift that wouldn't be too personal, but just personal enough to remind him of her. She settled on a pocket watch and had his named engraved on it. It seemed to please him. He presented her with a beautiful leather-bound volume of Longfellow's poems. It touched her deeply.

"Your Mother made the bookmark, but I put it in its place," Wes told her.

Lizzy immediately wanted to look at the passage he'd marked, but Jason spoke up.

"If I might," he said, pulling a slender box from his jacket pocket, "I have a gift for Lizzy as well."

Lizzy couldn't hide her surprise. Jason had gifted no one but

Mother, and to her he gave a lovely music box. He told them he'd purchased a few things while in Kansas City, knowing he would spend the winter at the ranch.

"When I purchased your mother's present, I saw this and couldn't refrain from buying it. You might think it a bit extravagant, but I felt it so perfect for you, especially given my thoughts for the future."

Lizzy took the box and opened it. She gasped at the sight of a jeweled necklace. A large yellow topaz was set in gold and hung on a delicate gold chain.

She looked up to find Jason grinning from ear to ear. "I thought it complemented your eyes and hair. When I saw it, I knew you should have it."

"I, ah, I don't know what to say." Lizzy closed the lid. "It's much too expensive, and I cannot accept it." She looked to her mother for support.

Mother came forward and took the box to examine the necklace. Lizzy stepped back and caught sight of Wes across the room. His eyes were narrowed and his brow furrowed. He put down his plate of food and left the house. Lizzy wanted to go after him but had no idea what she'd say to him. She thought she'd made it very clear to Jason that she had no interest in becoming more than friends, but his gift clearly suggested he still wanted things to be otherwise.

"Lizzy's quite right, Mr. Adler." Mother smiled and replaced the lid on the box before handing it back to him. "It's a beautiful necklace, but she couldn't possibly accept it."

Jason looked around the room. "It was only a token . . . a gesture of my appreciation that she is staying on with the show another year. I meant nothing else."

"Still, it's a very expensive and personal item." Mother took Jason's arm and patted his sleeve. "You were very thoughtful, but please understand. I cannot allow her to accept it."

The room fell silent, and Lizzy held her breath. If Jason protested, she feared it would spoil the Christmas spirit. The situation had already driven Wesley from the house.

Mother, however, seemed completely at ease. "Now, I want everyone to come with us to the barn. I have one final gift for Lizzy. It was something her father and I planned."

Lizzy felt her chest tighten. Father had been part of this gift. How wonderful. She could almost feel him at her side. She followed her mother to the barn, not even bothering to put on her coat. The winter chill didn't bother her at all. The thought of her father having planned this gift with Mother left her warm.

By the time they reached the barn, Lizzy was giddy with excitement. She knew the gift must be a horse. When her eyes adjusted to the dimmer light, she could see that she was right. Wesley stood holding the halter of a feisty buckskin colt. Phillip was nearby just in case Wes needed help.

"Merry Christmas, Lizzy dear," Mother said. "This fella was born earlier this year. When your father first saw him, he told me that he knew you should have him."

"He's beautiful." Lizzy stepped forward for a closer inspection. Her gaze met Wesley's, and she smiled. "I suppose you were in on this too."

He smiled, seeming to have forgotten the earlier matter. "I was with your father when he purchased him last January. He wasn't even a month old but was already the finest quarter horse we'd ever seen."

She marveled at the beauty of the colt. He was skittish, but Lizzy spoke softly. "It's all right, little fella. We're going to be good friends, I just know it." She looked at Wes. "Where did you get him?"

"Over in Billings. Remember last winter just after Christmas when we made that trip?"

"Yes. I wanted to go but had a cold and felt so lousy that

Mother kept me in bed for a week." The colt's coat was the color of tanned deer hide, and his mane and tail as well as the lower half of his legs were black. He was regal in his stance, almost as if he knew how fine he was.

"I love him, and I love that you have kept this surprise from me." Lizzy gently touched the colt's black muzzle. She glanced at Wes and saw the pleasure he took from her joy. She'd never wanted to kiss him more than in that moment.

"He is a magnificent animal," Jason said. "What will you call him?"

Lizzy didn't even acknowledge him. Instead she offered Wes a smile. "Emerson. For Ralph Waldo Emerson."

Wesley shifted his grip on the halter. "I suggest you keep him for breeding." The colt was clearly getting agitated. "For now, however, I think I'd better put him back in the pen. He's going to start kicking up his heels."

"And I think we should go back to the house for more hot chocolate and breakfast," Mother declared.

Lizzy went to her and linked their arms together. "I quite agree."

The day passed in merriments. They sang Christmas carols, played games, and ate until they could hold no more. Lizzy wasn't at all sorry, however, when it was time to go to bed. She was exhausted from the day and fighting to keep her emotions in check. The gift of the colt had overwhelmed her. Knowing her mother and father had planned it since early in the year truly touched her heart.

Standing at her bedroom window, Lizzy gazed out into the dark night. "I miss you so much, Father. But today, it almost felt as if you were here with us." She drew a deep breath and pulled the curtains. She wasn't going to let her feelings take charge. She needed to be strong.

She walked to her bed and saw the book of poetry Wes had

given her. She crawled into bed and snuggled under the covers before opening it to the place Wes had marked.

"'Memories,'" she read aloud, then continued in silence.

> Oft I remember those whom I have known
> In other days, to whom my heart was led
> As by a magnet, and who are not dead,
> But absent, and their memories overgrown
> With other thoughts and troubles of my own,
> As graves with grasses are, and at their head
> The stone with moss and lichens so o'erspread,
> Nothing is legible but the name alone.
> And is it so with them? After long years,
> Do they remember me in the same way,
> And is the memory pleasant as to me?
> I fear to ask; yet wherefore are my fears?
> Pleasures, like flowers, may wither and decay,
> And yet the root perennial may be.

Something inside her stirred to life despite her desperate attempt to bury her heart. It wasn't really a declaration of love, but it was more than she'd had before. Dare she hope that love might still grow between them? Did she want it to?

She thought of the painful sorrow her mother had experienced losing her husband. Lizzy had always admired the deep love her parents had for each other. They always seemed so happy in each other's company. No matter how bad the situation, they always had each other. Now Mother was alone. Even Lizzy's company couldn't keep her from feeling Father's absence.

"How could I bear it if something happened to Wes?"

She tucked the book under her pillow and blew out the lamp. Settling back on her pillow, Lizzy stared out into the dark, letting her eyes adjust.

The muffled sound of her mother sobbing filtered through

the walls. This was her first Christmas without Lizzy's father. Lizzy ached for her—wished she could go to her and take the pain from her so that Mother could have a decent night's sleep.

"Please, Lord, take away her pain. Help her to endure this sad time. I don't know how to help her, but I would give my life to make things right again."

Tears dampened Lizzy's eyes, but she refused to cry. She wiped her face with the sleeve of her nightgown and pulled the thick quilt up over her head. Then she did likewise with her pillow to block out the sounds. To block it all out so that she didn't have to feel anything.

Mary Reichert sat opposite Zeb and Thomas at one of the bunkhouse tables. She'd asked specifically to speak with them, knowing they had taken August under their wing and taught him what they could about working for the Brookstone show.

"Did he say anything to either of you when he came back to the train for the liniment that night?"

"Said there was some trouble going on at the farm," Zeb replied before taking a long drink of coffee.

Thomas nodded and swirled the contents of his mug. "Some fella there accused him of snooping around, and when August tried to tell him all he wanted was liniment, the man threatened him."

Mary perked up. "Threatened him?"

Thomas shrugged and put down the cup. "Yeah, told August he'd have to answer to Mr. Fleming if it happened again."

Her shoulders slumped. "But he didn't threaten August with physical harm?"

"Not that he said. Why all the questions, Miss Mary?"

"I think someone did my brother harm. I don't think he'd ever go near the Fleming colts, especially not after being warned about snooping. August wasn't the kind to cause problems. He told Lizzy what happened only because he wanted to make sure Mr. Brookstone knew where he'd gone when he left the farm. He wasn't seeking retribution for being driven out of the stable. I doubt he would have mentioned it at all if he hadn't been worried about his absence being noted."

"That seems about right," Zeb said. "Never knew that boy to buck authority."

"He wouldn't have. Nor would he have gone into tight quarters with those green colts if he hadn't been asked to. And if he was asked to, then someone at Fleming Farm did the asking—knowing full well the danger."

"Did anyone see him gettin' trampled by those colts?" Thomas asked.

Mary shook her head. "I don't think so. It's unclear. From what Mr. Adler recalls, someone said August was found that way—already dead—in the pen of the colts." She felt the words stick in her throat and found it impossible to go on without dissolving into tears. Getting to her feet, Mary forced a smile. "Thank you for answering my questions. If you think of anything else, please let me know. I think for now it's best I go practice my shooting."

"Would you like some help with the targets?" Thomas asked, pushing back from the table.

"No. I think I'd like to be alone."

❖⟝ NINETEEN ⟞❖

Prince, come," Mrs. Brookstone commanded the pup. The dog had quickly learned to obey and fell into step at her feet.

"You have him eating out of your hand," Wes teased as he led them into his bunkhouse office.

"Well, it has been nearly a month, and Barney did a good job of getting him started," the older woman said with a smile. "Prince and I are good companions. I couldn't have asked for a better Christmas present."

"I'm glad." Wes knew that her spirits had been considerably brighter since receiving the dog. "Especially given that everyone plans to take off at the end of next month."

"Which brings me to the reason I asked to see you." She took a seat in front of his desk, then snapped her fingers at the pup. "Prince, sit." He instantly obeyed. Rebecca Brookstone turned her attention back to Wesley. "I want you to go with them as head wrangler."

"What?" He hadn't anticipated this idea at all.

She raised her hand. "I know you love the ranch and prefer the work here to that of the show, but I'm concerned about Lizzy."

"Is something wrong?" He tried not to sound too worried.

"No, but neither do I want there to be. Oliver has taken Mark's death quite hard. He's sober now, most of the time, but that only makes him sadder. I fear once he's on the show circuit, he'll take to the bottle again."

"And you think I can keep him from doing that?"

"I don't know, but I know you care about him. Maybe just having a friend will help him remember his priorities. Regardless, I know Lizzy will need your support. Especially if Oliver does start drinking again." She paused and lowered her gaze to her hands. "Speaking of Lizzy brings me to another aspect of my request."

Wes and Lizzy had seen little of each other since Christmas. Wes had been busy with calving season, while Lizzy had been practicing daily with Ella for hours on end. He knew from Phillip that Lizzy often came to visit Emerson, but that generally happened when Wes was tied up elsewhere.

"Jason Adler intends to marry Lizzy."

This blunt announcement brought Wes back to the present. He knew Adler's intentions. They had been clear from the moment he first arrived at the ranch. "I know."

"Lizzy isn't in love with him and has made it clear that she has no desire to marry him. Still he pursues her, and I fear that once they're on the road, he will continue to do so. I think Jason is a nice enough young man, but with the plans he has to take the show to England, I fear his persistence might wear Lizzy down. And that, combined with my concerns about what Oliver will do . . . well, it might leave Lizzy vulnerable."

"So vulnerable she'd marry a man she didn't love?"

Mrs. Brookstone shrugged. "Who can say? Lizzy hasn't been herself since Mark died. I just feel that if you were there for her, it would make all the difference in the world. I know you love her, Wes."

He wasn't ready to admit to his feelings aloud. So far he'd done good just to sort them out for himself.

"I'm not pressing you to admit your feelings," Mrs. Brook-stone continued, fixing Wes with an understanding gaze. "That should be shared between you and Lizzy first. I just felt that I needed to speak to you about this while Oliver and Jason were gone, making final arrangements for the show."

The two men had taken off the previous week for Chicago. They would soon be back, however, and it wouldn't be long before the rest of the performers showed up to start their daily practice runs for the show's new routines.

"I have no idea what Oliver's condition will be when he re-turns. I hope he will refrain from drink, but who can say. I've already told Oliver that I think he should ask you to come on board. Jason has trimmed the number of men down consider-ably, and I fear that if you aren't there, things may take a turn for the worse. Jason doesn't know how much work it is to keep those animals in shape for their performances."

"I don't know why Adler thinks he knows better than Mark and Oliver when it comes to the show."

"Moneywise, I'm sure he will manage things better," the older woman assured him. "I truly believe Jason to be a good man with the show's best interests at heart. But I agree with you where the animals and their care are concerned. Jason is used to handling bookkeeping, and I'm not sure he realizes the degree of work that goes into traveling with so many animals. But you do. You helped in the early years, and you know how difficult things can get."

"I do, and I know how pushy Adler is with Lizzy."

"So you'll do it?" Her voice was hopeful.

Wes couldn't give her an answer. Not at that moment. He needed time to think. Maybe he could talk Lizzy into staying home. That would solve a lot.

"Who will run the ranch?" he asked.

"I will. Along with Sandy and Cookie and whoever else you

tell me is competent enough to fill in for you. I can handle the bookwork, and the men can tell me what they need. We've got a good crew here—men who've been at this long enough to know what's expected and needed. And since Jason has eliminated jobs for some of the older men, they can stay on here and help. I can't bring myself to put them out completely."

Wes nodded. He'd hoped that would be the case. "I need to think on it, Mrs. Brookstone. I need to sit down with Oliver too. I think it ought to be his idea, asking me to come along. Don't you?"

She considered this for a moment, then nodded. "You're right, and I know he does intend to speak to you about it, so I'll leave it alone." She got to her feet. "Thank you for hearing me out. Prince, come." The pup jumped up and started wagging his tail as if they were about to head off on a grand adventure. "I don't usually advise men to think with their hearts, but I hope this time you will—at least in part." She gave Wes a smile, then left him to ponder all they'd discussed.

Since leaving Kentucky, Ella had awoken every morning concerned that her father and former fiancé would show up at the Brookstone ranch and demand her return. That fear overshadowed everything, even the longing she felt to see her mother again. But today was her twenty-first birthday, and Ella finally felt a sense of relief. She was certain now that no matter what else happened, she was safe from having to marry Jefferson Spiby. Safe from having to return home.

What continued to haunt her, however, was the knowledge that she knew what had happened to August Reichert. At least in part. She knew her father and Jefferson were responsible, and she still couldn't keep the nightmares at bay.

Every day she prayed for wisdom. Today was no exception. She opened her Bible to pick up her daily reading. She had marked her spot at Ephesians five and began to read. Verses fourteen through seventeen drew her attention.

> Wherefore he saith, Awake thou that sleepest, and arise from the dead, and Christ shall give thee light. See then that ye walk circumspectly, not as fools, but as wise, redeeming the time, because the days are evil. Wherefore be ye not unwise, but understanding what the will of the Lord is.

She wanted to walk in wisdom—to redeem the time. Most of all, she wanted to understand what the will of the Lord was for her life.

"What should I do, Lord? What is Your will for me?" she prayed aloud.

Truth. The word seemed to echo in her soul. *Truth.*

She looked at the Bible verses again. *Wherefore be ye not unwise, but understanding what the will of the Lord is.* Ella bit her lower lip. Truth. She needed to tell the truth. That was God's will for her. She remembered hearing a sermon in their Kentucky church in which the pastor said that the truth would set you free.

"It could also cause the Brookstones to put me from this house and their company."

"Hey, Ella, are you ready?" Mary called from the other side of her bedroom door.

Ella frowned. "I'm getting dressed." She put the Bible aside and gathered her clothes. "I'll be right there."

She quickly combed and braided her hair, then threw off her nightgown, shivering from the chill of the morning. Never had she dressed so fast. She was still shivering when she made her way downstairs to breakfast. Everyone else was already seated and awaiting her arrival.

She offered them a weak smile. "Sorry I'm late. I was reading my Bible."

"Never have to be sorry for that," Oliver Brookstone said, smiling. He looked tired, but given he and Jason had just returned from Chicago, it was no wonder. "I'll share the verses I read this morning and then pray for our meal."

Ella settled into her chair. She was seated between Mary and Mrs. Brookstone and gave each a smile and nod while Mr. Brookstone read from the Psalms. After he prayed, Mrs. Brookstone reached for Ella's hand and gave it a squeeze. "Happy birthday, Ella."

The others joined in, wishing her well for the day with the promise of cake that evening. Mrs. Brookstone had even gone to the trouble to make Ella's favorite—pound cake.

She couldn't help but feel safe and loved. These people cared more about her well-being and happiness than her own family did. How could she not give them the truth?

Going through her paces later that day while Mary and Lizzy watched, Ella pondered how she would come clean and tell Mary what she knew. The truth would be hard to hear, but Ella knew it would help her friend move forward. At least she hoped it would. A part of her feared it would only cause Mary more grief. After all, few would ever believe that George Fleming and Jefferson Spiby had committed murder. And those who did believe it would be too afraid to do anything.

Ella felt a tightness in her chest. She loved the life she had here with the Brookstones. She had worked harder than she'd ever worked at home, but there was also a greater satisfaction in her accomplishments. She'd grown stronger in the last few months and now had little trouble saddling her own mounts or performing the various tricks Lizzy gave her to try. She'd even managed to renew her love of Roman riding using the Brookstones' horses. All in all, she was delighted with the way her life had turned out. What if the truth changed all of that?

"It's not like I know exactly what happened," she whispered

to Pepper as she leaned low over his neck. She saw Lizzy and Mary at the other end of the arena. She liked both women very much and didn't want to lose their friendship or her place in the show by admitting what she knew.

Nothing I say will bring back her brother.

That thought constantly stayed at the forefront of Ella's mind. Confessing wouldn't change the fact that August Reichert was dead, nor did she believe it would make a difference in seeing justice done for him.

"You're better at those Cossack drags than I am," Lizzy declared as Ella brought Pepper to a stop in front of her and Mary.

Ella slid off the horse and gave him a generous hug. "He's such a good horse. He always anticipates my every move." She glanced at Mary and noted that she was wiping her eyes with her handkerchief.

Lizzy's gaze followed hers. "Mary's having a rough day. She's talked to everyone who was with us on the show, but nobody has any answers for her regarding August."

Guilt washed over Ella in waves. "Would it matter so much if she knew what really happened?" Her voice was barely a whisper, but despite that, Mary's head snapped up.

"It would matter a great deal." Mary came to where Ella and Lizzy stood. She looked at Ella. "My brother deserves justice."

"What if there was no justice to be had?" Ella hadn't meant to get drawn into this conversation, but now that it had happened, she knew she'd have to continue.

Mary gripped Ella's shoulder. "You know something, don't you?" Her tone was accusatory.

Ella swallowed the lump in her throat. "I . . . I can't. . . ." She bit her lower lip. How could she admit to knowing all these months? Especially when she had no proof except what she'd overheard.

"Ella, if you do know something, you must tell us," Lizzy urged.

Tears slid down Ella's cheeks before she could stop them. She had always been given to crying when under pressure.

Lizzy put her arm around Ella's shoulders. "Come. Let's sit down."

She led Ella to the bench in the tack area. Ella sat, and Lizzy and Mary took their places on either side of her.

Mary took Ella's hand. "I'm sorry for snapping at you. It's just, well, you know how this is for me. I've tried so hard to find answers regarding my brother. Please—if you know something—help me."

Ella couldn't bear her pleading. "It won't help."

"Let me be the judge of that," Mary said, squeezing her hand.

"Ella, I know you've been living in fear of what your father and fiancé might do if they find you," Lizzy began, "but you are twenty-one now. You don't have to worry about that anymore. They can't force you to return home."

"You don't know my father. You don't know Jefferson. They are powerful and cruel."

"Did they have something to do with my brother's death?" Mary asked.

Ella's words caught in the back of her throat. She felt the room closing in and knew she had no choice but to tell the truth.

"Please," Mary begged, "I must know what happened."

Doing what she could to compose herself, Ella drew a deep breath and nodded. "I've wanted to tell you. All these weeks now, I've lived with the guilt of knowing what I needed to do." She got to her feet and faced both women. "You have no idea how it has tormented me. I don't want to lose your friendship—it means more than life to me."

Lizzy shook her head. "You aren't going to lose my friendship. Not ever."

"Nor mine," Mary assured. "Lizzy has told me how terrible things were for you. I promise I'll always be your friend."

"I've prayed so much about this. I don't know the details. I can only tell you what I overheard." Ella paused and met Mary's gaze. "Believe me, if it could have brought August justice, I would have said something immediately. But nothing I say will help you with that. My father and Jefferson Spiby own the entire county and part of the state. They have friends in powerful positions, and they will never be called to account for the things they've done."

"What have they done?" Mary asked.

"I don't even know. I overheard my father and former fiancé speaking. They said someone had seen too much. I don't recall the exact words, but the conversation ended with them resolving to take care of the matter. The next thing I knew, your brother was dead. I wasn't even sure the two events were connected. I had already planned to run away, and I knew that my chance to leave depended on being able to slip away unnoticed.

"When Father told us August was dead and the sheriff was coming, I knew I had to take advantage of that narrow bit of time. I was nearly caught coming down the back stairs of the house, but I managed to hide myself when I heard my father and Jefferson. It was then that I overheard Jefferson say that he had killed your brother."

Mary gasped and clamped her hands over her mouth. Lizzy's mouth dropped open, and her eyes grew wide. Ella felt a sense of relief that the truth was finally out there, but she had no idea what would happen now.

"I didn't see him do it, nor do I have any idea what August saw that made them think he had to die. I never dreamt my father was capable of such a thing, but I could believe it of Jefferson. I've heard horrible things about him. He even admitted to my father that this wasn't his first time to kill and it wouldn't be his last."

"We have to stop him," Mary said, lowering her hands. "He'll just keep killing people for whatever reason he deems necessary."

"I know." Ella could hear the resignation in her voice. If only they understood the hopelessness of it. "But no one will listen to me."

"You don't know that," Mary said, getting to her feet. She looked down at Lizzy. "We have to do something."

"But what?" Lizzy rose and looked from Ella to Mary. "She's right. I've met these men. They have money and power, and no one is going to speak against them."

"But Ella will. Ella can tell what she heard."

"But that's just it, it's hearsay. It's her word against theirs." Lizzy shook her head. "Ella's right, no one would dare come against them."

Ella could see in Mary's expression that she finally understood as she sank back onto the bench. "Then August's death will never be avenged. He'll never have justice."

"God will give him justice," Lizzy said, sitting beside her. She put her arm around Mary's shoulders. "God knows what happened, and He won't let evil win. We must give this over to Him and pray that He will show us what to do."

"If only we had some equally powerful men we could go to for help," Mary murmured. Her head snapped up. "What about Jason? His father is wealthy and a man of power."

"He's an Englishman. He doesn't hold any power here in America," Lizzy replied.

"But you said yourself that Jason is half American, and his mother's family is rich. He and his family must know powerful people here."

"Perhaps."

Ella could see where Mary hoped to take this. She wanted to do whatever she could to help. "If we can find someone—anyone—who will help us, I will happily testify to what I heard. I don't know if that will matter at all, but I will do what I can to help you, Mary. Please don't hate me for not speaking up sooner."

Mary's eyes met Ella's. "I don't hate you, Ella. You were afraid, and fear is something we have all experienced. I appreciate that you would tell me now, even though your fear is still very real. I knew my brother couldn't have been trampled by a horse. I know you're afraid your father and fiancé will come here and cause you harm, but I will do whatever I can to protect you from their wrath."

"We both will," Lizzy assured her.

Ella knew they were both sincere, but their words gave her very little peace.

⊷⊱ TWENTY ⊰⊶

Corabelle and Betty won't be returning to the show," Uncle Oliver announced. Some of the performers had already started arriving at the ranch as planned, while others had sent letters of regret. "I just learned that Corabelle's back injuries will keep her from performing. She twisted it pretty badly when we were on the road, and apparently while at home, she suffered a fall that caused the problem to worsen."

Lizzy looked at Ella. "She did both trick riding and Roman riding. Do you suppose you can learn some of the Roman riding act before we head off on the circuit?"

"I'm sure I can."

Uncle Oliver nodded. "I was hopeful of that." He looked at Gertie, a young woman of medium build in her early twenties. "What about you? Do you want to take on some of the Roman riding?"

The brunette shrugged. "I'm willing to give it a try, but I doubt I'll be proficient enough by the time we're on the road. I'm better with the trick riding."

"I can help," Lizzy said and turned to Jessie and Debbie, their other Roman riders. "I haven't done it in a while, but at least I've had experience. I'm sure with all of us working together, we can figure something out. If nothing else, we'll change the routine."

The ladies nodded.

Jason sat beside Lizzy and offered her a smile. "Are you certain? I remember you once saying that it is best to focus on just one area of stunt riding. If need be, I'm certain we could hire another rider."

He'd stuck to Lizzy like glue since returning from Chicago. She knew he wanted to endear himself, but being overly concerned wasn't the way to do it.

"I'll be fine. Once Ella knows the routine, they'll be back to a team of three. You said that we needed to learn each other's jobs so we could cover for one another in times of injury or absence. Ella and I have even been training with Mary, although I'm not much good at sharpshooting."

"I'm not as likely to get injured as you are," Mary threw out. "Besides, Alice is coming back. She wrote and told me, I just haven't had a chance to announce it. Since Teresa left, Alice didn't want to train with someone new, but when she found out I was rejoining the show, she decided to come back so long as her husband is rehired as crew."

Everyone looked to Jason. "Which one is he?"

"Carson Hopkins. He was my brother's best friend," Mary replied. "He wasn't sure he even wanted to return, but I encouraged him to do it in memory of August."

"Ah, yes." Jason looked to Oliver, who was nodding. Jason smiled. "He was definitely invited to return."

"Alice shoots bow from horseback. I think we can give her more time in the act," Oliver said. "Perhaps she'll have some ideas for how we might make the act even more exciting."

"I think I could add some things as well," Mary declared. "My job isn't as physically taxing as what the others girls do. If you need me to, I could do some additional tricks, even have more audience participation."

"I say, that's a capital idea," Jason piped up.

Lizzy listened as the conversation continued about how they would make the show more exciting and add some local interest as well. Jason assured them that having some contests for the locals would bring people in from far and wide.

"A sense of competition will always encourage attendance. We could have something of a challenge between the genders, perhaps?" His face lit up at this.

"I'm not sure I understand what the purpose would be," Mary commented.

Jason's expression suggested he'd just struck gold. "Imagine this. We could have an open competition at the beginning of each event—just prior to the show itself. We invite men to pay to shoot against Mary and Alice. Mary could use her rifle, and we could set up targets. Alice could have a similar contest with the bow."

Oliver nodded enthusiastically. "Yes! Yes! I can see that being very compelling. Imagine the men wanting to prove themselves against the women. Would you be willing to add that to your responsibilities, Mary?"

"Do you really suppose the men would pay to shoot against me?" Mary looked to Lizzy. "What do you think?"

"I think men tend to be ninnies any time women are involved," Lizzy said without thinking. Jason raised a brow as he glanced her way. Lizzy wasn't going to get caught in this discussion. "I have some new tricks I need to work on. I think whatever you decide will be fine. I'm sure there will be plenty of money to be made if the men think they can outshoot Mary. Goodness, if you made a kiss from her the reward, we're sure to be swimming in gold."

"There's an idea!" Uncle Oliver said, turning to Jason.

Lizzy didn't stay to hear where the rest of the conversation led. She made her way to the pens and collected Longfellow before heading to the arena. Once there, she saddled the horse and began galloping around the arena. She liked to warm him up before heading into any kind of maneuver. As they made endless circles, she thought of Wesley. He'd been so busy with the calving season that she'd seldom seen him. Mother said that Cookie was packing up food each day to send out with the men, but sometimes they didn't even make it back in before nightfall. There was so much to do, in fact, that Phillip and the older men were out helping.

Mother had also mentioned that she and Uncle Oliver wanted Wes to go on tour with the show. They felt confident that since he had experience and could be trusted, he was the perfect choice to fill August's role. Lizzy hadn't known what to think of that. The idea of Wes being with them made it much riskier for her. How could she hope to keep her feelings under control?

She signaled to Longfellow that they were going to start their routine. She brought him to a stop at the end of the arena. "Good boy," she said, stroking his neck. She slipped the reins under the bridle headpiece. "Now it's time to work."

She put him through his paces doing simple tricks—vaults, spins, and layovers. Longfellow knew what was expected and performed without flaw. When Lizzy felt they were both amply warmed up, they tried a few harder tricks. She knew better than to practice alone, but with Uncle Oliver and Jason wanting to go into details with the others, Lizzy felt the best way to spend her time was in practice. Besides, she and Longfellow rarely had trouble.

For weeks now, Lizzy had been planning out a series of tricks she could do at a full gallop, and she wanted to add one additional element that would allow her to vault from the ground into a squat on the saddle. From there she would stand up, then go head first to the left side of Longfellow, somersaulting to hit the ground with her feet and vault backward and back up. It needed to be fluid or it wouldn't look right. She hadn't quite worked out all the problems, but she was close.

She put Longfellow into a gallop and went into the pattern of vaults and spins, but when she tried the new elements, she lost her grip while vaulting backward, slammed her shoulder hard against the saddle, and lost control.

She hit the ground face first, knocking the wind from her chest. She stayed completely still, trying to force her lungs to take in air.

"Lizzy!"

She would have moaned in frustration at the sound of Wes calling her name, but she couldn't draw enough air. Of all the people to catch her in this situation, it had to be him.

He rushed to her side and rolled her over, drawing her into his arms. "Lizzy, are you all right?"

Thankfully she was starting to get control of her breathing. "I'm . . . fine."

His worried expression made her think back to what he'd told her about Clarissa.

She struggled to speak without gasping. "Really. I'm fine."

"You scared the life out me when I saw you lying here. What are you doing, practicing without someone here with you?"

He was still holding her, and Lizzy wasn't in any real hurry to get away, but his accusing tone was more than she wanted to deal with at the moment. "I had work to do." She drew a deep breath and ignored the ache in her side. "As you can see, I haven't quite perfected my new trick. Now, if you don't mind, I'd like to get up."

Wesley helped her to her feet. "You need to quit this. You're too old to do these dangerous tricks."

She put her hands on her hips. "Too old?"

"You know what I mean. The older you get, the more you risk hurting yourself in a bad way."

"Is there a good way?"

"Lizzy." His voice was full of irritation. "I don't think you should go with the show this year."

"Well, I don't think you should either."

He stared at her as if trying to figure out what to say next, but Lizzy saved him the trouble.

She reached down and picked up her hat. "I don't need you telling me what to do. If you want to be useful, then be supportive and encouraging. If you only want to find fault, you can find it with someone else."

She dusted off her backside and whistled for Longfellow. He came immediately, but Wesley took hold of his bridle. "You need to listen to reason."

"What seems to be the problem?" Lizzy's mother asked, coming to join them. Prince stuck close to her heels.

Lizzy rolled her eyes. "He's the problem. I fell off my horse, and he acts like it's the end of the world."

"I found her on the ground, not even moving."

Lizzy stretched to her full height on tiptoes and pressed her face closer to his. "I was trying to breathe. That's why I wasn't moving."

His lips bore the tiniest hint of a smile. "Breathing wouldn't have been a problem if you hadn't been thrown to the ground."

"I wasn't thrown, I lost my grip. Now give me my horse."

"No. You need to rest and make sure you aren't hurt. Go sit down."

Lizzy heard her mother chuckle and stepped back to glare at her. "This isn't the slightest bit funny. I have a routine to perform in just a few weeks, and if I can't get the trick right, then I will have an even bigger problem." She looked at Wes and shook her finger in his face. "Stop bossing me around. You are not my father or my brother." Seeing he wouldn't yield, she let out a growl and headed for the door. "Fine. You take care of his grooming and make sure that saddle is put away properly."

She slammed the door on the way out—just for good measure.

Wes could see the amusement on Rebecca Brookstone's face. He shook his head. What could he say?

"Now that Lizzy has clearly established what you *aren't*," the older woman said, "maybe you should figure out what you *are*."

"She's impossible. I thought she was dead."

Lizzy's mother put her hand on his arm. "Wes, you can't keep her from harm. She loves what she does and daily scares the life right out of me. But I can't tell her she can't do what she loves. She'd only hate me for it. She'd hate you too."

"But she could have been killed."

"Like Clarissa."

He swallowed hard and frowned. "Yes. Like Clarissa."

"Wes, Clarissa is gone. Lizzy is her own woman, and if you want a future with her, you'll have to accept her for who she is. To do less would be to change her. Love and marriage are all about give and take. Lizzy's ready to stop riding in the show, but if you tell her she can't do it . . . she's only going to keep doing it out of defiance just to prove she can."

"I don't know how to win her heart." Longfellow was getting bored with the conversation and began to shift around. Wes gave him a pat on the neck.

Rebecca Brookstone smiled. "You've already won her heart, Wes. Now you just need to show her that you don't see her as a child or someone to boss around, but as a partner—someone to share your life with, to grow old with."

"But she won't grow old at this rate."

Rebecca grew thoughtful. "Mark didn't grow old either, but

he wasn't doing anything more dangerous than sitting in a chair when he had his heart attack. None of us know when our time will come. Mark and I had some wonderful years together and a beautiful daughter. The dangers and risks were worth it. You might not have felt that way with Clarissa, but you two didn't marry for love."

He tried to hide his surprise, but Mrs. Brookstone shook her head. "You don't have to say anything about it. I know when a man and woman love each other. That's why I know you and Lizzy are in love—even if you're both too bullheaded to admit it.

"Come, Prince!" The pup snapped to attention and hugged her heel. Mrs. Brookstone took a few steps, then turned to glance over her shoulder. "If you're smart, Wes, you won't waste all your time trying to make Lizzy into someone she's not. After all, the woman she is now is the woman you fell in love with. If you force her to change, you risk losing everything."

He watched Lizzy's mother leave by the same door Lizzy had just slammed moments ago. Was she right?

He sighed and looked Longfellow in the eye. "What am I supposed to do?"

~·= TWENTY-ONE =·~

Lizzy was still seething over Wesley's attitude a week later. The last of the performers had arrived only the day before. They were full of excitement about the 1901 show calendar, and Uncle Oliver and Jason had called a meeting for that afternoon. Meanwhile, Jason had done everything in his power to get Lizzy alone. He hadn't succeeded, thankfully. Lizzy had no desire to spend time in private discussions with him when she had Wes on her mind. The trouble was that Wes was always on her mind.

As everyone gathered in the large living room, Lizzy sat in the corner, wondering why Wesley's opinion mattered so much. She felt bad for the way she'd acted. He had good reason to hate trick riding, and she knew he only wanted her to be safe.

Mary plopped down beside her. "You look like you've got the weight of the world on your shoulders."

"I'm still upset over what happened last week with Wes."

"He hasn't even been around to pester you," Mary reminded her. "Your mother said the men have been so busy with calving that she's not seen much of them."

"Yes, but Wes will be back soon enough. I ran into Phillip, and he said Wes intends to take the wrangler position with the show."

"But that's a good thing. You'll have all year to work on your feelings for each other."

"Thanks everybody for being here so promptly," Uncle Oliver said as he brought the meeting to order. "We've got some exciting news. Next year's show schedule is fully set, and I'm delighted to announce we will be going abroad in the fall to England."

There were gasps, and several people had questions that spilled out all at once. Uncle Oliver held up his hands. "If you'll just quiet down, we'll give you all the details." He proceeded to explain how they would tour extensively throughout the Midwest and move toward the East Coast. They would perform almost every day but Sunday.

"The schedule will be grueling, but we will have a nice rest when we sail to London in August. We will perform in England for much of August and September, then sail home to finish out at the Pan-American Expo in Buffalo, New York."

It was exhausting just listening to the details. It was worse still when Uncle Oliver explained they would do all of this with half the crew.

"You expect us to keep a schedule like that and take on other duties?" Alice Hopkins asked.

"Not many," Uncle Oliver assured her. "We want our performers to be well rested. We realize a daily performance is going to be hard enough. We haven't worked out all of the details, and some of them won't be known until we're actually in the throe of things.

"Now, Agnes has agreed to do part of the year with us, and while she's with us, she'll continue to train her niece Brigette, who's been her assistant the last two years, to handle costumes and laundry for the troupe. Meanwhile, Brigette's good friend Sally has joined up and is training to cook and clean. By having these two on board with us, we've been able to eliminate two positions, and once Agnes retires, we'll be down another. All of this will save money in the long run." He looked to Lizzy's mother. "I presume training has been going well?"

Mother nodded. "We've only just started, but it's going well. Sally had experience in cooking for large groups, so she's quite capable." Everyone looked at the shy young woman who sat beside Agnes and her niece. "She'll be ready when it's time to go."

"Brigette too," Agnes assured everyone.

"Wonderful." Uncle Oliver flashed a big smile.

The meeting went on for over an hour before Uncle Oliver finally brought it to a close.

"I want you all to finalize the performances you plan to give so that Jason and I can review them with you one by one. We want to pack as much into the show as we can. The acts will be in twenty-minute increments as before. This year, however, two hours prior to the show, there will be a local shooting contest that each individual town will advertise. The top three winners will compete against Mary. We'll offer a prize of five dollars for the man or woman who can beat Mary."

"But it isn't likely Mary will lose." This came from Gertie.

"Exactly. No matter the outcome, Mary will pose for newspaper photographs with the three top shooters. It will all be quite celebratory, and as word gets around from town to town, more people will be driven to try their hand."

"What if I do lose?" Mary asked.

Uncle Oliver chuckled. "Given the fees we'll charge to participate in the contest, it won't be that big of a loss. If a man beats you, we'll play it up that you were distracted by his stunning good looks or something."

Lizzy put out her own thought. "What if another woman beats her?"

"Then we'll hire her on," Uncle Oliver said with a shrug, making everyone laugh. "There's more. We've also made arrangements with the towns to handle concessions. The one provision is that they must carry our banners and programs and be prepared to give back our inventory and money immediately at the close of the program. Jason will be responsible for managing this, as well as the ticket sales."

Always in the past, a couple of the older men were responsible for these things. Lizzy thought it only right that if Jason was getting rid of the men, he should be responsible for taking on their jobs.

When the meeting finally concluded, it was understood that the staff working with the horses had been cut by half and those taking care of household duties had been cut by three. Jason had also eliminated the need for two of the train cars and had re-outfitted the others. Gone was the family car, as Lizzy and Oliver both agreed they could bunk in with the others. Jason also explained how new, up-to-date arrangements for the horses allowed them to need fewer cars for the animals. She hoped—prayed—that he knew what he was doing. Transportation was hard enough on the animals.

Glad to be out of the stuffiness of the house, Lizzy started for the arena, then changed her mind. There was plenty of time, and she wanted to work with Emerson. The colt was making great strides. Phillip and Lizzy had been working with him whenever time allowed. Soon, however, she'd be gone, and the responsibility would fall solely to Phillip. She didn't want to miss an opportunity for the colt to become more familiar with her.

At one end of the barn was the extended stall where Emerson was kept during the night. Temperatures had been brutal lately, and everyone felt it wise to afford the yearling extra protection. Lizzy grabbed a lead and went to the stall gate. Emerson was used to her now and came over in search of a treat.

"Show me what you can do, and then I'll give you a reward," she told him, attaching the lead to his halter.

She opened the gate and led the colt out of the barn. He was quite good on the rope. Wes had told her they'd worked through the summer with him, and it showed.

The air was crisp, but the temperature had warmed to the mid-twenties, according to Cookie. With the sun out in full, the intensity of its heat was welcoming, and Lizzy lifted her face to let the rays wash over her. All the while, she walked with the colt beside her.

She stopped several times, teaching him to respond to her commands. When he performed correctly, she praised him. "Emerson, you are quite the little stallion. I think you'll be an amazing sire."

She continued down the main drive, stopping and doing turns with him from time to time. It was important to keep him working on these skills. While most ranchers would have put him in a field until he was three and then have someone break him in hard and fast, that wasn't Lizzy's style. She wanted to form a solid relationship with the colt. She'd trained Longfellow and Thoreau, and both now handled as if they were extensions of her own body. She didn't plan to use Emerson in the shows, but she would still like to ride him.

Lizzy had started the colt back to the barn when she saw Jason Adler making his way toward her. She sighed. "Well, we didn't need his company, did we, Emerson?"

"Goodness, Lizzy, you are hard to find at times," Jason said as he reached her side.

"I have work to do." She reached up to stroke Emerson's face. "A lot of work, actually." She started walking toward the pens. "What can I do for you?"

He chuckled. "I would be brash and say *marry me*, but I doubt that would get me any further than my previous proposal."

"No. It wouldn't get you anywhere at all." She glanced up to find him frowning. "Did you enjoy Chicago?"

"Very much. I prefer city life in the winter."

"Only the winter? I figured you were sold on the city year-round."

Jason kept pace with her, and when they reached the pen, he opened the gate for Lizzy. She led Emerson inside, then took off the lead. Reaching into her pocket, she pulled out a few slices of dried apple. The colt was to receive them, then took off to join the other horses and see who he could push around.

Lizzy laughed at his antics. "He's such a fine animal. I'm more and more impressed with him."

Longfellow and Thoreau made their way over to her. Lizzy gave them each some apple, drawing the colt's attention.

"He's definitely pushy," she said, refusing to give him anything more.

"A fella has to be around here to get any attention," Jason replied.

She ignored the comment and attached the lead to Longfellow. "Don't worry, Thoreau, I'll send Ella to get you next." She walked Longfellow from the pen, grateful that Jason was happy to manage the gate.

"Thank you," she told him as she moved off toward the arena.

"Don't you have even a few minutes to talk with me?" Jason called after her.

He sounded so disappointed that Lizzy motioned for him to follow. "I can take a couple of minutes while I check over my saddle straps."

Jason nodded and caught up with her in two long strides. Inside the building, Lizzy tied off Longfellow, then went to the equipment stall.

"So what's on your mind?"

"You are, of course. I missed you, Lizzy. If anything, the time away only proved to me how much you've become a part of me."

She had figured he'd take this line and decided to change the subject. "I see you managed to talk Uncle Oliver into England.

I'm sure that pleases you." She checked the saddle from top to bottom and back to front. She'd worked with Zeb to add a new strap for her latest trick.

"It pleases me because it will allow me to show you London and our country estate. I know you'll love it, Lizzy, and I know my parents will love you as well."

"Yes, well, I generally get along with everyone." Pleased with the saddle, Lizzy grabbed a blanket. She was about to take it and the saddle to Longfellow, but Jason was at her side, pushing her hands away. He spun her around so quickly that she nearly lost her footing.

"Please, Lizzy. Won't you at least give me a chance? I've fallen quite madly in love with you." He held fast to her arms. "You know that I want us to marry."

"But I don't." She decided against any attempt to sugarcoat her words. "I don't ever intend to marry. Not you or anyone else."

"But that's not even reasonable. You're a beautiful woman with so much to offer. Marry me, and I'll give you anything you want."

"You can't give me what I want, Jason." Her throat went dry, and she bowed her head. She didn't even know what she wanted. "Please try to understand. I like you well enough." She forced herself to look up as he let go of her. "But I don't love you."

"You love him, don't you?"

She didn't need him to use a name to know that he meant Wesley. "Yes." She hadn't intended to admit such a thing to Jason, but now that she had, she felt the need to continue. "I never set out to, and God knows I have no intention of doing anything about it. But I do love him, and because of that, I won't give you false hope."

"You don't plan to marry him either?"

"No." She tried to keep all emotion from her voice. "As I said, I don't ever intend to marry—not that Wes has asked."

"Then he's a fool."

Lizzy smiled. "I don't think so. I think he may be the only smart one."

Jason let go a long breath. "I don't intend to stop trying to win you over and change your mind."

His statement only furthered her frustration. "What happened to us just being friends?"

"I lost my heart to you. That's what happened. I can't imagine taking any other woman for my wife."

"I am sorry, Jason. I made it clear from the beginning that I didn't want anything more. Now, please, leave me to work."

She thought he might argue with her, but thankfully her mother appeared from the shadows of the doorway. Prince was faithfully at her heels.

"Lizzy, here you are."

Jason gave Lizzy a slight bow and exited the arena without another word. Mother came to Lizzy and glanced back over her shoulder. "I thought if I made myself known, he'd leave you be."

"Thank you. He can be a pest." Lizzy leaned down and scratched Prince behind the ear. "I am so impressed with how quickly you've brought him in line."

"He's a smart dog and learns quick."

Lizzy gave him one final pat and straightened up. "I wish everyone would learn as quickly."

"Are you speaking of yourself or Jason?" Mother asked with a smile. "I'm sorry, but I overheard a great deal of your conversation. I was in the back room taking inventory."

"I didn't realize anyone else was out here, but that's all right." Lizzy lifted the saddle in her arms. She carried it to Longfellow and placed it on the ground beside him. "I didn't say a thing to him that I wouldn't have said with you at my side."

"Why did you tell him you never intend to marry?" Mother asked.

Lizzy put the blanket atop Longfellow and smoothed it out. "Because I don't."

"That doesn't sound like you. You've always talked about wanting to marry and have a family."

"That was then." Lizzy planted the saddle atop her horse, then rocked it back and forth to make sure it was in the right place. She'd secured the cinch and flank billet before Mother put her hand on Lizzy's arm. Lizzy looked up. "What is it?"

"Why have you changed your mind about marrying? I know you still have deep feelings for Wes. I heard you tell Jason that you love him. Why don't you want to marry him?"

"First of all, Wes sees me as a child—the daughter of the man he works for . . . or worked for. Second, he doesn't return my feelings. Third . . ." She fell silent. Looking in her mother's eyes, Lizzy knew her reasoning would only cause pain. "It's not important."

"I think it is, and I want you to tell me."

"I don't want to hurt you more by remembering what you once had."

Mother's eyes narrowed slightly. "Is this about your father and I?"

"Yes. I know what it cost you to lose Father. Your love for him and his for you was such a strong and beautiful thing. Now that he's gone, you're left with all this misery and pain. I hear you cry at night, Mother. I know how much his loss has meant."

"Yes, it's been very hard," Mother admitted. "But I wouldn't trade a single day we had together to be free of this sorrow."

"You wouldn't?" Lizzy found that hard to believe.

"Do you honestly suppose I would?" Mother sounded as if Lizzy had just suggested the most ridiculous thing in the world.

"I can't imagine that a few years of happiness is worth the pain you feel now."

"That's how little you know about love." Mother put her arm

around Lizzy and drew her away from Longfellow. She led them to the bench. "Sit with me a moment."

Lizzy took a seat beside her mother, and Prince settled on the ground between them. Mother clasped her hand in Lizzy's. "My darling girl, is this why you're avoiding Wes?"

"I'm not really avoiding him. He's been very busy with the calving."

Mother smiled. "I first met your father when I was just fourteen. I lost my heart to him almost immediately. I think he'd say he did the same. We were nearly inseparable from then on. We knew we'd marry and hoped we'd have a large family. Of course, the latter didn't happen. You were the only child we were able to have, but you were such a blessing. Your father often said that instead of giving us ten beautiful and intelligent children, God put the equivalent characteristics into one perfect child."

"I'm far from perfect, but I know you and Father love me dearly. I never lacked for love from either of you." Lizzy squeezed her mother's hand.

"I'm glad. I know I've never felt a lack of love from you and certainly never from your father. I don't even feel that lost to me now, which is why you must listen to me. Lizzy, avoiding love because you're afraid of losing it will leave you a very lonely and empty woman."

"But it will also keep me from knowing the pain you now know."

"Life is full of sorrows and pain. But it's also full of joy and love. Would you turn away from me because of the pain you've experienced losing your father? Would your fear of losing another parent result in you leaving me for good?"

Such a thing was unthinkable, and Lizzy was quick to say as much. "Never. That would be beyond reason."

"So too is hardening your heart against falling in love. You love Wes, and I believe the two of you belong together. Don't avoid love because you fear what might happen should he die. Don't sacrifice what is real for what may never be."

"But everyone dies." Lizzy felt her emotions welling up inside and pushed them back down. "You can't say that it may never be, because death will come."

"Yes, because it's part of life. But Lizzy, your strength is found in the Lord. I remember when you were very little and asked me what happened to us when we died. Do you remember that talk?"

"I do. I was five years old, and one of Grandmother's cats had been killed by the dog. The dog had threatened her kittens, and she died protecting them."

"Yes." Mother brushed a strand of brown hair from Lizzy's face. "I told you that when a person died they would either go home to be with God or they would be forever separated from Him."

"And I asked why." Lizzy smiled. "I used to ask why all the time."

Mother laughed. "You did indeed. But that was perhaps the most important time of all."

Lizzy remembered it well. "You told me about Jesus dying on the cross for me to take away my sins. It made me cry because all I could think about was how that poor cat had been killed."

"I know, but it was a good way to teach you about Jesus dying for us. He saw that we were in a bad way without Him. Satan was always threatening His children, just as that dog threatened the kittens. He gave His life so that we would be able to escape Satan's torment."

"You told me that if I put my trust in Jesus and confessed my sins, I would never really die."

"And you got confused and thought I meant you'd never die at all." Mother smiled. "Death in this life isn't the end. We certainly needn't fear it if we have given our hearts to God. We will see your father again. Of this I'm certain, even though it is hard to be without him now."

"It is."

Mother got to her feet and drew Lizzy up with her. She hugged her long and hard, and when Mother pulled back, Lizzy could see the tears that streamed down her cheeks. With her guard down, Lizzy could hardly bear it.

"Lizzy, I want you to know the truth for what it is. I would bear this pain and even more. Your father's love was worth the price. Just think about that, will you?" She kissed Lizzy's cheek, then walked away. Prince cocked his head to one side as he looked at Lizzy, then took off after his mistress.

"Yes. I will." Lizzy sank back onto the bench.

The door to the arena opened, but Lizzy didn't look up. She heard Mother say something but paid no attention. No doubt Ella was coming to work on their act.

"Lizzy?"

Wesley's voice so surprised Lizzy that she jumped to her feet. He stood only a few feet away, watching her. He looked tired and worried. Had Mother said something to him?

"I'm sorry, I was lost in my thoughts." She smiled and squared her shoulders. "What can I do for you? How's the calving going?"

"Everything's going well. We're ninety percent done. I think everything will finish up by the first of the month."

"That's good." Lizzy made her way back to Longfellow to finish saddling him. She took up the breast collar and secured it in place. "I'm sure you'll be relieved to have it all done before you head out with the show. Although I still don't understand why you said yes. You hate the show."

"I do not." He moved to stand beside Longfellow. "I never hated it."

"Then why do you give me such a hard time about performing?" She straightened and raised her brow.

"Because I don't want you to get hurt. Those stunts you create are dangerous. They're getting more and more dangerous just so you can thrill an audience."

She sighed. "Stop acting like an overprotective big brother."

Wesley growled and pulled her into his arms. He kissed her with great passion, nearly bending her over backward. Lizzy gave in to the moment and let the love she felt for Wes surge. It surely couldn't hurt just this once.

When he straightened and let go of her, Lizzy could only stare at him. Her pounding heart and panting breath hardly allowed her to speak. Slowly, rational thought returned. "Why . . . why did you . . . do that?"

His eyes never left hers. "Because I want to be clear on one thing: I do not think of you as my sister."

"Then what—what do you think of me as?"

He pulled her back into his arms. "My heart."

He started to kiss her again, but a scream sounded, and Lizzy pushed back.

"That's Ella!"

Ella flew through the open door. She was nearly hysterical.

"What's wrong?" Lizzy went to the crying girl and took hold of her. "What is it?"

Ella's eyes were wide with fear. "My father . . . Jefferson . . . they're here!"

TWENTY-TWO

Lizzy was glad that Wes agreed to return to the house with her and Ella. When they arrived, they found Mother, along with Uncle Oliver and Jason, sitting in the front room.

"Ella!" Mr. Fleming jumped to his feet. "I've been half sick with worry over you." He started to come to her, but Ella backed away. He stopped and looked at her with a frown. "Whatever has come over you?"

"Stay away from me. I want nothing to do with either of you."

Jefferson joined Ella's father. "What in the world is wrong, Ella? You've had us frantic for months in search of you."

"I left because I couldn't abide being there. I have no intention of returning home, so please go and leave me alone."

Lizzy put her arm around Ella. She could see the anger in Jefferson Spiby's expression, while Ella's father just looked confused.

"Why don't we all sit and discuss this in a civilized manner?" Mother suggested. "I'll have Irma bring us some coffee." She turned to go.

"I'd prefer something stronger," Spiby called after her.

Mother looked back and smiled. "I'm afraid we do not drink spirits in this house, Mr. Spiby. You'll have to settle for coffee, tea, or milk."

He glared at her. "Very well. I'll have coffee."

Lizzy was already ushering Ella to the far side of the room. There were two chairs by the door to the music room. If things got uncomfortable, Lizzy could take Ella out that way. Since the music room adjoined the library, which led to the hall, they could escape if need be.

Ella was trembling when Lizzy let go of her. She felt sorry for the younger woman. Ella's fear of these men was evident. Men like Mr. Fleming and Spiby counted on intimidation to get their way, and Lizzy wasn't about to stand for them trying that here. She saw Wes take up a spot by the hallway entrance. He crossed his arms and leaned back against the doorjamb, all while watching Spiby and Fleming. Lizzy found herself wishing she'd confided in him regarding Ella. What in the world must he think?

"I'm not sure what this is all about, Ella, but your mother has been sick of heart since you ran away. She took to her bed and has hardly been up since you disappeared. I thought perhaps you had gone to your sister in Chicago, but our investigation soon proved otherwise." Mr. Fleming turned to eye Uncle Oliver. "I sent a man to ask if you were with the Brookstone group, but he was told you weren't."

"In all honesty, Uncle Oliver didn't know," Lizzy announced. "I snuck Ella onboard and hid her. He knew nothing of her being with us until days later."

"I should have known." Ella's father looked at Lizzy in disgust. "You are a most willful young woman."

"Which is better than being one who cowers and lives in fear," Lizzy countered.

Ella said nothing and kept her gaze on her folded hands.

Mr. Fleming made a dismissive noise and continued. "Ella, as I told Mr. Brookstone, we've come to take you home. I've spent a small fortune hiring a Pinkerton man to find you, and now that I have you safely in my care, we must return home. We appreciate the hospitality he and Mrs. Brookstone have given you, but you've a wedding to plan. The date has been rescheduled for April."

Ella's head snapped up. "I'm not in your care, and I won't marry Jefferson Spiby."

Jefferson gave her a hard, cold look but remained silent. Ella's father, however, wasn't about to do the same.

"You *will* marry him. We made that arrangement long ago, and you knew your obligation to him."

"I won't." Ella looked from her father to Jefferson. "I will not marry. Those were your arrangements, not mine." She focused on her father and crossed her arms. "I'm twenty-one now, and you cannot force me to marry or return home with you."

Her father seemed to have forgotten this fact. He looked momentarily confused. Lizzy wondered if it were possible he hadn't realized Ella had come of age. Surely he knew the date of his own daughter's birthday.

Mother returned with Irma close behind. The older woman carried a tray with coffee and cups. Mother had a platter of cookies. "I hope you will enjoy these," Mother said, putting the cookies on the table between Jefferson and George Fleming's chairs. "Irma just pulled them from the oven. They're oatmeal. They will hold you over until lunch. I do hope you'll join us for the meal."

Lizzy admired her mother's grace and gentility. She was no happier to see these two men in her house than Lizzy was, but Mother maintained a polite, welcoming spirit.

"As we told you, Mrs. Brookstone, we are only here to retrieve Ella, and then we must be on our way."

"I'm not going anywhere with either of you." Ella was quickly growing bolder.

"Ella, I am deeply wounded. What did I do to cause you to run away?" her father asked.

Lizzy wondered if her friend would be truthful in this gathering. No one but Lizzy and Mary knew about Ella overhearing Jefferson Spiby's confession.

Mary. Where was she? What would happen if she heard that these men had come?

A log in the hearth shifted, startling Ella. She bit her lip and looked at Lizzy, eyes wide. Lizzy patted her arm and decided to jump into the conversation.

"Ella wants to perform in our show. She's going to trick ride with me. She's very good."

Spiby chuckled. "So she ran away to join the circus. How amusing."

"Not amusing at all," Mr. Fleming declared. "I wondered at your . . . manner of dress." He paused momentarily, as if considering all that had been said. "Ella, this is ridiculous. No daughter of mine is going to be a common performer. Furthermore—"

"I'm sorry, Father, but that is exactly what I am going to do."

He looked at Ella as if she were a stranger. "This is outrageous. I demand you refuse her, Mr. Brookstone." Mr. Fleming looked at Uncle Oliver. "If not, I will discontinue doing business with you and ruin your show."

"I'm not a man to be threatened, Fleming." Uncle Oliver crossed his arms. "Especially in my own home."

"And I'm not a man to be refused," Fleming countered. "Especially where my own daughter is concerned."

Silence fell over the room, and with it, the tension increased. Lizzy didn't figure either side would resort to violence, but she knew that Mr. Fleming and Mr. Spiby hadn't anticipated anyone taking a stand against them.

Then, as she had feared, Mary appeared in the doorway. Lizzy had no idea how she'd found out about the men's arrival, but she could very nearly read Mary's thoughts. She kept her expression void of emotion, but her eyes seemed to burn. When her gaze met Lizzy's, it was clear that she wanted nothing more than to use the guns strapped at her side.

"Ah, Mary," Mother said, smiling. "Mary is our sharpshooter."

The men barely nodded in acknowledgment before returning their attention to Ella. Lizzy wondered if her friend would be able to hold her temper. Mary knew these men were responsible for the death of her brother. If they had killed Lizzy's father, she knew she wouldn't find it easy to do and say nothing.

Finally, after what seemed an eternity, Ella spoke. "I wonder if I might speak privately with my father."

Lizzy knew what she intended to do. It was Ella's one chance to be rid of her father and Mr. Spiby. No doubt Ella figured that if she threatened to tell what she knew, then perhaps they would be willing to leave her alone. That was how Lizzy would have played it.

"I would be happy to speak with you, Ella." Her father's expression looked hopeful.

"Come with me to the dining room. It won't take us but a moment."

Ella left the gathering without so much as a backward glance. She was terrified of her father and Jefferson but knew she would have to face at least one of them. Her father seemed the lesser of two evils. Jefferson was a killer, after all. She could only hope and pray that wasn't also true of her father.

Once in the dining room, Ella pulled the pocket doors closed and went to the far side of the room. Her father followed.

"Why are you doing this, Ella? You know your responsibilities."

She put the table between herself and Father. Her voice was barely a whisper. "I know what you and Jefferson did." She decided the direct approach was best. "I know Jefferson killed August Reichert."

Her father paled. "You know no such thing."

"I overheard you two discussing it." She gripped the back of the chair. "I know that August saw something you didn't want him to see. I know that you felt he had to be dealt with, and I heard Jefferson confess to murdering him. I also heard Jefferson say that he has killed before. I'm prepared to go to the authorities."

Her father considered this for a moment. Then, as Ella had feared, he shrugged off the entire matter. "You know as well as I do that no one is going to come against me or Jefferson. No one is going to believe you—an ungrateful child, a frightened bride-to-be. You have no proof."

"You don't know that."

"I do." Her father's confidence had returned. "No one back home is going to lift a finger against either one of us, so you'd do well to get your things and come back with us now. I'm willing to overlook all of this, and once you're married, I'm sure Jefferson will as well."

"Jefferson has never overlooked nor forgiven any infringement against him, Father. You know that as well as I do. Would you truly turn me over to that man, knowing what he is capable of doing?"

"Rumors—all rumors. He would never hurt you. He loves you and will give you everything your heart desires." Her father pulled out a handkerchief and dabbed his forehead. "Now, get your things."

Ella eyed him suspiciously. "Why are you so determined for me to marry him? You know he is evil, even if you won't admit it to me. Do you really want to give your child to a murderer?"

"Jefferson will never harm you, Ella. We have an agreement between us."

"What agreement?"

Father pocketed his handkerchief. "It's none of your concern.

It's enough for you to know that a contract was arranged, and your marriage to Jefferson is part of it."

"It's your contract, not mine. I will not marry him."

"If you can get him to release you from it, then I'll have no more to say on it. However, I'm fairly confident Jefferson will never let you go. He loves you, Ella."

"Jefferson Spiby doesn't know how to love." Ella skirted the table. Once she reached the doors, she pushed them back and turned to her father. "It's best we join the others so I can make it clear once and for all where I stand."

"Be careful what you say, Ella. Words once spoken can never be taken back."

Ella marched across the hall and entered the living room. She pointed a finger at Jefferson, who had jumped to his feet. "I am not marrying you. I know exactly what you are and"—she paused, glancing at Mary—"what you've done." She returned her gaze to Jefferson, and from the look in his eyes, Ella knew he understood. "I will never marry you." The other men had also risen, and she looked at them. "I do not wish to cause you any problem with the show, so if you prefer that I leave, I will. However, I would very much like to continue with you."

"I'm happy to have you stay on, Ella." Oliver Brookstone looked at Jefferson and then her father. "I won't turn you out. They may threaten as they wish."

"You'll be sorry you took a stand against us," Ella's father said, moving to Jefferson's side. "I am no longer asking, Ella. I'm prepared to take you by force if necessary."

"I think it might be best if you two returned to town," Mrs. Brookstone interjected. "There's a lovely hotel there, and I believe you will be quite comfortable. That will give everyone some time to think. You could return tomorrow and join us for lunch—if you're prepared to act in a civilized manner."

Father began sputtering. "After I offered you the hospitality of my home, you would send me to a hotel in that poor excuse for a town?"

Mrs. Brookstone nodded. "I'm sorry, Mr. Fleming, but our house is full to overflowing. Not only that, but our party posed no threat to you or your family when we stayed with you. You're threatening to remove one of my guests by force."

Ella watched as her father assessed the situation. She prayed he wouldn't resort to violence. It had never occurred to her until that moment that Jefferson probably carried a gun. Would he dare to threaten this family? She was about to yield to her father's demands when he spoke up.

"Very well. We will retire to a hotel for the evening and re-turn again tomorrow at noon." He fixed Ella with a hard look. "You will return with us. No matter what you think you can do or say—I will not allow you to remain behind." He looked at Jefferson. "Let's go."

Jefferson looked as if he might refuse, but then to Ella's surprise, he nodded and threw Mrs. Brookstone a broad grin. "I look forward to joining you for dinner tomorrow."

She gave a gracious smile. "I hope we all enjoy a more ami-able time."

Lizzy all but held her breath until the two men exited the house. She wondered if her mother might later send a note taking back the invitation to lunch. She never wanted to see those men again. They were clearly evil.

"Oliver! Are you all right?"

Her mother's urgent voice seized Lizzy's attention. Her uncle had paled and sunk onto a chair, clutching his chest. Lizzy froze. It was just like Father.

Wes and Mother were at his side. Mary quickly joined them and began loosening her uncle's tie. "What is it, Oliver?" Mother asked.

"I think that was a bit more than I was up to," he replied. "I suppose I'm not entirely recovered from my trip."

Lizzy was taken back in time to when her father had his heart attack. He had been sitting and talking, doing nothing strenuous, when he'd grabbed his chest. She would never forget the look of fear in his eyes. It was the same look as in Uncle Oliver's.

"Wes, can you get him upstairs to bed?" Mother asked.

"Sure thing."

"I can walk." Uncle Oliver got to his feet, but his legs gave out, and Wes lifted him in his arms.

"It's all right, Oliver. I'll carry you. That way if it's something more, you won't be exerting yourself."

"Mary, tell Irma I need her. Lizzy, go find Phillip. Have him go to town and get the doctor. Tell him to say nothing to Mr. Fleming, however. I don't want them knowing how their visit affected Oliver."

Mary hurried off, but Lizzy stood frozen in place. She could barely breathe.

"Lizzy!" Mother's raised voice broke through her daze. "Go send Phillip for the doctor!"

Lizzy nodded as she forced her feet to move. Half stumbling forward, she fought to get ahold of her emotions. She searched the pens and then the barns for Wes's younger brother and finally found him working with one of the saddles in the tack room. She felt close to hysterics.

"Phillip! You need—you have to go right now. We need a doctor."

He stepped toward her. "What's happened?"

"Uncle Oliver." She found it difficult to make sense of what she wanted to say. "Oh, Phillip, go to Miles City and get the doctor. My uncle may be dying."

Phillip started for the pen to get his horse, but Lizzy stopped him.

"Wait!"

He turned, and Lizzy rushed to his side.

"Mr. Fleming and Mr. Spiby were just here. They upset Uncle Oliver, and Mother said to say nothing to them if you should cross paths. She doesn't want them to know their effect on my uncle. Just get the doctor without making a scene and say nothing to them."

"Sure thing, Miss Lizzy."

After he'd gone, Lizzy felt her chest tighten as her thoughts ran wild. What would happen to them if Uncle Oliver died? It would mean the end of the show and perhaps even the ranch. What would she and Mother do then?

Tear came to her eyes as she fell to her knees. *God, why is this happening? Isn't it enough that we lost Father? Must we lose Uncle Oliver too? Must we lose everything?*

She wasn't able to hold back the rush of anguish. How could God take all the best they had and leave them with nothing? Father had been everything to her and Mother. She could still see him lying on his deathbed. His face was pasty, almost color-less. She remembered lifting his hand to her cheek. The tips of his fingers were bluish gray, as were his lips. He was dying. She knew that but couldn't bring herself to accept it.

There on the barn floor, Lizzy buried her face in her hands and wept. Nothing would ever be the same without him. It hurt so much to know he was gone and she was all alone.

You aren't alone, Lizzy.

The words echoed in her heart, and she knew the truth of them. She had Mother and Uncle Oliver, but they would die too. They would die and leave her with no one. Then there was Wes. She had loved him for so long and wanted noth-ing but his love in return. But now that he offered it—now that happiness was within her grasp—Lizzy was terrified. He would die too.

276

Mother had said, *"I would bear this pain and even more. Your father's love was worth the price."*

Lizzy thought of the love she'd shared with her father. He had comforted her when she was afraid, encouraged her when she was sure she couldn't go on. Father had taught her so much about life and love. Wasn't this pain worth the love they'd shared? Lizzy wasn't sure she could answer that question. It hurt so much to be without him.

She felt strong arms wrap around her and pull her close. She knew without even looking that it was Wes. The thought of his death, of having to say good-bye to him, only made her cry all the more.

"It's all right, Lizzy."

Why couldn't he understand? It wasn't going to be all right. It was all wrong. Life was just one painful experience after another, and she wanted no more of it. How could she bear even one more loss?

"Go," she sobbed. "Just go."

Wes tightened his hold. "Sweetheart, you cry all you want. I'm not going anywhere. I'm never going to leave you."

His words were whispers of comfort, but they were also lies. Lizzy pulled away, but Wes refused to let her go. She was blinded by her tears, but she could see the love in his expression.

"Yes, you will," she said, struggling to break free. "Everybody leaves. Everybody dies. You'll die too, and I can't bear the thought. I'd rather be dead myself than lose anybody else . . . especially you."

TWENTY-THREE

Mary did what she could to help Mrs. Brookstone, but all the while she wanted nothing more than to ride after Fleming and Spiby and shoot them both. She burned in anger. It wasn't right that they should go about their business while her brother lay cold in the ground.

"Stop fussing," Oliver Brookstone demanded of his sister-in-law. "I'm just fine."

"You haven't been 'just fine' since Mark died," Mrs. Brookstone said in blunt honesty. "You have carried the burden of grief and responsibility like the weight of the world, and now it's catching up with you."

Oliver's face reddened as he struggled to sit up in the bed. "Nonsense. Just let me get my breath, and I'll be fit as a fiddle."

Mrs. Brookstone glanced at Mary. "Take off his boots."

"You don't need to do that," he protested.

Mary didn't listen to him. She removed his boots and set them by the bed. She had no idea what was wrong with Mr. Brookstone. Lizzy said he had started drinking again during the show tour and that he had once been quite the drinker. It was clear that he wasn't under the influence of spirits at the moment, but that might have been the problem. Mary had heard that folks who drank a lot got liver-sick when they went without a drink for a while. Grandma said it had something to do with the liver expecting a certain amount of alcohol—needing it, so to speak. Mary thought about suggesting a drink but decided against it. The Brookstones weren't ones to keep liquor in the house or even on the property, and if Oliver Brookstone was hiding some, he wasn't going to say.

"Mary, please ask Irma to come back up here. Then you go about your business. I know you have to practice for the show."

"I'm happy to stay if you need me." She glanced at Oliver Brookstone and smiled. "I'm rather fond of Mr. Brookstone and would do anything to assure his quick recovery."

"Nonsense. I'm fine. I just let Fleming get me worked up. I can't abide a man who thinks he can push around little gals like Ella and not have to answer for it. I don't care if he is her father. Given what Ella has told us and what we saw with our own eyes . . ." He fell silent, leaned back against the pillow, and let out a breath. "I can't abide cruelty."

Mary nodded, knowing their cruelty had also gotten her brother killed.

Mrs. Brookstone patted his arm. "You're clearly exhausted. I knew you shouldn't have taken that trip. We're both getting too old for this kind of life." She glanced at Mary. "Go ahead, dear. I'll be just fine."

Mary left and found Irma ironing in the kitchen. "Mrs. Brookstone asked that you come help her again."

"Happy to." Irma put the iron back on the stove. "Did she ask me to bring anything?"

"No. Just to come."

Irma nodded. "Well, I'll take a little coffee and some cookies just in case. Could be Oliver just needs something to eat."

Mary grabbed her coat and headed outside. For a moment she stared down the long drive from the ranch. It would take hours for Ella's father and Jefferson Spiby to drive back to Miles City. She could get her horse and cut across the land. She had taken several rides with Lizzy and on her own. Mary figured she knew the lay of the land well enough to ambush the men responsible for her brother's death. The temptation to confront them and learn why they had killed her brother was strong.

The air had warmed the night before, and most of the snow had melted. Despite the cold temperatures, Mary knew it would be difficult to slog her way across some of the open range. She knew too that killing two men in cold blood wasn't the right thing to do. She wasn't even sure she could pull the trigger with a man in her sights, even if that man was her brother's killer. No, as much as she wanted them to pay for what they had done, she knew it was better to go about it legally.

Mary stuffed her hands in her coat pockets and turned toward the arena. She and Alice were supposed to be practicing their horseback shooting act. She glanced at the cloudy skies overhead. "I promise, August, I will get justice for you."

Ella was in the arena when Mary came through the door. She was sitting alone, and there was no sign of Alice.

"Are you all right?" Mary asked.

"No. I doubt I'll ever be all right again. I can't abide that my father and Jefferson Spiby will get away with murder."

"You don't know that," Mary said, sitting beside Ella.

"But I do. I told my father that I know what happened."

Mary took Ella's hands and turned her. "What did he say?" She studied Ella's face for any clue.

"He said what I knew he'd say. No one will believe me, and he has friends enough to make sure nothing ever happens to cause him problems."

"And Mr. Spiby?"

Ella shook her head. "Something intricately connects the two of them. So much that my father would force me to marry a man known for his cruelty and abuse. Not only that, but Father knows him to be capable of murder, yet he would give his daughter away to such a man."

"I am sorry, Ella." Mary sighed. "I considered riding after them."

"To kill them?"

Mary was surprised by Ella's matter-of-fact manner. "Yes." She barely whispered the word. She wasn't proud of her desire to see them dead. After all, bad or good, they were human beings, and life was sacred. If she killed them, she'd be no better than they were.

"I'm sorry. I'm so sorry I brought anyone else into this."

Mary put her arm around Ella's shoulder. "You didn't. They did this. They brought it on themselves when they decided to kill my brother. Whether you had come here or not, I would have eventually ended up there to question them about what happened. I might have ended up dead as well."

"I just don't know what to do. My father has threatened to ruin the show if I stay, yet I cannot return. I won't give myself to Jefferson. I would rather die." Tears slipped down Ella's cheeks. "Maybe that's the answer."

"No!" Mary hugged her close. "No more death. I want justice for my brother, but not at the price of your life."

Ella pulled away and looked at Mary. Her face was contorted in grief. "Then what are we going to do?"

Mary shook her head as she got to her feet. "I don't know. I suppose we must pray even more about it than we have. God won't be mocked, Ella. He knows the truth of what happened, even if no one else does. Surely He will show us what must be done."

"I won't leave you, Lizzy." Wes wanted nothing more than to bring her peace of mind and heart. "I promise."

"You can't." She jumped up from the barn floor. "You can't make promises like that. One day we will all die. You. Me. You can't promise to never leave."

"All right." He stood, at a loss as to what he could say. Only one thing came to mind. "But you know that death isn't the end of things."

Lizzy began to pace. "I know that. I know Father is with Jesus, just as the thief on the cross is. But it doesn't help. If Uncle Oliver dies, Mother and I will be alone to face overwhelming circumstances. If Mother dies . . ."

"You won't be alone." Wes took hold of her. "So long as I have breath in my body, you will neither one be alone. And even if I die, you'll still have God. Have you forgotten that, Lizzy?"

He walked her over to a bale of hay and made her sit. Lizzy didn't protest, much to his relief.

"Look, I have a few things I need to say to you. First, I have to beg your forgiveness for how I've acted the last couple of years. I was wrong to put a wall between us. I was wrong to blame you for what happened to Clarissa." He pushed back his dark hair. "I felt guilty when Clarissa accused me of being in love with you. Not at first, because I didn't see it that way. I cared about you very much, but I cared about your entire family. I came to this ranch when I was just eighteen. I'd left my mother and father and brother, hoping to make my own way. I wanted to prove myself. Your family was more than gracious and took me in like a son."

"Father always said you *were* a son to him," Lizzy murmured.

"I know. He told me that as well. I loved him, Lizzy. He was like a second father to me, especially after mine died. I'll never forget how he helped me get past my grief. He told me just what I've been saying to you."

She looked up. "He did?"

Wesley nodded. "He said that death, while hard on the ones

left behind, was nothing but joy for the man or woman who loved God. He told me we should learn to put aside our grief and rejoice for the one who'd gone home."

"I know." Lizzy sighed. "But it hurts so much. It's like a burden on my shoulders pressing me down."

Wes knelt beside her. "I know. It weighs on me too. But maybe it wouldn't be quite so heavy if we bore it together."

She touched his cheek, much to his surprise. "I never thought about how much Father's death would hurt you. It was selfish of me only to think of my pain. I'm sorry."

He pressed his hand over hers. "I know you are, just as I'm sorry for how much you're hurting. Just don't let that pain cause you to wall yourself away from everyone. I can tell you from experience, it doesn't take away the pain."

He stood and drew Lizzy up with him, then looked for several long moments into her brown eyes. Why had it been so hard to see how much she meant to him—how much he loved her? "Lizzy, I—"

"Hello? Lizzy? Are you out here?"

Wes let go of her at the sound of Ella calling Lizzy's name.

"I'm here." Lizzy held Wesley's gaze a moment longer. "Thank you for talking with me. For your kindness."

She squared her shoulders and headed to the front of the barn. Wes could hear her speaking with Ella, but not enough to know what was being said. He wanted to run after Lizzy and declare his love—force her to admit hers for him. But for all his desire, Wes felt there was a better time and place. Right now, she needed to come to terms with her fears, and he felt that such a declaration would only interfere with God's plan.

Not only that, but he still had unfinished business.

Later that afternoon, after hearing that Oliver was suffering nothing more than exhaustion, Wes rode out to the little family cemetery. The Brookstone cemetery sat atop a rolling rise that overlooked the river. Wes had helped Mark and Oliver Brookstone bury their parents here. Together they had put a fence around an area twenty feet by twenty feet, and prayed they wouldn't have to bury anyone else there for a long, long time.

He remembered how Mrs. Brookstone had fought against all the elements Montana had to offer to grow a small collection of pines to stand vigil over the graves. He'd helped her water the trees and protect them from animals and the wind. There was little Wes had ever seen Rebecca Brookstone attempt without success, and this was no exception. The small seedlings she had planted the summer after losing her father-in-law were now sturdy, mature trees. They bore up under the drought and snows much as the family had over the years.

Wes dismounted his horse and made his way to Clarissa's grave at the far side of the fenced area. Due to the shelter of the trees, there was still some snow here and there, and her headstone was covered. With his gloved hand, he wiped the snow aside and read the inscription.

Clarissa DeShazer
1872–1898
Beloved Wife and Daughter

He stood back and took off his hat. "But you were neither, and for that I am sorry."

He stared at the stone for a long time. He knew Clarissa wasn't there—just her earthly body—but still he felt the need to speak to her, and this seemed like the only reasonable place.

"We never lied to each other about why we married," he began. "We both knew it was wasn't a love match, although I cared about you and I think you cared about me." He looked out across the cemetery to the river. "I thought I could keep you safe—protect you. I thought I could save you from the world and all those folks who would hurt you, and instead I ended up hurting you myself.

"It helps to know that you understood it was never intentional, Rissa, but it's burdened me nevertheless. I never meant to wrong you. I honestly never thought of Lizzy as a potential wife—at least not then. I cared about her and wanted to keep her safe, and I know I talked a lot about her and what she was doing. I didn't figure I was committing adultery, but maybe after a fashion, that's what it was. Either way, I let her come between us. I cared a great deal about her—loved her—but not the way you thought I did. But now I do."

He turned the black Stetson in his hands and shrugged. "I guess I wanted to tell you that I'm sorry. I'm sorry I didn't put everything in God's hands rather than do what I thought best. I learned a painful lesson about trying to take God's place. I'm sorry too that I could never give you the love you deserved. I know, though, that you finally have it. I know, given you put your trust in God before you died, that you finally know the only love that truly lasts forever. Just the same, I hope you forgive me."

Wes felt a peace settle over him. He could finally lay Clarissa to rest.

Gazing at the heavens, he continued. "Lord, I ask You to forgive me too. I was such a fool. Young and ignorant. I tried to take Your place. I thought that I could make things right and fix the problems Clarissa had. I thought I could do that with Phillip too. I've made a poor savior, Lord.

"From now on, I just want to put everything in Your hands. I'm asking You to make me a better man. Help me hear Your voice and heed Your directions rather than take my own counsel."

He thought of what had transpired earlier in the day with Lizzy. "Help her, Lord. She's hurting, and I know I can't make that better. I want to. I truly do, but I know she needs to come to You with it and not me. I love her, Lord. I don't know why it took me so long to see it or to understand that she's the only woman I want to spend my life with, but now that You've helped me realize it, I'm praying You'll help me be the man Lizzy needs. I'm praying You'll make me a man after Your own heart so that I always put You first and seek Your direction for my life."

Wes glanced one last time at the headstone. He'd done what he'd come to do and felt assurance deep in his soul that he could put the past behind him now and focus on the future. Whatever that future might hold.

ᐳ⟨⟩⊨ TWENTY-FOUR ⊨⟨⟩⊰

A strong wind had blown most of the night, and that, coupled with the memory of all Wes and her mother had said, kept Lizzy from sleeping. At one point she sat up in bed and drew her knees to her chest. At times like these, she knew there was nothing to do but pray.

"Lord, I'm so afraid." She hugged her arms around her legs. "Wes cares for me just as I've so often prayed he would. I love him, but I can't bear the thought of him dying. I know death isn't the end. I know Father is there with You now, so why can't I let go of this pain—this fear?"

Rocking in bed, Lizzy tried to remember all the Bible verses she'd ever memorized, but nothing came to mind. It was as if in putting up her wall of protection, she'd pushed out the Holy Spirit along with everything else. For a moment, she panicked. Had God left her alone because of her hard heart?

She fumbled for the matches on her nightstand. Finally she found them and lit the lamp. The glow did little to comfort her. She pulled open the nightstand drawer and retrieved her Bible. Just having it in hand helped soothe her spirit. It was only then that she realized she hadn't read it in a long time. A very long time. In fact, she hadn't read it since her father died.

"Oh, God, I'm so sorry." Tears trickled down her cheeks. "I didn't know. I didn't see. I was so lost in my pain that I pushed You away with everyone else." She began to sob and cradled the Bible against her chest.

After a few minutes, there was a light tapping at her door. When the door opened, Lizzy saw her mother's worried face.

"Lizzy, are you all right?"

"No. No, I'm not." Lizzy cried all the harder.

Mother sat beside her. She pulled Lizzy close as she had done when Lizzy was a child. "There, there, my darling. Tell me what's wrong."

"I'm what's wrong." Lizzy buried her face against her mother's neck.

"What are you talking about?"

Lizzy's voice was ragged. "I pushed God away. I didn't want any more pain, so I was determined not to love. I didn't realize that's what I was doing, but it was."

Mother nodded. "I know."

"Can He forgive me? Will He come back?"

"Oh, Lizzy." She brushed back Lizzy's dampened hair. "He never left you. He's just been waiting for you."

"Are you sure?"

"Of course. God promised He would never leave us nor forsake us. Even when we walk away, God is still there. But if you don't believe me—talk to Him. I promise He's listening. He's right here with us now."

Lizzy knew that her mother spoke the truth. She could feel it in her heart. For the first time in a long time, she could feel God's presence.

"Forgive me," she whispered, bowing her head. "Forgive me for pushing You away."

The peace that had been missing for so many months washed over her in warm waves. Lizzy felt herself relax in her mother's arms. For a long while she stayed in that loving hold, knowing that nothing in the world could hurt her.

After a time, Mother lifted Lizzy's face. She looked quite serious.

"What is it?" Lizzy asked.

"I hope you realize that your comfort just now is from the Lord, not me."

It was as if she'd read Lizzy's mind. "But it's your arms around me."

"And His around us both. Lizzy, I love you so dearly. You are my child—my only child. I could not have been happier with a dozen children. But I'm only human, and one day I will go home to be with God. I don't want to worry that you'll fall apart and leave your faith behind."

"I can't imagine life without you." Lizzy shook her head. "I couldn't imagine it without Father either." She thought of all her mother had said and began to see the truth. "I suppose God gives us people at different times to teach us and help us."

"To love us too," Mother added. "It's not good to be alone—at least not for long. God knows exactly the right person to send along on our journey. Whether it's parents when we are young or friends . . . or a mate. But it's God Himself who is our mainstay, our comfort, our hope. People do what they can, but they will leave or die . . . just as I will one day. It doesn't mean we can't cherish them while they're here, but we mustn't depend on them for our hope. That comes from God alone."

It seemed so simple, yet it had taken Lizzy such a long time to see the truth. "I understand, Mother. I do. I see it now. I put my trust in my earthly father rather than my heavenly Father."

"People make poor saviors." Mother smiled. "I had to learn the truth of that myself. I think God has been working to teach us both the same truth. He is enough, Lizzy. No matter who else walks in or out of our lives. God will fill the empty places in our hearts, but we must allow Him access. He never forces us to receive Him."

When Lizzy woke hours later, she found her Bible still cradled in her arms. Mother had gone, but the covers were neatly tucked around Lizzy, reminding her of when she was a child. She waited for the pang of loneliness and sadness to come, and when it didn't, she smiled. God had filled the empty place left by her father's death. God had taken His rightful place in her heart.

A million thoughts went through her mind as she made her way downstairs for breakfast. She felt freer than she had in months, but there were still a lot of problems. What would happen with Ella's father and former fiancé? What kind of trouble could Fleming and Spiby cause for the Brookstone show? And then there was Wes. What in the world was she supposed to do about him?

"Are you just now going down?" Ella asked.

Lizzy turned to see Ella following her down the stairs. She had dark circles under her eyes. "Yes. And you?"

"I couldn't sleep at all for fear of what Father and Jefferson have planned. I just wanted to pull up the covers and hide in my bed." Ella reached Lizzy's side. "What am I going to do? Do you suppose they'll come back today like they said?"

"All we can do is take it moment by moment. I honestly believe, however, that God has already taken care of all this. He will show us what to do and say. I feel sure of it."

Ella paused on the step. "You sound different today. Did something happen?"

Lizzy nodded. "I realized how foolish I was acting. I was trying to hold God and everyone else away from me so that I could avoid getting hurt. Mother helped me see that and some other things. I can tell you more after breakfast, but I honestly feel as though I've come back to life."

They reached the bottom step and heard voices in the dining room. Ella grabbed Lizzy's arm. "They're back. They're here."

"Your father and Mr. Spiby?" Lizzy asked in a whisper.

Ella's expression answered for her. She looked terrified. Lizzy held her back from going into the dining room. She waited to hear what her mother would say.

"Gentlemen, you are very welcome to sit and partake of breakfast with the rest of us. My brother-in-law, however, will not be joining us. He's been under the weather since traveling to Chicago, and I made him promise he'd remain in bed today."

"That's not a problem, Mrs. Brookstone." Lizzy knew that voice but couldn't quite place it. It wasn't either Mr. Fleming or Mr. Spiby. "We wouldn't want to inconvenience you."

"I assure you, Sheriff, there's plenty for everyone," Mother replied. "Please have a seat. We all eat together. I can make introductions to the show's performers in a moment when Lizzy and Ella join us."

Ella grew paler. "They brought the sheriff here?"

Lizzy leaned close. "Apparently, but that's a good thing. With the sheriff here, they won't cause any trouble."

Ella's expression was still panicked. She shook her head and backed away. "I don't want to face them."

"I know, but I hardly see how we can avoid it. Come on." Lizzy took Ella's hand and led her into the dining room.

"Ah, there they are," Mother said, smiling. To Lizzy's surprise, she wasn't wearing her black mourning clothes. Instead she wore a simple brown skirt and white blouse. Apparently God had worked in her heart as well.

"Sorry we're late, Mother," Lizzy said. She released Ella and went to her mother's side. "You look lovely this morning." She kissed Mother's cheek, then glanced at the three men who stood at the end of the table. "Good morning, Sheriff. Mr. Fleming. Mr. Spiby."

The men gave her a nod of greeting, but none spoke. Ella avoided them altogether and took the chair between Mary and Alice. The other performers lined the far side of the table, looking as uncomfortable as Lizzy felt.

Lizzy helped her mother into a chair. "I'm hungry enough to eat a bear." She claimed her seat as Wes walked into the room.

He glanced at the trio of men standing at the end of the table. "Morning, Sheriff. Gentlemen." He looked at Lizzy and her mother. "Sorry I'm late."

"You're fine, Wes. Lizzy and Ella just got here themselves," Mother declared. She looked again at the trio. "Gentlemen, I must ask you to either join us for breakfast or wait in the front room until we've concluded here."

The sheriff smiled. "I'm no fool. I know better than to pass up a good meal." He took a seat beside Wesley.

Fleming and Spiby exchanged glances, then took the empty chairs at the end of the table.

Mother gave a nod. "Wes, would you offer thanks?"

Everyone bowed their heads. Lizzy wondered if Ella's father and fiancé would have the decency to at least pretend to pray. She couldn't resist raising her head just enough to spy on them. Spiby sat rigidly, observing the occupants of the table while Wes said grace. Lizzy's gaze met his. Spiby smirked like he'd caught her stealing eggs from the henhouse. There was something so dark, so evil in his nature, that Lizzy could feel it. His expression left her cold.

"Amen," most everyone murmured.

Lizzy turned to her mother. She kept her voice low. "I see we have uninvited guests." There was enough noise going on with the passing of food that she felt certain no one could overhear her.

"Yes, they showed up just as we were coming to the table. I think they're figuring to use the law to get their way." Mother handed her a platter of biscuits. "Although with Ella being of age, I'm not sure what they hope to do."

"You won't turn her out, will you?"

Mother shook her head. "Of course not. She can stay, whether she works in the show or remains here with me."

Lizzy kissed her mother again, then took two biscuits and passed the platter to her right. "Thank you. And thank you for last night. I am truly renewed."

"As am I," Mother said, nodding. "I think your father is probably smiling in heaven to see us moving forward and putting our sadness behind us."

The conversation around the table mostly lent itself to the upcoming tour. Jason Adler didn't show up until they were nearly done. He explained that he'd had breakfast with Uncle Oliver in his room.

"I need to go over some of the show's details with the crew as soon as they conclude their meal. I'll wait in the living room." He left as quickly as he'd appeared.

"What's that all about?" Lizzy asked her mother.

"I believe Jason and Oliver made some changes to the way the acts will be presented. At least, that's what they were discussing this morning when I took your uncle a tray."

Little by little, the ladies excused themselves to seek out Jason. When only Lizzy, Mother, Wes, and Ella remained, Ella's father pushed back from the table.

"I don't wish to seem ungrateful for the lovely meal, but I would like to be on my way back to town."

"Of course," Mother replied. "Feel free to go whenever you choose."

Ella's father frowned. "That isn't the point. I've come for my daughter, as you well know."

"Yes, I do realize your purpose here," Mother said. "However, I also know that the young lady has reached her majority. If she chooses to remain here with us, I am perfectly content with that decision." She looked at Ella and smiled.

"She will return home with us," Mr. Fleming insisted. "I brought the sheriff so there wouldn't be any trouble."

Mother looked at the sheriff. "You know us well enough to know there won't be trouble. I'm sorry you came all this way. Mr. Fleming and Mr. Spiby were here yesterday, as they might have mentioned. Their daughter told them then that she intended to remain here to perform with the show."

The sheriff looked at Mr. Fleming. "You led me to believe your daughter wasn't of age."

"She's not qualified to make decisions, whether she's of age or not. She is rather simple-minded, and I am trying to protect her."

"From what?" Lizzy couldn't help interjecting.

Mother put her hand on Lizzy's arm. "It's best that you let them work this out. Why don't you and Wes meet with the others? I'll stay here with Ella."

Lizzy didn't want to go, and she was certain Ella didn't want her to leave. Still, she didn't want to dishonor her mother by arguing. She put her napkin on the table. "Very well."

The minute she stepped outside the dining room, however, Lizzy stopped. Wes nearly ran into her.

"What are you doing?" he asked.

She put her finger to her lips and pulled him away from the door. To her surprise, however, Wes all but dragged her into the living room, where Jason was talking about how Mary and Alice's act would play out.

"I think the timing will be better in the long run," Jason declared. He smiled at Wes and Lizzy as they entered the room. "Ah, Mr. DeShazer. I was hoping you might speak to the group about how you and your men will handle the animals and equipment."

Lizzy moved to where Mary sat by the music room door.

She waited until Wes had begun talking to nudge Mary. When several of the girls started asking questions of Wes and Jason, Lizzy pulled Mary into the adjoining room.

"I want to hear what Ella's father and the others are saying. I figure you want to know as well."

Mary nodded.

Lizzy led her through the music room into the library. From there, they slipped out of the library via the hall door and made their way to the kitchen's rear entrance. Lizzy spied Irma and put a finger to her lips as she and Mary snuck over to the dining room door. It was open only a fraction, but it was enough to hear what they were saying.

"I'm sorry you made the trip all the way out here, Sheriff. I can vouch for Miss Fleming's sound mind. She is not at all feeble nor incapable of reason. I believe her father has only suggested this because he plans for Ella to be married to his business partner."

"Is that true, Fleming? Is this the only reason you came here?"

"She's my daughter, and I demand she return with us."

"She's twenty-one," the sheriff replied. "Mrs. Brookstone, I'm sorry for inconveniencing your day."

"It wasn't an inconvenience at all. It was good to see you again."

Lizzy and Mary exchanged a glance. Would that put an end to it?

"I wonder if I might speak privately for a moment with my fiancée?" Jefferson Spiby asked. "Perhaps we could take a walk?"

"I have no desire to speak with you, Jefferson." Ella's voice sounded stronger than earlier. Perhaps she felt confident, given Mother's support.

Lizzy opened the door just a little wider to hear better. She knew from where everyone had been sitting earlier that the only person who might notice her was Ella.

"I'm not asking for much, my dear. I'd simply like to speak to you. If you are still determined to remain here after that, I won't protest."

Ella glanced up and caught sight of Lizzy. She bit her lip as she seemed to contemplate something. Lizzy wondered what she was thinking.

"Very well," Ella finally said. "I will take a short walk with you, but keep in mind that it is rather cold outside." She looked again at Lizzy, then got to her feet. The sound of other chairs moving left no doubt that the men were getting to their feet. "If it's too cold," Ella said, meeting Lizzy's gaze, "I can show you where I train."

Lizzy pulled back. "Get our coats. We're going to follow her. I don't want Ella to be alone with that madman for even a moment."

Mary nodded and quickly left the kitchen. Irma looked at Lizzy with concern. "What are you planning now?"

"It's nothing to worry about. If anyone comes looking for us, however, I'd appreciate you not mentioning that we were here."

"I won't lie, Lizzy."

"Nor would I ask you to." Mary returned with their work coats, and Lizzy quickly slipped into hers. "Just don't volunteer anything."

Irma smiled. "I suppose I can do that much."

Lizzy and Mary slipped out the back door.

"It is rather cold out, my dear. Is there someplace we might speak privately without subjecting ourselves to this bitter chill?" Jefferson asked Ella.

She nodded. She'd seen Lizzy watching her from the kitchen door and prayed that her friend was even now continuing her vigil. "As I mentioned, we can step into the arena where I train."

"Honestly, my darling, I don't know why you would do such a thing. It's hardly the calling of a proper young woman."

"Perhaps I'm not proper."

Ella opened the arena door rather than allow Jefferson to do so. She stepped inside, grateful that large windows on either end allowed for decent light. Some of the girls had been training earlier and had lit the large lanterns that further brightened the arena. Ella walked out to the center, knowing that if Lizzy had made it to the equipment room to hide, she'd be able to see what was going on.

"Say what you wish to say, Jefferson, and let's be done with it."

He looked at her thoughtfully. "You've certainly grown bold."

She shrugged. "Let's just say I've learned my value."

"You hardly dress as if you know it. Look at you."

Ella glanced down at her outfit. Today she'd donned a dark navy split skirt that had been banded at the knee like her other performance skirts. On top she wore a loose yellow calico blouse, and over this a canvas coat Lizzy had found for her. Her boots and gloves completed the outfit.

"I see nothing wrong with the way I'm dressed." She looked back up.

Jefferson scowled. "It's most inappropriate for a young lady. Especially one who is to be my wife."

"Jefferson, I'm going to be training with Lizzy in a few minutes, so it's quite appropriate that I dress in this manner. If I were attending a formal ball, then it might be different. Furthermore, I am not going to marry you."

He stepped toward her, and Ella backed up a few steps and put out her hands. "Stay right there. I won't be manhandled by you."

"You're wrong there, Ella. On both accounts. You will marry me, and I will handle you as I please."

She shook her head. "I have only to scream, and half the

hands on this ranch will come to my rescue. Heed my warning, Jefferson."

He stopped advancing and cocked his head. "You need to learn your place. Your father has let you have your way long enough. Call for your ranch hands if you must, but I will not allow them to come between me and the arrangement I have with your father."

"Your arrangement with Father is just that. Your arrangement. Not mine." Ella could see she was only making Jefferson angrier, but she didn't care. Movement behind him gave her confidence that she wasn't alone. She saw Lizzy and Mary only momentarily, but it was enough to bolster her courage.

Unfortunately, after taking her eyes off Jefferson, she didn't realize he had closed the space between them. He grabbed her throat and held her fast.

"Go ahead and scream for your friends. By the time they get here, I will have snapped this scrawny neck of yours."

"I see. Well, you did say that killing August Reichert wouldn't be your last time."

Jefferson's eyes turned dark and his expression cold. "So you know what I'm capable of."

"Yes, but not why. You killed the Brookstone wrangler because he'd seen too much. But what exactly did he see? Did he witness you kill someone else? Goodness, how many people have you killed?"

"That's none of your concern. What's important is that I will add you to the number if you continue this nonsense."

Ella looked into his eyes, unafraid. "Then kill me. I would rather be dead than married to you."

⊰≡ TWENTY-FIVE ≡⊱

Lizzy felt an icy chill run up her spine at Ella's declaration. It had been ominous enough to hear Jefferson Spiby admit to killing August and others, but to see him threatening Ella with death was too much. Mary moved beside her, as silent as the grave. Lizzy turned to see what she was doing and nearly gasped at the sight of her friend taking aim with her pistol.

She reached out to Mary and shook her head, but Mary merely moved Lizzy's hand away. The look in her eyes was determined. She intended to kill Spiby.

Lizzy put her lips against Mary's ear. "You can't do this. We've heard him admit what he did. Now we can bear witness to the sheriff."

Mary shook her head. "He deserves to die." Her words were barely audible, but Jefferson Spiby's rang through the arena. Both Lizzy and Mary returned their attention to the scene in the arena.

"I won't kill you . . . just yet. But if you don't do as I command, you'll wish you were dead." Ella said nothing, and he continued. "We will marry this afternoon in Miles City before boarding the train. That way you will never get the chance to do anything like this again."

Ella tried to pull away from his hold, but it only angered him more. "You think your friends here can keep you from danger, but I promise I'll make them suffer. I'll make each of them suffer for your defiance."

"They've . . . done . . . nothing wrong." Ella was barely able to speak.

"I don't care." He lowered his voice, making it hard for Lizzy to hear what he was saying. "I will hurt them. I will kill them."

Ella tried again to break free, but Jefferson held her fast.

"I thought you'd rather be dead," he said.

Ella gasped for air and tried to pull Jefferson's hands away from her neck. Lizzy looked at Mary. If she was going to kill him, why didn't she? At least now she had a good reason. If she didn't shoot him, he would kill Ella.

Mary stared straight ahead. Lizzy thought she looked frozen. "Mary?" she whispered. "Mary?"

Lizzy looked again toward Ella fighting for her life. She got to her feet. "Stop!" she yelled.

Jefferson didn't even seem to hear her.

Lizzy looked down at Mary. "Do something."

Mary pulled the trigger. The sound echoed in the arena, and Jefferson let out a roar. He held his arm as he scanned the room to see who was responsible. Rage marred his face.

Ella stumbled away from him. She coughed and sputtered, but at least she was alive.

"Don't move, or I'll shoot you again," Mary declared from her perch.

"You'll pay for this." Jefferson growled in pain. "You will pay for this."

The arena doors flew open, and Wesley and the sheriff rushed in. They stopped at the sight of Jefferson holding his arm, writhing in pain.

"What's going on here? We heard a shot," the sheriff said, looking around the arena.

Lizzy stepped out of the shadows. "He tried to kill Ella. He admitted to killing August Reichert."

Wesley closed the distance between them with incredible speed and took hold of Lizzy. "Are you all right?"

She saw the worry in his expression. "I'm just fine."

"Sheriff, I demand you take that woman into your custody. She tried to kill me," Jefferson declared as the sheriff approached.

This brought Mary out of hiding. She walked toward Jefferson with her pistol still at the ready. "She didn't shoot you. I did. I could have killed you. God knows I wanted to, given you admitted to murdering my brother."

Jefferson looked at the sheriff. "She's mad. I admitted no such thing."

Lizzy stepped away from Wes. "He did so. He threatened to kill my family and friends here if Ella didn't do exactly as he wanted." She looked at Jefferson, who seemed almost confused. "We can both bear witness to what he said, Sheriff."

Ella joined them, still rubbing her neck. "He tried to strangle me."

Jefferson seemed to gather his wits. "They're making this up. They're trying to keep Ella from returning with us." He pulled back his hand to reveal the blood on his arm. "I'm the injured one."

The sheriff looked at Ella and then back to Jefferson. "It looks like we'd better get you some help. I suggest we go back to the house."

He took hold of Jefferson but looked at Mary. "You can put that away. He's going nowhere for the moment."

Mary lowered her gun. "All right, but I'll be right behind you." She looked at Ella. "I won't let him hurt you again."

The two girls followed the sheriff and Spiby from the arena, leaving Lizzy and Wes alone. Wes watched her with grave concern.

"I'm fine, Wes. Stop looking at me like I'm going to die."

"I thought maybe you had."

She pulled his face down to hers and kissed him on the lips. He didn't have time to react before she stepped away with a grin. "See? I couldn't be better. Come on, we need to follow them. I heard and saw it all, including Jefferson Spiby confessing to killing August."

Wes followed her back to the house, but she knew he had to be confused about everything that had just happened. Especially the kiss. She felt bad that she hadn't explained anything to him.

There was utter chaos in the living room when Lizzy and Wes entered the house. The sheriff was trying to calm everyone down. Thankfully, the other performers and Jason had gone.

"Take a seat, folks. We may be here awhile," the sheriff said, pushing Spiby onto a wooden chair.

Everyone with the exception of Ella's father sat. Mr. Fleming, however, was indignant and paced back and forth. "What in the world is going on? Who shot this man?"

"I did," Mary admitted. "Because he was about to kill your daughter."

"Bah! I don't believe it. Jefferson would never harm a hair on her head." He looked at Ella. "Tell the truth."

"He tried to strangle me," Ella said, her voice hoarse.

"I did no such thing." Jefferson vehemently denied the accusation while writhing in pain. "You and your friends lured me to that place in order to kill me."

The sheriff looked at Mary. "Why were you there?"

"To protect Ella."

"That's right, Sheriff," Lizzy interjected. "I was listening when you were all talking in the dining room. I knew Ella was terrified of Mr. Spiby and her father and wanted to keep an eye on her."

"This is madness," Ella's father declared. "She isn't terrified of me or of Jefferson. She's merely been listening to the bad counsel of this woman and her family."

"That's uncalled for, Fleming," Wes said. He put his hands on Lizzy's shoulders. "This family has done nothing wrong. They're good, godly folks who took in your daughter when she ran away."

"I suggest that Elizabeth Brookstone encouraged her to run away."

"I did," Lizzy admitted. "Not only that, but I would again."

"See there!" Fleming yelled, pointing his finger. "She admits it."

Mother came into the room with Irma on her heels. Irma held a tray of bandages and other medicinal articles. Mother went to Jefferson and helped him out of his coat. She then ripped open the already torn sleeve to get a better look.

Everyone stopped talking for a moment, almost mesmerized by her ministering. When the wound was clean, Mother smiled. "It's nothing more than a graze. Hardly even that. We'll bandage it up, and you'll be fine. Probably won't even notice it in a day or two."

"I'll notice it plenty, and it'll be a wonder if I don't get blood poisoning. I need a drink," Jefferson grumbled.

"I can't accommodate you there, Mr. Spiby. I have no alcohol on the property. We don't allow it."

Jefferson swore at her, much to everyone's dismay. Mother said nothing, however, and instead reached for a bottle and poured a generous amount onto the wound.

Jefferson came up out of his seat, cursing all the more. "Are you trying to kill me?"

Mother pushed him back into his chair. Wes left Lizzy's side and stood behind Jefferson. He put his hands on the angry man's shoulders. "I'll help you stay still," Wes said sarcastically.

"This is my own special concoction, Mr. Spiby," Mother said. "It will help ensure you don't get blood poisoning."

This seemed to calm everyone down again, and the sheriff looked to Ella. "You say this man and your father were responsible for killing a man in Kentucky. Did you see them kill him?"

"No. I heard them talking about it as if they'd done nothing more than kill a rabbit."

The sheriff looked at Ella's father. "What about it, Mr. Fleming? What happened to the Brookstone wrangler?"

"He was trampled by a horse. Nothing more. The county sheriff was there, as well as the local doctor. If he was murdered, the authorities would never have said it was an accident."

"Yes, they would have," Ella countered. "Because you own them. They're all so obligated to you and afraid of you that they wouldn't dare have said otherwise."

This seemed to silence the older man. He finally took a seat, shaking his head. "I have given you everything, and this is how you repay me."

Jefferson balled his right fist and pounded it on his knee. "I'm telling you, it's this place and these people. They're all a bunch of hooligans."

The sheriff shook his head. "Mister, I've known these folks for most of my life. I can't say the same about you or your friend." He looked at George Fleming. "As far as I can see, you have no rights where this young lady is concerned."

"Well, I have rights," Jefferson declared. "I have the right to file charges against that woman." He pointed at Mary.

Ella stepped forward. "You do that, and I'll press charges against you for this." She opened the neck of her blouse to reveal the bruises that were already starting to show.

Jefferson clenched his jaw. The sheriff looked at him, as did everyone else in the room. "Very well," he muttered. "Let the devil have them both."

"He can't, Mr. Spiby," Mother said as she finished with his arm. "The Lord already has them, and the Good Book says He

306

won't let them be plucked from His hand. Seems to me you might want to seek Him out as well. Maybe then you wouldn't be so inclined to anger."

Jefferson pushed away from Wes and got to his feet. He grabbed his coat. "I've had enough of this place, George. Let's go."

The sheriff put out his hand. "Not so fast. There's still this matter of murder back in Kentucky. I think you and Mr. Fleming better accompany me back to Miles City. I need to hear from the officials in Kentucky as to whether you're wanted."

"This is madness!" George Fleming got to his feet. "Pure madness. We are highly regarded in our state. You have no right to hold this man."

Lizzy went to Ella. She clasped the girl's hand and gave it a squeeze. With any luck at all, they'd soon be rid of these men and get justice for Mary's brother.

"I am willing to testify to what I've heard Mr. Spiby say," Ella said, causing everyone to turn to her. "And Father, if you have any decency left in you, you'll bear witness as well."

Her father shook his head. "You don't know what you're saying. You stupid little fool. You'll be sorry for this."

Lizzy pulled Ella close. "You're hardly in a position to threaten her."

"I'll never forgive you if you go through with this nonsense, Ella." Her father's eyes narrowed. "You'll never be welcomed back. You'll be forever estranged from your family."

Mother stepped forward. "She'll always have a home with us. I'm happy to have her here with me or with the show. Whatever she chooses."

"You're all fools," Fleming sneered. "You'll be sorry for this." He looked around the room. "I'll destroy you and your show!"

"Mr. Fleming, you do what you feel you must, but I will tell you this much. We have long lived under the protection of God Almighty. Your threats are no concern to me." Mother looked at the sheriff. "Now, I will take you up on the offer to escort them away from here." Her gaze went from the sheriff to Spiby and then settled on Fleming. "Gentlemen—and I use that term with great hesitation—you are no longer welcome on Brookstone property."

———◆※◆———

After the sheriff left with Fleming and Spiby, Wes wanted nothing more than to be alone with Lizzy. She'd kissed him, and in that moment, he'd known something had changed. But there'd been Spiby's injury and Ella's accusations to deal with. Then, just as he thought they'd have a moment to themselves, his brother had shown up, announcing problems that needed his attention. What in the world were they all going to do if he went on the road with the show?

By the time he was free to seek Lizzy, she was busy training in the arena. He thought of what Rebecca Brookstone had said about not trying to change her daughter. Wes had prayed a great deal about this matter and knew she was right. Lizzy was nearly ready to give up the show on her own. What Wes needed to do was give her a reason to leave trick riding. He smiled to himself. She had kissed him, so she must love him. He just had to persuade her that she loved him more than performing.

In the arena, all the trick riders were gathered to go through their acts from beginning to end. Lizzy was critiquing and instructing from the sidelines as Ella, Debbie, and Jessie went through their Roman riding and acrobatics.

"That's good. Really good," Lizzy called to them. "You've got that looking smoother than ever."

Wes watched as Jessie stood atop a team of horses. She held them in a steady line while Debbie and Ella did a variety of maneuvers. It was funny how he didn't feel at all nervous watching them, yet their tricks were just as dangerous.

The ladies finished their act and came to where Lizzy stood. "I think you've got a winner. The more motion, the more the audience will perceive danger and thrills." Lizzy grinned. "It's all about making the ladies faint and the men cheer for more."

"It does look good," Wes offered.

Lizzy turned and met his gaze. "I didn't know you were here."

"I came to see you."

"I'm glad you did." She looked back at the trio of riders. "Go on with your practice. I'm going to speak with Wesley." She pulled on her coat and motioned him toward the door. "Shall we?"

He followed her outside. The skies were filling with clouds. Cookie had told him that morning to expect snow because his lumbago was acting up. In Montana, it could snow most any time of year, but you could be guaranteed of its arrival if Cookie said as much.

They walked a ways down the long drive before Wes worked up the nerve to stop Lizzy. He turned her and looked into her eyes for a long moment.

"I love you." There. He'd said the words, and now the chips could fall where they would.

She grinned. "I've waited nearly a lifetime to hear you say that."

"You're only twenty-eight, so it hasn't been that long."

Lizzy laughed. "You were just telling me the other day how twenty-eight was ancient."

"I said no such thing." He could see the change in her. "You're different. Something's happened to you."

She nodded. "Yes. It has. You might say I had a 'come to Jesus' moment." She shrugged. "I've been wrapped up in fear ever since Father died. I couldn't bear the thought of losing one more person, so I tried to close myself off to everyone . . . including God, although I didn't realize it at the time."

"What happened to change that?"

"Everything. You. Mother. I suppose even Ella and her troubles all moved me to see that I couldn't stop loving people just because of my fears. Then last night I was truly at a crossroads. I couldn't bear it anymore. I realized I hadn't even picked up my Bible in months . . . not since my father's death."

Wesley nodded. "I know how that can be. With me it was shame and guilt that made me want to hide from God. Just like Adam in the Garden of Eden."

"We've both come through a great deal, and I'm ashamed to say that I didn't perform very well."

He chuckled. "If we're being rated on performance, then we're both in trouble."

"Thankfully, God doesn't do business that way."

He shoved his cold hands in his pockets. "So what happens now?" She still hadn't declared her love for him, and Wes felt a little concerned. In her new understanding of heart, was there room for him?

She stepped closer. "It's cold out here. You do realize there are much warmer places to be."

He drew out his hands and wrapped his arms around her. "Like here in my arms?"

Lizzy nodded. "For one. Wes, when you are near, I feel whole. Complete. The way Father made my mother feel. When he died, I was heartbroken, but it was nothing compared to what my mother was going through. I didn't want to love you if it meant hurting so badly. Then Mother talked to me. She said she wouldn't trade what she had with my father for anything. She said the pain was unimportant compared to the love they'd shared, and I started to see that she was right. I want your love, no matter the pain."

"No doubt there will be some." He reached down to cup her chin. "But I know that with God, there is nothing we can't face."

"I agree." She gazed into his eyes. "I love you, Wesley. I've loved you since I was ten years old, and it amazes me how that love has changed and grown and become what it is today."

"And what's that?" he asked, almost afraid to know the answer.

"Ours." Her voice was filled with tenderness. "It's not just mine or yours. It's ours."

"I like the sound of that," he said, lowering his mouth to hers. "I like it lot."

Sign Up for Tracie's Newsletter!

Keep up to date with Tracie's news on book releases and events by signing up for her email list at traciepeterson.com.

Also from Tracie Peterson

In the early 1900s, Camri Coulter's search for her missing brother, Caleb, leads her deep into the political corruption of San Francisco—and into the acquaintance of Irishman Patrick Murdock, whom her brother helped clear of murder charges. As the two try to find Caleb, the stakes rise and threats loom. Will Patrick be able to protect Camri from danger?

In Places Hidden
GOLDEN GATE SECRETS #1

 BETHANYHOUSE

Killing
RUBY
ROSE

JESSIE HUMPHRIES

SKYSCAPE

SKYSCAPE

Published by Skyscape, New York

www.apub.com

Amazon, the Amazon logo, and Skyscape are trademarks of Amazon.com, Inc., or its affiliates.

ISBN-13: 9781477820063
ISBN-10: 147782006X
EISBN: 9781477870068

Book design by Krista Vossen

Library of Congress Cataloging-in-Publication Data available upon request.

Printed in the United States of America

To Nanny, who would have loved this the most.

Truths and roses have thorns about them.
—Henry David Thoreau

CHAPTER 1

I hid in the shadows, scanning the dark parking lot to assess the threat level. So far I'd identified three potential informants I'd have to evade when making a break for it. I didn't need my 4.0 GPA to know that being seen leaving the city library at 9:00 on a Friday night wouldn't win me any points on the SPA (Social Point Average), on which I was definitely flunking. Avoiding detection was key.

Maintaining position under the library's dark awning, I took a quick breath of briny ocean air to gain my bearings. The parking lot's sickly yellow lights flickered behind the suffocating fog, making it hard to tell whether the rain was misting down from above or wafting in sideways from the shore. In any case, the blacktop lay slick, full of potholes, and speckled with math-club kids who would have just loved to report a sighting of Reclusive Ruby Rose.

With a practiced stealth, I dashed through the night. Even in my new Prada peep-toe pumps—aka my Penelopes—I had speed. I moved light-footed through the blind spots, like I was navigating one of my dad's SWAT obstacle courses, until I found cover in the driver's seat of Big Black, my overly tinted SUV and current best friend. I gripped the steering wheel. "Ready to do this?" I asked Black, ignoring my therapist's voice in my head telling me to stop personifying the *things* in my life and start concentrating on the *people*. She didn't understand. *Things* couldn't break my heart.

Big Black's tires spun out, fighting for traction against the wet asphalt. No more denominators, dusty textbooks, or depressing thoughts. Instead, my mind changed gears to the last subject of study for the night. A study I'd so far kept strictly to myself. One that required night-vision binoculars, a police scanner, and my .38 Smith & Wesson handgun—all carefully hidden beneath the false bottom of the driver's console.

Rebel energy flowed through my veins as I allowed myself to imagine tonight being the night I caught my mark—Mr. Charlie LeMarq—in the act. I had thirty minutes until he got off work and headed to his favorite dive. A creature of habit, he hadn't deviated from his Friday-night routine for five weeks. And neither had I, as I'd waited for the evidence that would finally put the violent predator away for good.

I hit the Pacific Coast Highway with momentum, grateful for a break in the rain. With the windows cracked and the stereo up, the whipping wind and heavy beat refreshed my senses. Something about the brewing storm beyond the ocean's black-and-blue horizon spoke to me. It was a foreboding that simultaneously quickened my heart rate and eased the ever-present heartache.

I enjoyed the moment—until my phone vibrated against said heart like a minidefibrillator shocking me back to reality. The sad reality of a *semi*normal seventeen-year-old girl and not the sleek sleuth I pretended to be. (Only *semi* because *totally* normal girls don't wear four-inch Prada heels to the library, or stalk criminals, or wear four-inch Prada heels while stalking criminals.)

Pulling my cell out of my cleavage, I found the screen lit up with my best friend's face—my real-life, living-and-breathing best friend, Alana. Though breathing as a determining factor in a best friend seemed slightly overrated.

I had a choice to make. The red "Decline" button versus the green "Answer" button. Red: Avoid the call now, and keep declining all night because Alana Kailua (aka the only un-laid-back Hawaiian in SoCal) would never stop. Green: Put up my dukes to defend myself and be forced into lies. So, basically—lose-lose.

"Hello, caller, you're on the air," I spoke into my Denali's Bluetooth speaker system. I was nothing if not a law-abiding citizen who'd taken "The Pledge to Put It Down," the promise to "put down" handheld phones while driving. District Attorney Jane Rose (aka my absentee mother) had come up with that catchy slogan for her latest campaign.

"Girl, where are you?" Alana banshee-shrieked, forcing me to make an unsafe jerk of the wheel to turn down the volume.

"I'm driving home," I said, fully aware she wouldn't believe me. She knew I hated going home to an empty house.

"It's nine p.m. On a Fri—day!" she groaned. Our high school's fight song played so fervently in the background that victory could be the only cause. Other than the abuse of energy drinks. "I know you're not going home, so just get your antisocial A-S-S over here right now. There's gonna be a killer after-party, and you're coming!"

Sparring match commenced. Lately, every conversation with Alana felt like a brawl at the dojo. Like, even though I'd put away my black belt months ago, I couldn't stop fighting.

"I'm tired, Alana." *Lateral defense move.*

Checking my rearview mirror, I caught Huntington Beach High School's stadium lights fading away. Year-ago me would have been there at the game with Alana—giggling, cavorting, and playing along. *That* girl (with the 4.0 SPA) had long since faded from view. "I'll catch you tomorrow. We'll go to the beach or something." *Submissive bow out.*

"Ruby, I know you miss your dad, but your self-imposed solitary confinement isn't helping. *He* wouldn't want this." *Provoking palm-heel strike to the heart.*

"Please don't pretend to know what he'd want." *Double-handed hooking block, protecting the weak spot.*

"It's been over six months since he died," Alana said with worn-out delicacy. "It's time to snap out of zombie mode."

"I didn't lose a puppy, Alana," I said. *I lost the most important person in my life*, I didn't say, as I tried to suppress the billowing emptiness I felt inside. "I need more time."

"Yeah, so you say." *Elbow to the mouth.*

"I don't know *what* you want me to say." *Bleeding.*

"Say you'll take off your loner trench coat and come have some fun. It will be good for you."

"Not tonight, OK?" I begged, feeling the familiar anchor of guilt tugging at me, heavier every time I blew her off. "I promise we'll go to the beach or the mall tomorrow. Whatever you want."

"You know, Ruby, I should start calling you Rubik's Cube, because no matter how hard I try, I can never figure out what I'm supposed to do with you," Alana said. "And it's such a shame, because despite the fact that you've gone from being the slightly intimidating Brainiac Barbie to the totally antisocial Hermit Barbie—there are still several dudes I know who'd be willing to offer their shoulders to cry on . . . or their laps to sit on . . . or their lips to—"

"Alana!" I interrupted. "I'm sorry, but my life doesn't revolve around boys and parties like yours does, OK?"

Her long pause meant I'd pissed her off (more than I wanted to), and I drove past the street where I'd wanted to turn. My blood boiled as I realized my stupid mistake. I *rarely* made mistakes. And I *never* lost sparring matches, physical or verbal. I had the karate and debate trophies to prove it.

"Well, I promised I wouldn't say anything, but if I can't lure you out of your hole by myself . . . I have no choice." Alana must've moved into the girls' bathroom for privacy, because most of the background noise had vanished. "Your boy has something planned tonight." *Side stance, luring wave to come closer.*

"What are you talking about?" *Careful approach.* "I don't have a boy."

"Liam Slater, *Rubik's Cube.* Don't play stupid with me. I know better. I gave him your number last week, and I'm pretty sure he's going to text you tonight. And in case you feel like blowing him off, too, just know . . . he's going to ask you to Homecoming." *Roundhouse kick to the temple.*

Click.

She hung up on me.

I pulled Big Black into an empty beach parking lot along Bonfire Row, my ears still ringing from both the imagined blows and the real news.

Could I believe it? Mr. Elusive, Mr. Preseason Favorite for Most Beautiful Eyes of the Senior Class, Mr. Too Cool for School was going to ask me, Miss Too School for Cool, to be his Senior Homecoming date?

Surely not. Alana had to be messing with me. Liam and I had barely spoken about anything other than equations or our Advanced Calculus teacher's "sexy comb-over." I didn't even have Liam's cell number. Sure, I'd been crushing on the guy for almost two years. And yes, the boy had impeccable taste in shoes. But since my dad died, I hadn't been in the mood for flirting. Or anything else that required the pretense of happiness.

Plus, I thought he was going to ask Taylor Jennings, the cheer-leader not-so-secretly voted Nicest Rack. She'd been hanging her aforementioned lady parts all over him a lot lately. It wasn't enough that she was my sole competitor for the valedictorian race—she also had to compete with me for everything else, including the only boy I not-so-secretly liked.

I hoped he was smart enough to withstand her and her consid-erable ass-ets. He seemed smart. He was on last year's honor roll. But, then again, he'd probably paid for his grades with touchdowns and devilish grins. Not that I hadn't benefited from the way his smile could light up the room. These days, the thought of Liam's eyes on mine was sometimes the only thing that brought me back to school at all.

My phone vibrated again, but this time it was a text from an unknown number:

Hey Ruby :) It's Liam. Could you meet me at 366 Water Street as soon as you can? There's something I want to ask you.

He was texting me already?

Flourishes of goose bumps scuttled up my arms. Part of me felt ecstatic, thinking about the possibility of more than his eyes being on me tonight. Maybe his hands, maybe his lips—

But then little red flags began flying across my over-analytical brain. Actually, they were more like red flares lighting up the night sky in my mind.

Red flare: The mere thought of Homecoming! I'd have preferred for Liam to just ask me out to dinner without the rented tuxes, slutty sequin dresses, and group-sex parties. I didn't *believe* in high school dances. Beyond all the forced awkwardness of pinning corsages and posing for cheesy pictures—and never mind all those pesky statistics about higher rates of drunk driving and sexual assault—the whole idea of high school dances gave me anxiety.

Then again, how long had I been dreaming about spending any amount of time with Liam Slater? He could've asked me to go swimming with the sharks, and I'd have considered it.

Red flare: Water Street. Such a strange location. The old shipping harbor was hardly romantic. I hadn't pegged Liam as one of those guys who asked girls out in an overly dramatic way. Just today in English class my eyes had almost rolled right out of my head when Alana told me about a boy asking out a girl by having her name and the word "Homecoming" written in the sky. Gag.

But there was no way Liam would stoop to that level. He was the complete opposite of gaggy.

Red flare: "As soon as you can." The team should still be in the locker room celebrating, showering, and patting each other in inappropriate ways that only athletes are allowed to do. Had Liam already left for Water Street? I hoped he'd at least managed a quick shower, because I never pictured sweat as part of my fantasy make-out sequence with him. Though even that wouldn't be a deal breaker, considering it might mix with the drizzling rain running down our bodies, and we could have one of those epic kisses straight out of *The Notebook* . . .

Red flare: I already had plans—tailing Charlie LeMarq, one of the most prolific child abductors and murderers in my dad's profiles. My own kind of "*killer* after-party."

Sure, I knew that stalking criminals was a bizarre after-school activity for a seventeen-year-old girl. But ever since SWAT Sergeant Jack Rose (aka my fallen father) was killed "in the line of duty," I'd needed an outlet. A way to honor his memory. A challenge to focus all my efforts on. And yoga wasn't doing the trick.

Since the Department wasn't talking, or releasing any information on the "continuing investigation" into his death that seemed more like a "discontinued investigation," I had to do *something* to overcome the gnawing need for justice that never came. Obsessing over catching a predator my dad had hoped to put away had become that *something*. It wouldn't bring Dad back from the dead, but it had brought *me* back from wanting to die. I could no longer afford to be the helpless little girl who cried herself to sleep every night. I had to find a reason to live.

And Sergeant Jack Rose hadn't made me a weapons specialist and combat expert for nothing. For as long as I could remember, he'd trained me to be able to defend myself and protect others. Between sparring lessons and shooting practice, a spooky sound track had played in my head as he went on and on about what a dangerous world we lived in.

Nowhere was safe.

He and my mother had enemies because of their high-profile positions.

I should prepare myself for the day I'd be tested.

Somewhere around age fourteen, I turned off the broken record. The only threat I'd ever faced in my sheltered life was the threat of being suspended from school for fighting. So much for being prepared to defend myself when it was the very thing that got me into trouble! Which was the exact argument Mom always used with Dad after she got home from arbitration meetings with my principals.

But he'd stuck to his guns, or "our" guns, as they actually were, and never stopped training me.

Sometimes I chalked it up to his undiagnosed post-traumatic stress from his time as a Marine, or the violence he saw every day in law enforcement, or simply that I took the place of the son he never had. Whatever the reason, he kept on with my training—and I took to it.

Like a fish to water.

Opening the false bottom of my console, I looked down at the shimmering weapon—aka Smith, my .38 Special Revolver with built-in laser sight that I'd gotten for my Sweet Sixteenth. Gleaming underneath Smith was the accompanying laminated concealed-weapons license that Dad had personally signed for me two weeks before his death. As I ran my finger over his signature, I couldn't help wondering (for the umpteenth time) what he'd think of seeing his little girl and her gun now. Surely, he'd never envisioned his young scholar turning into a vigilante stalker.

Yeah, well, I never saw him being ripped from my life without any answers, either. So, whatever.

I grabbed the manila file labeled "LeMarq" and flipped through the pictures, timelines, and notes, focusing on my target instead of my sorrow. I knew almost everything about the sicko by now.

He liked prepubescent girls. He liked violating them, choking them, and leaving zero forensic evidence behind. Some of his cohorts called him Cherry Charlie, not only because of the string of cherry tattoos he sported on his left forearm, but also because of what each cherry represented: the theft of a young girl's innocence—and, inevitably, her life.

I'd never been able to zoom in close enough to be sure, but I'd counted at least a dozen cherries on his arm. A crop that should have earned him at least a dozen life sentences.

My dad died before he could catch LeMarq, but shortly after, another detective nabbed the creep. My mom was the lead prosecutor. I stared at the newspaper clippings in my hands now, remembering the injustice. His expensive attorney (provided by a rich relative), a procedural technicality (provided by an inept member of my mother's prosecution team), and a hung jury (provided by the great State of California) sent him walking. It was only a matter of time before he killed again, and neither my mom nor the police were likely to stop him. They only had another 113,000 or so registered sex offenders to worry about.

I slammed shut the file, disgusted with his ugly mug, his stupid baby-blue pedophile van with Louisiana plates he still hadn't registered (not even a misdemeanor crime), and the infuriating lack of evidence against him. I knew he'd be skipping jurisdictions again before long. If I didn't catch him soon, he could keep getting away with murder forever—and those little girls would never see him coming.

I shoved the file back into the console and looked out at the beach parking lot. The five-foot replica of Bill Brandon's toothy grin stared back at me. Brandon was my mom's increasingly nasty mud-throwing opponent in the upcoming District Attorney race. His campaign poster was plastered on the side of a parked advertising truck: "A Vote for Me Is a Vote for Change."

"What'dya think, Bill?" I asked. "Should Unruly Ruby change? Should I take a night off from my rogue ways to be wooed by one of the hottest guys in school?"

He just smiled with that charming set of veneers only money could buy.

I looked at the dashboard clock. I still had thirty minutes before LeMarq would get to the bar. Once there, he never left his drinking hole in less than an hour. I had a window of opportunity. I could go play Regular Ruby for a minute, find out if this whole Homecoming thing was happening, and get back to LeMarq before he left the bar. If there was any chance Liam really wanted to ask me, I had to find out.

I blew out a deep breath and plugged the Water Street address into my GPS system. With a stomach full of butterflies that felt more like fully equipped hornets, I let my GPS's Mary Poppins voice guide me toward the terrifying unknown. That's right—I felt more comfortable trailing a known murderer than being asked out on a date.

At least with LeMarq, I had a secure vehicle, a weapon, and a cell phone to use in case I needed to call for help. But if anything went wrong with Liam, I had nothing.

No protection. No backup. I'd be totally vulnerable.

The closer I got to the little destination star on my GPS screen, the more I questioned my decision. Every song that came up on my shuffle seemed to have strange overtones or dark undercurrents—"A White Demon Love Song" by The Killers, "I Will Follow You Into the Dark" by Death Cab for Cutie, and even my man MJ had to pipe in with "Thriller." I finally turned it off.

As I drove farther downtown and into the dark heart of the shipping harbor, I wondered how Liam was going to pull this off. Rose petals and candles hardly seemed dreamy among empty beer cans and broken meth needles. I imagined a trail of Hershey's Kisses leading me through a camp of homeless people until I found a balloon with a note inside reading, "I'd pop if you'd go to Homecoming with me!" Or something equally idiotic.

I really hoped Liam wasn't *that* guy. I wanted to give him the benefit of the doubt—maybe he had something totally non-lame planned. Yet, looking around this neighborhood, all I had were doubts—and an increasingly bad feeling.

"You have reached your destination," said the eerily pleasant Mary Poppins voice.

"If you could see where I am, Mary, you wouldn't be so chipper," I responded in my best British accent, realizing I'd rather sit in the car and have conversations with billboards and GPS systems than real people. My therapist would be so disappointed.

I brought Big Black to a stop outside an industrial-sized warehouse. Building 366's entrance was barely visible through the low-lying harbor fog. Only a few sickly yellow patches of light glowed over the large roll-up garage doors, all of which were closed.

Growing anxiety and a waft of fish-flavored air prompted me to raise the windows. I pushed aside all my instincts to bolt by convincing myself that leaving Liam hanging would not be socially acceptable. Or nice. Which lately wasn't a very strong argument for me, but this was Liam Slater.

So where was he? What if this was some kind of mean joke?

Easing off the brake, I let Big Black roll around to the side of the building. I flipped on the windshield wipers for a quick clean—and rubbed my eyes to do the same.

That's when I saw it.

Beside an open door was the familiar old blue van I'd been following for months.

And it wasn't Liam's.

CHAPTER 2

It took a few stretched-out seconds for me to process the fact that the text wasn't from Liam at all.

My stomach plummeted as I realized who owned that van: Charlie LeMarq. I fumbled to double-check the locks, pressing the lock a few extra times to be sure. My heart thumped in my ears. And my mind reached out for some invisible chain of logic.

Had LeMarq discovered I'd been trailing him? Had he brought me here to teach me a lesson? But how could he have known? And how would he know to fake a text from Liam?

I grabbed my night-vision binos and zoomed in on the threat. Written across the back window's condensation was the dripping question: "You think you can stop me?"

Then a bone-chilling scream from inside the building stabbed me like a dagger—a young girl's desperate call for help. He had a child in that warehouse.

Simultaneous flashes of heat and penetrating coldness warped my senses, debilitating my instincts to move, while images of horrifying scenarios consumed me.

I fought the escalating pins and pricks of panic. I had to act.

I reached into the false bottom of my console again and traded the heavy binos for the lightweight steel of Smith. Curling my fingers around the revolver's grip, I dialed with my other hand.

Almost immediately, I heard, "911, what's your emergency?"

"Send all available units to 366 Water Street. There's been a child abduction . . . and if help doesn't arrive soon . . . a probable homicide." I tried to sound in control.

"OK, 366 Water Street." Pause . . . typing . . . "Help is on the way. Please tell me your name."

"Ruby Rose. Daughter to District Attorney Jane Rose and the former SWAT Sergeant Jack Rose—"

"Sweetie," she cut me off. "Did you say Jack R—?"

"I have to go," I said, pressing "End." She didn't need to call me sweetie. Right now I was anything but *Sweet* Ruby, and I wasn't going to wait for the sirens to tip off Mr. LeMarq so he could slit the girl's throat and escape. I knew his MO: no survivors, no witnesses. Just lifeless little girls with no forensic traces of his filth. I had to get in there. Whoever just screamed had no chance if I didn't at least try.

I exited Big Black and raised Smith securely in front of me with both hands, just like Dad had taught me. My hands trembled, like they knew this wasn't pretend—this wasn't a simulation. I stared at the van and the dark brick building looming behind it, wondering if I was capable of stopping a dangerous man like LeMarq. Especially without my father.

I could almost hear Dad whispering over my shoulder. Telling me to slow my breathing, raise my awareness of every sound and movement surrounding me, and slowly put one foot in front of the other.

You can do this, Rue. You have to.

I did as he said and crept past LeMarq's decrepit van, cursing when I inadvertently stepped in a puddle of muck and felt the nasty water enter Penelope's peep toe.

Another scream escaped out the cracked warehouse door ahead of me. A weaker, more defeated cry. And something swept through me—an inner surge of strength, a shot of adrenaline, a wave of determination. Whatever poetic crap it was, I used it to fight the fear. I wouldn't let her die.

I entered the building and found cover behind the metal skeleton of what used to be a large piece of machinery. Dad wouldn't have fit, but I did easily. He always said my small size was one of my biggest assets.

At the far end of the sprawling space full of old machinery left to rust and rot like robot corpses, the shadow of the grotesque monster stood dark against the wall. The only light in the warehouse emanated from his corner. As I rounded the perimeter, I hushed my Penelopes by moving on the balls of my feet. I tried to hear what he was saying, but he was too far away. Steadying my breath, I checked my watch—it had been approximately ninety seconds since the 911 call. I had another ninety seconds, maybe, before the sirens would be heard. Somehow I had to get close enough to trap LeMarq. I moved through the shadows and around the haphazard machines until I was close enough to his voice to stop and find a vantage point.

I crouched behind a large, dead, steel apparatus. Its wires and electrical board had been ripped out like a medieval disembowelment. I raised my head up enough to catch LeMarq's wicked eyes flicker in the unnatural blue light of a camping lantern he'd set up on a makeshift table. The sight of him caused shots of fear to rip through me. I clenched Smith tighter.

And then I saw the girl. Sitting on the ground, her back against the wall on my right. Tied at the wrists and ankles. I was no more than thirty feet away from her, yet I was miles away from knowing how to save her with LeMarq standing between us.

My heart missed more than one beat when I focused on her face.

She looked—exactly like me! Well, me when I was about ten. We could have been twins. That had to be a coincidence . . . didn't it? *There's no such thing as a coincidence, Rue,* I heard Dad remind me.

"Just wanted to say thanks for the *delivery*," the monster said. But he wasn't talking to the girl. He was on his cell phone. Who was he talking to? "Just beautiful." He stared at her on the floor, admiring his catch.

I looked again—her long blonde hair parted in the middle, her pale-gray eyes, her petite frame. Mini-Ruby was trembling with terror.

"OK, ten-four, brother." He shut the phone and moved toward her.

The girl's eyes were full of fear as she shuddered under his gaze. Reaching into his back pocket, he pulled out a shining blade. She screamed again and tried to push herself further against the cement wall, as if it might give way and save her.

No, only I could save her now. But there was no way for me to position myself between them. As soon as I announced my presence, he'd be able to grab her and use her as a shield. And he'd kill her. What other option did I have, though? He reached out toward her and—

"Stay where you are or I'll shoot," I called as I cut out of the shadows to confront him.

He grabbed the girl.

"Who the hell are you?" he yelled in my direction with an expression I didn't quite understand.

I paused, wondering what drug he was on. *He'd* brought *me* here! I must've looked different with a gun in my hand. Or maybe he didn't expect me to get here so soon.

"I'm the person who's finally going to stop you from killing one more innocent girl," I said calmly. "Now, let her go!"

I raised Smith to a higher sharpshooting position, and turned on the laser sight, aiming the little red light directly at his overgrown unibrow.

He laughed. "You! You think you're gonna stop me?" He slid the blade under the girl's neck. Her eyes exploded with terror, and my soul exploded with rage.

I took two balanced steps forward, fighting my growing anxiety. It was clear he didn't take me seriously—after all, I wasn't much older than the girl he had in his arms. But he was wrong not to. "That's right, LeMarq. I'm going to stop you." I glared at him to make sure he knew I meant it.

"How'd you know my name?" He took two crooked steps backward, dragging the girl with him.

"Don't play games. You know who I am, just as well as I know who you are. You texted me. You wrote the message on your van!"

His face scrunched up like he was trying to manually restart his useless brain.

"Girl, I don't have a clue who the hell you are or what message you think is on my van, but if you want her to live, you'll drop your piece. Now!" He barked like a chained pit bull with more balls than brains.

Was he telling the truth? The surprise in his eyes seemed so genuine. And he didn't seem to have laid any traps. I studied his face for any tells, noting every strained gesture. If he *really* didn't know who I was, then someone else had brought me here. Suddenly, everything felt wrong.

I reanalyzed the situation: The police should arrive any second. He would hear them and drag her out as a shield—then kill her and run. I had no doubt that's how it would go down. This was the time. Dad's voice was loud and clear.

Take the shot, Rue. Find the largest target area and pull the trigger. Save the girl.

LeMarq's legs were well shielded despite the girl's small frame. His left bicep was exposed but wrapped around the girl's chest. The winged demon on his shoulder was practically calling out to be exorcised. But my bullet would pass through the girl's shoulder after his, and dangerously close to her heart.

My only shot was his forehead—the one exposed area that would mean a sure kill. As much as I despised him and wanted him punished, I didn't want to kill him. His life wasn't mine to take. I silently begged him to just leave the girl and run. Yes, there was the risk of leaving evidence behind, sending him to prison for sure this time. But the bigger risk was me pulling the trigger and sending his brains somewhere far worse than prison.

A wicked wind swirled across the space, and dust flew into my eyes. I was about to lower my weapon to shield myself from the grit, but the sound of sirens blared in the distance, pulling me out of my hesitation. It did the same for LeMarq. He pressed the knife into her skin. Blood sprayed. I pulled the trigger.

The deafening gunshot rang out.

Time stopped.

The world changed into a black-and-white movie with a river of red flowing all around me.

A ruby-red river of my own making.

I ran to the girl and carried her a few feet away, applying pressure to her gushing neck, and shielding her from LeMarq's dead body just a few feet away. She'd already been through enough. She didn't need to see that.

We didn't talk. We didn't cry. We searched for meaning in the gauzy haze of shock hanging over us. We waited in each other's eyes, the same gray eyes, communicating without words. She was scared of dying. I was scared I might not have saved her.

I willed her to stay alive.

Soon a swarm of uniforms, white gloves, and disembodied voices cut in and out of my consciousness. Questions were asked, one-sentence answers were given, and the girl was ripped out of my arms and strapped to the stretcher.

And then she was gone.

Even when my mom appeared on the scene, wrapping me in a scratchy police blanket to shield me from the arriving paparazzi and escalating interrogations, the darkness seeped inside.

I was a killer now, and nothing would ever change that. No matter how Dear D. A. Jane Rose played this one, I was guilty.

But of what, I wasn't quite sure.

CHAPTER 3

Alana wasn't much of a bodyguard—or publicist—but, bless her heart, she tried.

"Just keep walking," she said, her arm unnecessarily wrapped through mine, escorting me out of last period. "When Chanel stink-eye over there gets pregnant by her twenty-four-year-old boyfriend, they'll have a new scandal to talk about." Her voice was loud enough for Chanel's beady little eyes to turn to slits of spite. I wished Alana hadn't said that—I didn't need any more enemies.

It had been several weeks since the shooting, but I'd only been back to school for one. While the stares hadn't dissipated much, at least the camera crews had. Thanks to Mother Jane getting an injunction against the media to leave me alone at school, I'd only seen two paparazzi snipers hiding in trees today.

Despite the fact that no charges were brought against me, the jury was still out in my trial by public opinion.

"After I finish cheer practice and you finish your *shopping*, wanna come over?" Alana asked, putting undue emphasis on our code word for my psychotherapy appointments. She was the only person in the world besides my parents who knew about my long-term therapy. Therapy that I may or may not have needed before my dad died or the LeMarq shooting, but that I'd definitely needed since. She added, "We can watch a totally non-creepy, non-killing Halloween movie at my house. Maybe *Scooby-Doo* or something?"

"Sure," I said with my current version of a smile, keeping my head down as we crossed into the parking lot. "But do you mind if we do it at my house?"

"Ruby, it's time to get out of the dungeon." She shook her head. "Your tan is paying the price. You know what I always say: Tan makes fat look good!"

I pulled my head up to give her my *seriously?* look. "First, you're such a racist. White girls like me can't get a brown Hawaiian glow like yours."

"Hey . . ." She pretended to be offended, but instead began checking out her carefully maintained bronze forearm.

"Second, you're a stick."

"Not after that Tic Tac I just ate," she said with a wink. When Alana and I first met nearly a decade ago, she still had some of her "baby fat"—as she liked to call it. But even though she was now thinner than me, she was still self-conscious. It probably didn't help that half of her huge family (in size and number) still called her Baby Fat.

"Third, the breadth of your shallowness never ceases to amaze—"

A whistle that sounded more like a birdcall cut me off. I looked over to a group of guys hanging out on a classic yellow muscle car with ridiculous pinstripes. The guys reminded me of the *Macaws of the Amazon* series I'd been watching late at night on the Discovery Channel during my recent bouts with insomnia.

Display of brightly colored plumage: check.

Loud sounds to attract the female gender: check.

Posturing and puffing out of chests: check.

Then I saw Liam at the back of the flock. His rainforest-blue eyes caught mine, clouding my defenses. I'd been avoiding this moment.

I wanted to look away, I really did. But the way he was looking at me didn't speak of preening or puffing. More like worry—or some other emotion I didn't know how to read. He had to know by now *how* I got duped into going down to the docks in the first place—my ridiculous crush on him. Of course he knew. Everyone knew, thanks to a few corrupt cops and morally bankrupt tabloid reporters.

I felt like a fool.

"Call me later, Alana," I said, already flying toward my hermit's nest, where I could hide my pale feathers stained red at the tips.

"You'd better answer!" she called out after me.

Somewhere along the line I'd gotten the crazy idea that therapists' offices were supposed to be tranquil, with the soothing sounds of bubbling water or something. No such luck.

If I'd had a gun, I would've shot the damn clock for ticking so obnoxiously at me—an impulse that, admittedly, screamed "anger-management issues." But since my anger was directed toward an inanimate object and not a person, it was totally fine.

Or so I told myself.

Plus, my concealed weapons license had been suspended and Smith taken into evidence. I was harmless.

"How are things at home?" Dr. Teresa asked in her I-know-what-you're-thinking-better-than-you-do voice.

"Fine," I said, refusing eye contact. She sat only a few feet away in her oversized love seat, which made her appear intentionally under-sized. She wasn't the only one who could analyze others' choices.

"How's your mother handling the press?" she said. It was a nudge—a pleasant, patient push. I knew this tactic well. She was focusing the attention on someone else to make me more comfortable until I opened up naturally.

And if that didn't work, she'd move on to the crowbar-to-a-nail strategy.

"I'm not sure," I responded, biting at a cuticle that just wouldn't behave. I had tactics, too.

"Ruby," she said, lowering her voice into what I liked to call The Tone (a deeper version of her voice that meant it was time to drop the pretenses), "for me to help, you have to give me more than three-word answers."

I still didn't want to look at her, but I felt myself soften a little. The Tone had that effect on me. I was pretty sure she was part witch. But in a good way. I liked to think of her as my own personal Mother Teresa. At least when she was in one of those super-intuitive saintly kinds of moods where she seemed to be molding my soul like Play-Doh. In some ways, she was more of a mother to me than my own mom—especially during campaign season.

For the last eleven years, she'd been here for me whenever I needed her.

Signs of depression or withdrawal? *Call Dr. T.*

Night terrors and recurring dreams of being locked behind bars? *Dr. T can fix it.*

Fighting at school? *Get Dr. T on the phone, stat!*

Some years were better than others. In fact, in the last few I'd only been checking in with her every six months or so. But after Dad died, we reinstated our weekly Wednesday sessions at three. And since "the incident" with LeMarq, we'd been meeting every Friday, too.

Dr. T was one of the only people in the world who truly knew me—and still liked me.

She used to be my mom's therapist, too, but apparently the D. A. didn't need it (or have time for it) anymore. Jane Rose was now holding herself out as a beacon of mental health and stability, warming everyone with her powerful glow.

"Why don't you tell me what *you* would like to talk about today?" Dr. T uncrossed her legs and sat forward in her seat so only a few uncomfortable feet divided us—another one of her tactics to open me up. Next would be the crowbar.

I tucked my feet under my knees and bought myself a few more inches of personal space on the couch.

We sat in silence for a while. She would be patient—eternally, painfully, patient.

"Why don't I feel bad that LeMarq's dead?" I asked, point-blank.

"Because you did the right thing," she said without hesitation.

"Yeah, but killing is wrong. Morally, ethically, *biblically* wrong." Not that I'd ever read the Bible, but that sounded right. "And even though I hate the fact I had to do it, I sort of . . . don't hate that he's dead." I hung my head, knowing these words would be dangerous spoken outside this room.

"You killed to save a life. Defense of others is not only legally acceptable, but morally, ethically, and *biblically* as well." Her lips spread into a soft smile. "That's precisely why no charges have been filed against you. You *know* all this."

It was true. I *knew* all this because it had been carefully explained to me more times than necessary. And although my mind understood it, my heart and soul didn't seem to be getting the same message.

Part of me couldn't help feel a satisfaction in LeMarq being dead and gone. At least he would never kill again. And yet, nothing seemed to cleanse me from the dirtiness of being the one who'd pulled the trigger. I shouldn't have been forced to kill. I believed in law and order. I was born and raised with the principles of "innocent until proven guilty," and "justice is blind." Seriously, my mom sat me in front of that damn Justice statue every Saturday one summer so she could work while I studied. Turns out, Justice is a scantily clad, blindfolded woman holding a phallic sword and a set of scales— more like a Vegas stripper than an appropriate representation of fairness. And although I'd seen enough to know that our justice system didn't always live up to its ideals, I still believed it was the only and best solution for handling criminals. Who was I to have single-handedly sentenced someone—even someone like LeMarq—to the death penalty?

"The newspapers don't see it that way," I said. "They think the reason no charges have been filed against me is because my mom's the D. A." I looked out the window, wondering how many so-called journalists would love to be privy to this conversation. "It's been nearly two months, and they won't leave me alone."

"Don't pay attention to them," she said. "I keep telling you, don't give them the satisfaction."

"But aren't they right to question what happened? None of this makes any sense." I rubbed my temples, trying to put together a puzzle for which I didn't have all the pieces. "Somebody lured me there. Somebody sent me a text."

She straightened her back and ran her fingers through her dark hair. She always did that when she felt like she was losing control of the conversation. "Have they been able to trace the number that texted you yet? Or find out who LeMarq was on the phone with when you arrived?"

"They haven't said anything if they have."

"I'm sure they will. It's only a matter of time before they complete their investigation and clear you officially," she assured me. As if she was in a position to do so. "We all believe you did the right thing."

"Yeah, well, I don't think Detective Martinez *believes* me." I bit at that damn cuticle as though everything else would be OK if I could just fix my poorly executed manicure.

"Why would you think that?" she asked.

"You should have seen how he grilled me when he asked me to come into the precinct for more questioning. About why I had a gun with a laser sight in the first place, why my dad would give me a concealed weapons license, why I took the kill shot, why I would be so gullible as to respond to a text from an unknown number, why I didn't wait for the police, why I've been in therapy for most of my life . . ."

"Wait. He asked you about therapy?" Her eyebrows drew together, highlighting a few wrinkles her organic oils and yoga meditations hadn't managed to erase.

"Yeah, I'm not even sure how he knew. I guess that's why he's Mr. Big-Shot Detective."

"What did you say his name was?" She reached for her pen and pad of paper.

"Detective Martinez. With a capital *M* for Meathead. Why?" I asked.

"Did you know this detective before the incident?" She answered my question with a question. Why do therapists always do that?

"Yeah, he used to be my dad's partner, like twenty years ago. Before Dad switched over to SWAT," I said, trying to use the lack of personal space to my advantage for once and read the notes on her lap. Detecting the angle, she pulled the notepad up to her chest, removing the distraction. "That's why it sucks that he's the lead investigator. He hated my dad. And I think he hates me."

"Who told you he hated your dad?"

"My mom. She said something about bad blood between them, and I should never talk to him without her present."

Dr. T looked puzzled. "Though I'm sure you'd do well to follow her legal advice, I'm not so sure he would have any reason to hate *you*."

"How about that I killed somebody," I said. "I'm a Vigilante Teen Assassin. At least that's what TMZ called me. They can't get over the accuracy of my shot. They think that because LeMarq humiliated my mom in court, *I* might be the one who set *him* up."

"I told you not to pay attention to that filth—"

"They're very thorough, you know." I cut her off. "They found out my 'abnormally high' IQ results, my 'strange obsession' with combat training under my father's tutelage, my prolonged leave of absence from school after he died, and even my 'isolating behavior' at school since. They even quoted this girl in my class named Taylor, saying, 'She never really did fit in.'"

I shook my head, knowing Taylor's brutally public words were true. Even when I was little, I knew I wasn't like everyone else. Sure, I had the clothes and the shoes and the general skills to win superficial popularity points. But most girls, like Taylor, didn't go around knee-thrusting bullies in the crotch, even if they deserved it. And it probably didn't help when Dad reprimanded me for said crotch-kicking with a poorly concealed smile on his face.

In the last couple years, I'd managed to get involved in stuff like debate and student government, but I'd never managed to be, well, normal.

"And yesterday," I continued, "I saw this picture on the cover of a magazine—white rose petals dripping with blood, falling over an unidentified headstone—and above it in block letters: 'Ruby Rose: Teen Hero Bleeding with Grief Over Her Fallen Father? Or Drenched with Guilt Over Her Dead Victim?'"

Dr. Teresa must have sensed my latent insanity and put the pad and pen down to clear her throat and get my attention back.

"Let's not focus on that right now."

"But they're right!" I shook my head in defiance. "What the hell was I doing there? How did this happen to me?"

I knew exactly how this had happened, though. I'd brought it all on myself. I'd been tracking LeMarq (and a few others like him) for weeks, and *voila*—the consequences had arrived. I knew that what I was doing was dangerous. I just hadn't quite realized how killing a monster like him would make me *feel*.

"We don't know why this happened . . ." She trailed off, seemingly looking for the right words. She was always exact in her language, which made for long pauses. "But I'm sure your mother and the police will figure it out."

I felt the bubbling need to purge myself of my sin. I had to tell someone what I'd done. Someone safe.

"I want to tell you something." I made eye contact for the first time today. A risky move, and one I didn't take lightly. "Doctor-patient confidentiality, OK?" I knew the law.

"Of course." She uncrossed her flared-leg yoga pants and sat forward with anticipation.

"I was sort of stalking Charlie LeMarq," I semiwhispered, just in case there was a bug in the room.

There it was, the truth I'd been holding on to. The key bit of information I refused to give Detective Martinez so he could crucify me. The secret I'd never even told Mom or Alana.

Except Dr. T's eyes weren't lit up anymore. Shouldn't she be relieved at the breakthrough? I'd finally opened up. Granted, I'd done so with a real doozy, but she had to be used to my personality by now.

"Excuse me? *Stalking?*" She tried to sound calm, but her shock reverberated between us.

"I was tailing him. Doing surveillance," I said like it was a reasonable thing to do. "The guy was literally getting away with murder over and over again, and I wanted to catch him doing something so he would finally be put away. I had no intention of killing him. I swear." I held up my hands like that would convince her.

"So the night you confronted him, you were *not* following him?" she asked, suspicion snaking up between us.

"I was going to, but then I got the text that I thought was from Liam." I reached for my phone to prove it to her. Thank heavens the forensic team had let me have my phone back; otherwise, even I could have doubted this all really happened. "See, here's the text—"

"I believe you." She waved away the phone. "I just have to think about this. It should have been shared with me a long time ago."

"I couldn't," I argued. "You would've convinced me to stop following them."

"Excuse me? *Them?*" She angled her head at me as if she hadn't heard right.

"Yeah, I was sort of . . . following five different guys." I braced myself as she took her time absorbing my words. "You told me to find an outlet."

"Ruby," she said with a shake of her head, clearly indicating to me that my argument wouldn't work. "And you promise you're not doing this anymore?"

"Of course not. Please, Dr. T, you can't tell anyone. It would change everything. It would look like I planned to go there and murder him, and that would establish *mens rea*—the definition of criminal intent." I imagined the headline "Teen Sociopath Planned Killing All Along." And then there would be a trial. And sentencing. And those horribly loose-fitting orange jumpsuits with matching rubber shoes that not even Hollywood royalty can pull off—

"Don't worry," she said. "You can trust me, you know that." I believed her.

I waited to feel better now that I'd gotten it off my chest—but I didn't feel better. I rolled my shoulders and neck to see if that would help. Maybe medication *was* the answer.

"You have a bright future, and no one can take that away from you." She looked at me like she wanted to stamp the words across my soul. "No one."

"What about my mom's political opponents?" I could play devil's advocate all day. In fact, I was good at seeing the half-empty side of things. My Ruby Rose–colored glasses were actually quite dark. "Last week, Bill Brandon went on CNN, spouting off about poor gun laws in California. He wants legislators to pass retroactive legislation making it a felony to even own a handgun in California. I'll be a felon. Good-bye, Stanford." I waved adieu to my bright future with the grace of a well-trained beauty queen.

Dr. T got up and stalked toward her desk. "That's not going to happen. They're all just sensationalizing the incident for their own benefit. And that schmuck Brandon is crossing the line by involving you in his campaign against your mother. He knows his retroactive comments are ridiculous, but they give him more media traction. That's all it is. It would never pass."

"*Schmuck*. Is that a clinical term, doctor?" I asked, smiling for the first time today. I liked it when I wasn't the only one in the room with unrestrained resentment.

"I've used worse." She reached into her desk drawer and pulled out a white envelope before returning to her Throne of Discernment. "I was going to wait to give this to you, but it feels like now's the time."

"Is that my one Get Out of Jail Free card I've been asking my mom for?"

"It's a letter." She stroked its smooth face like it was a velveteen rabbit, and placed it next to me. It had no stamp or return address, just my name in bubbly elementary school lettering. "If you feel comfortable, I'd like you to read it aloud."

I had a good idea of what it was. And I wasn't sure I did feel comfortable.

I reached for it slowly, like it could jump away. I broke the envelope's seal and pulled out a piece of paper. A picture fell into my lap.

It was me. My blonde hair, my pale-gray eyes.

No, it wasn't me. It looked like my fifth-grade picture, but with a bandage on my neck.

It was the girl. The one I'd held at the warehouse. The one who'd clung to me as I tried to save her life. I'd been wondering how she was doing for weeks now.

A row of goose bumps raised across my neck.

"A therapist I know gave me the envelope to deliver to you," said Dr. T. "Can you read the note?"

I took another good look at the picture before unfolding the accompanying paper.

Dear Ruby,

Thank you for saving my life. No matter what anyone says, you will always be my hero. I'll never forget you.

Love,

Riley Bentley

My eyes found Mother Teresa's—hers had welled up with tears, while mine were profoundly dry from shock.

"Don't you think it's strange that she looks so much like me?" I said, holding up the picture of the girl. *Riley.*

"What?" It was Dr. T's turn to be surprised. She wiped her eyes to better study the small wallet-sized photo. "Well, yes, she does look a lot like you—but that's surely just a coincidence."

"I don't believe in coincidences. My dad always said that they're just clues." The emptiness echoed within me as I remembered his words.

"Well, what kind of clue would you suppose the similarity between you is?" she asked, clearly curious enough to indulge me.

I thought about it for a few seconds, though I didn't really need that long. I had been thinking about it for eight hours a night for over a month now.

"I think whoever lured me there was sending me a message." There, I said it. Talk about breakthroughs. Two secrets revealed in one session. This had to be my record. And saying it out loud only clarified it in my mind. Whoever was behind this planted a girl who looked just like me, to make sure I saw the connection. To make sure I protected her. To make sure I pulled the trigger.

That's who LeMarq was talking to on the phone—the one he thanked for the "delivery." There was a man behind the curtain, pulling the strings. A mastermind. But I couldn't fathom *who* or *why*.

"Maybe one of the other criminals I'd been following discovered me and was trying to get me killed or arrested," I said, thinking out loud. "Maybe someone who had a grudge against my mom."

"Ruby," Dr. T said, "why don't we break a bit early today. I don't want you to go *crazy* overthinking this."

I looked back to her, expecting a symbolic cookie for my hard work in "opening up." Instead, she'd said the C-word and started putting papers in her briefcase

I was about to ask what I'd said wrong when she stood and spoke first. "I'll see you on Friday." My mouth dropped open in shock—she'd never ended a session early. And she'd never reacted so brusquely.

Before I could voice my confusion, she promptly turned tail and exited the room.

Leaving me wondering what had just happened.

CHAPTER 4

Art, schmart. I didn't get it. And certainly not much of this stuff created for the Huntington Beach High School Art Fair.

I walked around the muggy, fried-food-scented cafeteria, just like the rest of the sheep, staring and *baahhing* at the individual pieces. I found myself lingering in front of a violent explosion of black, purple, and red paint on white canvas. I think it was supposed to be abstract, but it was probably just some emo kid's attempt to throw something together for a grade. To me, it looked like one of those inkblot tests psychologists used to determine a person's emotional well-being. Good thing Dr. T didn't use this kind of thing on me.

I pulled my notebook and pen out of my backpack and tried to formulate my thoughts. We were supposed to find two pieces of art that "appealed" to us and then write down why. It was an official assignment, which meant I had to do my best if I wanted to stay on the rails of my valedictorian train track. One that was increasingly steep and treacherous these days.

I took a sharp breath and narrowed my eyes on the textured colors.

The first words that came to mind were *blood spatter*, *grim reaper*, and—

"Seriously, do I have to force feed you normal?" Alana appeared beside me, looping her arm through mine and dragging me away from my morbid tendencies. "Come over and see the painting of La Jolla Cove that I did. It has blue skies and sunshine."

"Does it have chubby little baby seals in it, too?" I put my pen behind my ear and followed.

"No, seals are too loud and ugly and smelly. But maybe in the distance there's a certain hot boy in board shorts kissing a certain brown girl in a bikini." She licked her lips in a way I didn't need to see.

"Are you ever going to grow out of the boy-crazy phase?" I teased her.

"Don't be jealous," she said. "Kissing's no crime. You should try it again sometime. You know, like therapy. And I know someone who would be happy to help with the treatment."

"Alana, give it a rest, for, like, a day," I said, finally pulling away from the WWF armlock she had on me. Plus, who would want to kiss me anyway? My Social Point Average had taken an even deeper nosedive after the shooting.

"Just sayin'." She continued through the crowd to the center of the room, where I was beginning to suspect a trap. "Anyway, some guys think it's cool that you know how to use a gun. It's very Bond girl."

I stopped. Suspicion confirmed. "Is that Liam over there, *also* admiring your work?" It was a rhetorical question—Liam was hard to miss. He was like a man among boys, at least in stature. His face was different, though—somehow fresh, innocent, clear. Like all the extra light in the room found its way to him, and to his light-brown, sun-bleached hair hanging over those big, bright eyes.

Regardless of the light, I didn't like entrapment. I felt my fuse ignite—my highly flammable, dangerously short fuse.

"What? He likes good art." She stopped to face me with puppy-dog eyes and a guilty conscience. "Rue! He likes you, all right? He asked me to set this up. He feels like you're unapproachable. Sort of the story of your life!" She reached out to grab me by the shoulders, and I quickly deflected both hands. She knew better. After all, that's how we met. In fourth grade, when she moved to Huntington Beach from Hawaii, I found her in the corner crying while a couple of fifth-grade girls made fun of her tattered shorts and old flip-flops. I couldn't help myself—I had to tell the girls where to go. And when one girl tried to push me into the corner with Alana, I broke the girl's nose. Alana and I had been best friends from then on, and she'd seen my quick reflexes get me in trouble a few times since.

"I'm kind of going through something right now, OK?" I said under my breath so half the student body didn't witness the public confrontation. *Extra* would just love to interview Big-Mouth Taylor over there, who never stopped staring at the bleeding, withering Ruby Rose, now having a tiff with her best friend. Oh, how Taylor loved competing for the limelight and gaining the upper hand. If I didn't know better, I'd think she was behind the whole LeMarq incident just to ruin me. "I'm begging you, Alana, I just need some space right now."

"Liam wants to be your friend, Rubik's Cube. It's not like he's asking you to marry him," she argued, *not* under her breath. I could feel the crowd start to take notice. Deep down I knew she was only trying to help me. Under different circumstances I wouldn't have minded her matchmaking efforts.

"I don't need any more *friends* right now," I countered. "Not ones that don't understand boundaries, anyway." I clenched my jaw and stormed off.

Alana never stopped. It wasn't that I didn't still feel wildly drawn to Liam. It was that there was no room in my life for distractions.

"If you're not careful, you might not have any friends *left*!" she yelled after me as I disappeared behind a papier-mâché bust of a deformed alien. I almost reached out and punched that stupid warped head for staring at me like *I* was the weird one.

I wandered aimlessly until I found myself in the least populated corner of the cafeteria and slumped against the wall. The sticky linoleum floor was full of dust bunnies, long-lost Cheetos fragments, and other unsanitary droppings I tried to block out.

I concentrated on my shoes instead—a useful strategy I busted out from time to time. Oh, how I loved the strappy, black-leather Calvin Klein wedge heels hugging my feet. Classics. Always loyal, always kind. These little beauties would never surprise-attack me in the middle of school, would never care more about their careers than my happiness, would never die and abandon me to a life full of more questions than answers. Wait. *A scuff*?

"Damn it," I mumbled. I tried to wipe it clean with my thumb and a little spit. But it did no good. I'd have to wait until I got home and found my Kicks Kleaner.

Just great. Here I was, stuck in the proverbial corner of life—and not just because of the ever-sticky linoleum I was sitting on. Now I didn't even have anywhere to focus my disruptive thoughts. What, exactly, was I supposed to do? Stew in my guilt for snapping at the one person who still wanted me as her best friend? I wished I could distract myself by searching online for a new pair of shoes, but if I was caught on my cell phone I'd have more problems than I needed today. Cell phones weren't allowed during school hours.

Taking my chances of making eye contact with someone, I looked straight ahead. I still had to find another piece of art that "appealed" to me so I could finish my assignment. But I didn't want to get up.

I hoped I could see something worth looking at from here. Something that wouldn't inspire thoughts of death, betrayal, or scuffed shoes.

About twenty feet away I noticed a black-and-white charcoal drawing. It was a sketch of a young girl with long, straight hair parted down the middle. It was really well done. Perhaps a little too well done for this bush-league art fair. I stood and wiped stray guck off my red skinny jeans and made a beeline for it.

This had to be some kind of egotistical-Freudian-thought-processing-dysfunction, because as I got nearer, that girl in the sketch started to look a hell of a lot like me. Slightly upturned nose. Dimple in the left cheek. Long neck. What the H?

Who put this here?

In the bottom right corner of the picture, old-fashioned, scrolly letters read:

Love, D. S.

Who was that?

And now that I was up close, there was something very disturbing about this sketch. It wasn't just her face, it was the tattoo on her arm. A winged demon screeching at me, threatening to tear me apart. I'd seen that exact tattoo before on Charlie LeMarq.

Oh no. The world suddenly went fuzzy and dark, like I was seeing things through stained glass. I scanned the room for the nearest escape to fresh air, and instead of finding a clearly marked exit, I found another face that took the last of my breath away. Across the crowd, stood a man with a goatee who looked a lot like Detective Martinez.

A falling sensation rushed over me, and a sickening crack echoed through my skull.

"Ruby, can you hear me?" A raspy male voice lingered above.

"It's Ruby Rose!" a girl shrieked through the clamor. "Someone call 911!"

"No! Somebody just get me some water," Alana ordered.

I opened my eyes to find a three-headed monster looming over me. Then my vision cleared, and I made out Liam, Alana, and some tiny freshman girl, all fussing over me.

"No, don't call 911—I'm fine. I just need some water, like Alana said." I sat up and reached for the water bottle in front of me. As I drank, I felt the blood rush to my cheeks. Liam's arms were firmly wrapped around my shoulders—with at least a hundred inquiring eyes watching, and dozens of smartphones taking pictures.

So much for the "no cell phone rule" only I was dumb enough to follow.

Among the first of my unclear thoughts was: *The tabloids are going to think it's an early Christmas.* A close second: *This is impossible—Ruby Rose doesn't faint.* Lagging behind: *Is Martinez really here at the art fair? Couldn't be, because he'd be here now among the crowd.* Trailed by: *I hope I don't have leftover cafeteria Cheetos in my hair.* And finally: *I gotta get out of here.*

I got up and broke out of the literal and metaphorical grip Liam had on me. The sea of students parted as I made my way toward the exit—everyone moved except for Taylor. She just stood there gloating in all her non-fainting, anti-Ruby glory. With her arms crossed and dark hair pulled into a tight ponytail to accentuate her cat-like eyes, she said, "You OK, sweetie?"

"Excuse me," I said, as my shoulder checked hers, knocking her off balance. Maybe one day I'd get the opportunity to teach her how I really felt about her constantly calling me sweetie. But not today. I speed walked out the double doors, and then sprinted through the parking lot, begging the ocean breeze to cool down my red-hot cheeks and spinning brain as I ran. I was pissed. And light-headed. And losing control. I didn't even care if I got in trouble for leaving school early.

Shaking from anger and embarrassment, I climbed into Big Black and hugged his steering wheel. I immediately turned up the volume of my favorite "explicit language" rap song. I needed Big Black, I needed to be alone, I needed—a fat chocolate shake with whipped cream ASAP, and I needed to get out of this parking lot before Alana or Liam came running after me.

As I peeled out, images of the girl in the sketch kept floating to the top of my consciousness, no matter how hard I tried to push them back down. I had to find out who she was, and who'd put the sketch of her there. It was meant for me, I was sure. Well, not totally sure. I should have checked with Alana and asked if she saw it, too, just to make sure I wasn't having a psychotic split or mental breakdown. After all, I thought I'd seen someone who looked a lot like Martinez in that same moment, and he wasn't there. Plus, I'd never fainted before. Not like that, anyway. I passed out once during a karate match, but that was a one-off, and the only time I'd ever allowed a roundhouse to land on my body.

Fainting in the cafeteria was different: I'd had a visceral reaction to seeing that demon tattoo. It was the same tattoo LeMarq had on his arm. The exact same fangs and webbed wings. The exact same look of evil in its eyes.

Whoever lured me and LeMarq to the warehouse had also delivered that sketch to my school with the *Love, D. S.* signature. He was toying with me, communicating with me. There was no way that drawing was a coincidence. The girl looked just like me, just like Riley Bentley. These were clues. Whoever this crazy-ass D. S. was, he was speaking to me in a language I didn't understand.

When I was almost at the Dairy Queen (which I personally kept in business), my phone vibrated in The Cleave. I looked down at the screen to see who the culprit was. A picture of D. A. Jane Rose's new campaign poster winked back at me. Glamour Shots had nothing on this baby.

I had some headshots quite similar to this one, from back in the days when my mother had ceaselessly prodded me to compete in beauty pageants. Lame. Some things never changed, and not just because Mom's plastic surgeon kept it that way. She put a higher priority on appearance than anything else. Instead of the popularity contests, all I'd wanted was to compete in karate—something I was actually good at. If it hadn't been for my dad's training in negotiation and his willingness to take her bullets for me, I'd still be her beauty queen hostage.

I declined her call. The wall between us had grown to around shoulder height even before Dad died, and now it was well over eye level. I couldn't even see her anymore without a decent pair of four-inch Kate Spade platform heels.

Ten seconds later she called again.

She must have heard about what happened at school. There was no point in not answering. She'd track me down eventually, and I'd pay the price.

"Hey, Mom."

"What's going on? Where are you? I just got a call—"

"Mom, calm down." As a seasoned prosecutor, she should've been trained not to pose several compound questions at once. Very objectionable in a court of law. "I'm fine. I promise."

"Alana called. She told me you fainted and ran out of school?"

Objection: Leading question.

"Yeah, I don't think I've been eating my five major food groups. I just need some protein and some rest." I lied with a frightening ease.

"I don't believe you," she said flatly. "Alana said you were upset."

Objection: Hearsay.

"No, I'm not upset. Just embarrassed. I need to grab some take-out and lie down for a while."

"You've been acting very *strangely* lately."

Objection: Facts not in evidence. She barely sees me, how would she know?

"I'm very worried about you, honey."

Objection: Badgering the witness. I've told her a million times to stop calling me honey.

"Jane! I said I'm fine." Two could play the name game—she hated when I didn't call her Mom. "I'll see you tonight. That is, if you get home before midnight." Switching the focus to her always won the argument.

"No, I'll be home in fifteen minutes. We need to talk. You'd better be home then, too." She hung up.

As I pressed "End," I wondered what wrong button of hers I'd pressed. She never wanted to talk. She was never home before nine or ten. And she never hung up on *me*.

Great.

CHAPTER 5

I practically inhaled my chocolate shake—and it soothed every hot corner of my soul. Albeit temporarily.

I flung my backpack off my shoulder and collapsed onto my bed. I felt sick. Sick from the chocolate overdose, sick from my fight with Alana, sick with images of that sketch, sick with light-headedness from fainting, and sick with dread of the impending interrogation by my mother.

What was I going to tell her? The truth? Ha. She would feel obligated as an officer of the court to inform the appropriate authorities of all my *missteps*. Plus, my full and not-yet-entirely-disclosed side of the story was insane:

> *So, Mom, I didn't mention it before, but I had more of a hand in the killing of LeMarq than you thought, due to my OCD hobby of following killers in my spare time. And, oh yeah, there might be a chance that one of the other killers I was following is connected to the dude who lured me to that warehouse on Water Street. Oh, and now he's sending me messages through the school art show. But don't worry, it's all good. Let's just pretend none of it happened.*

Uh, no.

I crammed a pillow over my face so I could scream. But mid-scream, I realized *that* was about to turn into a throw-up, and I stopped.

The rumble of the garage door below let me know I had to get a grip on myself. I ran into the bathroom and washed my face with cold water, scrubbing off all my eye makeup in preparation for the inquisition. I would be stone faced. I would be savvy. Mom might have known how to intimidate criminals and suspects. But I knew how to box her out.

"Rue-girl," she hollered from downstairs. "I'm home."

"I'll be right there."

I stared myself down in the mirror and whispered, "You can do this."

I met my mom in the kitchen, where she still had her sunglasses on like she was some kind of hungover rock star. Even her stylish little A-line bob was askew. It looked darker than usual, so black that it maybe even had a hint of blue. She'd been going progressively darker since last year's polling data showed her darker hair produced a better Latino vote. If she thought I was a disappointment in my choice of guns over dolls, I felt the same way about her choice to embrace her Mexican heritage because it was convenient for political points. I'd never even met one member of her family. Her mother died when she was in law school, before I was born, and despite the fact that her father was still alive and unwell somewhere in San Diego, she hadn't spoken to him since he walked out on them when she was eight. I knew she had extended family spread across Southern California, but I stopped asking about them years ago when I learned my questions put her in a dark mood.

She was pouring herself a glass of wine. Liquid courage. Not fair—I didn't get any.

"Mom, it's only two o'clock." I grabbed an apple off the counter—Granny Smith was my only ally here. "Should *I* be worried about *you*?" I had to stay on the offensive.

"Ruby," she said, putting down the bottle. "Let's not do that."

"Do what?" I asked innocently, sitting down on a barstool across from her.

"Let's not shift attention to me, when this is about you." She finally took off her Gucci sunglasses, revealing puffiness around the eyes I wasn't expecting. She bit at her Restylane-injected lips—an old nervous habit, and one Dr. Syringe-Happy in Beverly Hills had warned her to break.

"Obviously not," I said, trying not to gawk at the hot mess before me. I'd never seen her looking like this—not even when Dad died. I knew she probably cried then, but it was behind her perpetually closed doors and perfectly coiffed facade. "What, did Bill Brandon call you a bad name in the *Los Angeles Times* today?"

She turned her back to me and rubbed her eyes with a clean dishrag next to the sink. This was highly unusual. I'd caught her in a real weak spot. Maybe I could actually win this one.

"No, this isn't about Bill Brandon." She faced me with renewed strength in her bloodshot, mascara-smudged eyes. "This is about you. Only you."

Oh, snap.

I told myself to think happy thoughts. I scratched at the thin wax coating on Granny Smith and imagined landing a sweet high kick. Buying a new pair of Steve Madden cowgirl boots. Kissing Liam Slater while we lay on the beach. Wait, where did that come from?

"Please stay with me," she said with a note of uncharacteristic hysteria in her voice. "I really need you to *not* do that thing where you close yourself off and think of other things and direct your attention onto inanimate objects."

I set down Granny Smith—like she'd ratted me out. "Wow, so you're a psychic now?" I asked. Since when had she paid attention to me long enough to figure out my war tactics?

"I may not be perfect, but I'm not stupid." She rounded the counter and stood opposite me. "I know we've been distant . . . and I haven't really been *here* for you . . ."

Not this conversation. I was so not in the mood for one of our strained heart-to-hearts.

"This past year has been difficult to say the least. Losing your father, fighting for my campaign, this whole LeMarq debacle. It's fair to say, I've really been thrown for a loop."

Excusez-moi? Did she just say that me shooting a man in the head had thrown *her* for a loop?

"I want you to know I love you very much." In my peripheral vision I saw her fiddling with her wedding ring, like her words weren't only meant for me.

I looked up. I hadn't heard her say the word "love" in so long. Something inside me felt soothed by that one simple sentence, reminding me of a better time when it felt true.

"I know I haven't been spending enough time with you and that I've been relying too much on Dr. Teresa for updates, which is completely unacceptable." She pinched her eyes shut. "But that's not the way it's going to work anymore." She opened her eyes and focused on me with a scary intensity. "And I need to start by telling you something important. Something I should have told you a long time ago—but never found the right time."

She paused and put her lips in position to say something, but nothing came out. This was becoming too painful to endure.

"I need you to know that everything I've done is to protect you, provide for you, and help you. And I will never stop trying to do that." With her hand over her heart, she nodded at me to make sure I understood. I didn't.

"What are you talking about, Mom?"

"Regardless of what has happened, or what will happen, I want you to remember that, OK?" A full-blown heat rash had developed on her neck. She started rubbing at it without taking her eyes off me. Her agitation did nothing to comfort me.

"Just tell me what you're talking about. Am I in trouble with the police? Are you going to have to press charges against me?" I gulped, not sure I wanted the answer.

"No, Ruby, that's not it. No charges will be brought. I don't want you worrying about that." She rounded the counter and brushed some of the hair off my brow. That simple touch felt like stars springing to life inside of me after years of living in darkness.

"It's about your dad." She hesitated, pulling away before I was ready. "I know I never showed much appreciation for the way the two of you spent so much time together, shooting and fighting and whatnot."

"That's a bit of an understatement," I said, wondering where she was going with this. "All you ever did was punish him, and me, for it."

"I know," she said with a grimace. "And I'm sorry."

Jane Rose said the S-word? And not in a sarcastic way?

"Turns out, he was right." Tears emerged in her eyes. "He was a good man, and he would have wanted me to tell you—"

A loud chime reverberated through the house.

"Are you expecting someone?" she asked, reaching up to smooth her hair.

"No." I shook my head, thrown off by (a) Mom's most sincere moment in years; (b) what Dad "would have wanted" my mom to tell me; and (c) the sound of the doorbell. Normally, people had to press the call button and get buzzed in to get past the entry gates. My parents couldn't be too careful with all the criminals they'd put away.

She grabbed the kitchen towel again and attempted to wipe away every sign of emotion before she took off toward the door, putting the Guccis back over her eyes.

As I absorbed the whiplash of emotions she'd just put me through and listened to the abrasively familiar click-clack of her heels on the tile as she walked away, I wondered who'd dared to trespass. Who was pulling my mom away just when she was finally opening up to me?

Before I had time to prioritize the feelings of annoyance at being interrupted and anger at Mom leaving me hanging again, I heard her gasp.

"What the hell!" She sounded scared. My mother was never scared.

I froze, allowing my mind to conjure all the fatal possibilities.

Just as I managed to gather myself to search the kitchen for some kind of weapon, the air pressure in the house changed, opening the front door with a gust.

I was out of time.

Clutching the steak knife I'd grabbed and listening for any indication that Mom was in danger and I needed to act. Why would she have opened the door if she was scared? Maybe she wasn't the one who'd opened the door at all.

"Hello, Jane." A deep Spanish-flavored voice boomed through our grand entryway. I knew that voice.

"Detective Martinez, is there some reason you didn't call my office?" my mother said in her trademark passive-aggressive tone.

My fingers uncurled from my weapon as I realized I no longer needed one—and that brandishing a blade wouldn't win me any points with the man investigating me as a murderer. I dropped the knife and cringed when it clattered into the stainless steel sink.

"I apologize," Martinez muttered, sounding entirely unapologetic. "But I did call your office. Several times, in fact."

"So you show up unannounced at my home?" my mother seethed. "This is hardly appropriate, Detective." She may have been irritated at his unexpected drop-in, but I was terrified. Even though he wasn't the first dangerous person who'd come to my mind when my mom gasped, he was dangerous nonetheless. Perhaps he'd found evidence to contradict my sworn statement. Maybe he was here to catch me in my lie—that I'd never heard of Charlie LeMarq before the night I killed him—and take me in with hands cuffed behind my back. Or maybe he really was at the art show, and he knew a lot more about the investigation than he'd been letting on.

"Have I interrupted something?" Martinez asked.

"No," she said, as if she'd completely forgotten that we were just in the middle of a rare moment of her opening up to me about my father. I tried not to let her lie sting.

"Good, because we need to talk."

"About what?"

"About the investigation, of course," he said, inviting himself in. "Is Ruby around?"

I tiptoed across the acoustic tile and peeked around the corner.

"Yes, but I would prefer it if we talked privately," she said, trying to corral him into her office. Instead, he walked around the foyer as if looking for something. He stopped in front of the framed family portrait, his face scrunching up in a weird way as he stared at my father's image. His goatee, his thick gold chain necklace, and unnecessary black leather jacket made him seem more like an actor playing a part on *Law & Order: LA* than a real cop. He was more good-looking than I remembered—and probably less good-looking than he remembered. Arrogant ass.

"Detective, please, my bureau if you would," she ordered, more aggressive than passive at this point, gesturing with her hands for him to move away from the picture and behind the closed doors of her *bureau*. Like using the French word made her office fancier, or more official.

He reluctantly followed her command, muttering something in Spanglish that I didn't understand. I knew she was only trying to protect me—my rights, my emotional stability. But I didn't like being kept in the dark. And I didn't think I could wait one second to hear what update he had on the investigation.

"Hi, Detective Martinez." I popped out right before the office door shut. His head swung around at my voice, and I saw a hint of excitement on his face before he narrowed his eyes into a stern-cop look.

"Hey, Ruby," he said. "Your mother and I were about to have a chat. But you're welcome to join us if you'd like."

I glanced at my mom. Her jawbone was about to break. "No, Detective, I already told you I would prefer if we speak alone."

"She's a big girl. She can decide for herself." He wasn't intimidated by my mom or her D. A. attitude. Huh—that was rare.

"Yeah, Mom," I said, walking past them into the *bureau.* "Don't you think I deserve to know what's going on?"

She followed me and whispered in my ear, "Listen to me. Don't speak, even if he asks you direct questions. Let me answer for you. Do you understand?"

"Mom, he's here to tell me what's going on, not to interrogate me," I whispered back, not believing my own words.

"Don't be so naive, Rue."

She sat me next to her on the couch, and motioned for Martinez to sit across from us in an armchair.

"So tell us, Detective, what news do you have to report?" she asked, firmly in command again. "What has the quick-as-snails Homicide Unit discovered?"

He gave her a look of disgust before focusing on me. "Well, it looks like your story has been corroborated by the forensics," he said, leaning forward, elbows braced over knees, practically oozing testosterone. If he was trying to establish some kind of male dominance here—good luck. "We dumped LeMarq's cell phone and found several texts and calls from an untraceable disposable cell. We know now that an unknown suspect promising a 'blonde delivery' lured

LeMarq there. We assume it was this same unknown suspect who texted Ruby that night."

I exhaled a little.

"This theory is also substantiated by the fact that LeMarq did not transport the young girl in his van. There were no hairs or fibers found in his vehicle, which leads us to believe that the unknown suspect, who lured both LeMarq and Ruby to the warehouse, also kidnapped the victim and used her as some sort of bait for both of them."

I felt my mom tense up. "Excuse me, Detective—*bait*?"

"That's right . . . bait." Martinez continued staring me down, not even bothering to look at my mom. "Why do you think someone would want to lure you there?"

"Detective, she is not going to answer that." Mom slung a hand over my lap like we were in a car and she'd slammed on the brakes.

He knew I was hiding something. He wasn't as dumb as his muscles made him look.

"Detective," my mother said, "I want to know *who sent that text*. I need that man caught."

The heat from her laser glare must have gotten to him, because he finally took off his stupid leather jacket. As he draped it over his leg, I noticed a tattoo on his right forearm. It looked like the Eagle, Globe, and Anchor Marine Corps symbol. Dad had that same exact tattoo, in the same exact place. I knew they'd been partners sometime before I was born, but matching tattoos? Maybe it was a common Marine thing—

"I'm working on that, Jane," he said, finally directing his focus to her. There was a venomous quality to his voice now. And he looked at her in a way that felt—inappropriate. Like he knew her better than I thought, and this wasn't the first time they were having a fight.

"Are you *working on it* with the same intensity as the department is *working on* finding my husband's killer?" she said in a raptor-like pitch. It startled me. Something strange was happening to my mom.

"Sergeant Mathews tells me that Jack's case has gone nowhere. It's unacceptable—"

"Jane, relax." He cut her off and stood with his hand up to her, as if he was blocking out her deathly atomic waves. "You know the department is committed to finding out what happened to Jack."

She rose to face him. She wasn't going to let him have the upper hand in anything, and certainly not in elevation—not with those heels.

I was wondering if he was going to bring up anything about the art show (since I wasn't going to)—or if I was legitimately delusional and waiting in vain—when my phone vibrated in my back pocket. My mom was standing in front of me, blocking me from Martinez's view, so I risked taking a quick look.

A photo text stared back at me. A girl tied up, gagged, and bleeding from a head wound. This one looked incredibly like me, too. At least, under the gag it seemed like it—blonde hair, pale-gray eyes. The message read:

11800 Ninth Street. This time, no police.

I blacked out the screen. I couldn't stand to look at it.

Maybe, hopefully, probably, it was a fake. Since the official story about the LeMarq debacle was leaked to the media, I'd received dozens of threatening texts purporting to lead me to more setups. Each time, I told my mom and she'd report it to the forensic-analysis team assigned to my ongoing case. Nothing ever came from any of them. According to my mom, the texts were sent by a series of punk kids from school, a dirty paparazzo, and an insane person who had nothing better to do with his time.

We'd finally changed my cell phone number. It had been three weeks since I'd received anything. Only Alana, Alana's big mouth, and my mom knew my number.

As Detective Muscle Head argued with my mom, I considered the odds of this message being real. None of the other messages had included photos, certainly not with a girl who looked so similar to me—and just like Riley Bentley. As far as I knew, no one had picked up on that detail yet.

I'd never been warned not to involve the police, either. Something about this message felt different.

"Is something wrong?" Mom's voice stopped my runaway train of thought. "Honey, are you OK?"

I looked up. She'd called me honey again. I ground my teeth, thinking about how to respond. The text said no police, and yet, a detective was standing right here in front of me. Despite the warning, there was no way I could heed it. If the message was real, that girl needed help.

"No." I shook my head. "No, I'm not OK." I turned on my screen so they could see the image. "And neither is this girl."

Mom grabbed the cell out of my hand like it was a bomb only she could defuse.

"Did this just come through now, Ruby?" she asked.

I nodded.

"Detective . . ." My mom turned back to Martinez, as though putting the picture closer to his face would help him react quicker. "This needs to stop. Get your forensic team to look into it immediately. If it's authentic, do something about it for once. I'm not sure how well my office, or your department, can handle another *incident*." She motioned for him to leave.

At first he didn't budge. He stood there, waiting, like a black chess piece eyeing his next move toward the white queen. Then his glare shifted to me. His eyes burned through me in a way that panicked me more than the photo did. Did he blame me for this?

"I'll have forensics trace the call immediately. Forward it to me, Jane—you know my number—so we can analyze the picture, too," he said, clenching his jacket in his fists.

My mom started sending him the text and picture. Did she have his phone number memorized? And didn't he need to take my phone with him? Or did he already have my phone tapped?

"But, Ruby," he said, moving in my direction and holding out a white card. "Take this. In case you need to talk about anything."

I looked away from him, trying to remember the research I'd done on what gestures marked deception or guilt. I was pretty sure I was doing all of them: rapid eye movement, hands near mouth, shifting in seat. I felt like the words "guilty stalker" were stamped across my forehead.

As I hesitated, my mom stepped in and took the card instead. "You should go now."

He stared her down for a good five eternities before leaving without another word, a potent trail of spicy aftershave following in his wake.

My mom threw my phone on the couch next to me and started rubbing her temples. She was definitely hiding something from me. I'd picked up a subtext in her fiery conversation with Detective Martinez. I was so busy keeping my secrets hidden that I'd almost missed hers.

"Mom, what's your deal with him?"

"Let's finish this conversation later. I need to make some phone calls." She made a dignified dash for her desk, like there was a VIC (only not a victim—more like a Very Important Conversation) that couldn't wait. "Go rest. I'll get some dinner delivered and we can talk then."

"OK, but what was that thing you were going to tell me before he got here?"

She finally looked up, and I watched the blood drain from her face.

"If it's about my case, I think I deserve to know what it is."

"You're right," she said, closing her eyes in defeat. "You do deserve to know."

Instead of coming to sit next to me, she took her place behind her desk.

"I don't know how to say this, so I'm just going to get it out," she said. "Before you came into our lives, I . . . had an affair. With Detective Martinez. It was the greatest mistake of my life, and not a day goes by that I don't regret it."

My stomach dropped along with my jaw. Why did it feel like she just admitted to cheating on *me*?

"And you're telling me this *now* because . . .?"

"Because, Ruby, it matters!" she snapped. "Things ended very badly between us. And now that he's the lead investigator on your case . . . let's just say he could make things very difficult for us."

I stared at the floor, not knowing what to say or think. All I could think about was my poor, loyal, dead dad.

"Believe me, I never wanted to burden you with this," she said, anger and guilt constricting her voice. "Damn it, I just needed you to know that you can't trust Martinez. Anything he says or does is dangerous."

She got up and crossed the great divide between us.

"Ruby, words can't express how sorry I am for my mistakes," she said, sitting next to me and pulling my chin up to face her. "But it was a long time ago and I need you to know I'm doing everything I can to make it right, OK?"

"OK," I parroted back, and turned away. Just when I thought she was making efforts to tear down the wall between us, it had grown even taller. Who was this woman? Was she ever the mom I thought she was? Had I deluded myself into believing we were ever a happy family?

"Why?" I asked feebly, too shocked and hurt to muster the emotion of anger quite yet.

"Why *what*?" She playacted that she was confused by my question, as if I had posed an irrelevant math problem.

"Why'd you cheat on Dad?"

She put her head in her hands. "You wouldn't understand."

Maybe even after all this time she still didn't understand it herself.

It took a few minutes for her to gather herself, and I let her. My usual MO was to react impulsively, aggressively. But right now, I felt stunned.

"Go lie down for a while." Not a request. "I'll get some dinner and I promise, we'll talk some more. But for now, I need to make sure this text you received is handled."

"Fine." I grabbed my phone and left her office. I didn't want to be near her anymore.

As soon as I got to my room, I threw down my phone and crammed the pillow over my face, no longer wanting to hear my mother's cold voice in my head, or hold the girl's image in my hand, or taste the tears running down my cheeks.

CHAPTER 6

My phone's vibration from my bedside table woke me up. Disoriented, I grabbed for it and cracked an eyelid to check the time. Five a.m. *What the . . .?*

I rolled over and rubbed my lids to try to un-paste the contacts from my eyeballs. I never fell asleep with them in—and this inability to blink without burning pain was why.

My phone vibrated again. I rubbed hard enough that one eye was usable. I had ten text messages! Three from Alana, each one increasingly more agitated by my radio silence, and the rest from two different unknown numbers. The first unknown number read:

> *Hey, it's Liam. Hope u dont mind Alana gave me your #. Just wanted to make sure ur ok. & I wanted to tell u something. Call me.*

I didn't mind. Actually, I couldn't stop the rising feeling of totally not minding. If a girl could shoot and kill someone, then pass out on the cafeteria floor like a lunatic, and this guy still wanted to talk to her, he couldn't be so bad. His abs didn't hurt his case, either.

The phone vibrated a third time.

I scrolled down to the rest of the texts, all from the same number. There were six of them, and I opened the first:

Check the Channel 3 news. You didn't listen, and you didn't save her.

The second and third and fourth—all said the same thing.

My heart palpitated. I switched on the news. Across the bottom, the scroll read:

Unnamed Teen Girl Found Dead Near Ninth Street.

All the warm and gooey feelings I'd had thinking of Liam and his ocean-blue eyes evaporated. A girl was dead. And it was my fault.

Something hardened in my chest. Like a cocoon had wrapped itself around my heart. And the darkness I'd worked so hard to dispel after losing Dad filled my mind. Guilt, sadness, anger, and despair all swarmed inside.

A normal person would cry at a time like this. Go running to Momma, to my dad's "trusted" friends at SWAT, and plead for mercy and help. But I was never normal, and definitely not in the mood for pleading. I was in the mood to find out who was doing this to me. And why.

I replied to the message:

Who are you?

Ten seconds later, the message came back undelivered.

I chucked off my comforter and slid to my knees beside my bed. No, not to pray. To reach underneath my box spring. I felt for the handles of my locked chest, pulled it out, and lined up the numbers of the combination until it clicked open. I hadn't opened the chest in weeks, foolishly trying to forget that it existed.

I rummaged through the case files I'd copied off my mom's desk until I found my notebook. I preferred paper notes just in case—I knew from my mom's trials that *nothing* digital *ever* disappears. And I wasn't going to be one of those defendants dumb enough to Google "how to catch a killer." No, I could easily burn these notes if I had to. And I always used my dad's computer for hacking into official criminal databases and evidence logs. I even had his access codes to get into higher-level police files. They were all neatly written on a laminated card he kept "safe" in his safe. Stupid bureaucracy hadn't even managed to shut down his accounts yet.

Thumbing through pages of comments, charts, and surveillance logs, I ran my finger over the name of each predator I'd been secretly following. All five of them—aka my Filthy Five. LeMarq was the first one I'd set my sights on.

The wind howled outside my window, and the branches of the orange tree scratched at the glass. I checked to make sure no one was there. Of course not—the creepy scraping noise was just part of a normal SoCal morning storm, not someone messing with my mind. Definitely not the spirit of the girl I should have saved.

The condensation from the night's rain on the windowpane distorted the world outside. And the images on the television next to the window distorted my world inside.

Television crews lined the Ninth Street crime scene. For some morbid reason, they kept replaying the coroner wheeling out the black body bag. I had never hated my high-def flat screen so much. At the moment, I didn't exactly want to "feel like I was there."

The police hadn't released the girl's identity yet, so the news team resorted to zooming in on the moment when the wind picked up and an unzipped portion of the body bag rose, revealing a blonde head. As the reporter went wild with excited speculation on who the victim might be, I couldn't help but wonder why they had to look like me, and what this guy was trying to tell me.

I felt like going on TV myself and warning every blonde-haired, gray-eyed girl in California to stay inside until I figured this out. But surely Detective Martinez or one of his chest-beating cohorts would see a pattern, and the public would be alerted to the profile of the victims. Or maybe the zombie media would figure it out on their own.

I could only hope the police didn't disclose my involvement. If they found out, the press's cycle of harassment would start all over again. A slimy paparazzo named Sammy tirelessly followed me around after Dad's death—he liked to call me the number-one victim of that senseless murder. More like I was the number-one victim of Sammy's invasion of privacy and national-exploitation tour.

I heard Mom stirring downstairs. Most likely making herself a pot of coffee, working on her usual three hours of sleep a night. I couldn't afford her barging in, and I certainly didn't want to talk to her about another death. I had to get out of here and find a safe place to gather my thoughts—alone.

The Pier.

I grabbed what I needed, and restashed all the evidence against me. After stuffing my notebook in my backpack and kicking my pirate's chest back under the bed, I headed to my bathroom to brush my hair and teeth.

I tried not to pay too much attention to that sickly looking girl in the mirror. Instead, I tried to look past her, to the open window, where I knew my spot under the Pier and its fresh after-rain breeze waited to wash away the dark lines and puffy skin around my eyes. But just the thought of puffy eyes made me think of my mom (not because we look anything alike, because we don't) and her admission of guilt in her office yesterday.

As I began to make progress on the rat's nest I sometimes called hair, I also wondered why she hadn't come up to see me last night. She said she would get dinner and we'd "talk some more." Typical Jane Rose. All promises—no follow-through.

Maybe, so she would start to care more about me than her career, I should start campaigning for Bill Brandon and leaking information to his campaign muckety-mucks on her inability to keep promises. The days of family breakfasts in bed and picnics at the beach had ceased well before we lost Dad. Right about the same time that she formally declared her ambition to run for District Attorney the first time, she unofficially stopped being a wife and mother.

I slammed down my brush a little harder than I intended to and frowned at the state I was in. Hardly my finest hour in the looks department. Even after a little mascara and blush, I still didn't want to see the girl in the mirror. Not even my mom's old pageant tricks of making myself "look better in order to feel better" were working. I needed a few moments with my oldest and dearest friend: Gladys—aka my shoe closet.

I rounded the corner of my bathroom and opened the door to the other "wing" of my bedroom. Clicking the light switch on, I watched the heavenly fluorescent light shine luminously on her walls. Happy to see me, too, Gladys and all her Pips stood at attention for my entry—except for my tan Dolce & Gabbana Catwoman boots, which had to be neatly hung to avoid damage or creases. I had to take care of my Sleeping Beauties.

"Gladys, I need help." My words echoed into the space. Sometimes it really paid to be an only child. This room had been meant for my sister or brother, but when they never happened, Dad knocked down a wall to give me a playroom. I was never really into toys—just shoes. I know. Weird. Dr. T told my mom I would likely grow out of it. No such luck. Dad thought it was funny. Mom thought it was expensive—but better than guns. And how could she blame me? She's the one who'd taught me everything I knew about high-fashion footwear. Shoes were "our" thing. Or at least they used to be.

"I'm going to the beach—and then to sucky school—but I need to be able to move," I said as if Gladys might talk back.

I walked around the shelves Dad had handcrafted just for me and the Pips, until I found them. My Juicy Couture Platino Metallic Gladiator Sandals named Hermes. I plucked them off the shelf and took them back to my room to get dressed, throwing on some yellow leggings, a Roxy hoodie, and my Spy sunglasses. I knew there was no sun, but like my shoes, they provided emotional support.

I slung my backpack over my shoulder and took a deep breath. A Courage Breath for the day—I didn't ignore everything Dr. T taught me.

Now I just had to sneak out without Hawkeye Jane catching me. I slithered down the stairs, into the garage, and into Big Black. For the quickest escape, I hit the garage-door opener at the same time as the ignition. It was already 6:00 a.m., and I only had eighty minutes before school started.

After sitting in the dry sand under the Pier for fifteen minutes, no effective thinking had taken place. Instead, I watched the light shift over the pink-and-purple horizon. Surfers lined up for their turns on the larger than usual sets rolling in. I hadn't surfed since Dad had died. It was *our* thing. And I missed it.

We'd sit out past the break waiting for the waves, and he'd tell me stories about combat as a Marine. About how hard it was to come back from the atrocities he'd witnessed as a soldier abroad. About the dangers still looming at home. About the line between right and wrong.

He'd called this beach his shoreline. He wanted to believe that— whatever he did—he'd always make it home, back to what was *sure*. His sure things included his integrity, his country, his freedom. His very own shoreline.

He was a broken record about me finding my own shoreline, about preparing myself for the moments in life when I'd be tested. There were times when his training and instruction felt like he was dragging me out into the deep waters of what my mom not-so-affectionately called his Post-Traumatic Stress Paranoia. Both in his time as a Marine and a police officer, he witnessed violence that most people can't even stand to watch on TV. So her words had merit, especially in the year leading up to his death. But now—his warnings and preparations didn't seem so crazy. In fact, it seemed like he might have known something (or *someone*) was coming.

Which made me wonder where my shoreline was anymore.

I grabbed my notebook and began OCD-organizing what was on my mind.

> *Problem 1: A girl is dead because I didn't respect the warning. I let her die.*
>
> *Dilemma 2: Whoever lured me to LeMarq is still toying with me. Trying to torment me. Or kill me.*
>
> *Predicament 3: I lied to the police about following LeMarq, and somehow Detective Martinez knows it. If he finds proof of my strange stalking habits, he'll argue that the LeMarq shooting was not, in fact, "legally justified." He'll claim that I had malice aforethought, intent, and motive—and that it was murder in the first degree.*
>
> *Disaster 4: My mom cheated on my dad—with the one man in a position to take me down!*
>
> *Mess 5: Mom's campaign opponent, Bill Brandon, is on a witch hunt to destroy the whole Rose family, and he doesn't mind using me to do it.*
>
> *Catastrophe 6: I am a killer.*

"Ruby!" A voice jerked my nose out of my notebook. "Hey, Ruby."

I looked up to find a half-naked Liam Slater jogging toward me through the sand with a surfboard under his arm.

This had to be some kind of psychotic delusion. Like my subconscious desires had fought to the surface. Or maybe I'd watched one too many episodes of vampire shows with shirtless immortals.

"I was hoping I'd see you here today," Liam said, a little out of breath. His unzipped wet suit hung dangerously low on his waist, exposing the muscular V-line in his hips that most girls would pay good money to see. His shaggy hair dripped salt water over his bronzed and chiseled eight-pack. Suddenly, I had a new problem—

Crisis 7: Acting like a total idiot in front of Liam Slater.

"I never heard back from you," he said as he sat down next to me. "Are you OK?"

"You hoped to see me? What made you think I'd be here?" I asked, semiviolently shutting my notebook like it contained national secrets.

"I've seen you out here before," he clarified. "My boys and I hit this spot before school occasionally for a session, and I've seen you here a few times *deep in thought*. I just never got the guts to actually come over and talk before."

"Really?"

"Really *what*?" he asked with a half smile.

"Really, you surf here? Really, you've seen me here? Really, you didn't have the guts to talk to *me*?" I was shocked by all three implications. Sure, I could be shortsighted and socially unplugged sometimes, but I couldn't have missed *him*.

He laughed, and I couldn't help but notice his perfectly straight white teeth against his sun-kissed face.

"I know we've goofed around in class, and said 'hey' in the halls and stuff, but you're sort of intimidating," he said. I could have sworn the sun came out just to do that shiny, sparkly thing off his teeth.

"I don't think *intimidating* is the right word," I said. "Maybe *unrelatable* . . . my therapist says I'm unrelatable." Why was I telling him I had a therapist?

"Oh . . . kay, unrelatable, unreachable, unattainable, sure." He looked over at me with raised eyebrows and a suppressed laugh. Seriously, dudes shouldn't have such long eyelashes. "You hit your head pretty hard yesterday. I hope you're OK."

"Did I?" I asked. I honestly didn't remember. Physical pain hardly ever bothered me. I'd gotten good at ignoring bumps and bruises.

"Right here," he said, reaching up to stroke my hair where my head had hit the floor. Now that he was touching it, that spot felt tender. But in this moment, I thanked the injury for giving me a rare moment of physical contact. Mom hadn't hugged me in years, and Dad's physical expressions of love (since I'd become a teen) consisted of sparring matches and pats on the head. In general, I'd always been pretty successful at keeping people within carefully controlled parameters. Even Alana had to hammer past my aversion to touch— what Dr. T said was part of my *autophobia*, or fear of abandonment. Which of course got ten times worse when my father was murdered.

But this uninvited touch from Liam? I didn't hate it.

"It doesn't hurt," I said, eyes down, blood pressure up.

"That's good." It took him a few strung-out beats before he lowered his hand. "Listen, I wanted to tell you something."

"OK, shoot," I said awkwardly. Not my best choice of words.

"Well, I don't want to come across as a creepy stalker kind of guy." He played with the damp sand in his hands. "But yesterday at the art fair . . . I noticed this guy. Well, a man. He was watching you."

"What?" I sat up taller. "What kind of man? A teacher?"

"No, I don't think he was a teacher. I would've seen him around school before. He was definitely out of place. He was watching you in an intense sort of way, and it was weird. I didn't like it."

Had he seen Martinez, too? Maybe I wasn't going crazy.

"What did he look like?" I asked, heart racing in a new way now.

"He was wearing a dark suit. No tie or anything, but a sort of athletic build, good-looking—like an older George Clooney kind of look." He grabbed a piece of kelp and crushed a bulb between his fingers.

"Was he Latino?" I asked.

"No, he was definitely a white dude. Sort of light, graying hair and stubble. Anyway, do you know someone like that?"

"No, I don't." If he wasn't talking about Martinez, then I had no idea who he was talking about (and I was officially crazy). None of my Filthy Five fit that description, unless one of them had hired a stylist and hit the gym like crazy for a few weeks. My fingers ached to open the notebook in my lap and write it all down.

"Then you passed out and he disappeared," Liam said. "Do you think this guy has anything to do with the text you got that night?"

His question caught me off guard. No one, not even Alana, had dared ask me about that night. Even though most of the details had been leaked to the media—including the fact that I thought the text was from Liam—I'd successfully given off the don't-talk-to-me-about-it vibe. Even without strict orders from Jane Rose, Esquire, I knew it wasn't wise to discuss the investigation with anyone.

"You know, the night you . . ." Liam paused, and I prayed he wouldn't say *shot that dude*. ". . . saved that girl? You think it might be him?"

I breathed a sigh of relief. "I have no idea."

"I *was* going to ask you to Homecoming—just so you know." He crushed another bulb. "I bought the flowers and everything. And I was on my way over to your house when Alana called me to tell me about—"

"Uh-huh." I didn't need to hear the end of that sentence. I knew what had happened next. I went into seclusion, and he'd gone to Homecoming with Taylor instead.

"I would've done the same thing." He turned to face me. "I would have pulled the trigger on that Charlie LeDouche, too. You did the right thing. No matter what anyone says, especially that Bill Brandon dude. I think you were brave."

I squirmed a little. He was sneaking past too many of my carefully constructed boundaries with his charm and sincerity. This is what I admired about Liam from afar—his ability to make people feel better about themselves.

"Obviously, I don't know *exactly* what happened," he continued. "Only what I've seen on the news or read in the papers, but it seems to me you were put between a rock and a hard place, and you ended up saving a little girl. That's totally amazing."

I felt for the picture of the girl hidden in The Cleave. Next to my other important stuff—cell phone, lip gloss—she was there.

Then I did something totally unexpected. I pulled her out to show Liam.

"She sent me this," I said, holding up the small picture.

His first reaction was shock—possibly at me reaching into my bra. Then his look changed as he wiped his hands on his wet suit and took the picture.

"Wow, this is her?" he asked.

"She sent me a letter, too, thanking me, telling me I'm her hero." I looked out at the ocean and the frothy waves crashing in. "But I haven't contacted her. The thing is, I don't feel like a hero. I mean, I don't regret killing him, because he deserved to die. He'll never hurt anyone again," I said, trying to stop the swell of truth gushing out of me, but unable to because it felt so good. "But it never should have happened. I never should have been put in that position. He should already have been behind bars. That little girl never should have needed saving—"

"She looks like you," he said.

My attention jerked back to him. He saw the similarities, too. Liam Slater was smart, observant, and protective. And he seemed to really want to help me.

"I know!" I said. "No one else noticed that."

"Well, they didn't release her name or picture," he countered.

"I mean the police. My mom. My therapist. People who saw her. None of them noticed."

"I don't know how they could have missed it." He stared sadly at the picture, running his finger over the bandage on the girl's neck where LeMarq had tried to kill her.

After a moment Liam reached up to his left ear and pulled his shaggy hair back over it. Through the wet strands I saw what he was trying to hide—a serious scar, pink and fleshy on the top part of his ear. I was surprised that, after all this time shamelessly staring at him, I'd never noticed it before. It must be why he always wore his hair long. I found myself desperately curious to know who'd done that to him and why.

The closer I looked now, the more I saw. His ear didn't bear his only scar. There were scores of little circles up and down the sides of his body. Like he had the chicken pox or—someone had used him as an ashtray. I teetered on the edge of asking, but I didn't dare. He was allowed to have his secrets, too.

He caught me examining him, and instead of being angry or ashamed, a look of little-boy sadness fell over him. He stared out at the sea with those eyes that changed a different shade of blue for every occasion. They were now a stormy slate, just like the clouded horizon.

Suddenly, I felt more truth bubbling inside me, and the urge to word-vomit everything. To share why I passed out in the cafeteria, the tattoo in the art, the *Love, D. S.* signature, the fact that I was stalking LeMarq, the photo of a frightened girl someone texted me last night, and the text blaming me for her death this morning. Another girl who looked like me. Liam already had more clues than the police did. He'd seen the guy who might be Mr. D. S. He could help me.

Or—he could hate me, despise me, and see me for who I really was. He could go to the cops, or worse, the media. Regardless of the way he was looking at me now, things would change. The truth would disgust him, repulse him.

The tide turned inside me, and my shell closed just like the oysters out in the ocean. I couldn't let these little pearls of truth escape. Ever.

"I gotta go," I said, grabbing the picture from his hand. As I shifted to get up, I felt his hand on my arm.

"What's wrong? What'd I say?" he asked. His touch and the worry in his voice almost cracked the shell back open.

"Nothing." I pulled away. "School starts in twenty minutes. I don't want to make you late." I speed walked through the clumpy sand, away from the emotional riptide that almost pulled me under.

"Ruby!" he called after me. "I'm sorry . . ." But the wind whipped away the last part of his apology.

As I climbed into Big Black, I resolved not to let Liam Slater get that close to me again. He could never hurt me if I never let him.

CHAPTER 7

I walked through the halls of Huntington Beach High wondering what it would be like to be that girl over there by the lockers—clearly in love with the boy next to her, and completely oblivious to every other concern in the world. Or that cheer chick in the courtyard, the one at the center of a gaggle of equally happy-go-lucky girls, laughing and listening to her glittery pink iPod. Or even that Goth boy by the water fountain, totally high as a kite. At least he *looked* happy.

I wondered what I looked like.

The bell rang, and I hurried to my Calc class at the end of the hall with my head down. Relieved not to be stopped, I slid into my seat at the back of the room and busied myself with my OCD preparations. Organizing my desk with the proper arrangement of my sharp mechanical pencil at my right, sleek calculator at my left, textbook center-right, notebook center-left, and bottle of water upper-right. A crack of the knuckles, and I was in the zone. A place where the only problems I had were mathematical.

When Mr. Holsum began to speak, I couldn't help but notice that Liam's desk was still empty. I told myself not to care. That it most likely had nothing to do with me. That he simply couldn't resist the storming ocean swells, and he was ditching so he could stay out with his boys. Surfers around here often did that. Even teachers were known to call in sick on big surf days.

So him missing class had nothing to do with me or my antisocial behavior.

Except, somehow I knew that wasn't true. He was genuinely worried about the guy behind all of this. And maybe even concerned about me. I could only hope he'd keep everything to himself. I didn't want him to get involved with the messiness of my life. He didn't deserve the whispers in the halls, the name-calling and speculation by the press, and he certainly didn't deserve to be tangled up in a police investigation.

"Psst, Ruby," Taylor whispered from her seat next to me. "Check this out." She hit me with a rolled-up newspaper.

I took it from her unwillingly, if only to stop her from bludgeoning me with it, and leveled my eyes on her. I unrolled the paper and clenched my jaw in preparation for the real blow. The headline read "Ruby Rose: Withering from the Roots."

Below the column header was a picture of me passed out on the cafeteria floor. And there was Liam with his bronzed triceps, holding me like a baby. I went from annoyed to humiliated to infuriated in a matter of seconds. My life was no longer my own, and now I was a joke, too. Taylor and her cheer cohort were snickering like a couple of playground bullies. And I never cared much for bullies.

Something snapped.

"You think this is funny?" I yelled at the suddenly snicker-less browbeaters.

"You think it's OK to make fun of me right in front of my face?" I stood now, and the screech from my desk chair might as well have been a whistle telling everyone to look my way. I didn't normally pick fights, but I knew how to win them.

"Ruby, is something the matter?" Mr. Holsum asked. He wouldn't get here soon enough to stop me from heel-kicking Taylor's front teeth out with my lovely Hermes sandals.

"We weren't making fun of you," Taylor said, so pathetically scared, so implausibly sincere. "I promise."

"Oh yeah," I said with a sneer I didn't particularly like in myself. "What were you laughing at, then?"

"It's Liam Slater we were *smiling* about," her nameless friend piped up, scooting her chair away just in case I decided to strike. "He's obviously so smitten with you. It's just interesting is all."

"What are you talking about?" I demanded.

"He's the only guy who's ever turned Taylor down," said Nameless Girl through her trembling, lip-glossed mouth as Taylor shot her a look of disgust. "We thought he was gay or something."

I looked at the newspaper scrunched in my fist. I didn't see "smitten." I didn't see "interesting." I saw privacy being deleted from my list of rights.

"Please, girls, that's enough." Mr. Holsum's voice sounded thin, just like his floppy comb-over. "Please, take your seats."

I looked at the declawed kittens in front of me and felt like a fool. They were petrified of me. Everyone was staring. They were all waiting for my next dramatic move.

"Never mind," I said, straightening my posture, then sitting back down. Even if Taylor was trying to humiliate or test me, it didn't matter. It wouldn't be the first or last time, and, as usual, I couldn't do anything about it. Other than ignore her.

I forced myself into a mindless coma for the next few hours. On autopilot, I planned to just get through the day and keep my head down until I could get my hands on some of the seriously strong Belgian chocolate stashed in the pantry at home. I focused on medicating myself with caffeine and getting to Dr. T's office.

Until I remembered how she'd closed up on me last time, presumably for sharing too much information. Maybe I'd finally done it and destroyed my sanctuary—just like I'd destroyed everything else.

• • •

"I hear you almost got into a fight today," Dr. T said calmly.

"Word travels fast." I stared out my favorite square window at the surf whitewashing the sand. Relieved as I was that my sanctuary appeared to be intact, I didn't feel like going so far as making eye contact. "Or is it that psychic thing again, and you *felt* the incident?"

"Your principal called me," she said, pulling her chair closer. "*And* your mom."

"All eyes on the withering Rose, eh?"

She released a small puff of air. "I'm a little worried. You're exhibiting an abnormal amount of *acting out* right now," Dr. T said carefully, with an *abnormal* amount of pausing. "Which is not altogether surprising considering the trauma you've experienced, but is nonetheless concerning."

Ugh. I hated when she went all intellectual on me.

"Nothing happened. It was a misunderstanding, not acting out," I argued, like maybe saying it out loud would make it true.

"You mean you didn't take some kind of karate stance in front of two girls today?"

"Karate stance?" I asked. Had I done that?

"Listen," she said with The Tone. Against my will, I relaxed. "I know you already know this, but violence is never the answer."

I finally looked her in the eye for the first time today. "I know that. Do you think I'm out of control or something?"

"I think you always have a choice," she said. "We always have a choice."

I didn't understand where she was going with this. "Are you saying I had a choice in shooting LeMarq? That I shouldn't have done it? That I was out of control and made the wrong choice—"

"No, no, no," she hushed me. "In that situation you made the right choice. I've told you over and over again that what you did was justified. I'm talking about other choices, those that will certainly come in the future."

It felt like she was alluding to something important. She had an uncanny ability to know things she shouldn't.

"What did my mom tell you?" I asked.

"That you received another message, and that you made the right choice again," she assured me. "You were right to report the text. You were right to trust the police."

"See, that's where I don't agree," I argued. "It couldn't have been right, because the girl is dead. Because of me." I knew I shouldn't have trusted ex-lover Martinez. Not only was he vindictive, but completely incompetent. He hadn't even bothered to call and tell me who the girl was. I had to find it out through my own (less than totally legal) lunchtime research at the library. I held my head in my hands, unable to support it anymore.

Her name was Sarah Jennings. Fifteen years old. Wasn't even reported missing, because her single mom was working a twenty-four-hour shift as a nurse last night. Only a freshman in high school, she'd never wear a prom dress, a graduation robe, a wedding gown. The terror she must have felt, the pain her mother must feel, the darkness of it all threatened to consume me as I allowed myself to—

"Ruby." Dr. T's voice felt awkwardly near. "Come back."

She wasn't just near. She was sitting next to me on the couch with one arm around me. "God offers to every mind its choice between truth and repose," she said quietly.

"Huh?" I'd lost my bearings. Dr. T had never put her arm around me before. "What are you talking about?"

"It's Emerson," she said, pulling away to shine her headlight eyes on me. "God offers to every mind its choice between truth and repose. Take which you please—you can never have both."

I wasn't drinking her Very Cherry Kool-Aid. And I definitely wasn't getting the message she was trying to send. Like the physical contact had created a spam filter and her message was just going to the junk file.

Normally, I liked to think of myself as a highly intelligent person, and not just because of the test scores. I wasn't one of those book-smart-only kids who could barely interact socially or drive without pissing off the entire State of California. Most of the time I could read people, situations, scenarios—and act accordingly. In fact, after I founded the Constitution Society, some people started calling me the "young Jane Rose," saying things like, "Maybe you'll be the District Attorney one day, just like your mom." Or, "I bet you make your mom so proud." Of course that was all before Dad died and I resigned from . . . everything.

Still, I should have been smart enough to decipher whatever Dr. T was really trying to say to me. But no. Her arm around me clouded my ability to think straight.

Perhaps sensing my rising discomfort level, she moved back to her chair, giving me some breathing room.

"Rue, tell me what you're thinking," she said.

Yeah, right.

"You know I have always tried to be professional with you. You are my client, and you deserve to be treated with every level of respect and dedicated care. But"—she paused, and I felt a blow coming—"I care about you very much."

That statement should have felt welcome, comforting. Instead, it felt loaded.

Dr. T didn't have any children of her own. My mom had told me about her series of miscarriages and subsequent divorce. I supposed it was completely natural for her to care about me, especially since I felt the same way about her. But, for some reason, it felt heavy for her to finally voice it. "I know what I'm about to say now may be hard for you to hear, but I am going to say it anyway because it's the *truth.*"

I took a deep Courage Breath, just like she'd taught me.

"It's time for you to let your mom in. You need each other now like never before."

Dr. T was right—that kind of advice was hard for me to hear. Wasn't it Jane's job, as the mother, to let *me* in? Not the other way around?

"You say that like it's an easy thing to do," I argued.

"I didn't say it would be easy. In fact I know just how hard it will be. But it's time." Dr. T checked her watch as if she was beginning to check out.

Until now, I'd pretty much relied on her to be a sounding board and nonjudgmental third party when I needed to vent about various neuroses. But now that I'd killed someone, indirectly caused an innocent death, and trapped myself in my own lies and illegal obsessions, I really needed her.

"We're going to end our session a few minutes early again today," she said. "We'll make up the time at another appointment." She stood to escort me to the door. But she hadn't even given me the chance to tell her about my mom's affair. "I want you to give what I said a great deal of thought. Truth or repose—you can't have both."

I honestly had no idea what she was talking about. But maybe with some distance I'd figure it out.

"See you next week," she said with a sympathetic nod. "Have a safe weekend."

"You, too," I said.

And she shut the door in my face.

CHAPTER 8

Equation of the night: Muggy air (smelling of equal parts beer and sweat) + hip-hop (blaring from the Napoleon-complex speakers) ÷ the throng of horny teenagers (rubbing up against each other like animals in heat) = sensory overload.

"I can't believe you brought me here!" I yelled into Alana's ear. "Can you get a ride home? I don't feel comfortable—"

"Oh, shut up and relax," she yelled back, fist-pumping to the music. "This is just what you need—mindless social interaction. No one is worried about you and what you've done or haven't done. They're too busy having *fun!*"

She was wrong. This wasn't *just what I needed.* I didn't *need* to be manipulated into coming to some stupid high school party when she promised we could talk. What I needed was to figure out who was messing with me. And fast, before anyone else got hurt or Martinez discovered that I'd been stalking LeMarq long before I put a bullet between his eyes.

As soon as I could, I was going home, locking myself in my room, and poring over my notes on the Filthy Five. There had to be a connection between them and my whole life falling apart.

I watched as Alana slipped into the pulsating heart of the dance floor. Her wavy black hair bopped to the beat, and her skinny little Daisy Dukes–wearing legs jumped up and down with the crowd. I couldn't help wondering why she still put up with me after all these years. Me, the epitome of Buzzkill. She remained ever loyal, even when I failed to reciprocate. I imagined Dr. T would probably say that as opposites, we needed each other to balance out our weaknesses and strengths. She kept me normal, and I kept her in excellent *couture*. Except lately, I worried I was more of an anchor, pulling Alana down into the depths with me.

As she got sucked further into the riptide of flesh, I found a wall to lean on, my anxiety growing. I shouldn't be here, hanging out, doing nothing. But I didn't want to feel the consuming guilt and anger threatening to break me, either. Maybe Alana was right: I needed a good distraction.

I scanned the massive room, observing other people's issues for once instead of concentrating on my own. It appeared that Declawed Taylor and unnamed friend were lushing their way to happiness. Jell-O shots and tube tops were all they needed. A pack of football players surrounded them as they slurped themselves into oblivion.

As my eyes roamed the room, I found so many examples of kids with major problems: Brianna Hartley, who'd spent last spring in rehab; Miles Brown, who'd gotten two girls pregnant in the same year; Ted Cohen, who'd once eaten a handful of worms on a dare . . .

But even after some therapeutic people watching, or as Alana liked to call it, "people judging," I still felt like a wolf in sheep's clothes. Well, a wolf in four-inch Jimmy Choo wedge heels. Yeah, these kids were crazy, but I was almost 99 percent sure that none of them were violent-crazy. Like me.

I caught eyes with a guy named Jace I dated freshman year—if *dating* meant kissing a lot and then being constantly harassed about "moving to the next level in our physical relationship." He was a charming guy, but his smooth talking got old. And when I told him I thought we should go back to being friends—the kind without benefits—he took it hard. If *hard* meant spreading rumors about what a boring prude I was.

While I was still looking in his direction, he shaped his hand into a gun and took aim at me. I couldn't believe it. He'd been a jerk-jar before, but this was crossing the line. I had half a mind to cross the room and break his little gun-shaped hand (and equally little boy parts) but the thought of the story getting leaked to *Access Hollywood* kept my back against the wall. When he cocked his hand and made a blasting gesture, I finally looked away. What a piece of—

"Don't pay attention to Jace." Liam's familiar voice caught me off guard. And his warm breath against my ear almost made my Jimmy Choos give way. "He only acts like an ass because he's never gotten over you."

I turned my head to find him leaning on the wall next to me, the disco ball sprinkling light on his face like diamond reflections.

When the freak did he get here?

"Oh, hey," I said, taking a firmer stance against those eyelashes. "Right. Jace. Ass. Totally." What was that? California Cavegirl–speak?

"It's hot in here. Wanna come out on the balcony with me?" This time his lips brushed the side of my neck as he leaned in. How could he still want to talk to me after I stared down his scars and then lamely left him at the beach?

I looked around for something to hold on to. A lifeline to keep me from jumping off this cliff. Where was Alana when I needed her?

I found nothing and no one. I looked down instead, trying to steel my resolve. Except his classic white Nike Air Force 1s might have just turned me on even more. This boy, his lashes, and his shoes were going to break me.

"Sure," I said.

He took my hand and weaved me through the bouncing bodies, up the stairs, through a master bedroom, and onto a balcony overlooking the shore with a spiral staircase leading down to the beach.

"Should we be up here? I don't even know who lives here," I said, out of breath. I wasn't trying to do that seductive-bunny voice girls like Taylor use to unhinge guys. Honestly. Hiking the massive staircase after months of no physical training and the close proximity of Liam's lips to my ear had sincerely winded me.

"Don't worry," he assured me, letting go of my hand and plopping down on a love seat facing the railing. "This house is just a party pad. You know Chase?"

"I think so. Is he on the football team with you?" I asked, even though I knew exactly who Chase was. Alana used to have a thing for Chase like I still had a thing for Liam. At one point, she'd even had the joint wedding all planned out.

"Yeah. Well, this is his uncle's third or fourth house. He's some billionaire from Texas or something."

"It's amazing," I said, still standing in the doorway where he left me.

"Yeah, I know—sick, right?"

"Totally. Sick." *I* felt sick. I had no idea what to do with my hands. Pockets, no. Behind the back, no.

"Come sit down," he said, sounding sort of winded himself. Which made no sense since he was in peak physical condition.

"OK." I rounded the seat and sat down next to him, wondering why I was being so weak. I had firmly resolved not to allow him to get close to me again. And here I was, obeying his every command.

"So, what's up with you leaving me high and dry the other day on the beach?" he asked with a slight hitch in his voice. Almost like he was just as tense as I was.

"There's this thing called school. And you aren't supposed to be late to it."

"Whatever. We had plenty of time." He leaned toward me.

It was a bright night, and the moon provided an unfortunate spotlight on my awkwardness—and a better view of that scar on his ear.

"Have you thought about what I told you?" he said. "About that guy watching you? Have you told the police?"

"No, I mean yes, well . . ." I stopped to gather myself. "Yes, I thought about what you said, but I haven't told the police."

"Have you told your mom?"

"No."

"Why not? Don't you think it's sort of pertinent?" He put his hand on my knee. I jerked away, far jumpier than necessary.

Of course I thought it was pertinent. But football players shouldn't use such big words. Or pretend to be seriously interested in me. And certainly not touch me like that, or look at me like this—with tenderness and intimacy.

"What's going on? Why wouldn't you help them protect you?"

"You don't understand. There's more to it."

"Tell me, then. Help me understand." He turned his body to face me.

I stared at his lips. Were they telling the truth? Or were they like chocolate—promising happiness, providing a few moments of heaven, then ultimately betraying me, going behind my back and putting junk in the trunk?

It didn't seem like a fair choice. Chocolate had total power over me—there was no denying my addiction to the dark, creamy crack. Those few moments of bliss were always enough for me to disregard the consequences. So, even if Liam was only chocolate, I wanted to taste a piece.

Just imagining the moment our lips would touch made me lightheaded. There was no denying how strongly I'd wanted this. An energy buzz overtook all my logic, all my pain. Overwhelmed by it, I gave in.

I softened.

Briny air swirled across the veranda, mixing with Liam's musky cologne. The scent swept over me, and I closed my eyes to breathe it in. But then something inside me turned over. It smelled like the same cologne my dad used to wear.

A deep pit formed in my stomach as I remembered him walking out the garage door for the last time. I didn't know then he would be ambushed and blown to pieces. I didn't know then that I would never see him again.

"I gotta go." I opened my eyes and started to get up. But Liam stopped me, reaching for my wrist. Instinctively, I rotated my hand clockwise and thrust it down with the full weight of my body to break his grip.

"Jeez!" He jumped up and grabbed at his wrist in pain. "What the—?"

"Don't grab at me then if you don't want to get hurt!" I moved behind the couch, to put some space, and furniture, between us.

"I wasn't *grabbing* at you," he said with a grimace. "I was just trying to stop you from running away from me *again*."

"First of all, you did *grab* me, and second . . ." I didn't really have a second. "Look, I'm way too messed up for you to bother with."

"I'm sorry, I didn't mean to *grab*," he said, moving toward me slowly, like I was a bomb in need of dismantling. "And just so you know, it's OK to be a little messed up."

"I don't know what you want from me." I backed up. "Or why you're acting so *interested* in me all of a sudden. Is it the fame thing? Do you want to see yourself in the newspaper next to Bleeding Ruby Rose again? Or did one of your football buddies bet you that you couldn't get laid by the most *dangerous* girl in school?"

Not likely. My virginity wasn't exactly a secret. One of those trashy magazines had even broadcast it in an article called "Ruby Rose: The Virgin Vigilante."

He stopped and looked at me with the mug of a kicked puppy. "Wow."

"Wow, what?" They were simple questions.

"I had no idea that's what you thought of me," he said, lowering his head to stare at the red marks developing on his wrist.

"Well, I told you," I said, a little less abrasively. "I don't know what to think. Things are complicated for me, and I don't know what your intentions are."

"My intentions?" he asked, as if he didn't readily know the answer. "I just wanted to help. That guy—he used me, too, you know."

"What? What do you mean he *used* you?"

"He pretended to be me when he sent you that text, remember? My name was in the police report. That Detective Martinez guy came to my house and interviewed me. And when it went public, reporters tried to talk to me. My friends never leave me alone about it. So, yeah, I feel a little *involved*, OK?"

"OK," I said, taken aback. I felt horrible that my stupid life had already affected him, and like the biggest B-word for giving him such a hard time. "I'm sorry, I didn't know—"

"Plus, I know what it's like to be misunderstood." He paused and did that self-conscious ear-touching thing. Again, I wondered what could have possibly happened to him. "It's a lonely place to be, and I can see how talented you are at pushing people away. Or maybe I should say karate chopping people away." A sliver of a smile formed in the crease of his eyes.

Oh, no. I was softening under his charm again. "But you're still not answering my question, Liam. *Why* do you want to help me? Are you upset that you're involved?"

He rubbed his forehead. "C'mon, isn't it obvious?"

"If it were obvious, I wouldn't need to ask."

"I like you, all right?" He was red in the face and clearly frazzled. "I've liked you for a long time, but you haven't given me the time of day."

It couldn't be that simple. He couldn't have wanted to help me simply because he "liked" me. I "liked" watching lobsters play in their tank at the restaurant, and I still "liked" to eat them. I didn't trust that word. For two years, I practically went all googly-eyed at him every time he looked at me. Now he was saying he "liked" me?

"I don't know what that's supposed to mean, but I've always given you the time of day."

"Let me be clear, then, so you know what I mean," he said, stepping forward again, a glutton for punishment. "I've been wanting to ask you out for a while, but when your dad died I figured you needed some time. Then, just when I got the courage to ask you to Homecoming, well, the bottom of your world dropped out again."

He knew that my dad had died. And he'd cared enough to give me time. I softened even more.

"So what about Taylor?" I asked, wondering why my brain had brought her up at a time like this. It was like my logical brain had a firewall and was trying to override the invading emotions.

"Taylor?" he asked back. His eyebrows creased together in confusion.

"You know, the girl you actually *did* take to Homecoming. The girl who's always hanging all over you. The girl nobody turns down." *Shut up!*

He reached out to take my hand, apparently unafraid of what other sudden movements I might make. And, inexplicably, I let him take it.

"I'm not going to say anything bad about Taylor," he said, moving his head even closer to mine. "But I'm not going to say anything good about her, either."

Wow. I couldn't help but be impressed with his maturity and refusal to trash-talk.

"But you on the other hand," he said, looking me in the eyes. "I think *you're* amazing. And brave. And totally different."

Firewall disabled, I let him pull me into his arms.

I let him put his body against mine.

I let my eyes close, appreciating the heat between our bodies. His heart beating against my ear drowned out all my wild, neurotic thoughts. I was giving in to him again. *I* was the glutton for punish-ment.

Until I felt a pinch on my neck. Like a bee sting, it burned. But surely there were no effin' bees at the beach this time of night. I tried to pull away, but by the time I reached to get the bee's stinger out of my skin, I realized I was dealing with something else entirely.

A syringe.

And I was losing consciousness.

CHAPTER 9

I heard the voices before I could identify where they were coming from. Swirling human forms floated around my mind. And pain. I felt that rising with my consciousness. In my head, mostly, but also on my wrists. They were bound behind my back.

I ordered my eyes to open, but they were as heavy as theater curtains. I needed pulleys or something.

When my eyelids eventually creaked open, I almost wished they hadn't.

I lay on the cold floor of a large metal cage, like one used for lions at the circus. I had awoken in my very worst nightmare. I hated bars. Like, I really, deathly feared them. Dr. T said it was a "seminormal/ common phobia," and not to give it too much importance, but that was easy to say when she wasn't the one with the recurring dreams of bars slowly closing in on her until she was crushed to death.

The men behind the echoing voices were nowhere in sight. Hyperventilation and claustrophobia drained me of my wits. I closed my eyes and tried to steady my breathing. I couldn't lose my cool now. I had to fight. I had to look past the bars and pretend like they weren't there in order to gather my survival instincts. The inanimate cage couldn't beat me when the very animate men beyond them were far more likely to do so.

Forcing open my eyes, I saw a spacious warehouse filled with boxes and old machinery, not unlike the one at the harbor where I'd put a hole in Charlie LeMarq's head. And I wasn't alone. There were two equally drugged and bound bodies just outside the cage, except they were tied at the ankles as well as the wrists. I wondered why they weren't in here with me—and why they weren't stirring.

I looked closer at them through the dim light. It was Alana and Liam. The last time I'd seen Alana, her dark hair was bouncing to the beat of the music. Now it was as limp as a doll's. And Liam's beautiful lips, the ones I'd come so close to kissing, were now gagged and covered in bloody cloth.

My chest tightened with a crushing force. I hated myself for getting them involved. If only I'd done a better job of pushing everyone away, they wouldn't be here.

"I'm not going to tell you again!" a deep voice echoed across the warehouse. "It's time, so make the call!"

"Come on, jefe, this ain't right," another man replied in a much younger and more hesitant voice, with an accent that made me think of the East LA gang crews. So not *bueno*.

I couldn't see them, and they couldn't see me behind the row of crates piled haphazardly toward the ceiling.

"What *ain't* right is you acting like a little bitch. Now get your phone out and make the call."

"Bro, calm down and think about it. All we're supposed to do is babysit these drugged kids for a while and then take the money and run? Rick, it's a setup."

Rick. I knew a Rick. Rick "The Stick"—one of my Filthy Five. But I'd never heard him speak, so how could I be sure if this voice belonged to him?

"You're wasting time," Rick said.

"You've done deals with this guy before?" the younger guy asked, sounding more skittish.

"Yeah, two nights ago, OK? It didn't go as planned, and I had to get rid of a girl. Let's just say he owes me tonight."

Two nights ago? Get rid of a girl? Could he have been talking about the girl on Ninth Street from the text I got?

"Didn't go as planned? Shit, man, you ain't exactly making me feel better."

"Look, I've done plenty of deals, and this one won't be any different," Rick said. "So just make the damn call and let's get this over with!"

"Why don't *you* make the call?"

"Because, you idiot, I don't have the number. The broker gave it to you."

The broker? What product—?

Oh, crap. We were the product. *I* was the freaking product.

"Here. Take the number that dude gave you. I'll go wait where the cops can't bust through that door in five seconds!" The younger guy was rattled.

"Look, you split, and you *lose* your split. You understand? That's twenty grand. And the *broker* is not *some dude*. He's big-time, working with Mr. G. You get in with G, and you don't get to mess around. So just shut up already!"

There was a pause and some shuffling.

"Can't I at least sample the product? Five minutes alone with the blonde?" My stomach turned, and my muscles tensed in revolt. Young or not, stupid or smart, this guy was dangerous. "If we get busted, at least it won't all be for nada—"

"How many times do I have to tell you? The broker said she's a virgin, and they pay triple for virgins. You're not touching her or her skinny little friend, no matter what. I need this score, all right?"

There was no longer any doubt in my mind—this was, in fact, Rick "The Stick." Number two on my list of the Filthy Five. The details I'd written in his file quickly came to mind. Formerly: Rick Rossi, champion featherweight boxer from South LA. Currently: notorious drug dealer and unmerciful murderer of anyone who got in his way. He earned his cute little nickname by screwing over one of his big-time drug partners, "sticking" him with the evidence that sent the guy to prison, and walking away with a sweetheart deal from none other than Dear Mother Jane Rose.

Before Dad's death, his team had responded to a tip on one of Rick's big deals going down. They recovered 500 kilos of cocaine, but not The Stick himself. He'd gotten away again. Since the bust he'd been lying low, staying away from the cartel guys. That must've been what he was talking about when he said he needed this score. He needed the money.

If I didn't do something quickly, they were either going to make the call and sell us, or they were going to talk each other out of it and get rid of us themselves. I cursed the man behind this torment. Who was this "broker" who'd convinced another one of my Filthy Five to participate in the systematic torture of Ruby Rose? Why didn't he just kill me himself? And why did he have to involve Alana and Liam? Sure, Alana was fragile enough to sell, but there was no market for six-foot-four tight ends who could knock out The Stick with one punch.

As they continued to argue about whether or not to get rid of us, I rocked back and forth until I could wiggle my hands under my legs and bring them in front of me. I was relieved to find my bonds were only plastic tie straps—and I had sharp teeth.

But minutes passed and I'd made no progress on the thick ties. My now swollen and bloody gums weren't helping, either. I was running out of time. If they hadn't heard me by now, it wouldn't be much longer.

I looked around for something sharp—a broken bottle, a piece of scrap metal, anything. But after too many minutes of blinking to try to focus past the bars, all I could find to saw the plastic were the sharp, rusty hinges on the cage itself. I swallowed the feeling that the bars were moving toward me as I crawled toward them, and I began sawing. I barely breathed as I used all my strength to grind through the plastic as silently as possible.

As soon as the ties snapped off, I felt around for a way to open the cage. In the top corner was a latch kept shut by a bicycle lock. A bicycle lock? Come on, no proper criminal uses a coiled three-digit-code bicycle lock! If it were a normal lock, I could have picked it with my earring like Dad taught me. But the only way to get this thing off was to know the code. And I didn't know it.

Wait. *Three* digits.

Suddenly, I had an idea. Mr. D. S. didn't seem to do anything without purpose or meaning. I doubted Rick had put me in this cage himself. It wasn't his MO. He was a vicious criminal who didn't mind beating people to death with his little bare fists, but as far as my research went, child trafficking wasn't in his repertoire. Plus, why cage me and not my friends? These bars felt very much meant for me.

The three numbers had to be significant. I mentally ran through all the numbers in my life—birthday, phone number, address—rotating the lock as fast as I could to any three-digit combination related to them. But nothing worked.

My heart thumped three times, as if willing my brain to figure this out for the sake of all the body parts. I let go of the lock and let my head fall against the bars.

I thought back to the text with the photo of the girl on Ninth Street. Any numbers? No. The sketch at the art fair? No. The text from Fake Liam luring me to the warehouse?

That message filtered into the forefront of my sore head: *366 Water Street.*

I squinted through the bars and put in the numbers 3-6-6. The lock clicked open, and I broke free.

"They're on their way," confirmed Rick's personal assistant in crime.

The call had been made. Whoever was coming to take us would be here soon. And I couldn't carry out both Alana and Liam on my back. Even if I could wake them up without making much noise, I had no idea how to get their ankle and wrist ties off in time.

I had to find a weapon, or see if my captors had one and use it against them. Maybe the men had a knife, and I could get back here in time to cut Alana and Liam free.

I crawled through piles of strewn trash, careful not to look too closely at it—and also careful not to cause any noise. Whether it was the drugs or the stress of the cage, time wasn't making sense to me. It took forever to get to the boxes separating me from the men. I peered over the clumsy piles, cautious not to knock them over like dominoes. Now I could finally see the enemy. Rick could have also been called The Stick because he'd been beaten by an ugly one. Or because he was as skinny as one. He and his coconspirator, who was far chubbier and softer than I was expecting, sat at a flimsy card table, anxiously staring at the door. Like either a dump truck full of money was about to back up through the cargo entry door—or a SWAT crew. There appeared to be only one revolver between them, and it sat untouched on the table. If either of them was packing another weapon, I couldn't see it.

That shiny gun was my target. I had to get it somehow. I imagined Dad walking me through it all—just like he had with LeMarq. Just like he always would, dead or alive.

Create a diversion. One of them will take the gun and check to see what it is. Take him out by surprise from behind. Grab the weapon and disable him with two bullets to the chest. You already know he will kill you, so don't let him have the chance. The second man will either flee or attack. If he flees, pursue. He could double back and ambush you before you're able to find a way to call for help, and you can't leave your friends in harm's way. If he attacks, you know what to do.

I took a deep breath. I could do this. There was no time to waver or second-guess. I had to save my friends.

I found an empty beer can nearby and chucked it toward the cage. It hit with a loud *clang!* Instantly, the men's chairs screeched backward on the cement floor. I hid behind the stack of crates again so when one man walked past me to check on the noise, I could spring.

"Go check it out," Rick ordered. I remembered his strange aversion to guns, and most likely the only reason he even had a tagalong with him was to pack it. Or to blame everything on later if he got caught.

"It's probably that stupid white boy waking up. I'd be happy to knock him out again," Tagalong said as he made his way to my hiding spot.

I lunged, simultaneously kicking him in the groin and twisting his weapon from his grip. I'd done it dozens of times in training sessions but never in real life. He howled in pain. This couldn't have been his first swift kick to the balls, but he sure acted like it as he rolled around on the floor with his hands between his legs.

"Rick, it's the blonde!" he moaned. "She's got my piece."

"Shut up or I'll shoot," I warned. I had no idea where Rick was. I hadn't heard him move.

"I knew this was a trap." He groaned. "Just shoot me and get it over with. I can't go back to prison. I won't go back. I'll kill you and both your friends before I go back." Real tears came spurting out of his pathetic eyes, and for a second, I almost pitied him. His baby face and purple LA Lakers hat turned sideways made him seem only a few years older than me. The guy should have been in college or working at the mall, not messing around with gangs and a guy like Rick. Dad's voice cut into my hesitation.

Protect yourself, Rue. Make sure the weapon is cocked, and take the disabling shots. You know he will do it to you, or worse, without a moment's hesitation if you let him.

As I made sure the gun was cocked, I noticed how familiar it felt. This was no street gun. This was a sophisticated piece. A gun I'd used before.

I heard the terrible cracking noise against my spine before I felt the pain. My knees buckled and I fell to the ground, face first. Either Rick had slammed me with a wooden two-by-four, which had splintered in half, or he'd used a steel beam and the cracking noise was my vertebrae shattering. But how had he gotten behind me?

I checked my senses to make sure I still had the gun. Its cold steel was still wrapped in my white-knuckled clutch. I looked over my shoulder. Rick's gaunt, pockmarked face loomed above me. And I knew he was hell-bent on making sure it was the last face I ever saw.

"Stop!" I screamed. I rolled over on my back, crunched up, locked my arms out in front, and raised the gun between my legs. "I'll shoot!"

He raised another two-by-four above his head, ready to destroy me.

I had no choice. He was going to kill me.

I aimed for the largest target area and pulled the trigger. The gun sounded like a bomb exploding in the vast space. His chest ripped open and his body lost momentum. As though in slow motion, he dropped to his knees and the life drained out of his eyes. He would never fight again.

The smoke from my gun rose, just as the dust particles under his body mushroomed from his fall, swirling with the sudden draft of wind.

I gagged on the taste of bile in my throat and grimaced as the tinny smell of blood and gunpowder choked the air out of my lungs.

I fell back, disgusted and disoriented.

Until I remembered the baby-faced gangster—who'd said he'd kill us all before he went back to prison.

I looked up and he was already running past fallen boxes and debris—toward Alana. He was going to play his last card and use her to bargain for his freedom.

I pushed myself up with renewed strength and chased after him, ignoring the splintering pain attacking my spine. I leapt over Rick's body and willed my drugged body to run faster than the pudgy threat. He couldn't fight me while I had a gun, but he could stomp on Alana's head or whip out a knife and stab her a few times before I got off a shot. I already knew he was going down swinging—or stabbing.

"Just wait, I don't want to kill you!" I yelled after him. I don't think he heard me, or believed me, because he ran faster. In my mind, I begged him to stop, to act rationally, to give me his phone so I could call for help, and to try his chances again at the failed justice system that allowed him to be on the street in the first place. Or just make a play for the exit.

"I won't shoot you if you leave!" I screamed while gasping for breath. "Please don't do anything stupid!"

My fears were confirmed the moment I saw him pull something metallic from his boot and go for Liam's lifeless body.

I stopped running to take aim—for the shoulder this time. I couldn't shoot a man in his back, and I didn't want to kill him.

Then I heard my dad again: *You don't have a sight on this pistol. You're too far away, and it's too dark. If you miss, he'll kill Liam. You have to do it.*

The truth seemed to sting my eyes. I pinched them shut for a millisecond to clear my vision and regain my resolve. Then I corrected my aim, took the shot between his broad shoulder blades, and held my breath for impact.

In midstrike, he dropped the dagger, dropped to the ground, and dropped off the face of the world forever.

A full minute must have passed before I allowed myself to exhale, because dizzy didn't begin to explain the fainting sensation welling up inside me. I looked down to the weapon in my hand. Its custom-polished stainless nickel-plate finish shined up at me, and I noticed for the first time that it was a Glock 30, .45-caliber handgun. The kind Dad had carried as his off-duty weapon. The one he carried with him during SWAT operations as a backup. I turned over the heel to check for an engraving. There it was—his initials: J. R.

I dropped the gun like it was a hot coal. If this was my dad's gun, it must've been taken off of his body by whoever killed him. I didn't even know it was missing. This couldn't actually be Dad's. No, it couldn't be.

He spoke to me urgently this time: *Rue. It's not over. They called someone. Pick up that gun. Never drop your weapon.*

"Nice work," a foreign male voice whispered in my ear, as arms clutched me from behind. "You just saved me a load of money."

My heart sank as I realized my mistake. Maybe my fatal mistake.

I couldn't see the new threat's face, but I could see Liam's and he was finally conscious. I wondered how long he had been awake and if he'd seen me kill the monster lying dead over his legs. By the wild look in his eyes, I was sure he had.

"No!" he screamed through his gag, trying to fight the bonds and get the dead body off him.

"Oh, I see," the scratchy voice breathed into my ear. "We have a boyfriend. Must've gotten in the way. I don't really deal in the boy market, but I'm sure we'll make do."

Instinct took over again, and I thrust my elbow into his ribs, twisted so his grip loosened, and—with every ounce of force I had left—slammed both hands down onto his wrists to break free. Now that I was facing him, I could go for the "sweet spots." I faked a kick to sweet spot number one—the groin—and got him in sweet spot number two—the eyes. I clawed at his face with my fingernails, and he screamed, "*Kuradi lits! Kuradi lits!*" Which sounded like he was saying, "Karate tits!" or "Karate lips!"—but probably meant something very different in his language, and nothing friendly, for sure.

With his hands now guarding sweet spot two, I promptly went for number one, releasing the kick of all kicks to the only place that matters. It connected with a crunch, and a guttural groan.

Followed by a protracted slide and click.

I didn't make that sound. A cold circle of metal pressed against my temple.

"Try something and I shoot," a different voice beside me warned.

"Ruby, don't move," Liam called out, panic in his voice. Somehow he'd loosened the gag enough to speak. "Don't fight."

Before I'd be able to swing around and make a play for the gun, my life would be over.

I dropped my throbbing head and listened for the answer. Where was my dad's voice now?

Gone. Just like my life in a few moments.

A backhanded knuckle-slap to my face cut me out of my ridiculous search for the voices in my head.

"Insolent brat," the first man spewed through his forest of facial hair. He reached into his jacket and pulled out a handgun—relieving the other man of gun-pointing duty—and stroked the side of my face with the barrel. "Your spirit will be broken soon enough."

"No," I said, coiling my springs. "I won't let you. I'd rather die than be handed off to one of your disgusting buyers." I tasted another round of fresh blood in my mouth and looked for the gun I'd so stupidly dropped. It was my one and only chance to survive.

"Please," Liam pled from the floor. "Ransom us. You don't have to sell anyone. My dad is filthy rich. He'll pay you whatever you want. I swear. You'll get far more that way." I didn't know Liam's dad was rich. He had to be lying. But it didn't matter—this was good. Liam was distracting them. Maybe I could find that gun in the dark and—

Thump. The violent sound caused me to turn. The second guy, with his stupid '80s mullet, was standing over Liam, kicking him in the side. With his hands tied behind his back, Liam couldn't defend himself. He was coughing and grimacing for air. The Mullet was going to break Liam's ribs or puncture a lung.

"Don't touch him!" I screamed. "Stop that—"

"Or what?" the first man breathed in my face. His oniony breath alone was nearly enough to kill me. "You'll use *this* against us?" He held my own father's gun to my head.

I didn't know which I was more pissed about: making the stupid mistake of dropping that gun or getting my innocent friends involved. Maybe if I had gone to save that girl on Ninth Street, this whole night wouldn't have happened. Maybe involving Alana and Liam was Mr. D. S.'s way of punishing me for my disobedience. Either way, I blamed myself. And who said dying would be so bad anyway? At least I'd be with my dad again.

As The Mullet made his way back over to me, I knew I had to act soon. I couldn't wait until they tied me up again. I had to die fighting *now*.

I took one last look at Liam suffering on the ground and Alana still in her unconscious ignorance, and I said good-bye in my mind. I could only hope my friends would put up a fight, too, if they could. Then I turned all my energy back on the first guy—the leader. I could disarm him, use him as a shield, and maybe get off a couple of shots before The Mullet could react. It was a long shot, but I had to do it if there was even the smallest chance it would save my friends.

I slouched my shoulders and heaved a huge sigh of defeat. Part of me meant it, and part of me faked it to lure the men to let down their guard. It worked—a smile formed through the dirty-nasty beard of the first man, and he relaxed just enough for me to make my move.

As I was about to spring, a small green dot appeared on his face. As though Tinker Bell herself had flown in to distract me, the light flickered before it steadied itself on his forehead. Before my brain registered what it was, the dot turned a burgundy-red and the man's body flew backward. He'd been shot in the head, just like LeMarq.

I spun, expecting The Mullet to blow me away, but before he could even raise his gun, he had two rounds firmly lodged in his chest.

For a moment I froze, not comprehending what had happened. Then adrenaline and relief coursed through me like an injected drug. Until it occurred to me that whoever just shot these guys might go for me next.

I looked down at the pool of blood near my feet and saw Dad's gun. As I reached for it, a strong arm wrapped itself around my body while a hand pressed a damp cloth over my nose and mouth. The harder I fought against the crushing strength, the faster I lost my own. The scent on the fabric stung my senses and made my eyes water.

My world quickly spun out from under me. Swirling. Darkness. Pain. The last thing I saw was Liam, still on the ground, soundlessly calling out my name.

CHAPTER 10

Either my face was dangerously close to a shallow pool of water or I was drooling. Or both. Gross.

I finally opened my eyes, and wiped my face with my sleeve. Wasn't heaven supposed to be all white and sparkly? I looked around for those pearly gates, some fat little cherubs, or some other heavenly clichés.

I sat up to make sure I wasn't in hell. This habit of waking up confused and bruised was getting old.

It didn't look like hell, though my back still hurt pretty hellishly. At least there was no fire, no brimstone. Not that I would even recognize brimstone if I saw it.

I was on top of an ocean cliff, lying in the middle of an isolated rugged bluff. The powerful surf crashed below me. The waters were angry, but that didn't mean anything. Maybe this was some kind of symbolic in-between.

A foghorn from a boat in the distance bellowed a deep belching sound. But in the weak light of dawn, I couldn't even see a vessel.

"Ruby!" a female voice called out. "Ruby, I'm over here."

I spun around—Alana!

She was lying on the ground behind me, twenty feet away. Still bound. And Liam was next to her, unconscious again.

I scrambled to my unsure feet and made my way up the slight incline and over the jagged sandstone rock to my poor, traumatized, lucky-to-be-alive, unlucky-to-know-me friends.

"Alana, I'm coming," I said, stumbling and falling on my already sore wrist. How did we get here? "I'm just a little dizzy . . ."

"It's OK, take your time," she said with a shaky voice. I could tell she'd been crying but was trying to be brave. "I don't want you falling off the cliff and leaving me and Sleeping Beauty over here for the vultures to peck on."

I finally made it to Alana and fell to her side. "I'm so sorry—this is all my fault."

"Would you just shut up and get something to cut off these ties?" She blew some wet strands of hair out of her eyes.

"Of course, I'll find something." I scanned the cliff top for a rock shard, a seashell . . . "Holy mother of . . ." I whispered.

On a small ledge twenty feet away sat a pair of heavy-duty stainless steel cutters. But that's not what stopped me short. It was the gun—my dad's nickel-plated Glock—sitting next to them.

"What is it?" Alana propped up her head to look.

I hesitated for too long, wondering why someone would want me to keep the murder weapon.

"Ruby! What is it?" Alana yelled at me.

"Some scissors. There are just some scissors over there."

"I've been lying here an hour, screaming at you and Liam to wake up, and there's an effin' pair of scissors over there?"

I ran over to the ledge and grabbed the shears. Making sure Alana was looking the other direction, I quickly tucked the gun into the back of my pants before I went to cut her free. As she rubbed at her raw skin, I crawled the few feet over to Liam to check his pulse before I cut his ties. His heart rate was scary slow, but he was alive.

"Liam, can you hear me?" I rolled him over so his head was in my lap. I brushed his shaggy hair off his eyes, willing them to open. "Please wake up." His face was clean and fresh, no more bloodied lip. Like someone had dunked his head in the ocean, or carefully wiped away any evidence of the beating.

"Is he all right?" Alana asked, now standing on wobbly legs.

"I think so."

"Who did this to us? Where are we? And where's my damn phone?" She started patting herself down like if she concentrated hard enough, her cell might miraculously appear in one of her skimpy pockets.

"Sit down, Alana," I ordered. "You're going to fall and break something."

"Did we get roofied? Is this some kind of sick practical joke?" she asked, refusing to obey. Her skinny little flamingo legs looked like they'd give out any second.

"No, this isn't a joke. Just sit for a minute."

"Why'd you say this is all your fault? What did you do to get us punked like this?" She began pacing, making me want to yank her to the ground for her own good. "If it's the football players who did this, I am going to *kill* them—"

"I told you, nobody's punking us." I cut her off, not comfortable with her talking about killing anyone. "It's not the football players." I turned my attention back to Liam.

There was no way to explain to Alana what had happened. She'd obviously seen nothing and never woke up to witness the carnage. She thought we just got dumped on the cliff. She hadn't even seen the blood on my shoes yet. I looked down, expecting to see my poor Hermes stained red with evidence of another crime scene, but instead it looked like I was wearing a brand-new pair of two-hundred-dollar designer sandals on my feet. And my hoodie, which no doubt once showed signs of blood spatter and gunshot residue, was clean. My brain couldn't process the amount of detail this guy had taken care of—

"Man, my mom and dad are going to be pissed," Alana said. Like her parents being angry was the biggest thing to fear at this point. She was so clueless. "How the crap are we getting home? I don't even know where we are."

Liam twitched in my arms. "Liam, wake up," I said, willing him to come back to me. "C'mon, wake up."

I thought of Dr. T's Emerson quote—truth and repose. Liam couldn't have both. None of us could. The truth was that a killer was holding him. And when he woke up, when his repose ended, that's what he would see when he looked at me—the truth. I was a killer.

I did what I had to do to save my friends and survive, but one death had been hard enough to take. Now there were four more. As I held Liam, I couldn't get my hands to stop shaking or my breathing to steady. I began rocking, trying to calm myself and dispel all the memories. Damn, I needed some Swiss chocolate right now.

Liam grimaced and his body tensed up. He was coming back.

"I'm right here," I said, touching his face. Intense relief rose in me. A profound sense of gratitude as I held him, knowing he was OK. I never meant to let myself feel this strongly about him—about anyone.

He finally opened his eyes, and they found mine.

They were a bloodshot blue this time. Not much sparkle at the moment.

"Are we alive?" he asked with the rasp of a whiskey-drinking smoker.

"I don't know how, but yeah," I said.

He blinked a few times and rubbed his eyes like he was trying to unsee something. "Where's Alana?"

"I'm right here," she said, snarling. He turned to see her standing with her arms crossed, clearly not as over the moon as I was to see him awake. "If your buddies think this is some hilarious prank, they're wrong!"

"Prank?" he asked, not to her, but to me. I knew what he was really asking, *She doesn't know?*

"Alana thinks we were roofied and dropped off here by your jock-head friends as a joke," I said with bulging eyes. *Don't tell her that I'm a raging sociopathic teen serial killer!*

"Oh." Liam let out a huge huff of breath. "*Ohhhh,*" he said again, but this time with a scowl as he held his sides. Then I remembered those kicks to his unprotected ribs.

"Do we need to get you to the hospital?" I asked.

"Hospital?" Alana's voice raised an octave. "What kind of friends are these guys? Is this some kind of hazing crap?"

"No, no hospital," Liam said, slowing his breathing.

He turned his back to Alana long enough for me to mouth to him, "I don't know what to tell her." My instincts warned me not to divulge anything she didn't need to know. Her loyalty to me could only go so far. Plus, I didn't want to scar her any worse than necessary. Maybe, for her own sake, the less she knew, the better. Like he could read my mind, Liam nodded.

"No, this is a football injury," he lied. "I must have been lying on it wrong. It's a bruise from last week's game."

I wasn't sure why he was playing along. I couldn't understand this guy. Always protecting me. I didn't even need to explain, and he was going along with my insanity.

"Well, can you walk?" Alana asked. "We need to find a way out of here. Maybe I can get home before my parents get up and decide to ground me for the rest of my life."

"Yeah, I can walk." He clenched his jaw and stood up with a swift grace. "I finished a game once with a dislocated shoulder. This is nothing."

"I'd be impressed if I hadn't just been drugged, kidnapped, and left to die on a cliff by your team of varsity a-holes," Alana said as she stalked away from the cliff's edge, presumably looking for a way to get out of here.

As soon as she turned her back, I whispered to Liam, "Thanks for lying."

"She really didn't see anything?" he whispered back, with a shaken look like *he* hadn't missed a thing.

"I guess not," I said softly, watching Alana. "Unless she's blocking it out because it's too awful." My shoulders bowed, remembering all over again what I had done.

"It was the same guy, Ruby," Liam whispered, taking my hand. Goose bumps raised all the way up my arm. "The one I saw watching you at the art fair. *He* drugged you with whatever was on that cloth at the warehouse. But he was dressed differently, like a special ops guy or something. Like Jason Bourne. Dressed in all black. I wasn't sure at first because he wore some kind of helmet, but right before he drugged me I saw his face."

I wobbled a little, as though a California tremor had just shaken below me. He steadied me as best he could and said:

"He looked me right in the eyes. He didn't say anything, but it was weird. He wasn't . . ." Liam paused and his eyes glassed over like maybe he wasn't really awake.

"He wasn't what?" I snapped my fingers in front of his face.

"He wasn't evil looking," Liam said with a question mark all over his expression. "His eyes were . . . I don't know . . . not intent on killing me. Not intent on killing you. It was weird."

I couldn't comprehend this. The motives of this Mr. D. S. evaded me time and time again.

"I think we should go to the police—" Liam said before I interrupted with my knee-jerk reaction to hearing "police."

"NO."

"Ruby, hear me out," he said.

"No. I don't know what *I* am going to do," I said, pulling away my hand. Not because I didn't desperately want his help, but because I felt guilty. I never should have involved him in this. He had a future. People who loved him and would be devastated if he was locked up for the rest of his life for two counts of conspiracy to commit murder, two counts of obstruction of justice, and who knows how many counts of seriously poor judgment for fraternizing with the known criminal Ruby Rose.

"Don't pull that on me," he said, taking my hand again, and this time tilting my chin up so I was forced to look him in the eyes. Those resilient eyes now turning a clear pale blue—almost the color of the horizon behind him. "We're in this together."

"No, *we're* not," I said, not pulling away, just clarifying. "*You* didn't do anything. *You* didn't pull the trigger. *You* didn't help me get away. *You* are not responsible for anything. This is my problem, not yours."

"I'd have pulled the trigger if I'd had the chance!" His voice raised above a whisper.

"Shhh," I quieted him. "Yeah, well, you didn't have to."

For a long minute, he stared at me. I'd tried to warn him. I'd tried to keep him away. Sheesh, I'd practically broken his wrist telling him to keep his distance.

"No one should have to go through this alone," he said, not backing down. "Whoever is doing this to you, to *us*, isn't going to stop. He's playing some sick, twisted, bullshit game with you, and you need my help." Suddenly, against my will, I was in his arms again. And I wasn't at all comfortable there at the moment. Last time I'd been there, I was drugged, caged like an animal, forced to kill two men, and dumped on a cliff.

I wanted to pull away. But I didn't.

"Sorry to interrupt your little *moment*," Alana called down from above, "but you might want to see this."

My guts fell like I'd just hit an unexpected drop on a roller coaster. What was it—a dead body? Evidence of what I'd done? My heart beat unnaturally fast as I scaled the cliff's steep face.

I almost burst when I saw him.

"Big Black!" My knight in shining armor. My SUV.

"At least those a-holes left us a ride," Alana said. "Now get in and drive me home before life as I know it is over."

"How in the . . ." Liam said behind me.

"I don't know," I responded, only to him. "Whoever this guy is, I guess he doesn't want me dead."

"Just traumatized for life." He feigned a smile. "C'mon, let's get out of here." He tried to lead me over to the passenger side door.

"I don't think so," I said. "I'm driving."

The drive home was sore and silent. After briefly discussing the last thing we each remembered at the party, which was basically nothing—except for Alana being told that I needed her upstairs—we let Mary Poppins guide us back to familiar territory. Turned out, we were only twenty miles down the coast, and it was going to take us about a half hour to get home. But the dread that filled the car was palpable. Dread that bodies would be found, parents would go ballistic, and lives would be ruined—any minute.

I figured no one wanted to speculate about what happened to us. No one wanted to discuss the looks on our parents' faces when we walked in and got the whole *I'm relieved you're alive, but now I'm going to kill you* speech.

I kept looking over to Alana in the passenger seat with her raw wrists, wondering what she really knew. Maybe some part of her subconscious had absorbed the gunshots, the sprays of blood, the smell of death. Maybe she was choosing repose over the truth—only postponing the twisted memories or dreams of me slaughtering two men. At least I had a good referral for a psychotherapist.

In the meantime, I had to find a way to convince her not to accuse the football players. That would just cause a chain reaction of problems I didn't need right now.

Even if they never found the bodies or other physical evidence (because of Mr. D. S.'s meticulous planning), Detective Martinez and my mom's campaign opponent, Bill Brandon, would tag-team up like a pair of brute wrestlers to take my mom and me down if they heard about this.

The butterfly effect would be disastrous. Not that killing three men was even remotely close to the ripple of a butterfly's wing. But whatever.

As I turned into Alana's neighborhood, Liam leaned over the center console and put his hand on Alana's arm. She quickly pulled away.

"Sorry, I didn't mean to . . ." Liam stuttered. "I just have an idea. Let's tell our parents that we had a bonfire at Newport, someone stole our phones, and we were stranded at the beach. Let's not tell them about being tied up, or about the cove. They'll freak."

"Why?" She turned to face him in the backseat. "You don't want to get your buddies in trouble?"

"If this was one of the football guys, I *promise* I will find out," he assured her. "I just don't think they would be capable . . ." He trailed off.

"Oh, really? And who would be *capable*?"

"Alana," I cut in, "you can't go around accusing people."

"Whose side are you on, Ruby?" she snapped.

"Nobody's. I mean—yours?" I didn't understand the question. Liam and I exchanged a worried glance in the rearview mirror.

"I don't know what you guys are trying to hide, but I am 100 percent not cool with being drugged, kidnapped, and dumped by *anyone*." Alana rubbed at her wrists like all of a sudden they scorched with pain. "All I know is that if you pull around this corner, and there are police outside my house because my parents called me in missing, I'm not telling any bogus lies."

I drew a last breath before rounding the corner to discover our fate. Alana's parents weren't normally the kind to worry, but I knew I had little chance of keeping up the ruse if they suspected anything.

I kept looking through my sunroof for any circling helicopters, or other signs of the whole LA cavalry out looking for our dead bodies after discovering the remains of four men at the warehouse.

Time skidded into slow motion as we turned onto Alana's street. The sun was up. Sprinklers cast rainbows over manicured grass, newspapers dotted the drives, and a yawning cat stared at us as we came into view—but there were no sirens. No black-and-white vehicles. No frantic mothers in Hawaiian muumuus on the drive. Nothing out of the ordinary.

We all exhaled. "Thank God," Alana said, dropping her head like she was really praying.

I looked in the rearview mirror. Liam's expression said *Now! Convince her now!*

"Look, Alana." I slowed my approach to her curb. "Will you just do one thing for me?"

She lowered her eyebrows. I opened my mouth, not even sure what I was going to ask her—but a beeping electronic device interrupted me.

Our eyes bulged as we recognized my text-message alert. I thought I'd lost my cell phone! The sound came from somewhere right between us.

I flung open the center console to find all three of our cell phones neatly placed next to each other. We each grabbed for our own, desperate to discover the fallout.

I had only one unread text message, from another stupid unknown number.

Check your mom's text log. All is well.

I scrambled to the history of text messages between my mom and me.

At 11:36 last night a text from my phone read: *Staying at Alana's tonight. See you tomorrow.*

At 11:38 Mom replied: *OK. Be safe.*

At 11:40 my phone replied: *OK.*

I looked up at Alana in disbelief.

"My mom thinks I stayed at your house last night," she said, looking at her own messages. "Someone texted her and told her so. Someone pretending to be me."

I watched her eyes and saw comprehension dawning. Like maybe she finally understood this had nothing to do with the football players, and everything to do with someone far more sinister.

"Let me see that," I said, taking the phone from her. It was true. Someone sent her the same text to check her mom's log. We were in the clear. All *was* well. At least in regards to not being busted yet. I knew it was only a small victory. Soon there would be a long list of other consequences such as the bodies being found, Liam turning on me, a very public trial, the inevitable destruction of my mother's life and career, and ultimately getting shanked in prison by a gang of "big girls" who didn't like my attitude. And to think that just a few months ago I was only worried I wouldn't make it to Stanford because of poor attendance.

"Same for me," Liam said from the backseat. "My mom thinks I'm at my buddy Chase's house."

A long and uncomfortable pause took over the car. I didn't know what to say or even what to think. I only knew that if Alana remembered something and wasn't saying anything to my face—it could be a problem. I could tell she didn't want to be in the car with me for one more second.

"I'll call you later," she said, not even bothering to meet my eyes before flipping the lock and practically sprinting into her house.

I wondered if I'd ever have a best friend again.

Not that it would matter if I didn't find out who had done this to us, and soon.

CHAPTER 11

As I slunk down in my tub, I wondered why I'd never thought to combine two of my favorite escapes before—a steaming bath and hot chocolate. If there was ever a time I needed them, it was now. I doubted prison would offer a massaging jet bath or carry this particular brand of imported French *chocolat chaud à la noisette*.

Not that I had done anything wrong—The Stick's murder was legally justified—but I wasn't naive enough to hope that everyone would see it as cut-and-dried. Not with my mom's enemies. And not with the psycho still out there attempting to destroy me.

Now that I found myself alone, it all started to sink in. I was on a collision course with disaster. No matter what I did, life as I knew it was over. Either I would be caught, exposed, and ruined, or I would have to live with the knowledge that I had betrayed everyone and everything I'd ever held dear by keeping my secrets and "obstructing justice."

Or, of course, there was always the third option: death.

No, not suicide. I'm not that girl. I'm talking a slow, tortuous death by Mr. D. S.-hole. By now, I knew this guy was in control. He was smart and capable enough of taking my life any moment he wanted. Shoot, he could very well come drown me in this bath right this second. Except that was obviously not what he wanted. So what did he want?

A wave of fatigue weighed me down. I needed to drag myself into bed before I accidentally drowned. Must've been the killer combo of the hot bath and having been drugged twice within the last twelve hours.

I grabbed a towel and wrapped it around myself, not even bothering to get dressed before I slid under my covers and turned on the TV to check the news. I had to know if they'd found the warehouse and the bodies yet. I flipped through the channels until I found Bill Brandon and his shiny white campaign teeth. That smile alone was enough to win over several thousand "cosmetic" voters who knew nothing of the candidates or issues, who admitted to voting based on good looks. "Cheap votes" my mom called them. In the last election she was the one collecting them against an old man with a bright-red bulbous nose. In Brandon she'd met her match—with his chiseled jaw and salt-and-pepper hair, he oozed masculine smolder.

"You see, Megan, there are just too many questions, and not enough answers," Brandon charmingly explained to the attractive news anchor, like he was at a bar and she was the lucky girl he'd take home tonight. "District Attorney Jane Rose is a rogue pirate captain on a sinking ship. There is not enough transparency. There is not enough justice. Too many violent offenders still roam the streets while she dines in the private chambers of her lobbyist supporters. Orange County needs a new captain. One who will right the ship. I have the experience as a former police officer—and the proven determination as a successful victims' rights attorney—to make it happen."

What a joke! Captain Jane Rose the Rogue Pirate versus Bill "Peter Pan" Brandon the Scallywag Hero. This guy couldn't be any more ridiculous.

"So tell us, Bill"—the reporter, and her implants, faced him—"where do you get your passion? Does this have anything to do with your family history?"

Talk about lobbing a softball question.

"Yes, I'm glad you asked." The Scallywag folded his hands and turned somber. "I get my passion from my daughter, Whitney. She's why I'm here. She was fourteen years old when she was taken from her bed in the dead of night by a multiple offender. As the police captain in our small community, I thought I was protecting her. I thought something like that could never happen to me. We didn't find her body until a year later. That's when I changed my thinking. I wasn't doing enough."

The smirk fell off my face. I felt stupid for not having known about his daughter. Had I only been selectively listening to information about him, and vilifying him because of my mom? There was more to this guy than I'd realized.

"The man who brutally tortured and killed my Whitney was still walking the streets. He wasn't convicted. His attorney persuaded the jury that my department had tampered with evidence because they wanted justice for me. Honestly, Megan, every day I considered finding him and . . ." He paused, lowering his gaze. When he looked back up at the camera, his eyes were alive with fire—instead of the tears I expected to see. He continued: "I considered finding him and killing him. Showing him the same respect he'd shown my daughter." He blinked and regained some of his composure, but I had lost some of mine.

"Of course, I came to my senses. I couldn't do that to my wife and two other children. Instead, I went to law school and helped create the program we now call Whitney Watch, which is a series of protocols that communities and police departments use to find missing children, prevent travesties, and obtain justice against offenders. I am resolved to get these multiple offenders off the street. No plea deals, no sloppy prosecutions, only justice. For our children, for our communities, for Whitney."

I couldn't believe it—this bully seemed sincere. He'd lost his daughter. He wanted revenge. He was just like me.

Before, I thought seeing him elected would be a bad thing, mostly because it meant my mom would be fired. Now, I wasn't so sure. Except that maybe I was one of those "multiple offenders" he vowed to put away.

I turned off the TV—everything was going hazy. Not just my eyesight from overwhelming fatigue, but my shoreline. That line Dad had tried so hard to show me—the divide between right and wrong—wasn't so clear anymore.

The shaggy green carpet tickled my cheek. I rolled around on the floor, giggling like crazy. Someone was tickling me, chasing me in circles. I laughed and fell, laughed and fell. I couldn't get away—I wasn't really trying. I looked up to the oversized smile above me and squinted through the belly laughs. I couldn't talk. I didn't have the words yet, but she did. "I'm going to get the little monster." Her long blonde hair was pulled into a high bun, so I could see her bright-blue eyes perfectly. I stared at soft, pink lips stretched out in a wide grin, making the dimple in her left cheek even deeper. She looked like the girl in the sketch at the art fair. It felt like I knew her.

Wait, was she me? She was my age. She looked exactly like me, except for the eyes. Like Baby Ruby was playing with Teenage Ruby, or the version of me that didn't include shades of gray and darkness—

All of a sudden the room went black, like the lights of the world had just turned off. I couldn't find her. I crawled around blindly, searching for her touch. Instead, I felt bars in every direction. Everywhere I turned the bars locked me in. The ground was sharp and hard.

"Ruby." My mom's cold voice entered my dream. If I didn't know this was a nightmare before, I knew it now. "I need to talk to you."

The darkness started slipping away to a fog, deep and heavy.

"Honey, wake up." Her impatient voice doused me like ice water, the silly pet name as annoying as always.

And yet, part of me was still glad to see her. There was always a seed of hope inside me that she'd surprise me, maybe whisk me off to Paris for fall shoes and chocolate crepes, like she did lifetimes ago. Pre-D. A. Jane used to be quite spontaneous. Post-D. A. Jane, not so much.

"I have to go," she said. Of course, she woke me up just to say good-bye. I never got used to her MO: offering me something I wanted, just to say I couldn't have it. *Here, Ruby, put these cookies in the cookie jar. And don't you dare eat them, they're for decoration. And shouldn't you be cutting back on the sweets? That metabolism of yours won't last forever.*

"It's fine," I said. Though it wasn't.

"You must've had one hell of a night," she said, eyebrows raised. Maybe it was all a dream. I let myself hope for only a second before I looked down to my wrists and saw the bruising.

"Yeah, you know Alana and me." I pulled up my towel and the covers to make sure none of me was exposed. "Party to the break of dawn." I faked a smile, but it probably looked more like a grimace.

"I know it's Sunday, but I have to go to the office for a little while, OK?" she said. Even though that "OK" with the inflection at the end indicated a question, which normally required a response, I knew better. She didn't need my permission. And even if I said no, what was she going to do—listen? Ha! Would she stay home and make me breakfast in bed like Dad used to do? The only recipe she knew was burned toast. Would she curl up and have a quiet Sunday in, watching episodes of *Law & Order* and talking about life? Come on, she was the star of her own real-life crime show.

And now with the whole affair thing hanging in the air between us, I wasn't sure I even wanted her around. I thought about what Dr. T had said—letting my mom in, us needing each other now more than ever.

"Call Alana," she suggested. "Do something fun today. I heard they're having a sale at Nordstrom."

"OK, fine. See you later, then." I wanted to grab my cell phone off the nightstand and check for messages, but I couldn't because of my bruised wrists.

"Don't be like that, Rue." She reached over to shift my hair out of my face, and I let her. Like a puppy starved for attention, I even leaned into her touch, hoping it would last longer. This was it—my opportunity to let her in. She was trying. I would try, too. My heart ached for Dad. And she had hurt me with her mistakes and selfishness. But I still needed her help. And for a second, I thought maybe I could tell her everything and she'd understand. Maybe it would all be OK. Maybe she'd believe me if I said, *Yes, I was stalking LeMarq, but no, I never meant to kill him. And I was also following this other dude, Rick "The Stick," someone I also killed last night. And, oh yeah, I killed his friend, too—*

"Why are you looking at me like that?" She pulled her hand away from my cheek.

"Like what?"

She blew out an exasperated breath and pinched her eyes shut. "Like you don't understand the stress I'm under or what's at stake for me."

I rolled my eyes. So typical—always thinking of Jane.

"I have a lot of important people relying on me, and I can't let them down now," she continued. "The governor wants to see me, and . . ." That's when I stopped listening. I was tired of wishing she'd consider me one of those *important people.*

"It's fine," I said quietly. I wasn't trying to guilt-trip her. I just knew I couldn't win this one. White flag raised.

"I *promise* I'll be back in time for dinner. We'll talk," she said, starting to get up. There was that teasing word again—"talk." I wouldn't hold my breath. "What do you want me to bring home? Chinese? Italian? A nice prime rib?"

"I don't care," I said, watching her speed walk out of the room. "It's your world," I muttered to myself, knowing she couldn't hear me. It was more likely she'd forget to call, and I would end up making myself mac and cheese.

"I'll surprise you, then," she hollered from the staircase. She must've been taking two at a time, even in heels. And I thought I'd inherited my agility from Dad.

After the garage door shut, I wondered if it would've been a blessing to her if I'd died last night. She wouldn't have to bother anymore with any of this mothering mumbo jumbo. She wouldn't have to come home *ever*. My death would probably give her a boost in the polls, and best of all, she wouldn't have to share the five million dollars of life insurance money my dad had left for me in trust.

So why did I still want her love and attention? If only Dad were here. He knew exactly how to buffer the tension between Mom and me. He'd make me some of his famous French toast with extra powdered sugar on top. He'd throw the wet suits and boards in the back of his truck and drive me down to our surf spot. He'd take me to the SWAT obstacle course and gun range to sweat and shoot my worries away.

I remembered now what it had felt like to hold my dad's gun for the first time when I was twelve. It was exciting—exhilarating, even. But last night that gun had felt so dangerous and wrong. The minute I got back home, I'd put it back in his safe where it belonged.

Which begged the question: How did Dad's gun even get there last night? Had someone stolen it from the crime scene? Taken it off his dead body for profit? Sold it to a pawnshop where Mr. D. S. had then tracked it down? My brain overflowed with ridiculous theories. Dad's entire SWAT team was with him the night he died. At least that's what I'd gathered from the few details I'd heard. So how could anyone have been able to take the gun—unless that someone belonged to SWAT? Could one of them have betrayed him? If it was possible for Martinez—his former partner—to betray him so deeply, then a wider SWAT betrayal was just as believable. Perhaps that's why his partner, Mathews, hadn't dared show his face around here since.

Crack. A sharp noise on the window made me jump. I looked over to see if it had shattered, but it was intact. Hugging the towel to my body, I got out of bed to make sure it was locked. Then I saw him—Liam.

He grinned up at me like I'd offered him an early birthday present: me, wearing virtually nothing. I jumped back, both relieved that he wasn't an ax murderer and totally pissed at him for scaring me and invading my privacy.

I ran to my closet to grab a robe, and in the space of a few feet my mind changed. I wasn't that mad. Maybe a little surprised, maybe a bit flattered, and maybe a bit curious about what it would be like to be in the same room as him wearing only a towel.

Two robes hung in my closet: a thick, purple frumpy thing I used at Christmas and the Victoria's Secret robe I used in the privacy of my own room. I couldn't very well go down there looking like Barney the dinosaur.

I wrapped the hot-pink robe around me and headed downstairs to talk to him like a civilized human being.

"Oy, you," I yelled out the front door. "There's this thing called a doorbell."

He came running around the hedge. "I was going for the whole Romeo-and-Juliet thing." He shoved his hands in his jeans and flashed that sparkly smile. Why did he look so happy to see me?

When was I ever going to understand this dude? Aside from Mr. D. S., he was the only person in the whole world who knew exactly what I was: a killer. And yet he wanted to play Shakespeare with me.

"You do know that Romeo and Juliet both ended up dead," I said, trying to sound unaffected by his charm, while inside I couldn't help feeling flattered—or maybe twitterpated. The black Hurley V-neck shirt he wore clung to his chest, revealing the muscular curves I'd daydreamed about ever since that shirtless morning at the beach. "And also, Romeo didn't chuck rocks and nearly break Juliet's window."

"Uh, yeah, sorry about that." He scratched his neck and wrinkled his nose. "Turns out throwing a rock twenty feet in the air *delicately* is sort of hard."

He stood on the welcome mat, looking like he felt totally unwelcome. Avoiding his eyes, I stared down at his feet. Under his impressively clean throwback Jordans, the mat read: "Life Is a Bed of Roses." Dad had given it to Mom a few years back. I used to think it was absurd. But after he died I started seeing it differently. Sure, we had our share of thorns, but we all loved each other.

"Have you heard from Alana?" Liam broke our uncomfortable pause.

"Not yet," I replied, unhappy to be reminded that my *best* friend had finally realized I was the *worst*. "Have you heard anything on the news about"—I paused for a second, ashamed to say what had happened out loud—"you know, the warehouse?"

"Nope."

I squinted at the sun, waiting for him to tuck tail and bolt.

"Well, aren't you going to invite me in?" Liam asked.

I looked down at my robe, feeling a little underdressed. It hadn't occurred to me that he'd want to come in. "Well, are you or aren't you?" he asked again, moving closer.

"I guess, but . . ." I didn't know how to finish that sentence. *If you promise not to turn me in to the cops . . . or seduce me.*

"Nice robe," he said as he pushed through the door and gusted in. I tightened the sash again. "We really ought to talk. You know, about that *math* problem," he said louder.

"My mom's not here," I said, relieving him of his need to speak in code. "We're alone."

His smile was wider than I'd ever seen it. Like twelve hours ago he hadn't been abducted and almost sold to an international drug lord who liked boys. This kid had the short-term memory of a goldfish.

"Good." He reached for my hand and pulled me to his chest, and I let him reel me in like *I* was the goldfish. "I forgot to thank you for saving my life," he said.

Er, wrong. I hadn't saved his life. I put it in danger just by knowing him—and caring about him—but I didn't say that. All I could think about were his eyelashes and his lips.

"You're welcome?" It came out more like a question.

"Look, I know this may sound weird or psychotic or something, but what you did last night was . . . freaking amazing." His eyes were lit up in a way that made no sense to me.

"What are you even talking about?" I asked.

"Ruby, those were bad guys. I mean really bad guys. They were going to kill us. Or worse." He grimaced. Finally, a look that made sense. "You not only saved us, but probably tons of other people they'd have messed with, too. I only wish I'd been the one to pull the trigger."

Whoa, whoa, whoa. I shook my head in complete disagreement and backed away.

"Liam, it's never OK to kill," I said flatly. He didn't get how it felt—hearing the crunch of bullet through bone. Seeing the spurt of blood. Living with the awful knowledge that I'd killed them. Not the cops, not my dad—but me. I had good reason to do it, sure, but that didn't make it "OK."

"Of course it is." He looked around like one of my mom's nude Greek sculptures would side with him and tell me how ridiculous I was being. "You don't really believe that."

"I believe in the justice system. I believe in the law. And I believe in the enforcement of it by those with authority to administer it," I said.

"And the law says a killing is *justified* in self-defense or in the defense of others. It's called excusable homicide," he said confidently. When I looked impressed, he added, "I Googled it."

I blew out an exasperated breath. Here I was standing half-naked in my foyer, arguing legal semantics with Liam Slater. I had so many problems that I couldn't even count them anymore. But first things first, I needed to put some clothes on.

"Come up to my room in five minutes, OK?" I said and turned to go up the stairs. "It's the second door on the left."

"OK." He smiled from perfect ear to scarred ear. I hoped he wasn't thinking what it looked like he was thinking. Or, maybe I hoped he was.

CHAPTER 12

I walked (completely clothed) to my window and opened it to make sure I could hear Mom's car if she came home. Not because I was going to be sharing a sex session with Liam, but because I was going to share something far more sinister: my research on two criminals, who just happened to have died by my hands.

"I like your room," Liam said from the edge of my bed. I detected an unusual amount of nervousness in his voice. "Very...uh...beachy."

"Bitchy?" I asked, teasing him for the stammer, and I joined him on the bed.

He grinned and shook his head. "It's like being at the beach. All the seashells and starfish and all."

"I'm just kidding," I assured him, grateful he hadn't seen my shoe closet. That one would be hard to explain, even to him. "I just wouldn't be surprised if that's what you really thought of me. Or worse."

"You should do that more often," he said, with suddenly soft eyes.

"What, misinterpret your words?"

"No, smile." He held my gaze. "It looks good on you."

My smile faded. Something about him pointing it out made it scamper away. Plus, I wasn't entitled to smile. I still had blood on my hands. Did *that* look good on me?

Except, Liam's expression made it clear that discussing my guilt wasn't exactly what he had in mind at the moment.

I had to change the subject. The tension radiating from him practically screamed "Let's Do It" like a flashing neon sign. I could even almost hear Marvin Gaye singing "Let's Get It On." And I could 100 percent for sure feel the energy sparking between his body and mine.

I'd opened the door wearing my hooker robe, invited him to my room, sat him on my bed, and *smiled*. Of course he could get the wrong idea. I think I was getting the wrong idea myself. On cue, images of him with his shirt off on the beach formed in my mind. His wet suit hanging low on his hips, his tan skin, his soft lips . . .

I felt like a hot teapot about to whistle from the steam inside me. Just as I was about to get up, he said, "I'm not trying to get into your pants, Ruby."

Huh? What about the neon sign—and Marvin Gaye? I'm pretty sure that my face turned Ruby Red.

"Er, that's not what I meant," he said, squirming again. "It's not that I don't want to. I mean, I totally do. Like you wouldn't believe— but that's not why I'm here." He rubbed his forehead like massaging it would help him articulate. "That came out weird."

"Liam, it's OK," I said, wondering what my personal neon sign was saying right now. "Let me show you something."

I stood and offered my hand to help him up. He looked up at me like he couldn't believe it. I was actually reaching out to him. I could hardly believe it, either.

He took it and something like an electrical shock zipped through me, head to toe. His clear eyes set me on fire; his scent burned me up. I forgot for a second what I was doing.

Oh yeah, the chest. I needed him to move so I could reach under the bed to grab it. I let go of his hand and fell to my knees beside him. With a grunt and a tug, the treasure came gliding out. I'd never shared this with anyone else. I couldn't believe I was doing it now.

I paused, wondering if I could trust Liam with this. He might not understand. But I needed help. A fresh set of eyes. I was too close. I couldn't see the forest *or* the trees anymore.

"What is that thing?" he asked, looking a bit worried.

"It's just some evidence I've been gathering," I said, trying to sound casual. "I've looked over this stuff several times in the last few days, but maybe you can help me find something significant." I fumbled with the code and popped the lock. Which made me remember the whole cage situation from last night. My body tensed up at the thought of the bars and the stupid three-digit bike lock.

"It's 366," I mumbled.

"What's wrong?" Liam dropped to his knees beside me.

"Just remembering a detail."

I told him how I was the only one put in a cage, glossing over how afraid I am of bars—not wanting to relive it. How I escaped, the combination number, and how they matched the address from the first shooting. About how there had been other cryptic clues or messages. Like the demon tattoo on that girl in the sketch at the art fair. Like the *D. S.* signature. Like the fact that the girl in the sketch looked a lot like me, just like the little girl Riley Bentley—the one I saved at the warehouse—and just like the one I didn't save on Ninth Street. Like making me use my dad's gun and then returning it to me afterward. Whoever was doing this to me was doing it for a reason.

"So, let me get this straight," Liam said, staring at the unopened chest. "This guy is sending you messages? Leaving you clues?"

"It feels like it. Like he's giving me pieces of some strange, twisted puzzle, and I'm supposed to put them together somehow."

"But why? To show you who he is? To exact revenge on your mom or dad? To lead you on a wild goose chase until he strangles you in some Satan-worshipping ceremony?"

"Jeez, Liam." I glared at him. "Way to make a girl feel better."

"Oh, sorry." He frowned and shook his head. "That was an insensitive joke and absolutely *not* going to happen. I was just thinking out loud."

"Whatever," I said, now focusing on the chest, wondering again if I should actually share this darkness with another human being. I could just see him on the witness stand. The prosecutor would ask him, "Then what did the defendant do?" He'd reply, "We were alone in her bedroom when she showed me her chest—her chest of horrors." *Dun dun dun!*

"Well, are you going to show me what's in this thing or not?" Liam asked.

"Yeah, of course." I flung open the top and pulled out a few of the most recent notebooks. "OK, before you start judging me, I just want you to know my therapist told me I needed an *outlet*. I was, like, comatose for two months after my dad was murdered. And one of the only things that got my mind off of his death was focusing on these guys." I laid out five files. "I call them the Filthy Five. Child abusers, murderers, and drug traffickers that either my dad couldn't catch or my mom put back on the street. I've been following them. Now two of them are dead." I stopped myself. I wasn't explaining it right. Maybe, if I just let him look at the records and connect the dots himself, he'd see something I missed.

He started thumbing through the thick green files and notebooks. And he stopped when he apparently couldn't read any more about what these men had done. He wiped his brow with the back of his hand as if he'd just eaten a hot pepper.

"Wow," Liam said quietly. "You did all this research yourself?"

"Like I said, I needed an outlet." I waited for him to look at me again, but he wouldn't. I could see the wheels turning in his head.

He was figuring out that if I was following them, that would give me a motive—which meant maybe I was really trying to kill them after all. And maybe I wasn't telling him the whole story. Which is what my mom, Detective Martinez, and any other rational person would think.

"Look, I know these guys are guilty," I continued. "The evidence is all there. But for one reason or another it couldn't be used in a court of law, or wasn't strong enough for a life sentence. I had to get new evidence in order to convict these guys for good. So I started tailing them." I knew I was rambling, and it sounded borderline psychotic, but I couldn't hold it back. "Anyway, whoever is behind this knows about my Five. LeMarq was number one and Rick is number two." I pointed to Rick's file. "You never saw him, but he was there last night. I killed him right before I killed the guy who fell on top of you. Oh my hell . . . I just admitted to killing two men last night."

"Shhh, Ruby, shhh," he said, holding me close. "It's OK." Was that him shaking or me?

"I never meant to do it, I swear," I said, covering my face with my hands and fighting surging tears. "I never wanted to kill anyone—"

"You didn't do anything wrong." Liam cut me off. "You don't have to work so hard to explain it to me. I've seen and heard enough to know that someone is manipulating you. We just need to figure out who and why."

A rogue tear escaped, and I wiped it away before it could reach my cheek. I couldn't let myself go to that place ever again. There was a time after Dad died when I let myself be crippled and debilitated by constant waterworks. I couldn't go anywhere or do anything without embarrassing myself. It had been at least three months since my last ugly cry. To survive I needed to see clearly, without the blurring pain.

As much as I needed and wanted Liam's touch, I pulled away to steel myself against the weakness threatening to destroy me. My walls were there for a reason: protection.

"Hey," Liam said, brushing my hair out of my eyes. "Why don't we get something to eat, check the news to see if there's a report on any, uh, crime scenes, and we can go through this in a little while."

I was hesitant to leave my research without showing Liam the three remaining criminals. There had to be another clue that would help me understand why all this was happening, or maybe prepare me for the next time around. Because by now, I knew there'd be a next time.

"C'mon, when was the last time you ate anything?" Liam asked, frowning and lifting himself off the floor. I could tell he was trying to hide the pain in his side from last night. "I had a bowl of Captain Crunch a few hours ago when I woke up, but I need some real food."

"Yeah, *real* food," I said, rubbing away any stray traces of emotion. "My mom doesn't do a lot of grocery shopping these days. I doubt there's anything here."

He offered me his hand and I let him pull me up.

"That's cool," he said, giving me that devilish grin. "I could really go for some In-N-Out Burger right now. A Double-Double, extra salt on the fries, and a big ol' whammer jammer chocolate shake. How about you?"

For the first time in a long while, Liam Slater made me laugh. I could only smile and nod in agreement.

"That was easy," Liam said, leading me toward the door. "You never do what I say."

"You had me at chocolate shake." I smiled. "And whammer jammer." I smiled even wider. But as I hit the top of the stairs I remembered I'd left all my "dirty laundry" spread out all over the floor. "Wait, let me just put away the chest. I'll meet you downstairs."

I put most of the files and notebooks back, and shoved the box under my bed. Admittedly, it wasn't the most original place to hide my deepest, darkest secrets. I stuffed the remaining three of five monster files in my backpack. They were heavy, but as I slung the bag over my shoulders, I couldn't help but feel lighter. I finally had someone to confide in. Someone who I could finally be myself around. He knew everything now—he was the only one. Not my mom, not Dr. T, not Alana.

My heart sank remembering the way Alana looked at me when she got out of Big Black early this morning. She wanted nothing to do with me anymore. I'd be lying if I said I didn't see it coming. Though she'd always made an effort to understand—and even sometimes participate in—my dad's training, she never loved it. In fact, in the year leading up to Dad's death, she was pretty much over it. Especially when it got in the way of parties, boys, shopping, and beach time. Which it always did.

I checked my cell phone to see if she'd called or texted, but her silence was deafening. I so badly wanted to tell her again that I was sorry for dragging her into all of this. Talk to her about how Liam made me laugh. She would practically drool over the phone if I told her about Liam's neon sign. How ironic that the only time I'd managed to push Alana away was also the one time I finally had something to say.

Suddenly, I heard men's voices coming from downstairs. Liam was talking to someone, but I hadn't heard the doorbell. I held tight to my phone in case I needed to call 911. I thought about getting one of Dad's shotguns, but first I peeked over the railing to see if I could catch where the voices were coming from and whose they were.

Liam stood near the open front door, arms crossed. I could see the outline of a man in black clothes standing opposite him.

This time, 911 wouldn't do me any good.

CHAPTER 13

I let the weight of my backpack pull my shoulders down. I was really getting tired of this whole showing-up-at-my-house-unannounced thing. A voice in my head whispered, *Police harassment.* Another whispered, *Abuse of power.* Yet another whispered, *Stop whispering. Unless you're building an insanity defense.*

And then a voice screamed, *Hide the files!*

I hurried back into the bedroom and flung my backpack under the bed, considering whether to call my mom for backup. But I couldn't just leave Liam down there all by himself with Detective Muscle-Head Martinez. I trusted Liam, but I didn't exactly want his trust to be tested.

I hustled downstairs to join them.

"Detective Martinez, what are you doing here?" I asked, not even pretending to be pleasant. I was angry, and I wasn't going to hide it.

"I came by to check on you," he said, not doing me the same favor of making it clear how he really felt. He casually turned away from Liam and squared himself to face me coming down the grand staircase. His gaudy gold chain flashed in the light of the chandelier.

"Check on me?" I asked. "Why would you need to *check* on me?"

He gave me a knowing look, but what he *knew* I couldn't guess. Maybe he knew I'd killed again. Maybe he knew that as we spoke, the CSI unit was meticulously analyzing the evidence off of four bodies that would put me away for good. Or maybe he just knew I was hiding something.

My foyer had turned into an interrogation room, and I was willingly waiving my right to counsel.

"Let's just say I was worried about you," he said, gesturing in Liam's direction, as if playing the noble father-figure card.

Step 1: Gain trust.

"Home alone, are we?" Martinez asked.

Step 2: Open with an easy question.

"Yeah, and I'm pretty sure my mom would have your badge if she knew you were here questioning me without her presence or consent."

"Whoa, there's no interrogation here." He held up his hands. "I only wanted to make sure you're *fine* and that everything is on the up-and-up."

Step 3: Reveal suspicion.

"Well, now that you know I am *fine* and things are looking *up,* you can go."

He studied me, his eyes trailing up and down my body as if looking for physical evidence. He moved closer. "I know what you're doing, Ruby."

Step 4: Make an accusation to invoke admission of guilt.

My facade of confidence faltered for a second. But if he really knew what I was doing, he should just arrest me already.

Liam finally stepped between us. "I think you'd better leave now." He didn't take my hand or put his arm around me, but his closeness steadied me.

Martinez's dark eyes left mine and narrowed on Liam. "Young man, you'd better be careful who you talk to like that."

Step 5: Use physical intimidation.

Liam was bigger than Martinez, but his eyes still dropped as the detective moved even closer, erasing the space buffer between us.

"Do you still have the number I gave you?" Martinez asked, maybe ten inches from my face.

Step 6: ???

"No." I pulled back my head. "My mom has it. You saw her take it."

"Here it is again, then," he said as he slid it into my hand and held it there a moment. "You just might need it one of these days. Do you understand?"

"I understand," I replied, totally not understanding, but hoping my compliance would make him let go, even though I knew he was waiting until I made eye contact. Damn, I didn't want to. But I wanted him gone. So I looked him dead in the eyes.

He blinked in acceptance of my token offering of surrender, and finally let go. He took one last look at Liam. "Remember what I told you."

As soon as he crossed the threshold, I slammed the door. We waited for a few minutes, listening for the sound of his car starting in the distance and then pulling away. I wondered how he even got past our gate.

"What the hell was that?" I asked myself, trying to wipe away the feeling of his hand on the back of my shorts. "When I tell my mom about this, she is going to freak."

Liam was strangely quiet. "What's up with you?" I asked.

"Nothing."

"It doesn't look like nothing," I said. "It kind of looks like *something*. What'd he say to you before I came down?"

"That guy, he just . . ." He avoided my eyes, and grabbed the door handle. "Never mind. C'mon, I think we both need a fat milkshake after that kind of police terrorization."

"Fine, just let me go get my backpack." I turned to go, but I could tell Liam was shaken. Detective Martinez must have gotten to him before I came down. And I couldn't help but wonder if sharing my research with Liam had been a big mistake.

Over the consumption of salt, fat, sugar, and near-illegal amounts of complex carbs, I continued to tell Liam the reasons why I couldn't go to the police about everything that had happened. Most of them had to do with Detective Martinez. My mom said he was dangerous and not to trust him. Their affair ended badly. Of course, I was still waiting for that "talk" with her for more details on their past. But this much I knew: I didn't like Martinez. If he could betray my father so deeply, then he could betray me if I confided in him about my Filthy Five.

Liam agreed we couldn't trust him but tried to convince me maybe there was another friend from Dad's SWAT team who would help. But I didn't want to talk about my dad, or his department. I couldn't go there. Not yet. They'd let me down and failed Dad by letting him die. All without giving me any kind of reasonable explanation.

Even Mathews, Dad's so-called best friend and right-hand man, had ignored me since that terrible night. The dude (Dad's replacement, by the way) had never even come to see me. And he used to be like a second father to me. In fact, he was the one who'd given me Smith for my Sweet Sixteenth. He said the laser sight would help me stop shooting like a girl. He used to love to tease me. Now, apparently, he loved to pretend like I didn't exist.

I had no friends in SWAT.

Liam never really told me what Martinez had said to him before I came down. He only alluded to Martinez warning him to "be careful" with me. I didn't press him because I had a feeling about what Martinez was really trying to do: use Liam against me. And yet Liam was inexplicably still here, despite the risks of being associated with me, enjoying a greasy picnic on the beach. Intermittently smiling and touching me, with a gentleness I'd never experienced.

"Did your parents say anything to you this morning?" I asked.

"My mom just asked why I came home so early. I told her I'd had a hard time sleeping and wanted to be in my own bed. She was cool."

"What did your dad say?"

"I haven't seen my dad in years," he said quietly. "But since he was a drunk, I'm sure he wouldn't have noticed or cared anyway."

"Oh." I paused, not meaning to bring up a hard subject. So he had lied about his "rich dad" ransoming us. "My dad drank a lot, too. But he noticed everything. Even when he was tanked, he could hear the scurrying of a cockroach. If he'd been here, I wouldn't have had a chance of sneaking in like I did this morning." I couldn't believe I was talking about Dad again. I hadn't been able to do this with anyone yet. At least, not without breaking down, cracking up, or shutting off. Maybe because I was trying to comfort Liam, it was OK.

"My dad was a mean drinker," Liam clarified.

"My dad could be mean," I countered. "He and my mom used to argue like a couple of rock stars in a hotel. Headphones came in handy on nights like those." In hindsight, now that I knew about the affair, maybe it explained why he was so angry with her for so many years.

"Yeah, well, I wish arguing was all my dad used to do." Liam pulled his hair over his ear again, and I longed to reach and out and touch him, reassure him. His dad must have given him that scar.

"I'm sorry," I said, panicking a little. I wasn't used to having real conversations about real things. I had trained myself to never talk about anything meaningful. Maybe Liam was right and I was completely unapproachable. "I never meant to bring up painful stuff—"

"It's OK, Ruby." He took my hand and soothed me. I must've had that about-to-self-destruct look on my face. "Before the sun goes down, let's have a look at those files in your backpack."

I looked up to the horizon. The sky was lit up like a melting bag of Skittles. Pinks and purples blended with yellows and oranges. We didn't have much time left before the light went.

I let go of Liam's hand and rummaged through my bag. "There are three guys left on my list," I said, laying the files out on the blanket in front of me, like we were just two teens about to do some homework. "I'm pretty sure Mr. D. S. knows about my Filthy Five list—or he at least knows I was following these guys and is trying to set me up to kill them all."

"Yeah, it seems that way." Liam nodded. "But why?"

I thought about it for a second. A theory was taking shape, but it had some serious holes.

"I think it has something to do with my mom."

"Uh-huh." He egged me on.

"No one has ever told me anything about what happened to my dad. Not even his best friend, Sergeant Mathews. I have no idea if it was a drug bust gone wrong, a robbery, a hostage situation, a terrorist attack . . . nothing. I only know that he was ambushed on Grissom Island, up the coast in Long Beach. That's it." I stared up the shoreline. Even though it was a little more than fifteen miles away, the lights of the busy harbor twinkled in the distance. "What if someone is trying to hurt my mom? Someone she put away or double-crossed or whatever. Step one: Kill husband. Step two: Send only child to jail. Step three: Destroy her career."

Liam didn't respond right away, and I could tell he wasn't convinced. He cocked his head like he was considering the theory. "But why not just kill her? That's a lot of work—and a lot of killing—for *her* to remain alive in the end. Plus, I thought you said you looked through your mom's cases and no one fits the profile of this guy."

"That's true," I said, throwing a cold fry to a seagull.

"What if this guy is just some crazy psycho who gets off watching you kill? Like that Jigsaw guy from *Saw*. He believes these guys deserve to die, too, and he thinks this is some game. Maybe he has a connection to one of these guys and that's what drew him to you. "

Or maybe Liam watched too many movies.

He flipped through the third file. It was Father Michael McMullin's. Seven suspected child molestations, two suspected child abductions, and five dropped charges. And that was only in the State of California. He'd been a priest in Michigan and Florida before that. District Attorney Jane Rose's press release blamed the failure to convict on the witnesses refusing to testify.

I took the fifth file on Stanley "The Violent" Violet—a sadistic video game genius, porn addict, and lover of small women with even smaller self-esteem. His "alleged" crimes consisted of binding, torturing, and killing innocent college-aged women.

My dad had dropped Violet with a through-and-through shot to the shoulder seven years ago during a standoff-hostage situation in a mall parking lot. Violet had gotten sloppy and tried to force a freshman coed into his Lamborghini. A search warrant produced four thoroughly bleached trophy keepsakes (small trinkets of nondescript jewelry that couldn't be linked to any missing person) from presumably four other victims who were never positively identified. His computer game success bought him a media-mongering hotshot attorney who convinced a jury that Violet was "legally insane and incapable of knowing right from wrong" because he thought he was in a video game. He got five years in a mental facility, then the bare minimum in parole supervision in the two years since he'd been out.

I glanced through the photos. I didn't have one of those two-foot lenses, so the pictures I'd taken were pretty low quality—mostly shots of Violet going in and out of bars, strip clubs, gas stations, and the odd videogame store. I don't think either Liam or I knew exactly what we were looking for, but it was better than doing nothing.

I opened the fourth file. Roger Vay—the worst of the worst. He'd literally gotten away with murder at least a dozen times. He was by far the smartest, slimiest, and scariest offender on my list. He studied his victims. He chose the isolated loners, the irresponsible partiers, and the professionals who worked long hours. By the time anyone noticed they were gone, so was any evidence connecting him to the crime.

The only reason we knew he was such an accomplished killer was his signature—a unique antique key he would later mail to the closest person in the victim's life. Each victim had his or her own handmade key. The thought of Vay creeped me out to the core. And how evil to mess with the family's minds, making them think that if they could just find the locked door to where their loved one was being held, maybe they could save them.

After years of fumbling around, the police finally figured out the glaring piece of "key" evidence and linked the cases—all twelve of them, spread out over twenty years. They started calling him the Key Killer.

Finally, someone got the idea to run a search on locksmiths in the criminal database, and they found the only one with an old rape arrest. They closed in on Roger Vay, gathered some damning forensic evidence tying him to the mailed keys, and put him on trial. During Prosecutor Jane's presentation of evidence, another woman went missing and a copycat killer sent another key. It was enough to create reasonable doubt, and the real Key Killer was set free. The justice system at its finest.

I stared down at the pictures in the file. Remarkably, Vay looked clean-cut, owned his own small business, and even had a wife and two kids. He also hardly went anywhere, so there were far fewer pictures of him to study.

"Hey, check that out." Liam pointed to one of the photos I'd put down. It was of Stanley Violet outside his gas station talking to someone in a vehicle. "See that black cargo van? It's the same one from this picture." He grabbed the photo I was holding and slid it next to his.

I gasped, my heart thumping in my ears. Could this be true? "Oh. My. Mother."

"It's the same vehicle, right? And part of the license plate shows."

"Liam, I can't believe this," I said, leaning in to him to see the photos better. "I totally missed that. But is that a *D* or an *8*?" I pointed at the plate.

"Are you blind? First of all, a *D* looks nothing like an *8*. And anyway, it's neither—it's a *zero*." He was clearly enjoying his break-through.

I squinted at the image, scrunching up my nose as though that would make the image suddenly clear. "It's definitely a *D*."

"Whatever you say," he said, imitating my expression. Mother Jane would be dismayed to know that a boy had caught me looking so unattractive. I didn't care. This was huge.

"Come on," I said, shoving the files into my bag. "Let's get back to my place before my mom gets home. I want to get on my dad's computer and check the plates."

CHAPTER 14

I didn't go into my dad's office very often. Only to do some research on the "official ongoing investigation" into his death, and some digging on the Filthy Five. Otherwise, it had been virtually untouched since he died—his gun case securely locked, the minifridge stocked with Corona Lights, and his dearly beloved semper fi flag hung on the wall. If I didn't know better, it felt like he might be coming home any minute to skedaddle me out of his man cave.

This time, as I prepared to do research with Liam, I noticed a large coin on the mouse pad. I picked it up to move it aside and realized what it was—my dad's Challenge Coin. What was it doing here? He'd always had it on him, and it wasn't here the last time I'd come in. Had he accidentally dropped it under the desk before he died, and the cleaning lady found it recently and put it somewhere we'd see it?

"What's that?" Liam said, as I turned it over in my hand.

"A coin that everyone in my dad's SWAT unit had," I said, trying to remember its significance. "It says 'Loyalty. Courage. Commitment.' Though, I'm pretty sure they just used it for bar games. When someone taps it, it's supposed to alert everyone to a challenge. The last person in the unit to pull out their coin and start tapping has to buy everyone drinks." I shook my head. "Like they need any more drinking in SWAT." I put the coin in my pocket anyway. It instantly made me feel closer to Dad.

I wiggled the computer mouse, and the last program used popped up. The large screen lit up with a photo from my sixth birthday party—my dad and me smiling at each other over a massive plate of sizzling fajitas and fruity drinks with umbrellas. My heart sputtered at the sight. I didn't remember looking at these photos the last time I was in here. My mom must've used the computer, which surprised me since I was under the impression that she hadn't stepped foot in here since his death. Maybe she missed him a lot more than she let on.

I closed the files and closed off my heart. No time for weakness now. Instead, I opened the license plate database, silently thanking Liam for not asking me any questions about the picture.

I typed in the letters and numbers I could see in the photo, filling in all the other fields I could—commercial van, black, standard California plates. Two-thousand-plus hits registered.

"Stupid overcrowded California," I mumbled, typing in a few variations. Three-thousand-plus hits came up each time.

"Dead end," I said and flopped back in my dad's oversized desk chair. A hint of musk from the leather and his cologne wafted up, and I pinched my eyes, pretending to feel frustrated, but really feeling like sobbing. If only my dad were here. He would know what to do. He would get his team to track down every lead and protect me.

"Ruby, are you all right?" Liam touched my leg and made me jump.

"I'm fine," I said, feeling stupid.

"You just looked . . ." He paused, searching for the right word.

"I'm sorry," I interrupted. "I'm good. I'm just not used to having someone around like this. Alana's usually here to create mindless diversions for me, but not . . . this." I gestured at whatever invisible *thing* hovered between us.

"Well, get used to it," he said gently, momentarily holding my cheek.

Flustered, I looked back to the blurry photo and studied it again.

"I wish I had one of those huge lenses so these effin' letters would actually be decipherable. One of those slimy paparazzi guys named Sammy had one that could probably take pictures of life on Mars. He's the guy who put most of those pictures of me in the tabloids. He was around here a lot when my dad first died, always saying these creepy personal things about me, baiting me to look at his stupid camera. After LeMarq, he was one of those sniper paparazzi hiding in the bushes at school. He's a real tool."

Liam sat up higher and laughed like I'd finally hit the punch line of a hilarious joke. "It's not that funny," I assured him.

"No, it's not that. I'm not laughing *at* you, even though it is pretty ridiculous," he said with a stupid grin I almost felt like wiping off him. "You just found the answer to the problem."

I stared at him. "I didn't know we were doing math tutoring. Which problem?"

"Let's go find this guy Sammy, and he'll have the photos we're looking for. If he was watching your every move with his privacy-invading camera, *and* the guy behind all of this was watching you, too, chances are there are more images out there. Maybe more than a license plate."

I sat there speechless, suddenly understanding. Not only would Sammy have photos, but insider information on the "Investigation" of LeMarq, and maybe even my dad's, too. Somehow these guys always knew more than they should. Like how many times I frequented the 31 Flavors on Main Street for Double Dutch chocolate scoops when I was "depressed."

Sure, there was a risk Sammy would take advantage of the fact I was doing my own investigations and asking my own questions. But that was a risk I had to take.

"Liam," I said, "you're a freaking genius."

"Rue! I'm home," my mom yelled just outside the door.

"Oh, snap, it's Mom," I muttered. Like a cat landing on all fours, I stood up, clicked off the monitor, and shut the drawer with my dad's passwords.

As my brain raced through how all this would look to her, I decided to play the awkward card. "Liam, she'll know I'm hiding something by being in here. Just pretend we were making out, OK? That'll really throw her off."

He stared at me for a few moments. "Really?" he whispered, eyes bright. "Won't she be totally pissed at me?"

"Who cares if she's pissed at *you*?" I didn't understand why he would even care how my absentee mother felt about him.

"Well, she could put me away for good. Everyone knows how tough Prosecutor Jane Rose is."

"For kissing?"

"For perjury," he said with a devilish grin. "You can't ask me to lie, can you?"

He moved in closer and put his arm around me, cradling my neck. He looked down at me with an intensity I almost couldn't handle, waiting for my permission. What was I going to do—say no?

Suddenly, he wasn't asking anymore. The moment our lips touched, my eyes fluttered shut in a rush of sensation. His hands, his body, and his mouth were slowly, tenderly, exquisitely consuming me. His warm breath and lips reminded me of melting campfire chocolate—soft and full, smooth and sweet, but dangerously hot. A tingling heat rose in my body. I'd been kissed before, but never like this.

I squeezed the back of his shirt into my fists and pulled him even closer. He didn't seem to mind as he brought both hands to my face, then to my shoulders, then to my hips. I didn't even know what to do with my hands anymore. I didn't mean to touch his abs, but there they were under my fingertips. Waves of adrenaline and desire surged in me with each kiss and touch.

I finally took a breath and realized how desperate I was for oxygen. He rested his forehead on mine, and we breathed the same air. I couldn't open my eyes yet—I was too dizzy.

"Wow, Ruby Rose, no wonder they say you're lethal," Liam whispered.

I playfully slugged him in the chest. "Hey, easy with the name-calling."

"Sorry," he said, kissing my cheek, then my neck, then moving back up to my lips. "At least we won't be lying."

I heard my mom just outside the door murmuring intermittent curses. She must've been going upstairs, because her voice trailed off around the third F-bomb. She definitely didn't know we were in here.

"I think she might have a case against me for assault," I said, looking at his wrinkled shirt and swollen lips. "You look like you just got mauled by a bear."

So much for restraint. As in every other aspect of my life, I was losing my self-control.

Liam smoothed out his clothes and tried to straighten up, but he couldn't erase the giddiness written all over his face. Which was good, because that was exactly what I needed my mom to see. I clutched my backpack and mentally prepared myself for the confrontation.

"C'mon." I grabbed his hand and led him out of the room. Once we hit the stairs, I yelled, "Mom, I'm down here."

A few seconds later, she popped her head out of my room. And one second after that, her eyes nearly popped out of her head.

"Rue, what . . . who . . . how . . ." she stammered. Poor D. A. Jane was at a loss for words. She was a mess, and she knew it. Shirt untucked, a few strands of unruly hair askew. As she descended the stairs, she straightened herself up as much as she could.

"This is my friend Liam. We were just studying for a Calculus test," I said.

"I wasn't expecting company," she said with a salty tone directed at me. "Though it's lovely to meet your *friend*." Liam smiled back, not knowing what to say. The look on Mom's face was bizarre at best. Was she pulling a cougar move on the first boy I ever let into my house?

Mission Awkward: Accomplished.

I watched as she accumulated the evidence against us. Messy hair, pink lips, guilty faces. I couldn't tell if she was mad or jealous. Or maybe she was just flat-out flabbergasted.

"We were just leaving, actually," I said. "Study group."

"It's almost eight o'clock on a school night!" she argued. "And I got dinner—fresh halibut from Duke's."

"Well, we have a big test tomorrow, and I already ate." I rebutted each point, just like she'd taught me. "I promise to be home by ten."

I turned to go. I wasn't exactly asking for permission.

Liam followed me to the door but stopped midway to do the proper thing. "It was nice to meet you, Mrs. Rose."

"It was nice to meet you, too, Liam," she replied, looking him up and down again. Even in her disheveled state, she was beautiful and she knew it.

I wanted to slap her right then. For how many reasons, I wasn't sure.

CHAPTER 15

Groggy didn't cover it. And third-period History wasn't helping.

To keep my head from collapsing on my desk, I supported my chin in my hands and propped open my eyes. Even then, the dim lights and gentle hum of the projector were luring me to sleep.

The long day and the late night with Liam had left me drained. Finding Sammy proved far more challenging than just calling *Star Magazine* and being connected to the desk of Sam Carmichael, who was credited with the "Hollywood Belles in Bikinis" pictures this week. We left a few messages and wrote a few e-mails before being forced into patiently waiting for a reply.

The endless early morning hours had left me exhausted—tossing and turning in bed with memories of blood and gunshots. And the warm room and Mrs. Monotone Voice weren't helping.

The only thing that kept me going was a steady intake of a very caffeinated soda in my thermos, and the invigorating memory of Liam's lips on mine.

Finally, the lunch bell rang and I hurried to meet Alana at her locker, just as I'd done every other school day for the last five years. As I approached, I noticed she wore long sleeves—despite the warm day. She was hiding the bruising from the ties.

"Hey, Alana," I said in my best lighthearted, glad-you're-alive tone, as I slid up to the locker next to her. She jumped at the sound of my voice.

"Hey," she said without looking in my direction. Instead, she kept her focus on switching the books from her backpack to her locker.

"Why haven't you returned my calls? I've been really worried—"

"Please, Ruby."

"Please, Ruby, what?" I asked.

"I gave you space when you needed it—now it's time to return the favor." Surely she was speaking to her textbooks, not to me.

"Uh . . . no, if you recall, you *never* gave me the space I wanted. And I understand why. You were only being a good friend." I put my hand on her shoulder.

She jerked away and turned to face me. "I was wrong. I should've listened to you. I should've understood. Now I'm asking you—"

"To what? Abandon you when you need me the most?"

"That's where you're wrong, Ruby. I really *don't* need you." She shut her locker with force. The crash of metal against metal was jarring.

"I get why you'd feel that way right now. But you have to understand that I never meant for you to get hurt."

"Look, I don't know what happened or why. I just know I don't want any part of it. Can you understand *that*?" She hurriedly zipped up her backpack.

"I do. But . . . you're my best friend." I looked down, searching for the words to convince her to forgive and forget. But mostly to forget.

"Consider this my best-friend breakup speech then," she said, slinging her backpack over her shoulder. I almost laughed. She'd threatened to "break up" with me many times over the years.

"Alana, you're being silly," I said, reaching out to her again.

She pulled away and took a few steps backward, shaking her head. "You know, all these years I thought the guns and the training were just more of your weird . . . *quirks*. Just a strange way to spite your overbearing mom, or a bizarre way to bond with your *dysfunctional* dad."

Hey! I thought she loved my dad. He'd taught her to shoot, too!

"Alana, don't . . ." I didn't need to finish that sentence. She knew my dad was out of bounds.

"But now I'm not sure what to think anymore. I've always given you the benefit of the doubt. Even when you killed that LeMarq dude and your mom took care of it. But the problem is"—she paused, with a look of sadness that turned to blame—"I know you too well, Ruby Rose. You've always been the one looking for the fight."

I ground my teeth in a flash of anger. OK, I got it—she was pissed. I almost got her killed and then tried to pretend nothing had happened. But attacking my family? Not cool. What was next? Burning my favorite pair of UGGs?

At the same time, though, she was right about one thing. Alana had known me too well, and for a long time. Of course, she didn't know the details—that I was stalking LeMarq and The Stick—but she knew I was more involved than I was letting on.

I closed my eyes, calling on my problem-solving skills to give me the words I needed to persuade her to freaking relax.

"You're overreacting, Alana," I said, opening my eyes to find her walking away. "Would you just wait? We need to talk about this."

"I'm sorry, Rue," she said, clearly not sorry at all. "But I'm sure Liam would just love to 'talk.' You two can share your secrets."

"What? Liam?" I looked behind me. Liam was at his locker, trying to pretend he wasn't listening. He gave me a sheepish smile, and I smiled back weakly.

When I turned back to Alana, she was already disappearing around the corner.

"She'll come around." Liam's gentle voice softened the blow. "As soon as we figure all this out, she'll understand."

"There's that *we* again," I said, backing up against the locker, still shaken from Alana's cutting words. "You sure you don't want out yet? A good night's sleep didn't give you more sense?"

He put his hand on the locker next to me and leaned in. "Not after the way you kissed me last night," he whispered.

The heat blossomed in my cheeks. Surely he wasn't considering kissing me right here in the hall? That would be highly inappropriate and at the same time freaking amazing.

"Any news on that schmucky Sammy dude?" he asked.

"Ha, no." I smiled. "He hasn't returned any of my e-mails or phone messages. You?"

"Nah, but he'll call. Don't worry." Liam gently touched my face. I really hoped no one was watching me melt right now. "Come on, let's get something to eat."

Every day Liam and I ate lunch at school (enduring Alana's spectrum of looks from disdain to disappointment), and every night we patrolled the Hollywood hotspots looking for Sammy and his missile-sized camera. But the schmuck was good at what he did. He was a ghost—just like Mr. D. S., the even bigger schmuck behind all this madness. And I was the haunted.

I didn't like being on the defensive all the time. I had to find a way to regain control of my life. Except I couldn't figure out how.

Until nearly two weeks later on Halloween, when the ghost finally called.

CHAPTER 16

The Pier was crowded for a Friday afternoon in late October. Unseasonably warm weather and the Halloween spirit buzzed in the air.

As I people watched, ghouls and phantoms roamed the beach. Some dude wearing nothing but skate shoes, board shorts, and a Captain Jack Sparrow wig played Bob Marley tunes on his guitar below me. Another kid, wearing one of those white masks from the movie *Scream*, casually rode his beach cruiser down the boardwalk. The souvenir shop in the middle of the Pier even had a huge grim reaper–shaped kite flapping around in the breeze.

The real ghost—schmucky Sammy—could be anywhere, watching me, taking aim to shoot me from afar. He had a camera lens for all occasions. Sammy had said to come alone, so I made sure I scheduled our little rendezvous for when Liam had a football game an hour away and would be gone all afternoon and night.

Liam and I had been together every other possible minute of the day for two weeks. I tried to act like it wasn't necessary, but he stuck by my side—which may or may not have had something to do with all the kissing. It seemed like whenever we had the chance, we'd lose ourselves in each other: at the beach, in my room, at the back of the library.

Shaking the images from my mind, I looked down on the beach for distraction. And what do you know—Jell-O-Shot Taylor and her still nameless sidekick lay tanning in their matching hot-pink string bikinis. I felt a larger than usual amount of spite rise up within me. Not only had Taylor most likely taken the upper hand in the valedictorian race, but she was embracing the seemingly carefree life that I'd never have again. She had a friend to hang out with, time to lie in the sun, and a future full of normalcy. If ending up incredibly successful and somewhat famous on the *Real Housewives of Orange County* is "normal." Better than ending up on *Cops*, though.

Taylor said something, and her friend's high-pitched laugh floated on the breeze all the way over to slap me in the face. Alana and I used to be like that—happy, silly, naive. I had no idea what she thought happened that night, or what she'd remembered since, but as far as I knew, she hadn't told a soul about being drugged, bound, and left for dead on a cliff.

I'd tried to call her. I texted her about twenty-five thousand times, with gentle questions like, "What's up?" or "Wanna hang?" or "Need chocolate?" I told myself she just needed more time. She'd been mad at me before and had gotten over it. After all, we were besties. It said so on the chain necklaces we got in junior high.

"Well, well, well, if it's not the infamous Ruby Rose." A thick and greasy voice sludged down my ear. Was he talking with his mouth full of food?

I turned to find an equally repulsive visual. Oily face, shiny bald head, and the unshaven jowls of a chipmunk about to hibernate. He took the last bite of the burrito in his hand and threw the yellow wrapper toward the garbage can about ten feet away. He missed.

I looked down at him in disgust—I mean I literally looked down at him because he was so short.

"Thanks for coming," I said, swallowing some pride.

"I brought what you asked for," he said, swallowing down the food and opening his jacket to expose a flat manila envelope tucked into his pants. What did he think this was, some kind of drug deal? The thought of touching that envelope made me want to take a shower in hand sanitizer.

"Can I see them?" I wished he'd just hand them to me.

"Let's discuss the terms of this deal first."

"What's to discuss? You said you'd help me."

"For a price." He stared at me like I was an idiot. "You didn't think this was free, did you?"

"Fine, how much dirty money do you want?" I stared back like *he* was clearly the idiot.

"I'm not talking money." He looked at all the girls in bikinis and licked his lips.

"If you think I'm gonna . . ." I trailed off, incapable of even forming words so vile.

"Relax, that's not what I meant." He patted his camera. "I meant some exclusives. I get some pictures of you doing *interesting* things, and you get pictures of a black van doing *uninteresting* things. By the way, do you think this black van has something to do with you blowing LeMarq's brains out?"

"What do you mean *interesting*?" I said through clenched teeth.

"You know—you in a bikini doing Tai Chi, you scantily clad in the arms of your hot new boyfriend," he said through a smile so big the pigeons were likely to crap on it. Then he dropped the smile. "Or a tip the next time a shooting goes down."

I hadn't given this snake enough credit. He saw a pattern and knew it would happen again. Maybe he knew it already had.

I nodded reluctantly. "We can work something out," I said, careful not to agree to anything specific.

He handed me the sweaty envelope, and I quickly took it.

"I knew your dad, you know." He took off his sunglasses and cleaned them with his dirty shirt. "Long time ago. He was a good guy."

"How would *you* know *him*?" I asked, seriously confused by how this lowlife could know a legend like my dad.

"He helped me out on a research paper I did in grad school. This was a few years back, before he became Sergeant, before I . . . got into this." He put his glasses back over his squinting eyes, like he was suddenly ashamed of himself. "I used to be a real journalist."

"That's hard to believe," I muttered. "So why'd you join the dark side?"

"Money," he said flatly. "Grad school ain't cheap."

And apparently, it's ineffective at teaching proper grammar. "What did my dad help you with?" I asked.

"Rooting out some *interesting* cops," he said with raised eyebrows, like I was supposed to know what that meant.

"OK," I said, raising my eyebrows in return.

"He made a few enemies back then, but I wasn't one of them. He scratched my back and I scratched his." He made another incomprehensible facial gesture. He thought we were speaking in some kind of code and I knew the subtext. But I didn't.

"They won't tell me anything," I burst out, knowing I was changing the subject. "They say my dad died in an ambush, blown up by explosives. But they have no idea who or why. Do you have any more back-scratching buddies left in SWAT?"

He dropped all the wise-guy pretenses. "Sure I do."

"Anybody say anything about what happened?"

"Sure, sure," he said. "I still got some buddies in SWAT who talk. Loyal guys. Guys still torn up about it. Yeah, word is someone was causing him problems. A high-ranking special operative—someone with a vendetta. There was a report, an official complaint your dad filed just weeks before . . ." He stopped to make the sound of a bomb exploding and illustrated it with his fat little hands. "They didn't tell you this stuff? Not even Mathews, your dad's replacement? I thought the two of you were close."

"A report?" I said in half disbelief, half rage. "No one ever mentioned a report! Certainly not Mathews. What did it say?" Could the "special operative" be Mr. D. S.?

"I'm not sure. I never saw it. This is just what I heard from Mathews, off the record. I'm not supposed to . . ." Uneasy, he started to look around. Like he felt someone watching us. "Look, that's really all I know."

"Can you find out? Could you ask Mathews again?" I knew I sounded desperate, but I didn't care.

"That's all I got," he said, nonchalantly running his tongue around the inside of his mouth as if he was checking for lucky leftovers. I had to force myself not to gag.

"I don't want to talk to you any more than you want to talk to me, but please, if you find out anything else, will you let me know?"

Either I'd said something that amused him or he found some beef jerky stuck in an incisor, because his goofy grin made him look far too satisfied.

"I'll tell you one thing, sweetheart," he said, backing away. "Talk to Detective Martinez. He knows more than you think he does. Waaaaaayyy more."

Sweetheart? Martinez? This loser knew just how to piss me off.

"Why him?" I started to follow the trail of slime, but he held up his hands like *I'll touch you with these greasy things if I have to.*

"Remember that corrupt-cop thing your dad and I were working on all those years ago?"

"You can't mean Martinez? If that was true, he wouldn't have been promoted to Detective."

"Let's just say that Martinez was good at getting in and out of more than just your mom's panties." He dropped his chins and grinned. A quick palm thrust would wipe that smug look off his face. "Not long after your dad found out about the affair, he turned Martinez in to Internal Affairs for some 'misplaced drug evidence.' Nothing stuck of course. Jack made the move to SWAT, and Martinez made his way up the ladder all the same. That's the thing about corruption, it's hard to know how deep it goes. But make no mistake, Martinez's hands weren't clean."

"But my dad couldn't prove it?" It was more a statement than a question.

"The thing is, Jack and Martinez were both damn good at their jobs. In some ways, they were a lot alike. Both highly trained, ambitious Marine brothers until the end of time and all that jazz. They were tight. But the *way* they did things couldn't have been more different. While Jack was all *letter of the law*, Martinez was all *spirit of the law*. Martinez bent the rules, did things his own way, and Jack didn't like it. Jack thought he could change Martinez. That as his partner, it was his duty or some shit . . . pardon my French. But obviously, that didn't happen.

"While Jack made his way up to Sergeant fairly quickly, Martinez built a reputation as a dirty cop. About a year ago, your pops *allegedly* began suspecting Martinez of suspicious dealings with a few drug rings." Sammy paused to make a full-circle motion with his chubby hands, then said, "So, when I heard Martinez's name came up in the personal complaint Jack filed the month before his death, I couldn't help but wonder—"

"Wait," I said. "My dad filed a report against Martinez one month before he died?" I couldn't believe the vast amount of information I didn't know. It kept falling on top of me like an avalanche.

"No, the report wasn't filed against Martinez. Remember, I said the complaint was against someone else—someone from both of their pasts. Somebody I don't know about, unfortunately. But Martinez was a *witness* to threats against Jack. Apparently it would've taken a lot more than a nearly wrecked marriage and an almost-destroyed career to break the Marine bond they shared. Water under the bridge." Sammy stared with skeptical eyes at the water slamming against the Pier's beams.

I shook my head in astonishment. Was he insinuating that Martinez didn't hate my dad anymore? That they made up, and he was actually helping my dad, trying to protect him from someone— maybe the same someone who'd been setting me up? Could I believe this dirty little slop of a man? Had I misinterpreted Martinez's concern all this time? Was he trying to protect me against the same man who murdered my father?

"Look, kid . . ." Sammy paused and glanced around nervously. "I gotta go, but don't forget to call. Remember, I scratch your back, you scratch mine."

The only thing I wanted to scratch was my skin in case some of his head lice had jumped onto my body.

But he really did know my dad—and in a way I never had.

I was supposed to go see Dr. T at 3:00. First, she pushed the appointment back, which I thought was lucky since that was the time Sammy had wanted to meet. But while I was on my way over to her office, she canceled altogether, saying she wasn't feeling well. That had happened like two times ever. Snow at the beach was more common. I wondered if I'd told her too much. If she was distancing herself from me because of what she knew I'd done.

I would've considered it another stroke of luck that the house was empty when I got back, but who was I kidding? My mother was never home.

I pulled the pictures out of the envelope and thought about burning it in the trash can to make sure all Sammy's slime was gone. But that would raise flags I didn't need, so I put it in the kitchen trash compactor and washed my hands four times. Just to be sure.

He had four pictures of the van. Clear, digitally enhanced photos. I pulled open my dad's database again and plugged in the plate number.

One name popped up: D. Silver. I almost couldn't believe my eyes. D. S. now had a last name *and* an address: 4081 Royal Hill Bay, Newport Beach, California—only twenty minutes from here.

Now I wished Liam wasn't away at his game. I shouldn't go—no, I couldn't go—to Newport without him. And yet it would be virtually impossible for me to sit here alone and twiddle my thumbs all night. Surely doing a simple drive-by would be a safe enough activity in my Mary Poppins–equipped Big Black. We could just go check out the address.

I closed out my dad's computer and headed over to his gun safe, putting in the pathetically simple code—911. The safe door creaked open, and I stared at the racks of weapons like a kid at a candy store. Since my handgun, Smith, had gone into the LeMarq evidence logs, never to be returned, I wanted something similar. Hanging on its hook was my dad's nickel-plated Glock, but I could barely stand to look at it, let alone touch it. Maybe I shouldn't be taking a gun at all.

I'd been somewhat successful at blocking out most of what happened that night at the warehouse. Liam and I had an unspoken agreement not to talk about it. But now, as I stared at the Glock, I couldn't help feeling the darkness of those deaths creep over me again. Why had Silver returned my dad's gun to me?

The only reasonable choice seemed like my mom's Ruger pocket revolver. It was tiny enough to seem like middle ground between a real gun and nothing at all. The only reason we even had it was because my mom once told my dad she wanted a gun small enough to fit in her small Coach purse, and he bought it for her anniversary present. She got so mad that he'd dared offer it in the place of a "real anniversary gift" that she never picked it up. I couldn't tell if it had ever been used. I knew my dad wouldn't have been caught dead with a little thing like this.

And I hoped I wouldn't be, either.

I slid it into my jeans pocket, next to the Challenge Coin I now carried with me at all times. As I was about to close the safe, the hilt of a knife caught my eye. It was one of those Rambo-type blades, with a leather holder that strapped on to the leg under clothing. I pulled up my jeans, tied it above my boot for good measure, and heaved a big sigh of relief.

I finally had a lead.

CHAPTER 17

I could barely make out the faded address sign on the decaying post at the entrance of the marina. "Bayside Buccaneer Yacht Club" had seen better times. Half of the old-fashioned street lamps were burned out, and half cast a faint Halloween-orange glow that did nothing to illuminate their surroundings. The place was littered with garbage, and the bitter reek of fish seeping through my rolled-up windows made it feel more like a deserted shipyard than a yacht club.

Aside from a few old beater cars lining the street, several abandoned-looking RVs in the parking lot, and a small office near the docks, no other evidence of life existed. This place was totally isolated. Even half of the boat slips were empty.

Could Silver live on one of these eyesores? It seemed unlikely considering his profile. Yet, as I sat safely inside Big Black watching a lonely plastic bag blow down the planked walkway toward the water—which I told myself *didn't* look like a ghost floating in the darkness—it started to make sense. This might be an ideal place for a criminal to hide. Nobody around except for the rotting fish.

The lights in the small office down the walkway flickered, catching my eye, and I toyed with the idea of jogging down there just to verify that D. Silver really did have a registered slip. But it was dark. And Halloween night. And logic told me to wait for Liam.

Except, logic also told me that I was fully capable of walking a hundred yards to ask one stupid question. Especially with the heat I was packing in my pocket. I grabbed my phone and quickly typed a message to Liam, telling him where I was and what I was doing, just in case. But as soon as I pressed "Send," the message came back undelivered with a huge exclamation point indicating no service. Just perfect.

I turned off the engine and reached down to make sure the knife was secure under my boot-cut jeans. Reminding myself of all my dad's training, I turned up all my senses as I walked across the parking lot and onto the creaking wooden causeway. I could do this.

The wicked wind picked up as I drew nearer to the office, and a tattered flag on a pole whipped and snapped at me. I knocked on the glass door of the small shack. Across the room, I saw the top of the guard's unmoving sun-spotted head behind his chair.

I could tell he was watching TV, not only because of the flickering blue light dancing across the ceiling, but because the volume was vibrating the floorboards beneath me. He was watching the USC versus UCLA football game—it was late in the fourth quarter, all tied up.

I let myself in.

"Excuse me, sir," I called over the front counter. The guy obviously had no peripheral vision left, because he didn't budge except to scratch himself in some wish-I-hadn't-seen-them places.

"Excuse me." I raised my voice even louder. He took a sip of a dark liquid I was sure wasn't Coke and adjusted his legs on the chair opposite him. Good gracious, was I going to have to give the guy a coronary just to get his attention?

I walked past the desk and rounded him so he could catch me in his peripheral vision. Instantly, his eyes bulged open, his legs and his drink went flying, and the old man overturned his folding chair and landed flat on his back.

"What the . . . !" he screamed. "Who the P-P-Pete are you?" he stuttered from the floor.

"I knocked," I said while helping him up. "I'm really sorry—I didn't mean to alarm you."

"What you d-d-doin' here, girlie? Making me miss my damn game!" he barked. "We ain't doin' no trick-or-treatin' round here!"

"I'm not here to trick-or-treat. If I could just get some information, I'll be out of your hair." Oops, he only had like five hairs left.

"Fine," he groaned, holding his back as he went over to the desk, motioning for me to evacuate his personal space. "What you want?"

"Could you please tell me where Mr. D. Silver's boat is docked?" I asked politely.

He blew out a stale-smelling breath and started poking at the computer keyboard with one finger. "What's the first name, girlie?"

"I don't know. Everyone calls him D. Silver," I said casually, not wanting to raise any red flags. Legally, he shouldn't be offering any information, but something told me this guy wasn't exactly a stickler for the rules.

"If it will get you out of here sooner . . ." he muttered, pushing up his sagging bifocals and leaning in to the monitor. "B-16. That's down the left side here—"

"Really?" I asked, craning my neck to sneak a glance at the monitor. "Do you know him?"

"Know who?" The old man tilted the screen away from me. So it was OK to tell me the info but not to let me see it?

"D. Silver," I said pointing at the screen. "Have you seen him around? Do you know what he looks like?"

"What's this about?" He took off his skinny reading glasses hanging for dear life off the end of his nose and gave me a see-here-young-lady look. I could tell he was gearing up to run me off when a staticky voice came to life from the ground. An ancient walkie-talkie.

"So B-16 is empty, then?" I asked as I backed out of the office, glancing out the window in the direction of the slip.

"I didn't say that." He bent over to pick up the walkie-talkie off the floor. "But ain't nobody out there tonight, rest assured."

"Thanks," I said, almost out the door already. "Sorry about the fright."

"Yeah, yeah, yeah," he mumbled as I left.

I turned left and made my way down to the B dock. I was operating on instinct now, not fear and certainly not logic. The guard said no one was out here tonight, so if I went and had a peek around the boat, it might pay off. And if he was wrong and I found any signs of life—lights, noise, or movement on the boat—I'd leave and come back later with backup. Lots of backup.

The wind was getting stronger, pushing me backward, but I was almost to the B dock when I heard a shriek.

A man's.

My feet—and my heart—stopped.

"Help, help . . . I'm drowning . . . please help!" The voice and the splashing water weren't far away, but I couldn't see where in the darkness.

I pulled the gun from my pocket and made sure it was cocked and ready.

Damn it. This wasn't good. I shouldn't have ever gotten out of Big Black. Or more to the point, I shouldn't have ever gotten *in* Big Black tonight. This was a setup. But how? How could he have known I'd come tonight? Was he watching Sammy?

"I can't . . . stay up . . . please!" The voice cut through my thoughts.

I grabbed my cell out of The Cleave. I had a choice to make:

A. Call 911 and go back to the security office, hoping the drunk and feeble old man could move fast enough to help me save whoever was out there;

B. Call 911, go back to Big Black and leave, knowing the police would trace my number and I'd have to explain myself;

C. Call 911 and go save the man myself; or

D. Don't call 911 at all, because I just remembered I have no effin' service! I held up my phone to the night, willing the phone gods to send me some little bars of mobile coverage. Curse words I'd never used before came flowing out of my mouth.

What choice did I have at this point but to get out of there, and fast—before it was too late? But if this was Silver's work, I already knew he wasn't afraid of putting innocent lives at risk. And what if the person in the water was someone I knew?

I took off toward the cries. Sprinting down the narrow, uneven dock, I nearly fell over some loose ropes. The poor lighting and slipshod care of the dock were dangerous.

In the moonless night, I couldn't get my bearings. I couldn't see anything in the water, and the sounds were echoing off the boats in every direction.

Until the light.

Like a spotlight centered just for me, a bright beam shone directly on the side of the old rickety houseboat at Slip B-16.

Its name, *Ruby Belle*, was painted on the side of the boat.

Time seemed to stand still. Information overload started falling into designated Tetris-like slots: The boat was named after me. It was docked at Silver's slip. And someone was in the water next to it, calling out for help.

He'd done it again. He wanted to toy with me. And I'd been stupid, impatient, and impetuous enough to walk right into his trap.

"Help," the voice called again. Whose voice was it? Whose life would I have to save, and whose would I have to take?

I jumped onto the boat—a motorboat with a small cabin—and raised my gun to prevent a surprise attack. The deck floor was wet and slippery as I found the bait in the waters beyond the front hull— the human bait meant for me. My eyes adjusted to find another familiar face, another monster fighting for his life.

Father Michael McMullin. Number three on my Filthy Five list, of course. Without his thick-rimmed 1970s glasses, I almost didn't recognize the pedophile priest my mom had prosecuted and failed to convict. Still wearing the white collar of God. But now, tied up in the silver chains of Mr. D. Silver. The thin chains tightly wrapped around his neck didn't look heavy enough to drown him, but the ties binding his wrists together weren't helping.

"Help!" he cried. "I can't swim."

Considering what he'd done to all those children, he deserved to drown. The chain around his neck couldn't have been more appropriate—several of his victims had been tied up with rosary beads.

As I watched this grown man (who'd never learned the basic skill of treading water but had most definitely mastered the skill of ruining lives) struggle for air, I couldn't help but marvel at how Silver had outdone himself. If I didn't save Father Michael, technically it would be me who killed him. I wouldn't have pulled a trigger, but he would be dead at the bottom of the ocean just the same.

But I wasn't a killer like Silver—or like Father Michael.

"Help!" he called again, more desperate now.

I scanned the deck for a flotation device, rummaged through the sparse galley, and even scoured the two other boats docked nearby. Everything had been removed, as though pirates had pillaged the place. Of course I knew there was only one pirate behind this sick trap.

I hurried back to *Ruby Belle*'s bow and found the only thing that might save Father Michael—a short mariner's rope with hooks at each end. I threw one end out into the water for him to grab, but it wasn't close enough to him to see in the dark night. Not that he was even looking for it. He was probably so blind without his glasses that I'd have to hit him over the head with it.

I reeled the rope back in and yelled, "I'm throwing you a rope. Grab it!"

He was too out of his mind, flailing about for air.

My choices became abundantly clear. Let him die—saving countless souls, and the justice system hundreds of thousands of dollars.

Or attach the rope to the boat, jump in to attach the other end to his body, and pull both of us back into the boat—risking not only my life, but others' lives in the future.

I put the gun and my cell phone down along with my boots and jacket, hooked the rope to a rod at the tip of the stern, and jumped in. The cold Pacific water shocked my system like an abrasive alarm screaming, "This is a mistake!" My clothes suctioned to me, strangling me like a thousand sheets of icy blankets. Each stroke I took felt like a bad dream where my muscles wouldn't respond to my brain's commands.

As soon as I got to him, I hooked the rope onto the chains around his neck (knowing it wouldn't feel awesome to be strangled as I dragged him) and tried to pull us back in, but his flailing legs made it impossible to even move in the right direction.

I swam around to face him, hoping that when he got a good look at me—even without his bifocals on—he'd calm down. But instead, his eyes bulged and he started screaming. "No, no! Not you."

"Relax, I'm trying . . . to . . . save you!" I screamed, choking on seawater. What the hell was he so scared of? A skinny little teenager trying to save his life? Had Silver warned him that I would hurt him? "I'm going to cut you loose . . . so you can grab the rope."

But he couldn't hear me. He was too busy repeating Hail Marys between gasps for air. I took a huge breath and dipped under the water, away from his splashing blows, to try to get at the knife strapped to my leg. With frozen fingers, suffocating clothes, and collapsing lungs, I almost thought I wasn't going to be able to do it.

Just as I thought I was doomed, I let go of the rope, gave my pant leg a tug with both hands, and slipped the blade out of its sheath. Air had never tasted so good.

Clenching the knife in one hand and taking the plastic tie binding his wrists in the other, I sliced and his hands were free—with or without cutting some of his skin. I neither knew nor cared.

But as soon as he realized I'd freed him, he didn't try to swim. He grabbed my head and tried to use my body to stay above water. The moron didn't understand that he was connected to the boat now, and all he needed to do was grab hold of the new line and pull himself in.

I gasped for air and tried to tell him, but he was past listening, past feeling, past reason. I tried to fight the sting of the ice water burning my lungs with the adrenaline kicking in to save me. I was drowning, I couldn't break free of him, and I couldn't fight—he was too strong, and my reflexes were too weak from the numbing cold. Time and again my head went under the pitch-black water, disorienting me, freezing me, threatening to choke me. I knew I only had one choice left.

I gripped my knife and gave him a warning stab in his arm— only meaning to hurt him enough to get free of his grasp. Instead of the cut weakening him, it enraged him even more. He was like a shark incensed at the smell of blood—thrashing and clawing at me with more force than I could handle. He grabbed me by the neck and tried to choke the remaining air out of me. My mind went fuzzy.

I fought back—for precious oxygen, for life—but instead, I inhaled two mouthfuls of foul salt water mixed with blood. I was going to die, right here, at the hands of Father Michael.

No. I would not be another one of this man's victims. My dad didn't train me to survive only to have this pathetic sadist drown me.

I renewed my grip on the knife and slashed once as hard as I could, until I felt the blade slide through tissue and hit bone. He went limp.

Oh, crap. Where had I stabbed him that made him give up so fast? I'd only wanted to make him let go of me. But in my choking, frozen, and blinded state, I hadn't had the senses for precision.

I released the weapon, too weak to even pull it out, and swam as far away from him as I could. It wasn't until my fingers felt the slivery wooden ladder that I even turned back. But by then, he was already underwater.

Chances were he was dead, but I had to at least keep trying to save him. My soul couldn't take any more deaths.

I scaled the ladder, shaking in the night wind. I charged to the stern and grabbed the rope, pulling with everything I had left. I heaved until my arms felt like they would come right out of their sockets, with no progress. He was too heavy. Maybe even stuck on something below. If he hadn't been killed by the knife wound, he had to be dead now after several minutes underwater.

I let go of the rope, falling to the floor of the boat, and sunk my head between my knees.

How much more of this could I take? I tried to breathe, but my lungs were burning and I could only gasp in agony. My hands shook with the bitter cold.

What was I supposed to do now? Call the cops and tell them I'd killed yet another man? Watch them pull the priest's body up with my knife sticking out of his chest? My stomach clenched in disgust.

Try to explain (again) that it really wasn't my fault? How would I even justify my presence here—or his?

The whole truth would need to come out, only to be twisted and used against me. Used to destroy me, my mother, my dad's good name. My heart stung with rage.

I let out a wild cry, banging my fists on the boat's wet floor and letting the tears fall.

I hated myself, I hated Silver, and I hated what he'd made me.

He was Dr. Frankenstein, and I was his monster—forever tainted by the shedding of so much blood.

My tears mixed with the salt water still dripping from my sodden hair. I shook with anger—in near hypothermia, and in horror. Alana was right. I was always the one looking for the fight. I'd chosen to follow these men that I'd killed. I'd chosen to put myself in a place I shouldn't be, carrying weapons I shouldn't have.

Yes, part of me had wanted the priest dead, but not at my own hands. Yes, he had deserved to die by injection or old age in his lonely prison cell, but not by stabbing. Yes, he would never hurt another soul again, but what about me? I still had a soul. Perhaps a dark one—but it was a soul nonetheless.

I had to pull myself together and report this one. The four bodies at the warehouse were different. I had no idea where the damn warehouse even was. I would have looked like a lunatic.

But *this* body was right in front of me, dangling at the end of a hook like chum in the water. Silver may have made me into an executioner, but I wouldn't let him take away my integrity. I wouldn't leave Father Michael's body here for a poor old fisherman to find.

Plus, I still believed in the justice system, and believed that I would receive a fair trial. Despite the mess of everything, I could rely on a jury of my peers. Well, maybe. As long as my mom employed a high-powered defense team (using up all my dad's life insurance money meant for my college education); as long as I portrayed myself as sympathetic (which I had no idea how to do); as long as no juror had a secret hatred for any member of my family (not likely, since the polls showed that at least 25 percent of Orange County strongly disapproved of my mother's tenure as D. A.); and as long as the press stopped calling me a Teen Vigilante (they'd probably come up with something worse).

OK, so maybe I didn't believe the justice system always worked. But I still needed to call 911. I forced my boots back on and pulled my jacket over me for warmth.

As I stood, a new light caught my eye—there was a car up on the street. No, a van.

A black van—pulling into a parking spot. It stopped in mid-turn as the beams of light landed on me like I was the star performer in his sick show. I couldn't see him, but he could most certainly see me.

I grabbed my gun and phone and sprinted up the rickety dock to the street. When the van's tires squealed and it roared away, I changed course to get back to Big Black.

My nerves and icy fingers had me shaking so badly that I could barely get Big Black's door open. Silver was getting away. Finally, I was in and I screeched out onto the street. I knew the general direction he was going: south. If I could get close enough, I could shoot out his tires and stop him.

I pushed the engine down the empty street until it opened up into a busier area. I barely blinked, waiting and watching for something to show me where the van had gone. Suddenly, about two stoplights away, I saw a black vehicle turn left and disappear behind a building. I blew through two yellow lights and turned in after it down a narrow street, which became a claustrophobically thin alley with nowhere to hide. It seemed like I was on the butt-end of a strip mall, where workers came to throw out the trash and sit on milk crates to smoke. Except no one was around—and probably hadn't been for a while.

Big Black's headlights finally lit up the gate at the end of the alley. The sign on it said: "Dead End."

He must have somehow gotten through this gate and relocked it. I flashed Big Black's brights on the sliding gate. Either I was delirious or that heavyweight padlock was still swinging.

I thought about doubling back and finding out where the end of the alleyway led, but that was ridiculous. Silver was long gone. A thousand steps ahead of me—a million miles away. He'd outsmarted me again and lured me away from the crime scene. I could just see myself on the witness stand trying to convince everyone that I wasn't the stupidest girl in the world. Not that my defense team would ever let me testify.

I had to go back to the marina and use the Security Guard of the Year's phone to call it all in.

"S-s-say what?" the guard stammered as he slammed down his remote control. What was he so irritated about? His stupid, inconsequential, non-life-threatening football game was over.

"I said, can I please use your phone? There's been a terrible accident." I looked a mess—soaked and matted hair, smudged eye makeup I couldn't wipe off, still-sopping clothes, and my poor, innocent, formerly light-brown Diesel ankle boots crusted with salt water and debris.

"What kind of accident?" he asked, grabbing his walkie-talkie.

"A man drowned out there," I said, trying to sound calm. "I tried to save him, but he was tied up. I need to call the police right away. Please, where's your phone?"

"Hold on there a minute," he said with his hand up, suddenly alarmed. "What man? Where?"

"We don't have time for this." I didn't want to explain anything to this guy. He was drunk, and my words could be twisted. "Can we just call the police?"

"Look here, young lady," he said. "There ain't no phone around here. This here radio's all I got. Budget cuts. So you'd better tell me the location so I can report it."

"Fine," I said. "B-16."

He started jabbering into his walkie-talkie, waving me to follow him to the dock and describing me to whoever was on the other end as a juvenile delinquent and possible meth head. Through the static noise and unintelligible war codes they were using, I presumed the police had been notified. The guard was surprisingly sprightly and nimble through the darkness, and we were back to the *Ruby Belle* in no time. Maybe he would have been able to help me save Father Michael after all.

"Where?" he demanded.

"Right there," I said, pointing to the rope leading over the stern of the boat.

He climbed aboard, and I followed him up to the edge of no return. We stood there looking down into the dark water. In just a few moments, he would pull on the rope and make the most ghastly discovery of his life. Inch by inch, he pulled at the dead weight. The rope made a sickening grinding noise against the metal of the boat. Either this guy was shockingly strong or Father Michael had already lost most of his blood and limbs to the bottom feeders.

Finally, the end of the rope came into sight. My knees buckled, and my lungs locked up.

Where was the body?

CHAPTER 18

I stared at the rope, incapable of forming a logical thought. All that was left of Father Michael was his shirt.

"Better call off the fuzz, Jimmy. We got a false alarm here," the crotchety old guard complained into the radio, staring at me with what looked like a mixture of sympathy and disgust. "Just a dumb Halloween prank."

A prank? That's what he thought this was?

"Somebody put an old shirt in the water." He held the shirt in the air to demonstrate what a stupid blonde I was. "Girlie, you need some new friends."

My legs felt like overcooked spaghetti noodles. My brain was telling me to sprint out of this haunted harbor, but I couldn't make my feet move. I felt trapped, watched, manipulated. So much for standardized testing and its assessment of my "elite" intelligence—I was an elite idiot to have come here without Liam. His presence might have prevented this. Or at a minimum, he'd be here holding me now.

"Are you OK?" the guard asked.

"Of course," I lied.

"You're trembling. Are you cold or somethin'?"

"Yeah, cold," I said.

"Well, c'mon back to the hut with me and I'll fetch you a blanket."

"No, I'm fine," I said, because I still couldn't move. But I suddenly noticed the stink of bleach.

Somehow, Silver had managed to come back and destroy all the evidence that Father Michael had ever been here. But that was impossible. How would Silver have had enough time?

"What did you say you were doing out here?" the guard asked, staring at me.

"I didn't say," I responded flatly. And I walked away.

As I drove, I kept shoving all the harbor images out of my mind. I tried to think about Liam instead.

The closer I got to home, the heavier my guilt became. I should've called 911 and reported what I'd done. Yet, how could I do that with no body? Not even a shred of evidence that anything at all had occurred? Only a discarded wet shirt. Just like with the warehouse killings, I had nothing to back up my story.

I had to get home, to get warm. Maybe then my brain would start working. My ice block of a foot lay heavy on the gas.

I peeled onto my street, anxious to escape the darkness of the worst Halloween night of my life. Luckily, my neighborhood was too snooty to participate in trick-or-treating, so I didn't have to worry about running over any little witches or wizards. But Big Black—and my heart—skidded to a halt when I neared my house and a dark shadow materialized next to a parked vehicle outside the gate, exactly where the paparazzi usually lined up. Except, the car wasn't Sammy's old Pinto.

No, it was Liam Slater's red canvas-topped Jeep.

I jumped out of Big Black without even bothering to shut the door behind me. Running to Liam, I buried my face in his chest and let his arms encase me. I breathed him in and instantly felt safer.

After a second, he pulled away from me—probably because he'd realized my hair and clothes were wet, not to mention I smelled like blood and fish guts. With his hands on my arms, he scanned my disheveled state with eyes as dark as the night.

"Oh, Ruby," he said. "What did you do?"

I told Liam the whole sordid story, and he just sat there in my bucket seat, staring down the radio dials like they'd done something horrible to him. Or maybe it was the heater vents. Oops, he was probably sweating in the hot car. I was still cold from being in the dirtiest part of the Pacific Ocean. I turned down the heater, and my seat warmer up. Damn, I wanted out of this car and into a hot shower, but Liam deserved to know what had happened

I wondered when Liam was going to yell at me. Ask questions. Storm off to the police station. Or any other rational response.

"Liam, I'm really sorry I didn't wait for you. I was impatient and cocky, and maybe in the back of my mind I felt like you didn't deserve to be dragged any further into this mess." I slammed my head back onto the headrest. "I win the contest for Most Screwed-Up Girl and Idiot of the Year."

I flinched as his fist connected with the dash. Out of all the reactions I could've foreseen, that wasn't one of them.

I gripped my armrest, unsure of what he might do next. I'd never seen this side of him. He was furious.

"Yeah, Ruby, maybe I'm a little pissed that you went to see Sammy without me. And maybe I think you're absolutely crazy for hunting down this guy alone. But what I'm the most upset about is the danger this dick, Silver, is putting you in. You could have died!" he raised his voice like I wouldn't get the message at a normal volume.

"Relax, Liam." I slid my hand halfway over the console between us. "I didn't die. I'm right here."

He saw my gesture (which was no little thing for me) and was quiet for a few moments. Taking a deep breath, he grabbed my hand

and squeezed it in both of his. "Ruby, this guy is smart and patient. He knew you would go to the boat dock. He had it all planned out. He made it so that either you had to watch the priest die or risk yourself to save him. He obviously told the priest that you were dangerous to ensure the priest would fight back and you'd have to kill him in self-defense. Then he lured you away so he—or his accomplice—could go back and take the body and leave the priest's shirt, knowing you'd call the cops. He's not trying to get you caught. It's almost like he's trying to protect you." As he said it, some of the puzzle pieces started shuffling around in my mind, but they weren't fitting neatly into place.

I pulled my hands away and slumped back in my seat, massaging my sore head. "If that's true, then he has split personalities or something. First, he puts me in these dangerous situations, forcing me to kill, and then he defends me and cleans up to make sure I could never be prosecuted. The dude gave me back my dad's engraved handgun! Why would he do that?"

"I don't know, but no matter what, it's like he's ten steps ahead of us." Liam paused and pursed his lips. "I know you don't like it, but I think it's time to go to the police, Ruby. Maybe Sammy was right and Detective Martinez would back us up if he knew what was going on with your dad."

"No." I stared at him. "No, no, and no."

"Things are getting out of control—"

"Things have long been out of control, Liam. I have killed, or been responsible for . . ." I stopped to count with my fingers. "Seven deaths now. Seven!"

"That's not true," he argued.

"LeMarq, the girl I didn't save, The Stick and his friend, the two other gangsters . . . or whoever they were . . . and now Father Michael. How would I ever be able to explain that?"

He blew out a breath, and clenched his hair in his fists.

"You aren't responsible for any of those deaths. *He* is," Liam said. Who was he trying to persuade? Himself?

"*He* didn't make me carry that knife. *He* didn't force me to pull any triggers," I said, playing prosecutor. "*I* put myself in those positions. *I* am the one with motive, intent, and—worst of all—very little remorse for the *victims.*"

"Ruby, *he* put you in impossible situations. And in every single case, you did the right thing. Every one of them deserved to die, except for the girl. But now the right thing is to tell the authorities. Maybe the FBI or CIA can help." He reached for me again, but I didn't want his touch. I put up my signature warning hand.

"Yeah, so they can *help* destroy my family and escort the both of us to prison for the rest of our lives," I said, my voice rising an octave. "No matter who we go to, it all trickles back down to the detective assigned to my case—Martinez. And if Sammy was wrong about Martinez, he'll take you down with me. Because, as you recall, you were present for some of this."

"Don't worry about me. I can take care of myself. I've been doing it all my life. Believe me, I can handle whatever the police throw at me," he said with a weird smirk.

"What are you talking about?" I asked. I glanced over at his disfigured ear.

"Never mind. I didn't mean that literally," he said, shaking his head—a move I now knew he did to make sure his hair covered his scar. "I just meant that we have no choice but to trust the system—"

"What happened to you?" I cut him off. He knew my secrets. It was time for me to know some of his.

He glared at me with *how dare you* eyes, but I held his gaze like we were having a blinking contest. "Liam, c'mon, you know I won't say a word—"

"I have a record, OK? A juvenile record, that is. It's sealed, and supposed to be expunged or erased, or whatever, when I turn eighteen next year. But it exists. And somehow Martinez knows about it.

That's what he was talking to me about that night he came to your door. He warned me to stay out of this, and away from you, or else he'd make sure my record got longer."

"What?" I lost the blinking contest. "Back up. What did you do?"

"It was a long time ago, Ruby. I've never told anyone about it."

"Are you freaking kidding me? Whatever you did can't compare to what you've witnessed me do," I said, irritated that he was holding back when things were so lopsided in the bad-deeds department.

"I nearly killed my father," he said point-blank, staring at his hands as if they might still have blood on them.

"Because he did that to you?" Not only did I ask the question we'd been avoiding for weeks, but I actually reached over and touched his ear. At first he flinched away, but then he hung his head and let me move his hair aside to run my fingertips along the disfigured skin. I could feel him cringing as I prodded his head to the side to allow the blue light of my console to shine on the scarring. My heart ached for Liam's embarrassment, and it burned for the father that had done this to him.

"Well, yeah, I reacted to defend myself from him, but really to protect my mom and brothers." Before he looked away, I saw that his eyes were now full of sorrow and rage. "He used to abuse her right in front of us, our whole lives. He'd come home wasted, knock her around, call her every name in the book, accuse her of things—and if my brothers or I got in the way, we got it, too."

"You have brothers?" I asked, wondering how I didn't know this.

"Christian is twelve, and Tug is only eight."

"Tug? That's his name?"

"Well, his real name is Tomas, but my mom always says 'If you're not careful, he'll tug your heart right out,'" Liam said, smiling painfully and looking out into the night. "Not to mention your arms if you don't take him surfing when he wants."

"Good to know," I said, hoping I'd get the chance to meet them someday.

"Anyway, one night, when I was thirteen, I just couldn't take it anymore. He came home from work late, drunk and out of his mind. He was angry about . . . everything. He went after my mom. Slapping her, pushing her, accusing her of having affairs when everyone knew—well, I knew because I was the oldest—that he was the one sleeping around. He threw Christian across the room for getting in the way and was about to go after Tug for crying when I snapped. He got me in the ear with a broken beer bottle, but I . . ." He closed his eyes as if talking about it made him relive it.

I put my hands on his cheeks and made him look at me. It was my turn to comfort him. "It's OK—if there's anybody in this world who'd understand, it's me."

"I would have done anything to protect my mom and brothers, even if it meant killing him." Liam swallowed hard, like he regretted letting his dad live. I finally understood why he liked me—I was just as damaged as he was, if not more.

He was big and strong and gorgeous, but broken. Cracked inside—just like me. We both put on our best show, but underneath we couldn't stop the suffering for those we'd lost and what we'd done.

"Where is he?" I asked, wondering if I needed to go kick his ass right this second.

"He still lives up in NorCal. I haven't seen him since the trial."

"Trial? He pressed charges on you?" I gasped and placed my hands over his balled-up fists.

"Yeah, and they stuck. They said I should've spoken up about the abuse—*if* it really happened." He squeezed my hand. "They didn't believe me after the fact."

"What? Didn't your mom and brothers testify to back you up? Surely they had bruises or other physical evidence to corroborate your side of the story."

"Things got complicated, Ruby." He shook his head and pulled his hands away from mine. "My dad was smart. He rarely left evidence of his abuse. Even that night, I was the only one hurt. Christian had carpet burns and my mom had red marks, but as usual, the real damage was on the inside." Liam cracked his window and took a breath of fresh air. "Plus, my dad has a lot of money and he hired an attorney to file a petition to terminate *her* parental rights, arguing that my mom had poisoned me against him. That she actually brainwashed me into trying to kill him for the money. My brothers were little, and I couldn't bear to see them being put through all that. And, we didn't have any money to fight him. He agreed to drop the petition and let her have custody of us if I copped to the assault charge. So I did. He kept his good name along with his multimillion-dollar business, and I took the blame."

I grimaced at the reality of the situation.

I had been taught—ingrained with the belief, really—that the justice system worked. That the police investigate the crimes, the D. A.'s office prosecutes them, and the Constitution protects it all. Sure, there were glitches, but overall it was the best system in the world. And I preached this at my high school Constitution Society meetings. True, I only founded the stupid club to pad my resume, but I still believed it.

Until now.

Now, I didn't know what to believe if abusers like Liam's father and murderers like Father Michael could get away with so many premeditated crimes, with *malice aforethought* and *intent to do harm*. Liam had none of that, I had none of that, but we could go down in flames.

"If I'd reported the abuse earlier, documented it, documented some evidence against my father before it all blew up? Maybe he'd be the one with the record and not me."

"You were just a kid, Liam," I argued. "How could *you* have documented evidence against him? That makes no sense."

"It doesn't have to make sense, Ruby," he said, shaking his head. "After the fact, it was our word against his. And his word meant a whole lot more than ours. He was a well-respected businessman who donated regularly to the campaigns of anyone who mattered in the City of Santa Cruz. The police couldn't help me even *if* they believed me."

"I get it, Liam. I know how much it matters to have connections. I've obviously been on the receiving side of that crooked line lately, and I have the same problem you did! I don't have any evidence. Silver has made damn sure of that," I said, burned out. Tired of being cold, sick of thinking, and weary of being me.

"I know," Liam said softly. "I know."

We sat in silence for a few minutes, staring into the dark night. There were no easy answers, and we had almost no one to trust.

"I just need some time." I interrupted the silence. "I promise, I'll think about it."

"In the meantime, is it OK if I come up?" he asked.

"Up where? To my room?" I said, surprised.

"I don't want to leave you alone," he said. "Your mom isn't home yet."

I looked at the clock. 11:02. "Yeah, I'm not surprised. She's probably having 'campaign drinks' downtown."

"So . . . yes?" he asked with raised eyebrows.

"Uh, I guess," I said, sure about wanting him near, but unsure about what a *yes* actually meant. "You might want to park your Jeep around the corner, though, so Jane doesn't immediately call in the cavalry."

"Cool, because there's something I want to show you," he said with a wicked gleam in his eye that my virgin brain couldn't interpret. Suddenly he was moving his whole body in my direction, and all the frozen blood in my body turned hot. Until I realized he was just leaning over to press the gate-opener button clipped to my sun visor. "I'll meet you inside," he said, his lips so close that his breath mingled with mine. "Let's do this."

CHAPTER 19

When I finally emerged from the shower, my skin burned bright red. I wiped some of the steam off the mirror and stared at my pitiful reflection, counting up the reasons why I resembled a Hot Tamales candy.

It could've been the scalding water I'd used to warm the icy marrow in my bones.

Or the vigorous scrubbing with my loofah to remove the evidence of ever having touched Father Michael.

Or the anger I felt toward Silver for turning me into something I hated.

Or the intermittent impure thoughts I had about Liam alone in my room.

I cracked the window to let the ocean breeze turn me back to a normal color before I got dressed and went out.

I opened the door to find only a bedside lamp was turned on. I'd forgotten for a second that I told Liam not to turn on any more lights in case my mom came home. This way she'd think I'd fallen asleep already.

As I let my eyes adjust to the low light, I discovered Liam totally relaxed (and fully clothed) on my bed. Disappointment (that he had no physical expectations) and relief (that he had no physical expectations) duked it out for control of my emotions. Then a third reaction won out—surprise—when I saw what he had in his hand. A photo. Of a man. With a well-groomed beard that could only be . . .

"Is that a picture of Silver?" I asked, racing to the bed to snatch it from Liam's fingers. "How in the—"

"You're not the only one with high SAT scores," he said, pulling the picture out of my reach.

"Really? I thought you got on the honor roll by batting your girl lashes at teachers," I teased back, grabbing the picture.

"Hey, I don't have girl lashes!" He pretended to be offended. "And I'll have you know, I study very hard to get my grades. Not all of us are naturally brilliant like you."

"Whatever." I smiled without looking back at him, staring at the photo.

It wasn't great. In fact, it was terrible. But it was something. Silver looked just like Liam described. Handsome, in that "look at my sexily groomed beard" kind of way. Well built. Well dressed. No more than forty years old, if that. What would a guy like this want with me? He looked too normal. This had to be the man that I'd seen across the crowded cafeteria as I was about to faint, and through my blurred vision I made a facial hair miscalculation, projecting my fear of Martinez onto someone else.

"Seriously, how did you get this?" I asked, not taking my eyes off the picture.

"You know Mrs. Peabody in the front office?" he asked. I nodded. "This morning, when I was supposed to be in second period, I took her some donuts. When she went to the break room to get her coffee, I took a peek at the security footage. It's all digital, so I typed in the date, zoomed in on the clearest image, and printed this sucker out. It was easy."

I finally looked up at him. Genius. Why hadn't I thought of that? And why did I keep underestimating, distrusting, and generally misjudging him? I could have reached over and kissed him in gratitude, but instead I said, "This is amazing. Thank you."

Our eyes lingered on each other's, until I had to look away, blushing. His neon sign was back on, and mine had blinking red lights. And in this situation the red lights didn't mean STOP.

I wondered if he felt the same. If he could forget all the awfulness of the evening. After all, we didn't need to go all the way. We could just—

"So now that we have proof of what he looks like, it should be enough for the police to ID him, right?"

OK. Not what I was expecting.

"What's wrong?" he asked. "Isn't this good news? This could help clear you. It shows that the guy is following you. He's somewhere he's not supposed to be." He reached toward me, not to touch me or comfort me but to take back the picture. "If we show this to the police, they have that face-identification technology—"

"I told you, Liam," I said, standing up. "I can't go to the police with this. Not yet. Just having a picture of some dude doesn't prove anything. How do we connect him to any of the abductions or killings? How do I prove he made me do anything?"

"Hang on," he said. "Just a few minutes ago, you were ready to plant one on me for getting this picture."

"I think it's time for you to go." I crossed my arms, ready to close the doors on the vault. I knew I was being ridiculous, but exhaustion, shame, and confusion were drowning me just like Father M—

"Look, I'm not going to do anything you don't want me to do. I promise." He held up his hands and moved toward me slowly, like he knew what I was capable of. "I'm just trying to help you."

I bit my lip, unsure of whether I should believe him. I couldn't even trust myself. Just moments ago I was ready to kiss him, and now I could just as easily knee him in the jewels if he said the wrong thing.

I dropped my head and ran my fingers through my damp hair. "I'm sorry. I just don't know how to feel anymore. I don't know who to trust or where to turn. I should probably just run away to Mexico where no one can find me, and then I wouldn't have to kill anymore or go to prison."

"OK, let's go," he said, smiling and moving in closer again. "Let's just get some sleep before we make a run for the border, all right? You've had a busy day."

It was true. It had been one freakishly long day, and I didn't want to spend any more energy or emotion recounting it. I was ready to collapse.

"Come and lie down." He took me by the waist and guided me back to the bed. Part of me wanted to steel myself against his charm, but there was no denying the larger part of me wanted to give in to him. I wanted to believe him that he wouldn't do anything to hurt me. He wouldn't do anything stupid behind my back, like talk to the police. Whether I was willing to admit it or not, the vault had been unlocked. I'd let him in completely somewhere along the way.

I was falling—*out* of control, *into* bed, and *for* Liam Slater. Falling hard.

I slid under the covers and felt him slide in right behind me. Within moments I was drifting. Not just into sleep, but closer to another human being than I'd ever been before. He pulled me tight to his chest, and I melted into him. Every part of him entwined with every part of me, like I didn't know where he started and I ended. My head rested on his arm, and our breathing slowed to match one another's. I'd never experienced anything like it. His hot breath near my ear sent prickles up my neck.

I lay there, waiting to feel his lips against my skin, or his free hand on my thigh. I wanted it. But apparently not as much as my body and mind wanted sleep.

The last thing I remember was his arm reaching over me to turn the lamp off, and the feel of his body against mine. I didn't even care if my mom came home to find him in my bed. What was she going to do? Kill me? She could get in line.

In the morning, Liam was gone, but his scent wasn't. I breathed in my pillow, the smell of his cologne and shampoo reminding me of his warm skin and soft hair. I longed to feel him again, to be held by him. So much for my aversion to touch.

I wondered when he'd left. It was Saturday, so he probably had early-morning practice or something. I hadn't even asked if he'd won his game last night. It didn't seem like it mattered at the time, but now my omission just felt rude.

My stomach rumbled. It had been nearly a day since I'd eaten anything. I rolled out of bed and went to the kitchen. The smell of coffee not only alerted me to my mom's presence but also spiked my awareness of a possible confrontation with her. I almost went back up to my room to search for a granola bar in my backpack when I heard her voice.

"Is that you, Rue-girl?"

I gulped and shuffled into the bright light of the kitchen. I felt like I needed sunglasses just to enter this side of the house. Maybe I had some kind of hangover from last night's horror.

"Hey, sunshine," she said.

"Hey, Mom." I went straight to the fridge without looking at her. As I searched for the quickest and easiest nourishment, I watched her out of the corner of my eye. She put down the paper and watched my every move. Why was she just staring at me without her normal assault of judgment or cross-questioning? She knew something.

"Good night's sleep?" she asked.

"Uh-huh," I said, grabbing the orange juice.

"Not too tired this morning?" she prodded.

"Nope." I filled up a glass and sipped the juice while studying the fruit bowl for something I could grab and get out of there with. But damn it, the bananas were too ripe and the oranges looked a day or two past edible.

I turned to the cabinet to snatch some bread instead while Mom continued staring. Had she seen Liam in my room—or had she seen him sneak out this morning? Did she know something about what I'd done last night?

"Is there anything you'd like to tell me?" she pushed.

We were exceeding our spoken word limit for the day. I didn't have time to toast this bread. Butter and jam would have to be enough.

"Not that I can think of," I said, throwing a fake smile in her general direction.

She took off her reading glasses, sat back in her chair, and crossed her legs. One of her signature D. A. moves that meant, *OK, I'm getting serious now.* I bet it worked great on unwitting criminals ready to plead out, but it wasn't working on me. At least, I was *trying* not to let it work on me. It would be a lot easier *trying* from my room. I started to go, but then she said, "Ruby, why do you lie to me?"

I skidded to a halt. I didn't even know which lie to cover for.

"I don't know what you're talking about," I said, turning and accidentally making eye contact.

"How long has this been going on?" she said.

What? Stalking people, killing murderers, or having sleepovers with a boy? "Could you define what you mean by 'this,' counselor?"

"It's not a game," she said, standing up and making her chair scrape against the tile floor. "You could be jeopardizing your future."

I needed a few more specifics. Everything I did lately was jeopardizing my future. "Seriously, Mom, just tell me what you're talking about."

"Well, we've never had this conversation, and it is probably overdue . . ." She put her arm around my waist and led me back to the table.

Two horrible "overdue conversations" sprang to mind: Either she'd found out about the deaths piling up around me or she actually wanted to have *The Conversation*. Yeah, like at seventeen I didn't already know about the birds and the bees.

I honestly couldn't decide which discussion would be worse.

I sat down at the table with my bread and butter as my only defense against her attack, jamming in mouthfuls of food so she couldn't expect me to speak first. She sat down across from me.

"I don't know exactly how to say this," she said, "but I hope you at least used protection."

As much as I suddenly longed for her to be talking about the gun and the knife, I knew she meant something else. And I wished she did know about Father Michael. Then she wouldn't feel the need to torture me with this awful subject.

"The last thing you need right now is to bring a child into the situation," she said, now talking more to herself than to me. "Believe me, a mistake like that would be devastating, not just for you—but everyone involved."

I stared at her, trying to read where this was coming from. Something in her eyes made it seem like she wasn't talking about me anymore. Like she was alluding to someone else. Maybe even herself. But that didn't make any sense. She was in her thirties when I was born. Right about the same time she admitted to her affair with—

"Please don't tell me that Martinez is my real father." I closed my eyes, unable to look her in the face.

"Ruby! Of course not. No, that's not it at all." She paused, speechless.

I reopened my eyes to make sure she was telling the truth.

"I'm talking about *you*," she said, straightening her posture to regain control.

"What about me?"

She hesitated. So un-Jane Rose. She was rattled, flustered. I'd never seen her thrown, so completely off her game.

"I know about you and that *boy*." Those words practically spurted from her mouth, oozing with disdain. "I asked him to leave this morning. I didn't wake you because I wanted to know if you would be honest enough to just tell me the truth. And apparently, the answer is no."

"Really?" I asked, cocking my head. "This is so interesting coming from someone who lies for a living." I set down my bread. I no longer needed it to defend myself. "You lie to the press, lie to the Court, lie to your only child—and you're accusing *me* of lying!"

"Young lady—"

"You promise the world to everyone," I said. "Promise the community to be tough on violent offenders and then cut them deals or allow enough incompetent mistakes to let them off." I ripped that one straight from Bill Brandon's talking points. I knew I should stop, but the words kept bubbling up.

"You promise your family that you'll be there for us, and you aren't." Just mentioning the "us" brought flames to my heart. There was no "us" anymore. Just her and me in our glorious isolation. At least she couldn't cheat on Dad *again*. But I didn't dare mention that. "So please remind me, *Jane*, where I was supposed to *learn* honesty."

"This discussion is not about me, Ruby, and I will not let you attack me to protect yourself. Don't think I've forgotten this is how you work. Dr. Teresa has told you over and over that this is not an appropriate way to communicate." She smoothed out her hair and narrowed her eyes. "*I* am the mother. *You* are the daughter, and you will treat me with respect. And you will tell me whether or not you are sleeping with *that* boy under my roof."

"OK, you want the truth? You want respect?" I said, narrowing my eyes right back. "No, I am not sleeping with *that* boy. We've never had sex. *I've* never had sex. He slept in my bed last night, but nothing happened. We didn't even kiss once." Part of me wished I had slept with him, just to throw it in her face. "And since you brought her up, Dr. Teresa is more of a *mother* to me than you've been in a long time.

At least she accepts me and tries to understand me. She never bails on me." Well, except for yesterday, but that was unheard of.

Mom deflated like I didn't expect. I'd hurt her. She sat still, shoulders slumped, a few tears suddenly running down her cheeks. Was she a wounded lamb or incensed tiger? I had no idea. I wanted to take back the words, even if they were partially true.

In the lingering, threatening silence, I braced myself for her response.

Even after she quietly got up and left the room, I held tight to the table for a while—just in case.

CHAPTER 20

For weeks I held on, waiting for my mom to lash out at me, punish me, forbid me to see Liam. Take away my credit card and shoe allowance. Surely, she'd come up with some retribution for my insubordination. But nothing happened.

I wondered if I'd really hurt her. My grandmother—my mom's mom—died before I was born, but I knew she'd worked more than one job to help put my mom through college and then law school after my no-good grandfather left. My dad had explained to me that one of my mom's biggest regrets in life was not having her mother there when she walked onstage to receive her law degree. Which was why she pushed me so hard. It was her way of honoring her mother and rising above the hardship she'd endured as a girl.

For days after our fight, she left early and came home late, which I liked to think wasn't *only* because of me—Bill Brandon's attack ads were picking up steam on every TV, radio, and Internet channel.

I went to school and to bed without seeing her. I reviewed the assassination of JFK (and Charlie LeMarq), the carnage of World War II (and Rick "The Stick" and his cohorts), and the dissection of frogs (and Father Michael). Everything reminded me of those horrible moments. Not even Liam's kissing skills, or several pounds of my mom's best imported chocolates, could make me forget. As if committing "legally justified murder" wasn't already hard enough on my soul, it was also taking its toll on my thighs.

And to add insult to injury, I had absolutely no new evidence to lead me to the answers I needed.

Liam and I checked the California databases for any additional information on D. Silver, but there were over a thousand results. Even after we refined the search criteria to an adult male, there were over a hundred. Early one Saturday morning, before Liam's football practice, we went back to Bayside Buccaneer Yacht Club. While Liam used his old scuba gear to search the shallow bottom of the boat dock for Father Michael's body, I scoured the boat for clues. Big surprise—nothing.

We went back down the coast—to the cliff we'd woken up on—to search for answers, but that was a bust, too. We had no idea where to start to find the warehouse we'd been taken to the night of the beach party. Liam even asked a bunch of kids if they'd seen anyone suspicious that night, but since it was a high school party full of all kinds of shady behavior, that didn't produce anything helpful, either. One of his friends, pleasantly nicknamed Johnson (and not because it was his last name), thought he "might" have seen Liam being carried down the back staircase over the shoulder of "some dude," but he said he didn't think twice about it because he thought Liam was probably wasted, too, and anyway he was a "little high," and in the middle of making out with a Swedish exchange student named "Molly or Marin or something."

It was like none of it had ever happened. Except that it had. Liam knew it, I knew it, Silver knew it, and Alana maybe knew it—she at least knew *something*, because she still wasn't talking to me.

Thanksgiving and the holidays were upon us, but no one would have known it at Casa de Rose. Not like last year when Dad and I got out the decorative fall wreaths and the miniature stuffed pilgrim set and spent days baking chocolate-chip-pumpkin cookies.

This year, there was only the scent of silence.

That is, until a bouquet of colorful autumn flowers arrived at my door, smelling maybe a little of marijuana. The delivery guy was clearly stoned even though it was only 7:00 a.m.

"Are you Ruby Rose?" asked the weed guy. I noticed that his eyelids were barely doing their job.

"That's me," I responded, ascertaining that his threat level was a mellow-yellow. I knew Silver likely had inside men helping him, but this dude couldn't be one of them. Just in case, though, I had a bedazzled butterfly blade Dad had once given me for Christmas hidden in The Cleave.

When he'd buzzed in from the video gate, I asked him to leave the flowers by the call box. He said he was given specific instructions not to do so. Out of curiosity and sheer desperation for any clues, I let him come to the door. But not without properly arming myself.

"Rad." He bobbed his head. "I've seen your picture on TV. You're way hotter in real life, though."

Gross. Even though he wasn't completely destitute in the looks department, slacker skater dudes in their twenties weren't my type. Especially not ones who may or may not be working with psycho manipulator of the year D. Silver.

"Are you going to give me the flowers or not?" I asked, holding out my arms. "I have to get to school."

"Oh yeah, totally." He looked down like he'd forgotten he even had anything in his hands. As he gave them to me, he said, "You know, if you ever get sick of the guy who sent these, I'm single."

"Good to know." I threw him a you-may-leave-now smile and shut the door before I got high simply from being near his clothes.

I practically sprinted to the kitchen to read the card sitting on top of the scarlet, white, and ginger blooms. Inspecting the envelope for any initial clues, I gingerly opened the seal.

Roses are Ruby red
Autumn lilies are orange and white
Let's do something normal for once
Will you go to the Sadie Hawkins dance with me tonight?

Oh—kay. Sure, in the back of my mind I'd considered the possibility that Liam had sent the bouquet. It probably made more sense than D. Silver, who was more likely to send me a cryptic piece of art or a creepy message.

So why couldn't I decide if I was relieved or disappointed? Excited or terrified? Appreciative or angry?

Despite my growing catalog of concerns, Liam was relentless about the dance. Even after I explained my aversion to underage binge drinking, awkward group dates, and cheesy picture stances, he still insisted that we go. All day at school, he went out of his way to make me smile, laugh, and forget. My answer went from a firm no, to a definite maybe, and then after his speech about being normal and going on our first real date, my answer turned into a hesitant yes.

After all that he'd done for me, it was about time that I did something for him.

I caught a glimpse of my androgynous ensemble in the reflection of his shiny Jeep door as it slammed shut in his driveway. "Sadie Hawkins, eh!" I said contemptuously.

"Come on, they're just T-shirts," Liam said, batting eyes the same color as our matching baby-blue Billabong Ts.

"At least we didn't have to go all matchy-matchy in footwear," I said, concentrating on my more flattering shoes. Sure, Liam could pull off the vintage checkerboard Vans, but I needed something with a little more lift.

"Well, I thought about getting matching shoes, but I can't rock the heels like you," Liam joked.

"Ha-ha." I couldn't restrain my smile. "These aren't heels by the way, these are my stripey blue-and-white wedge-pump Toms with a bow."

"And I thought *I* had a shoe problem," he said, grinning. I was already starting to feel more normal. "Come on, I promise this will only take five minutes. My family really wants to meet you and take a few pictures."

"Right." I shook my head in disbelief as we walked to the front door. Why Liam's mom and brothers wanted to meet the Vigilante Teen Killer was beyond me. Maybe they wanted to pat me down for weapons, or warn me to stay away from Liam when his back was turned.

"And just so you know, it was my bro Christian who helped me write that poem for you. He's the family romantic. Tug, on the other hand . . ." He blew out a breath. "Let's just say you need good reflexes. Watch out for flying objects." He winked and took my hand to escort me into his small house.

"Hey, guys," Liam said warmly to the two boys sitting in front of the TV. "I want you to meet Ruby."

At first, all I saw were eyes. Two big, bright brown eyes and two big, beautiful green eyes—looking up at me with the same excitement.

The older boy stood up and came over to shake my hand.

"Hi, Ruby. My name's Christian." He was thin, with short dark hair and glasses. He looked nothing like Liam. Actually, he was sort of the opposite of Liam in every way.

"Well, hello, Christian," I said, shocked at his polite and formal manner. Either he'd been prepped for this or he was the most charming twelve-year-old I'd ever met. "It's nice to meet you."

He smiled and returned to the carpet. Tug teasingly punched him and made a googly face. Tug had the same dark hair but was thick as a tank.

"Tug, be nice," Liam warned, though he was obviously amused. "Don't expect Tug to shake your hand, Ruby. He's got cooties."

"Hey," Tug said. A shoe went flying past Liam's head, barely missing his scarred ear.

"I see what you meant about reflexes," I said to Liam.

"Yeah, we'd better get going before someone gets hurt." Liam smiled. "*Mamacita! Estás lista?*" he called into the back rooms. I hadn't realized he spoke fluent Spanish.

A woman with luxuriously dark hair and eyelashes that went on for days came gliding into the room. I could see where Liam got his lashes and olive skin, but other than that I was confused. Liam had much lighter hair and blue eyes. And I thought *I* looked nothing like my mom.

"Oh, Ruby," she said, her dark eyes just as vibrant as the boys', but softer at the same time. She took my hand in both of hers, then swiftly pulled me in for a kiss on each cheek. "I've heard so much about you."

Oh, snap. Hearing things about me couldn't be good.

She pulled away to look me in the eyes. "Thank you for taking a minute to come by so I could take some pictures. Liam doesn't go to many dances. I have to seize my opportunities."

It was only now that I noticed she had an accent. And that kissy thing wasn't very American, either.

"Of course," I said, finding myself naturally drawn to her. Either she didn't know who I was and what I'd done—or she truly didn't care.

"OK, *vamanos*. I have to get to my shift, and you have to get to the dance." She motioned for me to follow her out the back door. "My name's Claudia, by the way—or Ma, as the boys like to scream at me." She swiveled her head around to smile.

Liam guided me through the house with his hand placed at the small of my back. True to his word, he made the whole thing painless. We took a few quick shots in the backyard flower garden, made pleasant small talk, and were out before his mom could ask any tricky questions.

When we got back into Liam's Jeep, his family came outside to wave good-bye. A pang of envy struck me as I absorbed the way they beamed at Liam. They were a family—perhaps a damaged, struggling family on some levels, but they were together.

A wave of fear came rushing in right after. What if they lost him because of me? How would they ever fill the hole that Liam would leave? It made me sick to think my selfish desire for his help could destroy their world.

"Was my family that bad?" Liam asked after a few minutes of silence.

"What? No." I shook the sour look off my face and attempted to smile. "It's not that. They're all lovely. Your mother is so beautiful. Where's she from, by the way?"

"Costa Rica. My dad was a big wave chaser." He grimaced a little at the mention of his father.

"What shift does she have to get to?" I asked, trying to get away from the dad subject.

He frowned. "She's sort of a . . . bartender. Works nights. It's not like she's the most powerful attorney in the county or anything, but she makes unbelievable tamales most Sundays."

I'd trade the powerful-attorney thing any day for a mom who would look at me the way Liam's mom looked at him. With obvious love—like he was the most wonderful thing in the world.

"What is it, then?" Liam said. "Did Tug put something slimy in your pocket when I wasn't looking? He does that—"

"No, Tug is hilarious, and Christian is a little heartthrob. Really," I assured him. "Your family is great."

"Then why'd you just go all *brooding brow* on me?" he asked, not paying nearly enough attention to the road.

I rubbed my forehead. "Look, I'd never forgive myself if anything ever happened to you because of me. Your family needs you."

"Well, *I* need *you*, Ruby," he said flatly. "You make me crazy, and constantly worried, but . . . I need you."

"Yeah, you need me like you need a hole in the head," I said, realizing immediately what a distasteful joke that was. I wasn't sure I'd ever been told that I was needed before. "Sorry, I didn't mean that."

He wrinkled his nose for a second, then reached out and touched my hand. "Let's make a deal, OK? Let's play pretend."

"Like pretend we have supernatural powers and can actually defeat the evil villain?" I shook my head. As if.

"Even better, let's pretend we're normal seventeen-year-olds, and we're going to a high school dance. Curfew is two hours later than normal, and nothing else matters tonight. You're just a girl—an insanely sexy, kick-ass girl, obviously. And I'm just a guy—a totally hot yet sensitive guy, of course." He smiled. "And we're going to rock this Sadie Hawkins dance tonight! That kind of deal."

I laughed. "OK, deal."

"Sweet." He turned up the stereo and started moving to the music. I laughed even harder. "I promise, tonight will be epic!"

As we pulled into the school parking lot filled with matching teen couples, I shooed away the creepy-crawly thoughts of Silver showing up to ruin my night. Just as I started imagining some terrible incident involving blood and punch bowls, Liam opened my door and reached for my hand.

As if he could sense my nervousness, he leaned in and kissed me, forcing the worries away. I tensed up at first, then gradually relaxed, my mind going blank as his fingertips threaded through my hair. Tasting him, breathing him, feeling him, wanting him, were the only ping-ponging thoughts I could find in the corners of my mind right now. Nothing and no one else mattered.

A tingling sensation of desire formed deep within me. I wanted to pull him back inside the Jeep and go someplace else where we could be alone.

He pulled away sooner than I wanted.

"If I have to do that every time I catch you brooding," he said breathlessly, "I will."

"Is that a threat?"

"It's a *promise.*" He pressed his lips together in a way that made me want to kiss him again. Then, taking my hand, he led me through the parking lot and into the gym full of handmade posters, dangling streamers, and so many strobe lights a girl could have seizures.

The first person I saw as we walked through the balloon archway was Alana. She saw me, too, but instead of brightening with a flash of excitement like the one I felt at seeing her, she looked away in a flash of something else. Anger? Hurt? Fear?

I wanted to run and talk to her, find out who her date was. Maybe slap her on the butt and say "good game" in a husky voice to make her laugh. That's what we did and who we were before. I wanted that back. Maybe Liam was wrong, and I couldn't be normal ever again.

"Why are you tempting me?" The sensation of Liam's breath on my ear made my knees come dangerously close to wobbling. "A promise is a promise, and I am a man of my word. Shall we dance?"

"Uh, don't you want to go see some of your buddies?" I looked over to his Amazon-birds entourage in brightly colored shirts—and did a double take. Four guys. Four girls. Four sets of T-shirts in solid colors. His best friend, Chase, and his girlfriend, Meg, in purple. His other friend Jett, with his date, in yellow. And the fourth couple, in red, Jace the Ass Face with none other than One-Up Taylor.

"Is this a group date?" I asked Liam, horrified.

They were all looking at us now, some of them waving us over.

"Not exactly," he said, holding his finger up to his friends, asking for a minute. "Traditionally, in high school, teenagers attend dances as a group. But . . ." He paused, looking at me. "*We* can do whatever you want."

I tried not to feel trapped. "Did you not hear my objection to the awkward group-date thing?" I asked, just a little too snarkily. "Liam, Jace *and* Taylor both hate me!"

"Whoa." He let go of my hand so he could cup my face. "I had no idea they were even coming. It's not like they asked my permission," he said, snarking right back. "But honestly, tonight we don't have to do anything you don't want to do. We can keep our distance."

"It's not like I want to be the jerk girlfriend, but . . ." I didn't know what to say without sounding *exactly* like a jerk.

"Hang on, did you just call yourself my girlfriend?"

Oh, double snap. Liam's eyes crinkled with amusement.

"I didn't mean to infer—"

"Wait." He put one finger over my lips, looking like a retriever who'd just heard one of those silent dog whistles. "This is my song. Come on!"

As we slow danced to the cheesy remix of an '80s love song, he drew me in tight and I laid my head on his chest. How many times had I dreamed of being this close to him? All I knew was that it was better than I'd dared to imagine. It was the way his hips moved against mine. The way his lips brushed my neck as he sang the ridiculous chorus lyrics. The way he assured me with every movement that he wasn't letting go.

He knew me for exactly what I was, and he was still here.

I was disarmed, in every way.

In order to avoid spontaneous combustion, I had to distract myself, so I peered around the dark gym watching the lights trickling over the crowd.

Suddenly, a movement caught my eye—the outline of a man with broad shoulders in the dark corner of the gym.

"Oh no," I whispered. "Not here. Not tonight."

I stopped dancing—and breathing.

"What's wrong?" Liam asked.

The figure couldn't have been more than thirty feet away, but in the darkness my eyes strained to see him clearly. A jock couple in atrocious lime-colored TapouT UFC shirts moved directly into my line of sight. I wanted to tap them out.

"Follow me." I untangled myself from Liam and pulled him through the crowd.

If it was Silver, what was he going to do? How would we stop him?

As we weaved around the dancing couples, my vision finally adjusted to the dim light. And there he was, plain as day—Mr. Holsum, our Calculus teacher, with his unmistakable floppy comb-over, pouring himself a drink.

I felt like a moron. Not to mention paranoid. "I thought I saw . . ." I trailed off, feeling suddenly shaky.

"Ruby," Liam shushed me with his voice and touch. "You don't need to explain. I get it."

I looked into his understanding eyes.

"Maybe we should just go," I said. "I suck at normal."

"What, before my song is over?" His eyebrows pinched together in dismay. "I don't think so."

Just as he drew me back in close, the song ended and I pulled away, thinking I'd ruined the moment and probably the night. But then the DJ announced another slow track.

I exhaled. "I'll try not to run away this time."

Liam held on to me for the next three songs. In fact, he barely let go of me for the next three hours as we danced, whispered, and touched.

But the fear never left me. The fear that one of the dark shadows I kept seeing out of the corner of my eye would materialize—and Silver would come back.

In fact, I knew he would.

CHAPTER 21

I'd really outdone myself this time. Not only were Alana and my mom still giving me the cold shoulder, but Dr. T was, too. She'd been distracted and distant in our appointments. I wondered if the fight with my mom was the cause. I didn't doubt Jane was vindictive enough to have done something to compromise my relationship with Dr. T because of my comment about my twice-a-week therapist being a better mom. Maybe she'd told her that it was unprofessional to get so emotionally close to a patient, or something like that. Maybe she was hoping I'd feel like I couldn't lean on Dr. T after all, and would break off the relationship altogether.

My suspicions spiked even higher when I got a text from Jane:

Meet me at Dr. Teresa's office after school today. 4:00 sharp.

She had never (as in *ever*) come with me to an appointment before. Something must have changed. I worried about what she could possibly want to say to me that she couldn't just say alone. Maybe she was going to tell us that she wasn't going to let us keep having our appointments or something.

It felt like an ambush, and I didn't like it.

The tension between my mom and me was at an all-time high. I felt like I was still sitting at the breakfast table, holding on to the edge with white knuckles, waiting for her wrath. Like I had been sitting at that table my whole life.

When she finally showed up in Dr. T's waiting room, she was late, of course. Gucci purse in one hand and a Venti Starbucks in the other, she came storming in like a celebrity.

"Hello, Ruby," she said with the aloof formality of a stranger.

"Hello, Mother," I responded with the sass of a neglected teen.

"Is Dr. Teresa not here yet?" she asked as she sat down next to me and started digging through her purse.

"I don't think so," I said. "I knocked a minute ago and no one answered."

"Is she usually late?"

"No, not really," I said, thinking back. Actually, I couldn't remember the last time she'd been late.

"Well, I don't have time for this," my mother said, standing and power walking over to the door to knock again.

Shocker: Jane Rose didn't have time for *this*.

"What's going on, Mom?" I asked. "Why are you even here?"

"Dr. Teresa?" she called through the door, ignoring me. "It's Ruby and Jane. Are you in there? Please open the door."

I rolled my eyes. If she were in there, she would open up. What if she was with a client and didn't want to be disturbed yet?

"Mom, are you even going to answer me?"

Apparently not. She pressed her ear against the door, listening for a sign of life, I assumed. "She should get a receptionist, for crying out loud."

"Mom?"

"What, Ruby?" she answered harshly, looking at me like I was a petulant two-year-old.

"Why are you here?"

"I'm here because we need to talk."

How many times was she going to give me that "we need to talk" crap?

"Then talk," I challenged. "Why do you need Dr. Teresa present to talk to me?"

She rattled the door handle. "I just do."

I was about to admonish her for being so evasive (something she loved to do to me) when the door swung open. It was unlocked and no one was inside, that much I could see.

I stood, surprised that her door was unlocked if she wasn't there.

"This is highly unusual," my mom said disapprovingly.

"Which part?" I answered, walking past her into Dr. T's room. "The District Attorney breaking and entering or someone standing you up?"

"All I did was check the door. It swung open on its own," she said defensively.

I'd never been in Dr. T's office without her being there. Curious, I wandered around the space. I'd always wanted to know more about Dr. T: her family situation, her failed marriage, her miscarriages, her history. Despite how hard she worked on me to open up, she never really returned the favor. All I knew about her came from my mother.

"What are you doing?" my mom asked, sounding suddenly uncomfortable.

"Nothing," I said, looking through some papers on Dr. T's desk. "Just checking to see if she left us a note or something."

"If she left a note, it would have been on the door," she argued. "Or she'd have sent me an e-mail."

True. This was so unlike her. Then again, after ten years of intermittent therapy, I wasn't confident I really knew what she was "like" anyway. I continued to search her desk for a family picture or keepsake that held some trace of who she really was. Instead, it was scattered with self-help books, medical journals, candles, and an assortment of coffee mugs.

"Come on, let's wait outside and I'll call her to see where she is," Mom said, digging through her bag for her cell.

I was about to leave the room when I looked at Dr. T's chair. My breath caught, and time jerked to a halt—like the moment I shot LeMarq, like the moment the blade went into Father Michael's chest.

A large, old-fashioned brass key sat in Dr. T's place.

I felt sick as I reached to pick it up. The panic rising in my chest threatened to consume me as I realized the key could only mean one thing—he'd taken her. The Key Killer, the fourth man on my list.

Attached to the rusty key was a red string and a small note. I pinched it up with my fingertips like it was a poisonous spider. The note read:

Find me.

The handwriting was Dr. T's—I'd seen it so many times before. Another one of the Key Killer's signature moves—forcing the victims to leave one last plea for help to their family.

My vision went starry. Air wasn't making it to my lungs.

Not Dr. T. Not the only person in the world who knew me best and loved me anyway.

I couldn't comprehend what kind of an evil person would crush minds and souls like this. How would I find her? None of his victims had ever been found. Not one of them. Twelve keys. Twelve missing persons behind twelve locked doors.

This had gone too far, become too personal. If the Key Killer or Silver were here right now, I would tear them to shreds. I looked back at the note, but it was turned the wrong way now—and there was a message on the other side, written in someone else's hand:

If you want the Doctor to live, <u>do not</u> involve Jane.

"She's not answering." My mom's voice sliced through my spinning frenzy. Why couldn't I involve her? "I'll leave a message."

As she waited to leave a voicemail on a phone that would probably never be found, my mind raced.

Wait, Dr. T's phone wasn't off. It rang before it went to voicemail. That meant it could be tracked. If I called the phone, the nearby towers would ping her location—and we might find her before he turned it off and demolished it. I had to act fast.

If there was ever a time I needed my mom, it was now. She had the resources to track the phone, and she cared about Dr. T, too. Surely, she'd pull out all the stops to find her. But a flashback of the blonde girl on Ninth Street stung my mind. Silver didn't bluff. I couldn't risk Dr. T's life by involving Jane. I'd have to find another way.

Suddenly, I knew where I needed to go. To the only person I trusted.

As my mom left Dr. T a voicemail, I escaped. Even when she yelled after me to come back, I kept running to Big Black.

"Slow down," Liam said, grabbing me by the wrists after I told him about the key. "Ruby, everything is going to be OK."

"No, it's not," I argued. "You don't understand. This can't happen to her. Not Dr. T."

Looking over his shoulder at half the football team and most of the cheer squad staring at us, he pulled me deeper under the bleachers for privacy. Even though Alana's back was firmly facing me, I wondered if it hurt her that I'd come running to Liam and not her.

"Ruby, just breathe for a second." Liam still wore his pads with his helmet pulled back on his head. He looked so normal, so All-American. And here I was, drawing him into my dark world, trying to fight a serial killer.

"So, what do you want to do?" he asked quietly

"I need someone with access to cell phone tower information," I said, knowing it was a ridiculous game plan. A Hail Mary.

"Well, who would have that kind of access?"

"A detective, I guess." I thought out loud. "Someone who could get a quick warrant."

"Well, how many detectives do you know who could help with that?" he asked, as if he already knew the answer.

I knew it, too, and the answer was "one": Detective "I'm Gonna Take You Down" Martinez. I put my face in my hands. I couldn't believe it had finally come to this. But if it meant Dr. T might live, I would willingly place myself at the mercy of a man I wasn't sure I could trust.

"It looks to me like you don't have a choice," he said, pulling my hands away from my face and nudging my chin so I'd look up at him. "Do you still have his card?"

"I think so," I said, fumbling through my backpack. "Yeah, here it is."

"Good. Let me just tell Coach I gotta go. I'll be right back, OK?"

I wanted to stop him. Tell him I could do this on my own. Tell him I'd go to Detective Martinez first and then call him. But the truth was, I needed him. Or maybe I just *wanted* him so badly that it felt like *need* at this point.

Maybe if Liam had been with me when Father Michael died, I wouldn't have fled the scene and lost the body. Maybe it would have prevented the whole thing. And maybe if Liam came with me now it would throw off some part of Silver's plan, and we could get the upper hand.

I gripped the rusty key until it left marks in my skin. I would never let go of it until I found her. How many other loved ones had the same thought about their key before the police took it away as evidence? The thought made a bad taste come to my mouth, as if the key was firmly lodged in my throat.

"I just have to go change," Liam said, suddenly in front of me again. "I'll meet you at your car, and we'll call Martinez together, OK?"

"Sure," I responded, feeling nearly defeated already. I was about to cross over the point of no return—go to the cops, hand myself over to the Detective my mom had told me to stay away from, the man who'd betrayed my father—without any certainty we would ever find Dr. T. I panicked at the thought of where she might be. If she was scared or confused—or even alive.

"Hey," he said, doubling back and reaching out to squeeze my hand. "It'll be all right. We'll find her. Remember, this guy keeps drawing you in. He wants you to save her, and he wants you to kill her abductor."

Of course. I wasn't thinking logically. I'd forgotten Silver's game. This wasn't the Key Killer acting alone, in which case Dr. T would never be found. This was Silver pulling the strings, and Dr. T was just bait. Not only would I find her, but I would have to kill another human being to save her.

I pulled away from Liam. I would kill again if it meant Dr. T would live. I didn't like it. I didn't want it. But I would do it if I had to.

CHAPTER 22

Liam leaned against the hood of Detective Martinez's unmarked police car while I paced next to it. Martinez sat in his driver's seat with his door open, silently staring at his computer screen. He held his cell phone like a hand grenade.

If anyone from school saw us right now, they'd think that Liam and I had just been pulled over by an undercover cop. But asking Martinez to meet us outside Starbucks on Main Street was the first plan that crossed my mind. The location was public (which made me feel better), close to the precinct (yet far enough away that I couldn't be thrown inside a detention cell), and near the Pacific Coast Highway (for a quick getaway to Dr. T). Too bad it was also busy. I could tell that a few people inside the café had recognized me. I turned my back to them and stopped pacing next to Liam.

"The warrant was issued at least forty-five minutes ago," Martinez grumbled. "Damn it, this shouldn't take so long."

Liam and I looked at each other, wordlessly communicating our confusion at his being mad at anyone but us.

Minutes felt like hours while we waited for a shred of hope. It made little sense that Martinez wasn't pounding me for answers, grilling me on the details. He'd simply taken my word for it that the

Key Killer had pounced again and, without blinking, he'd requested the warrant to access the cell phone information. I'd even shown him the key with the messages attached. All he did he was sit there steaming, texting up a storm.

I was about to ask Martinez if there was anything else I could be doing, when the two-way radio in his car rumbled to life with a staticky voice. The only words I caught from a few feet away were "last known ping," "Pasadena," and "Rose Bowl Stadium."

"Ten-four," Martinez said, staring into the distance. He typed another text into his phone.

"What are you doing? Is everything OK?" I asked. Was there something I'd missed over the radio?

Sweat beads ran down his cheeks despite the cool dusk air. He ignored me and continued texting. I didn't like it. As I was about to grab the car door, Liam blocked me with his arm, but I shoved him away.

"Detective, what's going on?" I asked, standing directly next to the open car door. "If you don't tell me, I'm going alone. I heard Rose Bowl Stadium. I'll just go—"

"I warned them," he said sharply. "None of this should've happened. None of it!"

"Who? Warned who?"

When Martinez wouldn't answer, I spun to Liam. "Screw this. Let's go. I don't have to wait for a police escort."

"Wait," Martinez said, getting out of his car. "Ruby, you're not going anywhere without me. Do you hear me, young lady?"

I ground my teeth. Young lady was better than sweetie or honey, but not by much.

"Well, I'm not going to sit around here listening to you spout off to yourself about who knows what!" I raised my voice. "Dr. Teresa could be dying right this second."

"Get in the car," he ordered. "You, too, Mr. Slater. Now."

He didn't have to tell me twice. Sirens could only decrease travel time.

As we drove, I wondered when he was going to call for backup. Instead, he drove north with a locked jaw and lead foot, occasionally shaking his head at me in the rearview mirror. Liam squeezed my hand as we slid around the backseat like bobble-head dolls.

I wanted to know how long it was going to take to get there and what we were going to do when we got there. But it was almost like we had an unspoken agreement not to ask questions.

"What do you think it means?" Liam whispered in my ear.

"Think *what* means?" I asked back. Was he talking about Martinez's bizarre silence, the new choice of bait, or something else?

"C'mon, the *Rose* Bowl? You didn't catch that twisted so-called coincidence?" His hot breath against my skin caused a physiological reaction completely contradictory to my rational one. I was turned on and turned off in one fell swoop—an inconsistency that unfortunately defined my life. Valedictorian contender—or death-penalty candidate? Founder of the Constitution Society—or vigilante lawbreaker? Protector and defender—or vengeful killer?

Whether or not the location was chosen to match my name, the truth was that when we reached the Rose Bowl, the chances of my committing murder again were high. This time, it would probably happen right in front of the detective who'd personally petition for my capital punishment. Why *not* do it at the Rose Bowl? The press would eat this up.

Instead of answering Liam, I stared out the window at the blurred lights. The billboards and neon signs off the freeway grew distorted and fuzzy as unwelcome tears welled up in my eyes. I hated what Silver had made me do, what I had to do now. And I worried this was it for me—that it would be my last night of freedom. The last time I would be able to hold Liam Slater's hand, touch his face, or . . . kiss his lips.

Without thinking it through, I leaned over and kissed him. He recoiled at first, most likely surprised at the timing, location, and the company—Martinez was less than two feet away with a fairly good view. But I didn't let Liam go. The kiss meant more than a possible good-bye. It was a thank-you, an apology, and a desperate hope for the best. When I pulled away, I saw the understanding in his eyes. "It might be the last time I get to do that," I said.

"Don't say that." He put his arm around me so that my head fell on his chest. "Everything is going to be OK."

I wanted to believe him as I savored the taste of his lips.

Now, I would be lucky if they let me have a choice between a firing squad and lethal injection. Though in California, they'd probably kill my soul with never-ending bureaucratic appeals, amicus briefs, and rubber knock-off Crocs sandals long before they killed my body. At least the Orange County prison had HBO, a luxury I used to think was preposterous.

I clutched at the key still piercing my hand. There was no hope left for me, but maybe some remained for Dr. T. This was all worth it for her. I would not let her die.

Suddenly, we weren't on the freeway anymore. Instead, we were in some kind of residential neighborhood. Old houses, apartment buildings, and winding streets.

I couldn't help myself anymore. "Detective, where are you going?"

Martinez didn't respond; he only clutched the steering wheel tighter. What was going on with him? What wasn't he telling me?

"Is this how you get to the Rose Bowl?" I sat forward and put my arms over the back of the passenger headrest. "When are you going to call for more units?"

"Damn it, Ruby!" he roared. "Just sit back and shut up. Trust me when I say that more units won't help in a situation like this. Or don't you remember the last time SWAT let you down?" He took a hard turn into an apartment complex.

I sat back, not expecting the aggressive snap or the painful truth. He was right—SWAT had let me down in the worst way possible the day they let my dad die.

He parked against the back wall of the bare parking lot and threw the car into park with too much force. An awful cranking noise escaped from the hood of the car. He flipped open his phone and started that texting crap again.

"Detective," I began, trying to sound respectful. "Please, tell me what's going on."

"You've got history here, Ruby Rose," he said, turning around to face me. "He's brought you back to the beginning."

That was it—Detective Martinez knew who Silver was. "The beginning of what?" I asked. "Just tell me why we're here. I thought we were supposed to be going to the Rose Bowl."

"The stadium is right behind that hill," he said, pointing behind the abandoned-looking apartment building. I could just see the bright lights of the stadium in the night sky.

"But we're not going there," he went on. "He's brought you back to apartment 4E."

I tried to make sense of the apartment number, but 4E meant nothing to me. I racked my brain and scanned the building for something familiar to jog my memory. And there it was, the address sign: College Village South Apartments—366 University Parkway. This was the third time Silver had used those three numbers in his sick game. He'd meant to lure me here all along, and Martinez knew it.

"Why here? What is this place?" I demanded.

When he didn't answer, I leaned over to see his face. His mouth moved like he wanted to say something, but nothing was coming out. Why was it so hard for anyone to tell me anything?

"We don't have time for this," I said, exasperated. Resolving not to wait for answers and to go find them myself, I reached for the door handle. But Martinez grabbed my shoulder with a death grip.

"*We* aren't going anywhere. *I* am going in, alone." He squeezed my shoulder tighter, with emphasis. "You two are staying here until I say otherwise. Do you understand?"

"No," I said, pulling away from him. "Dr. T is in there because of me. What if I'm the only one who can save her?"

He gave me a condescending smirk. "You're seventeen. Believe me, you're not the only one who can save her." He turned and got out of the car. "Just stay put," he said, glaring at us both.

He shut his door, raised his weapon in front of him just like my dad would've done, and disappeared under a dark archway of the building.

"I'm not sitting here," I said to Liam. "I'm the one with the key." I pulled it out of my pocket.

"Ruby, I'm begging you," Liam said. "Just wait."

He stared with concern at the spot where Detective Martinez had disappeared, but I knew Martinez was fully capable of defending himself. At least he had a weapon, which was something we didn't have. I searched the squad car for a stowed shotgun or a hidden knife, but I found nada. My only weapon now was the key.

After minutes that seemed more like wasted hours, I caved. I wasn't going to be a spectator anymore. As I was about to leap out of the car, the boom of a cannon sounded and fireworks exploded behind the hill. The home team must've scored. For a moment, the beauty of the scene blindsided me, and I couldn't help but watch the streaming colors fall from the sky. I grabbed the door handle. "Liam, you can stay here if you want, but I have to go in."

When he didn't move or respond, I waved a hand in front of his face to get his attention. He grabbed my hand and pinned it down, continuing to stare at where Martinez had disappeared.

"Are you listening to me?" I said, losing patience.

"Ruby, just wait," he said in a hushed tone. "I thought I saw something."

"What?" I strained to see what he was talking about. "Where?"

"I don't know." He huffed and finally pulled his tense body away from the window to rub his eyes. "Maybe it was nothing."

"Liam, what did you see?"

"I thought I saw a flicker of light in the apartment up there," he said, pointing to the second story. "I thought I heard something, too."

I looked up to where he was pointing but didn't see anything. "Are you sure it wasn't the fireworks?"

"I don't know."

"Well, I'm going to go check it out," I said, but he stopped me again.

"Wait, Ruby, it's a trap. You know that!" The intensity of Liam's eyes in the darkness was more effective than his python-like grip. "Just because Martinez didn't want to call for backup doesn't mean that we shouldn't—"

"No, I think Martinez was right. If we call it in, anyone from dispatch to SWAT could handle it wrong and Dr. T could die. Maybe Martinez knows what he's doing. He seems to know a lot more about Silver than we do." I shook my head in disbelief that I was actually siding with Martinez. "Look, Silver has a plan, and at this point I don't think killing me is part of it, so I'm going in there. And you are *not* going to stop me."

I got out of the car, and Liam climbed out after me. The building's entrance seemed more like a deserted mine than college housing. And given how close we were to the stadium, it felt odd for the area to be so forsaken.

A bluster of dust nearly knocked me into Liam as I moved toward the dark corridor's opening. All the exterior lights were either burned out or busted in. If anyone still lived in these apartments, I felt sorry for them.

Martinez must've somehow known exactly where 4E was, and he'd gone this way, so we followed the path until it opened up into a courtyard with a gated pool. The water looked like the greenish-brown algae color of swamps meant for gator huntin'—not bikinis and Pi Beta Phi keg parties. It even smelled like a rotting cesspool. Anything could be at the bottom of that water.

Signs were posted all around the gate, and I crossed the dying grass to read one. The place had been condemned. Scheduled to be torn down and rebuilt in a few months. Which meant it was abandoned, and we were alone.

"Great. No witnesses." Liam's words echoed my fears. "I don't feel good about this."

When had either one of us ever felt good about any of this?

Suddenly, a desperate groan came from the shadows behind us. We spun around to face a dark entryway at the back of a staircase, then we sprinted toward the sound.

It was Martinez—lying facedown, looking broken and barely alive. Blood poured out of his shirt. He'd been shot.

"I knew I heard something," Liam berated himself. "I'm calling 911."

I wasn't going to stop him. Though I doubted the cops or an ambulance would get here in time.

"Ruby," Martinez moaned so low I could barely hear him. I fell to my knees beside him as Liam made the call. The smell of blood mixed with the faint scent of smoke made me dizzy and nauseated. I didn't know Martinez smoked. I hadn't smelled it on him in the car.

"I'm here, Detective, right here," I said, holding his bloodied hand. "We're calling the paramedics. You'll be all right." I hoped it was true.

"Liam, help me turn him over."

As we carefully rolled Martinez over, I felt a bulletproof vest under his linen shirt. In the dark corridor I couldn't see where the bullet wounds were.

"I'm going to take your vest off, Detective—"

"No, Ruby, don't . . ." He spoke laboriously, like every syllable pained him. "I tried . . . to prevent it . . . to make them—make *her*— tell you . . . the truth."

He was losing consciousness.

"I told your mother not to do it. I told her to come clean. But how could . . . we have . . . known it would . . . come to this?" His body tensed up with a sudden shaking fit to match the tremors inside me. What had my mother done to bring this on us all?

As I tried to find the source of the bleeding, the metallic scent of blood and the scent of smoke grew even stronger. My eyes watered, my nose stung, and the glands in the back of my throat tickled— that feeling right before a vicious upchucking attack. A section of his flesh had been ripped open on his forearm, right where his Marine tattoo used to be. The same tattoo my dad had.

I watched Martinez struggle for breath, and some intangible part of me ripped as well. As much as I had hated him, I now felt stirrings of compassion and regret. I didn't want him to die.

"Hold on," I pleaded. "Help is on the way."

I looked up at Liam, now leaning over Martinez's body, and our eyes met. Through the darkness, I could see the fear in his expression. Did this remind him of the night his dad had cut open his head with a beer bottle?

I wanted to reach out and calm him, but my hands were bloodied, and I started coughing. Then it hit me. I looked around—black smoke was blowing our way.

Fire.

"I'm going up to 4E—you stay with him," I said to Liam.

"No, you can't . . ." Liam trailed off as Martinez gasped in pain. "Ruby, the police will be here soon, just wait."

"If she's in there, it will be too late," I said, letting go of Martinez. Clutching the key in my bloody hand, I bolted to find Dr. T.

From the center of the courtyard I scanned the six surrounding two-story buildings for the right apartment. It wasn't hard to find— flames behind the windows, not to mention the billowing smoke emerging out the open door, was a pretty good indication of which apartment would be 4E.

I scaled the staircase and covered my nose with the sleeve of my hoodie as the thickening smoke nearly knocked me out of my resolve.

Once through the door, I tried to orient myself among the flames. At the far end of the room, a large metal cage contained what looked like two lifeless bodies. The surging nausea rose again, but this time it had nothing to do with the smoke.

I urged my feet forward. I had no time to close my eyes and try to overcome my stupid psychotic fear of bars. I had to get to the bodies before the flames did, or we'd all die. Black smoke surrounded me. Dancing on the ceiling. Climbing up the walls. Suffocating everything—including a photo of a girl on the wall.

The same girl from the sketch at the art fair. What?

No, I couldn't think about that now. Another coughing fit hit me. I fell to the ground, aching for oxygen, desperate for clear thought.

Then I saw Dr. T. She was one of the bodies in the cage, blindfolded and duct taped. I crawled to the cage and searched for the lock that matched my key, but I couldn't find it. Tears in my eyes made it even harder to see—a pure physical reaction to the smoke.

Finally, I found a clunky metal lock and slipped the old key in. It clicked and turned, and the barred door swung open. I forced myself inside—reminding myself that I'd beaten the cage before and could do it again. I pulled Dr. T's limp body over and saw something written on the duct tape covering her mouth: "SECRETS." What the hell was that supposed to mean? I checked her pulse—it was slow but steady.

I didn't want to, but I reached for the other body, too. Eyes stinging and lungs closing up, I pulled on his shirt. It was definitely number four—Roger Vay, the Key Killer, with the same gray tape, same message: "SECRETS."

There was no way I could get them both out before the flames consumed us. Silver was making me choose. Making me condemn one to death.

I grabbed Dr. T's arms and wrapped them around my neck as I crawled out onto the green shaggy carpet. Once outside the cage, I dragged her by the shoulders with every ounce of strength I had left, trying to locate the door. The smoke was too dense, the flames too high, my legs too weak. As I searched for the way out, a flame seared through my cloth Toms. Of all my precious shoes, these had to be the most flammable.

The flapping flames framed the exit. Desperate for oxygen, I had no more time to think. I called on my last shreds of adrenaline and strength to pick up Dr. T and sling her over my shoulder. My knees almost buckled, but I steadied myself for the five seconds I needed to burst through the doorframe. I collapsed as soon as I sensed fresh air.

We were outside the apartment at least.

"Liam!" I screamed, coughing up a lung. "Help!" My head felt like it wasn't my own. I was disoriented and barely alive—I felt like I was choking to death. If I just lay my head down here, maybe it would feel better. Maybe Liam would come and we'd be OK.

A blanket of cool air swept over my body as I drifted in and out of consciousness. In a distant corner of my mind I was no longer in danger. I was weightless and free. I thought I was in the ocean, lying flat on my longboard. With the sun on my back, I let my arms dangle in the water. I heard my dad's voice in the distance, gently calling my name. The current was taking me toward him . . .

A jarring pain stabbed through my chest, and a coughing fit brought me back to reality.

The last thing I felt was being carried away in the arms of a strong man.

The last thing I saw was the reflection of flames in the man's eyes through the clear plastic shield of his black tactical helmet. Familiar eyes with an unfamiliar intensity.

The last thing I heard was my own voice screaming, "Wait, Dr. T!"

CHAPTER 23

Everything glowed too white. Too sterile.

I couldn't keep my eyes open with all these fluorescent bulbs trying to blind me. I could barely breathe with whatever was strapped to my face. I couldn't move with my arms bound.

Wait. I was tied up? Where was I?

I forced open my eyes to look down at the body that surely wasn't mine, even though it was attached to my very dizzy, throbbing head. An atrocious gown covered my torso, and sandpapery white sheets covered my legs. I didn't even want to think what kind of nasty wool socks covered my feet. I felt them scratching my heels, and that was enough to piss me off.

I jerked at the leather straps at my wrists and ankles, blinking wildly from light overexposure. My damn pupils stung like invisible fairies were taking archery practice on my eyeballs—

I had to be on drugs to be thinking like this.

The plastic mask covering my mouth felt sweaty and claustrophobic. I wanted it off. Now.

Was this some kind of torture room? Where was Liam? And Dr. T?

I closed my eyes and fought my restraints. I don't think I meant to scream, but it sure sounded like my voice echoing off the white walls and beeping machines.

"Relax, honey, relax!" A voice caught me off guard—a sharp, authoritative voice, accompanied by soft, heavy hands. I stopped fighting long enough to find out who was brave enough to call me honey when I was in such a foul mood.

All I saw were huge boobs. Not the usual perky Hollywood implants, but enormous mounds of flesh.

"It'll be better if you relax," the sharp voice warned.

I slammed my head back against the pillow. Whoever this lady was, she meant business. She'd probably been hired to carry out the torture. I wouldn't make it easy for her.

Step 1: Get free.

Step 2: Land a serious knee kick to her head. Striking her anywhere in her core would be like trying to punch Play-Doh. Hell, those breasts were as good as a bulletproof vest.

Step 3: Find clothes.

Step 4: Run!

Of course, this brilliant plan only had a chance if I could steady my breathing and get free. I didn't need the beeping monitor to tell me my heart rate was dangerously high.

"I don't want to have to increase your dose," she said as she fussed with my straps, my mask, my sheets. "But you're testing my patience."

"Please, just tell me where I am and what is going on," I said. But given the combo of not having spoken in who knows how long and the thick plastic mask covering my mouth, I doubted she understood. I lifted my thirty-pound bowling-ball head to plead with my eyes.

"I'm going to untie these wrist straps now," she said with less attitude and more tenderness than I expected. "You're going to be all right. Now that you're awake, no more thrashing around, OK?" She moved in and started working on the ties. I prepared myself for the moment when I'd be free, heel kick her in the jaw, and escape this strange, sterile dungeon. I'd find Dr. T and carry her on my back if I had to—

"Oh, thank God." A familiar voice came from outside the door. "She's awake? Can I see her?"

My mom! Did Silver get her, too?

The door swung open and she was there, hurrying toward me.

A short, wrinkly man in a white coat materialized behind her, carrying no weapons as far as I could tell.

Beyond them, a tall figure moving in the doorway caught my eye—Sergeant Mathews. His square jaw was set tight, yet his dark eyes were soft. My drugged brain couldn't make sense of how and why he was here.

Cool air tickled my wrists, telling me I was free. I wanted to rip the plastic mask off my face and bolt out of this white hell, but my mom's fingers wrapped themselves around the place where the straps had just come off. Not free enough.

"Oh, Rue," my mom said as she sat beside me and pulled down my mask. She looked unusually haggard and stressed. "I was so worried."

"Mom, what's going on?" I still wasn't sure if I needed to protect the both of us.

"You gave us a scare there," the wrinkly man said as he wobbled closer and nodded to excuse the woman I now understood was my nurse. "It's been nearly two days since you came in here kicking and screaming."

That made no sense. I didn't remember that. Why didn't I remember anything? Maybe that was why I was strapped down.

I searched my consciousness for a crack in the dam that held back my memories of when and how I got here.

"You suffered extreme smoke inhalation. We had to give you oxygen and keep you sedated so you could rest," Dr. Wrinkles said, patting my foot through the sheets.

Smoke. Yes, I remembered the smoke. So much smoke.

Crack.

"Luckily, you only have minor burns on your leg from the fire," the doctor continued.

Fire, sure—where there's smoke, there's fire.

Crack, crack.

"Give her a few more days, and your little heroine will be good as new," he said to my mom.

Heroine? Who did I save?

Crack, crack, crack.

The dam broke, and Dr. Teresa was behind it.

"Where is she?" I sat up tall in bed. "Dr. Teresa? Is she OK?"

"She's fine," my mom said, putting her thin hand on my knee. "She's in a room down the hall."

I exhaled in relief and went into a coughing fit.

"I have to go see her," I said, starting to get up. "I need to talk to her."

My mom's grip tightened. "I don't think that's a good idea."

I jerked away to climb toward the opposite side of the bed, but then I felt a sharp, pointy tug at my forearm. I looked down to find that a scary-looking IV connected me to the medical equipment lining the headboard. The thought of ripping it out made me dizzy and nauseated.

I held my head in my hands for a moment to fight the desire to dry heave. Another attack of the black lung made me double over the bed with a very unladylike hacking noise. Someone slid the plastic mask back over my face, and I concentrated on the cool, wet air replacing the painful darkness inside me.

I had no choice. I let my mom force me back in bed.

When my breathing steadied, I opened my eyes to find my mom standing at the foot of my bed. She had tears in her eyes. Not little ones or fake ones meant for TV, but real streaming tears.

"What is it, Mom?" I asked, pulling the mask away slightly.

"I need to tell you something," she said, looking at me so hard it felt like she was looking through me.

My heart felt as weak as my lungs. What did she *need* to tell me now?

"OK," I said, bracing myself.

Another tear spilled out, and she paused as if forming the words in her mouth pained her. "Detective Martinez is dead."

Deep down I'd already known, but it did nothing to soften the blow.

I remembered talking to him, feeling his warm blood on my hands as I tried to stop the flow. I looked down at my hands, wondering if they were still stained.

I closed my burning eyes.

"Rue, there's more," she said, prompting me to reopen my eyes for another hit. I didn't know if I could take it.

"The police found Liam with Martinez's blood all over him." She paused. "They've arrested him for murder."

CHAPTER 24

It took another three days before they released me from the hospital. This time it wasn't the IV or the coughing bouts confining me to bed—it was an armed officer standing at my door. My mom said the guard was there for my own protection, but it felt more like he was there for my own imprisonment.

Those three days seemed endless. I went over everything in my head again and again, trying to figure out what I could have done differently to keep Martinez from dying and Liam from going to prison. Where had I gone wrong? I needed to talk to my mother about my involvement in it all, but there was always someone else within hearing distance—a nurse, a doctor, a guard . . .

After telling me about Liam's arrest, Mom had explained the investigators' theory that he had set fire to the apartment complex to destroy evidence. That even though Liam's motive for the murder was still unclear, his involvement was indisputable. And until he started cooperating with the investigation, he would continue to be the sole suspect. The more she explained, the more guilt wrapped around me—the reason he wasn't "cooperating" was to protect me.

According to Jane, Liam was claiming ignorance. She rolled her eyes in exasperation and ran her hands through her hair when she recapped his side of the story in press conference bullet-point detail: "Martinez had been shot by an unknown third party, you and Liam went to his aid—hence the blood—you smelled smoke and went after Dr. Teresa, he'd tried to go after you, and someone knocked him out from behind. The next thing he knew a fireman was waking him up in the street outside the apartments."

At the hospital, I'd mostly just listened while biting my tongue. But once we got home, I knew it was time to come clean. In order to plead Liam's case, I had to tell Mom the truth. All of it. In the privacy of her office, I dropped every detail, spat out every fact. From me following Charlie LeMarq and the Filthy Five, to Silver's messages and five forced murders, to going to Detective Martinez with the key.

I wasn't sure she entirely believed me without any proof to back up my story. No bodies were ever found at any warehouse, harbor, or apartment complex. Well, except for Martinez's—his burned corpse and gold chain were all that remained in the complex's ashes.

I told her that Silver had to have been the one to knock out Liam. Of course he was. Stupid-ass Silver and his split personalities had done it again. This was his MO—set us up and then save our skins. But this time, he left evidence that tied Liam to Martinez's murder. So why didn't he just kill Liam like he did Martinez? Why ruin Liam's life when he could take it?

When I brought up Martinez's cryptic comments about me being brought "back to the beginning" and asked her what Martinez was talking about when he said he'd tried to warn her, she pleaded the fifth. When I showed her the picture of Silver from the art fair, she got that surly look on her face that meant she was going to take a coffee break, or a vodka break, or whatever other kind of break she needed to "think straight."

I was used to her hiding things from me, just like she was used to me hiding things from her—but under these circumstances it felt unfair. As I opened up, she closed down. Again and again I asked what she knew, but she was a vault of secrets. And I *never* had the code.

It took nearly all day, several shouting matches, and a few inter-mittent silent treatments to get out my entire side of the story and answer all her questions. In the end, she hated me for it. I could see it all over her face—the way she grimaced as I shared the darkest details. She didn't realize that I hated myself for it, too.

But I had to trust and believe she would exonerate Liam. This wasn't just about me, or my family, anymore. Liam could be put away for the rest of his life just because he'd gotten involved with the wrong girl. I couldn't let that happen. His mom and brothers needed him.

Silver was the one who needed to pay for his crimes, not me. And certainly not Liam.

Before I went to bed after our long day of disclosure (and non-disclosure), Mom stone-facedly assured me she'd take care of it. But I didn't know how she *could* do it with the media working against her. Most of the news outlets, from the local paper to CNN, had already judged Liam guilty—sensationalizing the whole thing for their own profit. Despite the fact that the police hadn't released even the most basic information from the crime scene (like the facts that Dr. T and the Key Killer were there at all), some of the nation's best-known criminal defense attorneys were called in on prime-time television to discuss how bad it looked for not only Liam, but D. A. Jane Rose and her bid for reelection. They argued that the only reason I wasn't in jail with Liam was because of the "abuse of her position."

Everyone knew I had to be involved; they just didn't know how. But with schmucky reporters like Sammy roaming around and opponents like Bill Brandon looking for dirt, it was only a matter of time before more damning discoveries were made.

But I believed in my mom's ability to fix everything—she was powerful, influential, and had an uncanny ability to get what she wanted. I had to trust that she was keeping the police away from me for the right reasons. And yet I couldn't help toying with the idea of storming into my dad's old department to see Mathews, or into Martinez's unit office and demanding that someone release Liam immediately as I revealed the details needed to exonerate him. Surely my sworn testimony would provide immediate proof of his innocence. But every time I thought through that scenario, I saw myself cuffed and escorted to a padded cell where I'd wait until Jane could come parading in to save me.

If worse came to worst, I was prepared to confess to Martinez's murder myself. I figured the probability of me going to prison for life was already so high that tacking on another murder to my rap sheet hardly mattered.

While Liam had been detained for six days now, the press was lined up and down our street, turning our house into my own personal detention center. Closed curtains, locked doors, and complete isolation. I roamed the house with a frenzied tension that became more unbearable by the second.

The only human contact I'd had all day was when my mom came into my room this morning. She stood at the foot of my bed and cleared her throat to wake me up.

"Ruby, I shouldn't have to say this, but I am going to make it abundantly clear. Don't do anything *stupid* today. Don't leave this house and don't talk to anyone. The two guards stationed outside will inform me if you try. Do you understand?"

Barely awake, I nodded.

When I sat up to face her, she was already gone, leaving me in the wake of her Chanel No. 5 perfume. It was like I had taken the role of one of her desperate clients—and she had taken the role of my distant high-powered attorney.

She didn't even say good-bye or reassure me that it would all be OK. Not that I expected her to. But that didn't mean that I'd forgotten the days when she did.

Now, I sat on the stairs and clutched my phone, wondering when my mom would call to give me an update. A shred of info, a scrap of hope. I'd already called her four times with no answer.

I scrolled down my contact list until I saw my backup mom's name—Mother Teresa. I hit "Send" knowing I wasn't supposed to talk to anyone today, but Dr. T probably wouldn't answer anyway. She'd blocked me at every turn. She left the hospital before I was granted permission to leave my room. And she hadn't answered one of my calls or texts since. Whatever her "SECRETS" were, she was hanging on to them like they were still duct taped inside. She had to know something that would help Liam's case, but she was staying silent. The call went to her voicemail, and I hung up.

I considered writing a letter to Liam, telling him how sorry I was. But what was I going to say? *Sorry I got you framed for the murder of a police officer. I hope your family's hearts aren't broken and that Tug doesn't cry himself to sleep at night. Oh, and I trust the guards aren't beating you too badly.*

He didn't belong in there. He belonged out here with me. Except, I worried he would finally come to his senses and decide to distance himself from me entirely. I wouldn't blame him, but I would miss him more than I wanted to admit. I ran a finger over my lips, remembering the last time we kissed. The taste of him was gone, but the memory of him would last much longer. Maybe forever.

I scrolled down to the next favorite on my contacts list—Alana. I pressed "Send" knowing she wouldn't answer, either, but just hearing her voice on her outgoing message made me feel connected to her again:

Aloha, you've reached Alana. I'm either at the beach, at the mall, or . . . at the beach. Leave a message at the beep.

Instead of hanging up, I inexplicably started to cry. Right there on her voicemail. My voice cracked as I tried to say, "I miss you." It cracked again as I sobbed, "I really need you." And then my heart cracked along with my voice as I begged, "Please call me back."

I hung up wondering what I'd just done. I'd never been the pathetic, pleading kind of girl. After all that time of pushing Alana away, all I wanted was her friendship back. As I held my head in my hands—ashamed as well as alone—I tried not to admit to myself that all my "irrational fears of abandonment" had been realized.

I was completely on my own. Just like Liam would be for "twenty-five to life" if my mom didn't pull a miracle out of her hat.

Out of complete desperation, I went to the family room and turned on the TV, flipping through the local news channels to see if my mom was being interviewed. The last few days I'd been avoiding the news like the plague, imagining all sorts of terrible headlines.

"Ruby the Death Rose—Involved in Yet Another Murder"

"Ruby Rose: Hot Damsel in Distress or Cold Psychopathic Killer?"

"Incumbent D. A. Jane Rose Drops Twenty Points in the Polls to Bill Brandon—Wayward Child to Blame"

Instead, what I saw made my heart plunge with sorrow. Coverage of Detective Martinez's funeral service showed huge crowds of uniformed police officers, decorated Marines, and hundreds of civilians dressed in black among the flags and flowers. So much sadness, so much pain. A fresh set of tears came to my eyes, and I wiped them away with both hands like windshield wipers, remembering my dad's funeral. The sight was so morbidly similar.

With a dark emptiness in my chest, I wondered whether Dad would've been there today. Had he and Martinez really put the past behind them? In any case, *I* should have been there. I should've been standing there next to his family, telling them the truth of what happened.

And then I spotted my mom at the head of the procession, walking through the graveyard with two Latina women. One was older, like grandma old. And the other was young, like my age or a few years younger. She looked vaguely familiar. Some part of me felt like I knew them. Martinez's mom and daughter, perhaps?

They were followed by Sergeant Mathews, who I didn't even realize knew Martinez. But there he was. At six foot six, he looked more like an NBA center than a cop. Then, of course, Bill Brandon and his perfect hair and teeth came strolling in last with his entourage.

I watched it for as long as I could. When the commentators came back on and began smearing Liam, I switched the channel. I couldn't watch anything anymore.

I paced up and down the staircase like a caged animal, trying to figure out how Silver had pulled this off. Even when I'd thought I was being clever with the license plate clue, he'd seen it coming and used it to lure me into another kill. He punished me for getting Detective Martinez involved with the cell phone tower signals by killing him and framing Liam for it. I wanted to run but had nowhere to go. And even if I had a destination in mind, two guards were stationed outside my house.

My heart was practically beating out of my chest—not only from climbing the stairs over and over again, but also from a growing sense of claustrophobia. I stopped at the top of the stairs and looked out the one window that wasn't blinded by drapes, the half circle of glass above the entryway. All I could see were blue skies, palm trees swaying—and an angel, walking up the driveway. A brown-skinned angel dressed in Daisy Dukes with a bright yellow flower in her hair.

Alana.

I rushed down the stairs and opened the door before she even had a chance to reach the front steps. She stopped when she saw me and cocked her head sideways with a *Don't jump on me* look.

Too bad.

I ran and threw my arms around her. I couldn't care less that the guards were probably freaking out about my unauthorized exit.

"I'm so sorry, Ruby," she said as she nuzzled into my neck. "I've been the worst friend ever. I just got your message. I totally sucketh—"

"Stop. You don't suck," I assured her. "You're here."

"I heard about Liam and that Detective. I just can't believe it."

"I know." I pulled back to face her. "Don't believe it, because it's not true. Come on, let's get in the house before those paparazzi leeches get any more ammunition. You never know if your butt will make the front page tomorrow."

"You think so?" she asked, sounding flattered. "It could be the start of my butt-modeling career."

"Miss Rose," Buff Security Guy Number 1 said, blocking the entrance. "We don't have clearance for anyone but you to enter the premises."

"Yeah, well, she's coming in whether you like it or not. She's my best friend. So go ahead and try to stop us."

Buff Guy Number 1 gave Buff Guy Number 2 a nervous glance.

"What are you going to do? Fight me?" I led Alana through the two of them and grabbed the front door. "Call Warden Jane if you want. We'll be inside."

Slam—that felt good.

As soon as we got to my room, Alana handed me a thick stack of papers.

"Your makeup work," she said. "Well, most of it. I actually got this two days ago and was going to bring it over yesterday, but I wasn't sure if you'd want to see me."

"Oh my gosh, thanks." I wasn't allowed to go back to school until this was all "cleared up." Not just my lungs, but the allegations piling up around me. But if there was a chance I could still graduate with perfect grades, I'd take it. I plopped it all down on my desk before joining Alana on my bed.

"So," she said warily, her eyes roaming the room as if looking for body parts.

"Look, Alana, thanks for coming. I know how *complicated* all this is, and there's probably nothing I can say to explain—"

"Then don't," she broke in. "You don't have to explain anything to me. I only came to make sure you're OK. I see your picture on the news. I hear your name in the halls. Everyone has a theory on your involvement with another murder. They're saying the craziest things. Like you put Liam up to killing that cop, that maybe you had something to do with your own dad's death."

Ouch.

"That you're going to go after me next," Alana continued. "And I just couldn't take it anymore. I almost punched Taylor in her big ol'—"

"Oh, I am so sure, Alana," I said. "You and what army? I won't be there to back you up, so don't go getting yourself into any trouble because of me." I couldn't bear to think of putting Alana in any more danger. All I had ever wanted to do was protect her. Even from that first day on the playground when I found her crying in the corner.

"I'm really worried about you, Rue," she said, looking me directly in the eyes. "Things just seem to go from bad to worse. When is it going to stop?"

"I don't know." My shoulders slumped. "Maybe never. Honestly, I don't see me coming out of this one unscathed, Alana. There's too much I can't explain. And my mom . . ." I searched for the words to describe the great divide between us. "I don't know if she's going to be able to stop me from going to prison for a very long time. Even if she wanted to."

"What are you talking about?" Alana tipped my chin up to face her. "Who is this person sitting here? And what have you done with Ruby Rose?"

"It's not that simple. My mom promised me she'd help exonerate Liam, but then behind my back she seems intent on using him as a scapegoat for Detective Martinez's murder. I'm getting desperate. I'm almost to the point of confessing myself even though I didn't do it. I swear, Alana, the man responsible for this is the same guy who made me kill LeMarq and . . ." I stopped there. I didn't need to bring up the laundry list of other bad dudes I'd killed.

"Shut up, I know you guys couldn't have done it," she said. "Not only do I believe you, Ruby, but I believe *in* you."

"But it's not over. He's going to find a way to lure me out again. I can't stop him, he's too smart—"

"Whoa, whoa, whoa—have you forgotten how freakishly brilliant you are? *You* are smarter than this guy. You are totally capable of beating him. And you don't have to rely on your flaky mom to do it."

Alana didn't get it. She didn't have all the facts. She was too naive and ignorant of the truth to understand that even if my mom came through on Liam, I couldn't let all those murders (that Alana didn't even know about) get swept under the rug. No amount of her Rah-Rah-Ruby cheerleading would change the fact that I would eventually have to confess to having killed these men, and my story was too unbelievable for redemption.

"You don't understand."

"Stop it, Ruby." She raised her voice and grabbed my hand. "Stop it with your glass-half-empty bull-crap. All is not lost. Your dad, Mr. Badass Jack Rose, didn't train you for all those years so you could give up."

"My dad?" I sat a little straighter at the mention of his name.

"That's right. Don't forget what he taught you. I used to think he was psycho—the way he made you his little Barbie Soldier. Turns out, he was psychic or something. He must've known this could happen."

I stared out the window, digesting her totally un-naive, non-ignorant wisdom. I had underestimated my incredibly loyal best friend, just like I'd underestimated Liam.

"He wouldn't let you give up, and neither will I. So tell me you're going to fight," Alana demanded.

The strength of my dad's soul surged inside me. Memories of us sitting on our surfboards past the break came crashing back. Days at the shooting range and nights at the dojo. It was true: My dad wanted me to be ready. He prepared me for the time my shoreline would be tested. I'm sure he never imagined it would be quite like this. But he knew someone was a threat to his family. He'd made sure I was strong enough, smart enough, and prepared enough to endure it.

And in all that time, he never let me hang my head.

So I lifted it. "I promise, I'll fight."

And suddenly, I knew exactly how to do it.

CHAPTER 25

Before Alana left, I assured her that if my plan didn't work, I unofficially bequeathed my shoe collection to her. In the meantime, we agreed that it would be best for her to keep her distance. She needed no further convincing of how dangerous it was to be my friend. Maybe one day soon we'd get back to working on our tans together.

But for now, I knew what had to be done: Get to Filthy number five—Mr. Stanley Violet—before Silver did. Or at least before Silver put me in the impossible position of killing him. I needed to warn him that if he did what Silver said, he would end up like the other four. I needed to make Violet my ally, not my victim. I needed him to help me not kill him.

Ha, I *was* insane. I was about to sneak out of my nice safe home and go looking for a rapist to convince him to help me. *Real smart, Ruby. Best idea ever.*

"Oh shut up," I said to my inner self, then went upstairs to get ready.

Within fifteen minutes, I had my mom's minigun holstered under my hoodie, my butterfly blade in The Cleave—and I'd scrawled a note to my mom:

I'm sorry that I did something "stupid," but I just couldn't sit here. I went to see the last man on my list, Stanley Violet. If I don't come back, you'll know where to start looking for me.

I left it on my desk, not hers, just in case I got back before her and she didn't need to know.

I cracked my window and threw the hook of my dad's Ranger Rappelling Rope around the tree branch nearest me. I'd done this kind of thing before at the SWAT training center, and once on a NorCal camping trip with Dad's team (including Mathews), I'd done it down the face of a mountain.

The adrenaline kicked in as I gripped the rope with gloved hands and steadied myself outside of the sill. I shut the window behind me and let myself down little by little, using my feet to slow the descent. I hit the ground softly with the balls of my feet and tugged at the rope from a 45-degree angle to get it to slide off the branch right. But it didn't. The line was stuck on something. I couldn't just leave the rope dangling. Soon one of the guards would make his rounds back here and see it.

I only had one other option since I didn't have time to climb the tree and untie it. I had to throw the rest of the rope back up into the branches and hope the guards didn't look up.

When I heard a man cough, I chucked the rope like it was a viper and ran. This time I'd thought ahead and was wearing my Dr. Martens combat boots—aka The Doctors.

I tore across the yard and jumped the wall behind my house. No paparazzi hanging out back here. Good thing, because the way I was dressed—black skinny jeans, black boots, black hoodie, my mom's little black gun hiding in my black shoulder holster—didn't speak highly of my intentions. I wasn't going to church, that's for sure.

Dr. Fenton, the anesthesiologist who lived behind us, had a Ducati motorcycle my dad drooled over. He used to tease my mom that one day she'd have to bail him out of jail for stealing it because

"Dr. Brilliant" always left the keys in the ignition. Little did he know it would be me doing the stealing.

I padded around the Fentons' gazebo and pool waterfall, making sure not to be seen, and I slid into the dark garage. I flipped the switch to find not just one shiny beast, but four—all lined up.

The red Harley Davidson, the blue Kawasaki, the silver BMW, or the black Ducati. After a full minute of needless indecision, I chose the Ducati in memory of my dad (and to match my outfit). I found a shiny-charcoal helmet that fit well enough and tucked my braided ponytail inside.

To avoid the roar of the engine, I walked the bike out until I hit an overgrown patch of ivy on the side driveway. Then I turned her on and thought about a few dirt-biking trips with my dad to remember how to make her go. Soon, I was peeling out in the direction of Mr. Violet's video game lair twenty miles down the Pacific Coast Highway.

The wind felt cleansing as it whisked past me at 90 miles per hour. For a while, the adrenaline erased everything. The emptiness and regret for a life without my father. The sadness for Martinez and his grieving family. The frustration toward my mom and her silent evasion. The guilt for Liam alone in his eight-by-eight cell. All of it was temporarily replaced with blind speed and mindless exhilaration. Until I realized that getting pulled over for a simple speeding ticket could set off a disastrous chain of events.

I slowed down and tried to focus, finally exiting the highway and turning onto a private drive right up the cove. Didn't need GPS directions for this one—I'd been here before.

A while ago, I'd followed Mr. Violet back here after a gamer conference he'd attended in San Diego. I'd watched him with binoculars, waiting for the moment he'd pull someone out of the trunk of his Ferrari. But when it never happened, I went home.

This time, I wouldn't be going home until we'd had our little chat. I knew he would recognize me, and at a minimum be curious why the infamous Ruby Rose was on his doorstep.

Not to sell Girl Scout cookies. Certainly not in this getup.

I slowed down and parked the Ducati in a patch of oleander bushes two houses away, hanging the helmet on the handlebar. Violet's place was too secure to sneak up on him, and I had no time for any drawn-out tactics. Instead, I was going to walk right up and ring the doorbell.

Over the cobblestone drive, through the ivy-clad entryway, and under the portcullis into the courtyard. Two large wreaths hung on the double doors, but instead of red ribbons or holly berries, the painted black sprigs boasted a silver snake and miniature swords. Where'd he buy this—HolidayDecorationsForCreeps.com?

I looked down to make sure that if I rang the bell there wasn't some booby trap under my feet that would land me in his dungeon forever.

A video intercom sprang to life before I could touch anything. Violet's shiny face leered down at me from a screen on the pillar.

"Who are you? What do you want?" His voice sliced through the speakers, surrounding me like I was in a cave.

"My name's Ruby Rose. I need to talk to you," I said, checking that my gun was still there. "It's a matter of life and death." That was the first time I'd ever used that clichéd phrase, and it was actually true.

He paused, and I heard the tapping of a keyboard. It sounded like he was playing one of his video games. Or maybe he was using face-recognition software to confirm my identity. Or putting in the command for his portcullis to fall and trap me—who has a portcullis anyway? This was Orange County, not Scotland circa 1400 AD.

"Ruby Rose, eh? Whose life and death are we talking about?"

"Yours." I tried not to blink.

Another pause. He started typing again, and I braced for what he might do. He could send a 911 text and have my own dad's SWAT team come take me out.

Instead, the remote-controlled double doors swung open. "Then by all means, come in."

As soon as I crossed the threshold, Violet rounded the corner and held out his small hand to formally introduce himself like a perfect gentleman—which I knew he most definitely was not.

His moist fingers wrapped around my hand, and it felt like I was being forced to shake tentacles with a dead octopus. It took everything I had not to throw him and his greasy ponytail into one of his antique swords and make him feel the pain he'd forced on too many innocent girls. I would have if it didn't involve touching more of his skin.

"Come." He motioned for me to join him in a strange sitting room full of skulls and serpents. "May I offer you something to drink?"

Yeah, so he could drug me and make me more *compliant*. "I don't think so."

All the windows were covered in black curtains, blocking out any late-afternoon light. I had to get this over with—and get out of here as soon as possible.

"Listen, I need your help," I said, hating the taste of the words on my tongue. "And you need mine."

"Oh . . . *kay*," he said, awkwardly sitting down on a claw-like couch—the back rose up in four sharp talons, so it seemed like any minute he could be crushed within his own living room. "Help with what, exactly?"

I took a long breath, searching for the best way to answer. "Your life in is danger, and I want to protect you."

"Right." He released a stifled laugh that was tinged with nervousness. He was scared of me. And the poorly concealed pistol in his track pants didn't seem to make him feel any better.

I paused, seeking the line between telling him as little as possible (to prevent him from going to the police with any information), and as much as possible (to prevent Silver from pulling off the fifth kill by my hand).

"Has anyone contacted you lately about 'product' you may be interested in?" I asked.

"Listen, Ruby—may I call you Ruby?"

"That's fine," I lied. "But you didn't answer my question."

"OK, Ruby, I know who you are." He pulled at the hem of his thin V-neck to expose scar tissue on his shoulder. "After all, it was your sharpshooting dad who gave me this."

He stared at me like I owed him an apology.

"You deserved it," I assured him.

"So is that why you're here? To give me what I deserve?"

"I told you, I'm here to help you. I swear."

"Help me like you helped that LeMarq fellow? With a bullet between the eyes?" He placed a pale forefinger to his oily brow, as if I needed a visual.

I clenched my jaw and decided to respond in kind. "OK, Mr. Violet, here's the truth, plain and simple: Someone has been setting me up to take out *killers*." I watched his eyes flinch. "I don't know who's doing this to me, and I'm not even sure why. But I do know that you're next."

I took a few steps toward him to make sure he understood me with perfect clarity. "He is going to try to make me kill you, and I *don't* want to do that."

A twisting silence slithered between us while he absorbed the truth. He stared through me with the eyes of a racked soul.

My head swiveled around just in case someone else was here. I put my hand inside my hoodie to grip my gun.

"Yes, someone has contacted me," he finally admitted.

"OK, then," I said, relieved he might actually cooperate. "I have a plan."

I flung my backpack off my shoulder and reached inside to grab my dad's vest.

"This is an Ultralight Concealed Goldflex/Kevlar Level IIIA Bulletproof Vest." I held it out to him. "Wear this day and night. I don't know when you'll need it."

He sat forward on the heel of the claw-couch and took the offering, inspecting the impossibly thin design.

"Wear it with sweatshirts to maximize the concealment," I said, channeling my father. "And you need to start thinking about other methods of protection. Hire more security, stay armed, and above all, resist any kind of bait he lays for you."

"Slow down, sweetheart, slow down—"

"Don't call me *sweetheart*, and don't you dare treat this lightly," I warned him.

"But I don't understand. You aren't making any sense." He held up his hands. "Why would—"

"You don't have to understand." I cut him off again. "Look, I don't have all the answers. I just know at some point he'll come for you. And as much as I don't give a damn about you, the only chance of this working is if you try to protect yourself. Any slight wrench in his plans might be the difference between you living and me killing you. If you value your life, you'll fight however you can."

Doubts fought against my hopes as he sunk in reaction to the word "fight." This small man was no fighter. He was scrawny and despicable. But he was my only chance.

I turned to go. I couldn't bear to be in his presence one second longer.

Before leaving, I said, "Regardless of what I think of you and the truly evil things you've done, I don't want to kill you. Please don't make me."

CHAPTER 26

The sound of the garage door cut through my thoughts. Mom was finally home. I shook off the memory of Violet's tentacles touching me, reassuring myself that my scalding shower had washed away all his filth. Man, my loofah was getting a lot of use lately.

I ran downstairs to meet her. I had to know what was going on with Liam.

"Hey, Mom," I said softly, trying not to scare her. It was well after 11:00 p.m., and most of the lights were off.

"Ruby!" She jumped like a skittish cat. "What are you trying to do, kill me?"

Was that a Freudian slip?

"Why are you home so late?" I asked, going for a gentle approach. "I've been waiting to talk to you."

"Yeah, well it's going to have to wait," she said curtly as she scrambled to pick up the files she'd dropped.

"What's wrong with you?" I asked, sensing something in her frantic movements.

She brushed past me and started hiking the stairs.

"Are you just going to ignore me forever?" I called after her. "You know, it was only a week ago that *you* asked *me* to meet at Dr. Teresa's to talk. Did you suddenly forget what you had to say?"

"Rue, it's almost midnight. It's been a long day, and I'm tired." She stopped and took off her heels—like that would give her more getaway speed.

"You told me you'd help him," I said, not even close to giving up. "You promised."

She turned and looked down at me.

"He's been in there forever. Why haven't you gotten him out?"

"It's more complicated than I realized at first. Do you know how it would look if I pulled strings to get my daughter's high school *fling* out of jail after he killed a veteran police officer?"

Whoa. I could not have heard that "he killed" part right.

"He didn't do it. I told you that. I was there!" I stalked up the stairs after her. "If you'd let me talk to the police, I would tell them that! They have no right to detain him. They have no evidence, no motive. He should have been released by now."

"Ruby, honestly, just stop. You have no idea what you are talking about. His bail was set too high, and his mom can't afford it. She's a bartender," she said condescendingly. My anger flared and the springs in my muscles tightened up, waiting for the release.

"What bail—what are you talking about?" I asked, staring her down.

"Arraignment was several days ago. The judge set bail at a million dollars." She turned to go, but I grabbed her wrist. This was escalating too fast.

"A million dollars? That's ridiculous. Why didn't you tell me?" I narrowed my eyes at her, knowing exactly why she hadn't told me. She saw this fight coming, and that's why she'd been avoiding me. I wanted to slap myself for believing in her and not finding out about Liam's situation myself. "Why haven't you told me anything? I trusted you, and yet you're the one allowing the charges to be brought!"

She pulled her wrist away. "My hands are tied. I can't go easy on him because you have a crush on him, Ruby. He had Martinez's blood on his hands—"

"So did I. I told you that Martinez had been shot. We *both* had blood on our hands because we were trying to save Martinez's life. And even so, that's not enough evidence for an arrest."

"I'm afraid it is," she said, her tone hot with impatience. "It may be circumstantial, but combined with other factors, it's evidence nonetheless. The boy has a record, Ruby. He almost killed someone before."

"What? He was only protecting his little brothers and mother from his *drunk* dad," I argued. "And how is that relevant?"

"Protecting yourself would be calling the police, not taking a baseball bat and putting your own father in a coma for seven days."

"You don't know all the facts," I said, a little thrown by the baseball-bat thing. Liam hadn't mentioned that detail, and I flinched at the image of him beating his father.

"Neither do you," she said flatly. "No matter what his father did, he didn't deserve to be nearly beaten to death. Contrary to what you might currently believe, violence is *not* the answer. The boy is a danger to society."

"I should've known you would pick sides with the abusive parent," I sputtered. "You *know* Liam didn't do this."

"That's not true. He won't even talk to me. He gave his statement to the police and now he is relying on his two-bit public defender," she said, rubbing her eyes and smudging her makeup even more. "The whole thing . . . it just doesn't look good."

"It doesn't look good?" I repeated. Of course, I should've seen this coming. "*Looks* have always been more important to you than the *truth*, Miss Botox California. Miss Sham Marriage, Miss Closet Alcoholic. I wonder how it would *look* if I decided to go see my paparazzo friend Sammy and gave him an exclusive interview on the *real* life of Jane Rose. Or call up our Bill Brandon and give him—"

"I'm going to bed," she cut me off, pinching her eyes shut and blowing out a dramatic breath of exhaustion. She was bluffing, and I was calling.

"Drop the charges, Jane, or I'll drop a bomb on your campaign you'll never recover from. Bill Brandon will have a whole new set of names to call you," I said, knowing I'd just crossed the line. But asking nicely wasn't working. Liam's life was on the line. "There is no evidence that can't be explained away. He's innocent, and you know it. I won't let you use him as a scapegoat."

She glared at me, and I almost lost my nerve, but instead of succumbing to her intimidation, I turned it up. "I will not be ignored by you anymore. I will not be neglected and abused because of your career. I will not let you scoff at what I have with Liam. It's not a *fling* or a *crush*. He's been there for me in a way you never have." It was all true, but instead of feeling relieved for finally communicating what Liam meant to me, I felt awful for the mean way it came out.

"I don't respond well to threats, young lady," she said. "Not from the criminals off the street, and not from the criminals in my own home."

I flinched, and for a second I thought she did, too. Her words stung worse than a slap to the face. Yes, I'd trailed the men I killed, I'd withheld information from the police, and I'd even "borrowed" a motorcycle from a neighbor without permission. But every life I took was taken either in self-defense or in the defense of others. None of what I'd done looked good—in fact, much of it looked horrendously stupid in hindsight.

But I thought I'd explained it to her, all very clearly. Yet here she was, calling me a criminal. Mothers aren't supposed to say things like that. They're supposed to love unconditionally, aren't they?

"You would do well to remember that I'm the one who's kept you out of the courtroom. *I've* kept you out of prison." Her red-wine breath made me back up. "So you don't care for who I am, I get it. Well, guess what, *honey*—I don't much care for who you are."

The look of disgust on her face was enough for my soul to scurry back into the hole it had come from. "Or not, at least, what you've become."

She turned her back and closed her double doors on me with deliberate force. Then she locked them. She was scared of me. Maybe even repulsed by me. And, until further notice, she was done with me.

I was officially alone in the world. Not that I didn't already feel it, but now I knew it. I had Alana again, but for now, the less contact I had with her the better.

I bit my lip trying to fight the sting of my tears. In the darkness, I felt the pain, the rejection, and the guilt roll down my cheeks. Maybe if I hadn't followed my Filthy Five in the first place, none of this would have happened and she'd still love me.

Never in my whole life had she so deliberately rejected me. Through all my failures to live up to her expectations, through all our differences of opinion, and even through the death of my dad, I had never seen her so cold.

If Silver was trying to demolish me, mission accomplished.

Everything I'd ever valued was gone.

I tried not to imagine my mom's gloating face as they took me away forever. She'd be happy to be rid of me, and my inheritance would only be a bonus. She'd get all five million dollars of life insurance funds held in trust for me.

Wait, the money! Why hadn't I thought of this before? I wiped salty tears from my cheeks.

Liam needed a million dollars, and I had it. Maybe I could call the estate-planning attorney and get the money wired by noon— Liam could be here by nightfall. The thought of his arms around me and the warmth of his breath on my neck made me lightheaded. Like a balloon expanding with air, I allowed myself to fill up with hope.

Unfortunately, my thin piece of ruby-colored rubber popped when I remembered who the trustee was: Wicked Witch of the West Coast Jane Rose. She controlled my trust fund, and there was no way

I'd be getting my hands on any of it. At least not until I was twenty-one. And even then, it had been explained to me that I would only receive one-third increments—presumably to prevent my spending it all on shoes in one year. Which, to be honest, was a bigger possibility than I cared to admit.

I gave my pillow a pile driver to the gut and threw it across the room. Not knowing what else to do with myself, I grabbed the remote. Part of me wanted to throw it like a Chinese star at the flat screen, but instead I pressed power. My TV had never done anything to me.

The only thing on was *Real Housewives of Orange County*, and—oh yeah, the late-night reruns of the talking heads speculating on the sanity of Ruby Rose. How would I ever get a fair trial with these bottle blondes spouting off about "mounting evidence yet to be released?" Not that I didn't like free speech—or getting a few highlights now and then—but please, these girls didn't know the difference between the day spa and a defamation charge. I doubted either of them would have called me a "disturbed and traumatized child" to my face. But it was cool to say it in front of the entire free world.

I listened to them hypothesize how Liam and I were like a teen version of Bonnie and Clyde. That perhaps the motive behind Martinez's murder was Liam protecting me from being investigated. That young love sparked his intent to kill.

Did these women smoke crack before going on air? How much more outrageous could they get?

The tolling of the grandfather clock downstairs brought me back to cold reality. It was 12:15 a.m., and I was no closer to sleeping. No closer to finding any answers that could save me from this nightmare called my life. I turned off the TV and sat there brooding until around 1:00, finally falling asleep in Gladys, my trusty shoe closet and most loyal friend.

CHAPTER 27

I woke up with a start. Gasping for air, I rolled over wondering who'd taken my pillow and why my comforter was tangled around me. It was 4:00 a.m.

"Oh jeez." I sat up to get my bearings. Light trickled in from my bathroom across the way. "No rest for the wicked."

Sore didn't cover the way my back felt. Even my mind felt stiff. Dreams of blonde-headed zombies chasing me with pitchforks hadn't been exactly restful. I looked around Gladys's dark walls for some comfort, but for perhaps the first time in my life, my shoes had none to give. They all just sat there, listless and inanimate. I must have hit rock bottom if I felt alone even among my shoes.

I finally scraped myself off the floor and headed to the kitchen for something to eat. As I hobbled down the stairs, I noticed my mom's doors were open. Maybe she couldn't sleep, either.

I perked up my ears for signs of her presence, but all I heard was the howling wind seeping in from outside. No TV coming from her room, no dishes clinking in the kitchen, no tapping of the keyboard in her office.

I couldn't help myself. I mounted the stairs again and peeked into her room. It would be so like her to lure me in there just to punish me for it. Maybe *she* was the mastermind after all. Or had employed Silver to make me into the assassin she couldn't be. If she couldn't put those killers away, she would have her psychopath child do it for her.

Now *my* speculation was getting out of control.

"Mom?" I called out. I hadn't been in her room for months. "Are you in here?"

The wind whistled back like it was trying to tell me something. The hair on my arms stood on end.

Her bed was unmade; the light in her walk-in closet was on. *Curious.*

Her briefcase and car keys were on the dresser. *Suspicious.*

I rounded the corner into the hallway leading to her bathroom but was stopped by papers scattered all over the floor. *Straight-up alarming.*

"Mom!" I called out again, this time with a tremor of panic. To be sure, I doubled back into her room to look under the crumpled bedcover, in the closet, and even on her balcony.

I ran downstairs and then back up, checking each room to make sure she wasn't hiding somewhere.

She wasn't here.

Silver had gotten her. I was sure of it. Somehow, he'd slipped in past security and taken her. Despite the anger I'd felt toward her last night, all I felt now was sick. I went back to her bed and put my head in my hands. She was my mom, and I still loved her. I needed her, even if she'd never need me back. She was all I had left.

Blood. Why could I smell it all of a sudden? I sniffed the air like a dog. The metallic scent was definitely coming from the bathroom. I'd followed the coppery smell over the trail of papers and into the excessively large master bathroom suite when the wind got kicked right out of me. My mom's sink was full of bloodstained water and more papers. The drain was actually blocked, holding it all there for me. I pulled out some of the papers and let them drip on the floor.

Red streaks covered the countertop and mirror. Mom must have resisted. I was horrified by my reflection—it looked like *I* was covered in blood. Like some magic mirror had finally revealed the real me.

Red Ruby Rose, stained in blood.

More papers were strewn across the drawers and shelves, all of them soaked in watery blood. I put them together on the bath mat to figure out what they could be. Knowing Silver, I had to assume they had meaning.

It was a pleading, and the caption read "In the Matter of the Custody of the Minor Child Hailey Bracken." It was a Notice of Hearing on a Petition to Terminate Parental Rights. I dropped to my knees, desperate for more information. I found pieces of the Petition with my mom's signature, then another signature on a paper titled "Affidavit of Guardian Ad Litem." She hadn't had physical custody of the child but had closely monitored the girl's care, nutrition, and well-being. That much I got.

Through the scattered and blood-soaked puzzle pieces, a story started to unfold. Fifteen years ago, my mom was appointed temporary Guardian Ad Litem of a baby. The baby's mom was on drugs, the baby had been neglected, and my mom terminated the bio mom's rights. No mention of any dad. All I could find was "Abandonment by biological father, name unknown."

During my mom's Family Court days, she must have been appointed Guardian Ad Litem for dozens of children. Did this have something to do with Silver? Was he the one who'd abandoned his child? Was my original theory correct, and he was paying my mom back by slowly taking away everything she had? Did he intend to destroy her by destroying me, too?

Suddenly, her phone rang, the high-pitched ringtone frazzling what was left of my nerves. I followed the sound back to the bed and picked up her cell. Unknown number.

"Hello?" My voice cracked.

"Hello, Ruby," a male voice said. It sent shivers down my spine.

"What do you want?" I demanded.

"Do you remember the last day you saw your father?" he said in a deep Batman-type whisper.

Of course I remembered. I remembered it every day. "Why? What are you planning to do to my mother?"

"Do you remember?" he repeated.

"Yes! OK, I remember." I tried to remain calm. "Listen, whatever she did to you and your family, she's sorry." It wasn't working. I was losing control. "*We're* sorry—"

"Then remember last night, because unless you get here fast enough to save your mother, it will be *her* last night."

I opened my mouth to scream, but nothing came out.

"Just so you know, Mr. Violet is also waiting for you."

My heart sank. He must've taken Violet right after I left. Or maybe Silver had been there when I visited earlier.

"We are both waiting for you," he said carefully. "I know I don't need to tell you this, but if you call the police, you might as well call the morgue, because she will already be dead. We're going to finish this just as it began—on Grissom Island. The place your father tried to bury the truth. More detailed instructions will be sent to your phone. Good-bye, Ruby."

I held my mom's phone long after the line went dead.

I had no idea what kind of delusional truth Silver was referring to, but a sharp reality lodged itself inside of me: This man had killed my father. I was sure of it now. My dad was murdered. Assassinated. By the same man who'd officially destroyed my life.

I'd believed knowing the truth would finally set me free. Instead, it crushed me. And hardened me. I vowed to make Silver pay.

If there was one way I could honor my father, it was to remember what he'd taught me. I couldn't react emotionally. I had to be logical and strategic.

Silver had said he'd know if I called the police, so either he had a scanner or a rat on the inside who would tip him off. In any case, he couldn't expect me to go in there alone. I longed for Liam. He was smart. He saw things I didn't. I needed him, and my own mom had made sure I couldn't have him.

I checked the call history on Mom's phone. One name stood out among all the others: Mark Mathews—the man who let my dad die and then took his place as SWAT Sergeant. Why was my mom talking to my dad's old best friend at 11:25 p.m.? And again at 11:52? Plus several missed calls through the night?

Was she sleeping with him, just like she had with Martinez? Or could it be they were working together on catching the man behind all this madness? Or both? My mom was a lot of things, but she wasn't stupid. She'd probably known from the night I killed LeMarq that there was someone manipulating me. That the same man who killed her husband was following me, luring me, torturing me. And she'd never said a word.

She'd betrayed me so deeply for so long. Lied to me, hidden things from me, imprisoned Liam—when none of it was even my fault. It was hers. This madman was tormenting me for *her* crimes. *Her* secrets. She'd destroyed his family, and now he was destroying hers, and mine. And also destroying Liam's to spite me.

Yet, she was my mother, and I wouldn't do to her what she had done to me. I wouldn't abandon her—I had to save her. I stared at the phone in my hand, weighing my options.

Go in alone, like he said.

Call 911 for help.

Trust Mathews—my dad's best friend, my mom's ally, the man who used to be like a second father to me but still refused to speak to me. Even after he came to the hospital after the fire.

Maybe all three. I would do whatever it took to bring Silver to justice.

I touched the screen over Mathews's name and waited for the ring.

"Jane, why haven't you been answering? I've been calling—"

"It's Ruby." I stopped him. "She's gone. He's taken her."

He paused, like he needed some extra time to process my voice.

"*Ruby*? What happened? Where are you?"

"I'm at home—in her room," I said. "There's blood, and papers. A man called and said to come to where my father tried to bury the truth. Grissom Island. And if I called the police, she'd be dead."

I switched hands holding the phone, thinking my hand was sweaty from nerves. But when I looked down at my pants, I realized sweat wasn't making my hand slippery—it was blood. Her blood.

"Listen, Ruby," he said calmly, just like my dad used to even when he was stressed. "Don't move. I'll send a team to your house to protect you. I'll take care of this."

"No, that's not how it's going to happen," I said with surprising authority. "I'm going in. Alone. That's what he wants. He's too smart. Too prepared. Anything else and she dies. Wait for my call. Then and only then you can move in."

"Honey, please don't—"

"Don't call me honey!" I snarled into the phone. "I've been through too much to be treated like a child. And you know me better than that."

"I'm sorry, I didn't mean it like that," he said, backtracking. "I just need you to understand who you're dealing with."

What? Did he know about Silver, too? Did everyone but me know my mom's secrets?

"Oh I *understand* who I'm dealing with all right," I snapped. "I think you and the whole police department are the ones who don't understand." I felt a wave of long-building anger rolling in. "It's been nearly a year since my father was murdered, and you and your SWAT brothers have conveniently forgotten about him and his case. So much for honor, courage, and commitment." I felt for the Challenge Coin in my pocket. "You let him die, and now you've let his memory die by ignoring the justice he deserves. I thought you loved him. I thought you loved me! How could you keep denying me the information I deserve *and* . . . sleep with my mom?"

Wow, where did that come from?

"Wait right there, Ruby." Mathews's tone shut me down. "First of all, I am not sleeping with your mother. That was Detective Martinez's mistake, not mine. Second, I did love your father. He was the most courageous man I ever knew. *He* taught me honor and commitment. And I love you, too. It was your mother who forbade me—forbade us all—to speak to you. She told us to stay away. That in your emotional state you couldn't bear it. I respected her wishes to keep you protected from the darkness surrounding their very public lives and your father's very public death. I see now that it was a mistake, and I'm sorry. As soon as I get the chance, I'll give you the whole truth. But not now. So please, just let me take care of this. Do you hear me?"

My mind raced to take it all in: First, Mathews wasn't the traitor I thought he was—and maybe I could even trust him. Second, there was no end to my mom's betrayal. And third, I had to get to Grissom Island before Mathews.

"Don't move in until I call you," I said before hanging up.

I ran to my bathroom to wash the blood off my hands, and then to Gladys to change into black clothes and shoes. Everything was already laid out—gun, holster, and all—just in case. I didn't bother with the window this time—just ran downstairs, opened the sliding back door, and bolted for the wall. I didn't even care if the obviously incompetent guards saw me. As soon as I made it to my neighbor's Ducati, it wouldn't matter anymore.

CHAPTER 28

When I was a kid, my third-grade class took a field trip to Grissom Island. I remembered learning three things that day:

1. Grissom Island was one of four man-made islands on the Long Beach coast named after fallen astronauts.

2. The islands were built to hide some of the nation's largest and most productive oil-drilling rigs.

3. From shore, they all looked like something you might see at Disneyland. Grissom Island was definitely eye candy—encased in an elaborate facade decked with swaying palm trees, huge waterfalls, and castle-like towers . . . all built to mask the dirty rigs.

I'd once asked my dad if princesses lived on the islands, and he said, smiling, "Only when they're on vacation."

I doubted he was smiling the day he went there and got blown to pieces.

Shaking off the image, I pulled into the harbor parking lot nearest the island. The sleek digital clock on the Ducati's dash read 4:46 a.m. It had only taken me twenty minutes at 100+ miles per hour to get here—even against the wicked wind trying to blow me back. The sun wouldn't show up for another ninety minutes or so, but the harbor security likely would. I had to move if I didn't want to be seen.

In thirty seconds flat, I parked the bike, removed the helmet, and took cover behind a building marked "Shoreline Yacht Club." I reached into The Cleave for my phone and pulled up the waiting messages.

One from Mathews read:

Don't do this. Call me immediately.

The next from Sammy read:

On my way.

I shook my head, not believing what I'd done. Halfway to Long Beach, I'd stopped and sent him a text.

I'm coming thru on our agreement. If u want the story of ur life, u and ur cameras better get to Grissom Island asap. Tell Sgt Mathews I told u to come. I need this on film.

Even seeing his name on the screen made me want to jump into the harbor and wash myself off. But he was my insurance. Like Liam pointed out all those weeks ago, the police would never believe me if I didn't have any proof. This time I planned to give them footage they couldn't ignore. It was a long shot—not just because Mathews might not let Sammy and his camera tag along, but because I could bet my life that Silver wouldn't strike a pose for me. But I had to try if it gave me a way to exonerate Liam.

I skipped to the last text, from the unknown number:

Find Boat Slip K-11—Gate K is wedged open. Take the orange kayak to southern rim. Meet us in the large white building at the heart of the island.

Great. I took a long hard look at the obstacle course before me.

The coastline was in darkness. But not Grissom Island. The decorative pink, yellow, and blue lighting lit up the sea. The sound of the crashing waterfalls consumed the area. If I hadn't known better, I could've mistaken this place for Fantasy Island. Too bad I knew exactly what it was—a veneer. A good place to hide secrets. Or even better, a great place to dig them up and bury them again.

A sliver of lightning cut through the sky, momentarily highlighting the entire scene and pointing out how isolated this place really was. It was basically in the middle of the ocean. Not only was getting on the island undetected going to be difficult, but the place was an underground maze. Even if Silver had taken out the island's private security team and I could make it ashore, I was essentially walking into a dark and potentially explosive trap.

Getting off the island would be another mess. That was assuming any of us would be getting off alive.

Worst of all, a thunderstorm was coming. The shape of the encroaching fog looked like a monster about to swallow this place whole. The thought of traveling over those turbulent waters on a kayak—in the dark—required courage enough.

Someone was going to die on Grissom, I was sure of it.

Maybe my mom.

Maybe Violet—the last man standing on my list.

Maybe me.

Silver had outsmarted me at every turn. The chances of this time being any different were low. I accepted my odds. But I still had a brain. Only half a soul, perhaps, but definitely a fully functioning mind.

And hope. I still had shreds of that, too.

I spotted Gate K—about fifty feet away.

All of a sudden I felt like praying. I didn't even know how—I'd never done it before. But I figured it certainly couldn't hurt.

I muttered some "please helps" into the phone I clutched, like maybe the cell had God's number on speed dial and like maybe I deserved the help (which I wasn't sure I did). I may not have been raised religious, but I'd heard of the Ten Commandments, and I was pretty sure the whole *Thou shalt not kill* thing was still high on that list. My mom's cell vibrated in my pocket. I pulled it out and stared at the angrily blinking red light, wondering if Silver had found out I called Sergeant Mathews and was now sending me a picture of my mom's corpse.

I tasted the bile rising inside me.

Pulling myself together, I turned on Mom's phone to see who the message was from. Mathews. It read:

DON'T GO IN. My team is eight min out.

My phone vibrated again. Another message from Mathews:

WE will take him out. I promise Ruby. I want justice for your dad just as much as you do. PLEASE don't go in. Respond.

Maybe he thought bombarding me on both phones would delay me.

But it wouldn't. I had to get inside, and now. I didn't doubt Silver's ability to kill and disappear. Just like with that girl on Ninth Street, if I didn't do something, my mom would die. How could I live with myself if I stayed out here and did nothing?

I typed:

I'm already in. DO NOT move in until I contact you. I have a plan.

Who did I think I was? Not in my wildest dreams did I ever think I'd be ordering the SWAT Sergeant around. If I just waited a few minutes, they could escort me in. Or we could come up with a plan together. After all, they'd have the schematics of the island. And ten guns had to be better than one.

Except ten guns hadn't been enough to save my dad. I couldn't put my mom's life in their hands when I knew with certainty what the result would be.

I wouldn't kill her by disobeying Silver's instructions.

I pulled my gun out of the holster inside my black hoodie and tried the gate. Just like he'd said, the heavy door was wedged open by what looked like a shoe. And not just any shoe. One of the $900 Christian Louboutin "Love Me" 100 mm heels my mom was wearing last night before she took them off to run away from me. This sicko was taunting me again. There was absolutely no need to bring such a perfectly beautiful pair of shoes into this!

I went through the gate and re-wedged the shoe behind me. Slip K-11 was hard to miss. It was the only slip without a million-dollar yacht. Waiting for me was more like a hundred-dollar piece of crap—a plastic kayak. I bit my lip as I descended the ladder, climbed into the unsteady craft, and began paddling toward the island with quick strokes across my body like my dad taught me.

It took me only a few minutes to navigate out of the dock and enter the open sea toward the southern perimeter of the island where the waves swelled around me. Ignoring the thoughts of what lay beneath and beyond, I concentrated on getting to the shore. The icy water slapping me in the face, the choppy wakes making me sick, and the fear bullying me backward wouldn't stop me.

Finally, I reached land. I shoved the stupid kayak onto the rocks and climbed the boulders to the top. Gun out, eyes up, arms wobbly from the paddling, I sprinted to the only big, white building I could see and hid behind a buzzing electrical box. I scanned the outside of the building until I found what I was looking for—a circular metal plate covering the ground. There was a chance in the darkness and fog that Silver might have lost sight of me (if he was watching) and wouldn't catch me entering from below.

I strained to pull up the plate, then lowered myself into the dark, relying on the feel of each metal rung of the ladder and hoping my eyes would adjust. I couldn't see how far it was to the bottom, but it felt never-ending. Like this tunnel led to China. Or straight to the fiery depths of hell—where Silver belonged.

For every inch I descended, my heart rate exponentially ascended. I couldn't take much more of this.

Finally, my feet hit the ground and my eyes detected light. I raised my weapon and took careful, balanced steps through the darkness toward a barely lit tunnel. As I moved, all I could hear was the slight squeak of my own footsteps, a rhythmic drip-drop of water, and the buzz of electricity.

I moved through the cold, dank air, listening for any signs of movement above or below. I prepared myself for attack from any side, analyzing every space I encountered for potential threats and sabotage. A calm focus took over as I moved swiftly through the snaking underground chambers. Maybe my dad had taken these exact steps.

His strength and courage filled me as I stole through the darkness.

One foot in front of the other, Rue, don't hesitate. Trust your instincts.

I clenched my jaw and moved forward. A faint sound came from above. I found a spiral staircase at the farthest west end of the bottom floor and began scaling it. *Arms up, shoulder cocked, weapon high and tight.*

I peered up to the first floor just to make sure no one was there. Then I continued up, my heart beating faster with every step. The air temperature warmed and the dank smell dissipated the higher I climbed.

Breathe, concentrate, keep your focus on the target.

My arms were tired, and my legs burned from the stairs. I took a moment to compose myself and slow my heart rate before I made the final steps to the point where I could see the room above.

There was a stifled cry. I peered up through the railings to locate the noise, my head shielded by metal rails.

My mom was sitting in a chair at the center of the round room. Her hands were bound behind her, and there was gray tape across her mouth. Two men stood in front of her with their backs to me, speaking in whispers. I recognized the small man as Filthy number five—Stanley Violet. Which meant the other one had to be Silver.

The dimly lit room appeared to be some kind of emergency antechamber with a cylindrical ceiling at least a hundred feet high. All the way up the walls I saw scaffolding and rungs of balconies for the different floors. Each floor was lit by small red lights. But on the main floor before me, there was vast empty space. No rigs, no machinery, no cover—except for the ring of shadows from the second floor scaffolding around the perimeter.

I bobbed my head back down and texted Sergeant Mathews:

She's in the westernmost area of the white building, center of the island. At least 2 levels down. I'm about to move in. Wait for my call.

I put away the phone, eager to finally see the man who had destroyed everything and everyone I ever loved.

The urge for revenge boiled inside of me. Dark, rolling, and spilling over with hatred.

I was so close to saving my mom, getting justice for my dad, and perhaps even proving Liam's innocence. It didn't matter that Sammy wasn't here yet.

If I shot Silver now, I could explain it all. Mathews would back me up, and when Sammy got here, his crime scene photos would, too.

How lucky was I to have found him just standing with his back to me, whispering tactics with Filthy Five *number five* and totally unaware of my location?

I slid the gun out onto the floor to steady myself. I only had one chance. I closed my left eye and focused down the barrel of the revolver toward the target. My finger itched to shoot. Just as I began to put pressure on the heavy trigger, he turned toward my mom and I finally saw Silver's face.

It wasn't him.

Or it didn't look like him.

At least not the "him" in the surveillance picture Liam brought me. This guy was clean-shaven and much older than I expected. The picture Liam showed me of the guy at the art fair had that silver-fox beard thing going on. Sure, he could have shaved, but he couldn't have aged twenty years. Now that I was looking, this guy also had weird posture, like he was seventy years old.

But if this wasn't Silver, where was he? And who was this?

"Hello, Ruby," said a voice from below. I almost pulled the trigger in surprise, but it was aimed in the wrong direction. "Put the weapon back in your holster."

Really? Not hand it over or kick it twenty feet away?

The man was only a few steps below me on the spiral staircase, his face hidden. I recognized his voice from the phone call. Silver.

"You may need it in a few minutes," he continued in that low, gravelly voice.

Of course, he still wanted me to kill. I thought about pretending to put my gun away and then turning it on him for a quick shot, but I wasn't ready for my first bullet wound. He'd stop me—not kill me. I knew that by now he wanted me alive in order to kill Violet, but he'd defend himself if I forced him to. I couldn't be impatient or hot-headed if I wanted to save my mom. I had to let it play out and take the chance when it presented itself.

"Listen, I know you think my mom's a bad person." I started to negotiate. "You don't have to convince me of that fact, but—"

"Shhh," he hushed me, using his gun to push me up the stairs. "There's plenty to say, but not just yet."

CHAPTER 29

I holstered my gun inside my hoodie like he asked and climbed slowly up the metal stairs. Each step I took sounded like the clicking of the tracks on a roller coaster as it climbed its way up to the big drop. The roller coaster came to a pause as I stepped out into clear sight of my mom and the two men. My mom's eyes widened with horror when she saw me, and she began jerking against the plastic ties binding her to the chair. One of her wrists was wrapped in bloodied white gauze.

The two men moved closer to her, as though they were protecting her from me. Like the way two lions would stand over their nice zebra dinner.

Who was the guy standing next to Violet?

I knew Silver was still behind me with a gun, but nothing prepared me for the moment he placed his hand at the small of my back to guide me toward the group. It was as if the roller coaster finally lurched forward from its pause on the precipice, making my stomach drop as the plunge took my breath away.

When I turned to face him, I found—Detective Martinez.

No, it couldn't be. Martinez was dead. Shot. Burned. How could he be standing here wearing a tactical helmet and the smuggest smile I'd ever seen?

"But I saw you bleeding." I talked myself through the memories. "From under your vest—"

"Blood bags, Ruby."

"But your arm was ripped open where your tattoo used to be." His arm was covered now, but the way he was using it showed no signs of serious damage.

"I had to make sure they found my blood on you or the boy. Plus, I'd been meaning to get it removed anyway." He glowered. "The man I got it with no longer has his, either."

My dad.

"But they found your body in the fire!"

"They found *a* body, Ruby. Someone in the coroner's office owed me one."

"I don't understand . . . Liam . . . why—?"

"You will." He motioned for me to keep moving toward the two other men and my mom. "We don't have much time."

"Time for what?" I asked, obeying his order while fighting for a sense of reality.

"I know you called in a SWAT team," he said evenly, no longer using the low whisper from the phone call. No wonder I hadn't recognized his voice. He'd been disguising it.

I turned to see his rage at my disobedience, but the anger wasn't there. He wasn't surprised by my decision. He'd known I wouldn't blindly follow his directions.

"I expected nothing different," he said, motioning for me to move forward. "But perhaps the good ol' boys in SWAT will remember to watch out for the more *explosive* parts of this building."

Oh no, he'd booby-trapped it. My instincts raged to obliterate this sadistic piece of scum.

I was almost to my mom when he stopped me, and the four of us stood in a misshapen circle around my mom's chair. She looked so helpless, so afraid.

"I believe some introductions are in order," he said, moving away from me and standing halfway between me, my mom, a very nervous-looking Violet, and the mystery man. I kept trying to make eye contact with Violet, but he looked terrified.

"As you all know, my name is Detective Martinez, deceased," he said with a very un-deceased smirk on his face. "To my right is Mr. Viktor Gulav. On the left, Mr. Stanley Violet, the last man standing on Ruby's little list. Then last, but certainly not least among us, we have District Attorney Jane Rose." He stepped closer to her and ripped the tape off. A piercing scream echoed off the cement walls around us. I flinched at the terror and rage in her cry.

"Are you done?" he asked squarely.

"What more do you want from me?" she shrieked. "I've already given you all of Jack's life insurance money. You said if I gave it to you you'd—"

"That I'd leave you alone?" He walked several feet away, stopping under the shadow of an overhang. Without the flickering flame inside the open incinerator grate next to him, I wouldn't have been able to see his evil grin. "Come on, Jane. You know me better than that by now."

"Then what do you want?" she yelled.

"Let's start with the truth."

My mom's eyes pivoted to me. She obviously knew what he was talking about.

"What truth?" I asked her. "What truth?" I asked him.

He never took his eyes off her, like he was waiting for her to answer first.

"OK, fine, I'll start with some truth," he said, unfolding his arms, gun still in hand. "You both already know Mr. Violet here. But you may not remember Mr. Viktor Gulav. Let me refresh your memory. Mr. G here is a skilled thief, arsonist, and international sex-trade and drug dealer."

I looked over to the small man, expecting him to be offended at this description. Instead, he couldn't have puffed out his bony old chest any farther.

"His services have been quite helpful in my little endeavor. His connections and legwork came in handy when it came time to place the various men in position for Ruby to discover. He was released from prison last year. Took a two-year plea deal, copping to three counts of aggravated assault. Does any of this sound familiar, D. A. Rose?"

My mom closed her eyes. Giving out weak plea deals was an everyday occurrence for her.

"Two years," he repeated. "Does that sound right for someone you know is responsible for thousands of rapes, hundreds of deaths? Yet you put him back on the street like it was nothing. Justifying your failures with sound bites like, 'Sometimes justice is constrained by the law.' All while you and King Jack sat on your thrones, accusing me of corruption."

Silence.

Meanwhile, Mr. Gulav's mouth was opening and shutting like a carp's, like he was searching for the right words to get him out of this situation. Like he was only just now realizing he'd been set up by Martinez. He took his black beanie and put it over his heart. He knew something bad was coming.

"Well, let's just say that I'm no longer *constrained* by the law—or by my old friend Jack, who relentlessly accused me of working with the likes of Mr. G and had become dangerously close to proving it." Martinez raised his weapon in the direction of my mom, Violet, and Gulav.

"No, wait!" Gulav shouted with his hands up. "I thought we had a deal! What about the big payout? What about the shipment?"

"Oh, the shipment will arrive per our agreement," Martinez said, slowly lacing his hands around the gun, enjoying every second of this production. "You just won't be there to profit from it. Good-bye and good riddance, Mr. Gulav."

Two deafening shots blasted, and Gulav went flying backward. Then blood. So much blood. It began gushing out near my mother's feet.

My mom released another guttural scream. I wished she would stop doing that. It wouldn't get us out of here alive.

Or, then again, maybe it would. I examined the shadows of the large room and the overhangs of the decks above us. Maybe Sammy was here by now; maybe he'd gotten that murder on camera; maybe SWAT's sharpshooter could take out Martinez from above.

I couldn't see any signs of infiltration yet. On top of that, Martinez had positioned himself under the scaffolding. Even if sharpshooters were up there, they'd have no shot on Martinez. Not only was he protected, but I could vaguely see a door behind him.

Martinez was holding the smoking gun casually at his side. He showed no remorse, no shame. He was entirely unaffected by the taking of a human life.

In the space of a few seconds, my mind spun away from me. The adrenaline kicked in, and I couldn't feel my own body. I was floating above this horror story, numb from the panic filling the room.

I still believed I had a chance to stop the madness. Not just for me, but also for the people I loved. For my good and loving father, for my selfish and manipulative mother, for Liam, for his family. But somehow Martinez had outsmarted me at every turn.

I'd let them all down. I could see where this situation was going. He was going to give Violet a choice: Kill my mom—or be killed.

Which really meant he was giving me a choice: Kill Violet or let him kill my mom, in which case I'd be responsible for another death. Ruby Rose, the serial killer.

I really hoped Violet was wearing the vest I'd given him. A sympathy pang for him caught me by surprise. He was a despicable human being, but still very human. And he was afraid.

"Don't pretend to feel sorry for this waste of flesh, Ruby." Martinez's voice kicked me in the gut. "Remember who he is, what he's done. What he's capable of doing again."

I remembered. Violet's greatest pleasure was other people's pain.

So why didn't Martinez just shoot Violet himself if he thought it was right? Why make me do it? Nothing about this made sense to me.

"Now, before it's Ruby's turn to pull the trigger, there's some more truth to be told," Martinez said, removing a glove from his right hand and an arm guard off his forearm. Without losing focus, he threw both into the fire pit next to him. Was he trying to dispose of any traces of gunshot residue? He wore another glove underneath the first. The extent of this man's planning blew my mind. "It's time to come clean, Jane," he said, turning to my mom.

She raised her head and gave him the scariest look I'd ever seen in my life. Her mascara had run and the demon glare she gave him made *me* flinch. "Don't do this," she said quietly. "For her sake. Don't."

"It's not up to you anymore. Both you and Jack had your chances, and you failed to take them. I warned you it would come to this." Martinez wasn't intimidated. His lowered eyes matched her defiant stare. "If you don't tell her, I will."

"I've been trying to tell her. I was going to, but—"

"What are you talking about?" I yelled. "Mom, what are you not telling me?"

"Ruby, I know I haven't been the perfect mother," she said, leaning toward me. "I know I've let you down, but don't let him—"

"Enough!" he roared. "We don't have time for this." Martinez showed his first signs of losing composure. If he was expecting my mom to cooperate, he was mistaken.

"Mr. Violet, you know what to do," he said with eyes narrowed on my mom.

Mr. Violet didn't look like he knew what to do at all. He stared back at Martinez with a pleading expression.

"*Now.*"

Violet scurried to a table behind him and came back to my mom's side with a long knife. "I don't want to do this," he whimpered, wiping his snotty nose on his sleeve.

"What, it's OK to do it to innocent young women, but not to the guilty?" Martinez asked. "You know your choices, Violet." Martinez raised his weapon and aimed it right at the shaking predator.

I couldn't stand it.

I started to move toward my mom, but Martinez stopped me with a bullet sparking on the floor six inches from my foot. "Ruby, be patient. You need to hear this."

"Really?" I screamed, finally pulling out my gun. "You want me to be *patient* while you let this freak with no soul murder my mom right in front of me?"

"She's not your *mom*," he responded. "She's a thief, a liar, and a murderer."

"No, Ruby, don't believe him," my mother called out.

"Mr. Violet!" Martinez called out louder.

Violet placed the knife against my mom's neck without conviction. A sliver of blood formed and ran down her skin. She screamed again.

"Stop!" I cried over all the madness, shooting ten feet to the left of Violet to scare him away. He cowered aside. "Do *not* hurt her."

I spoke directly to her. "Mom, just tell me what he's talking about."

"I'm your mother, Ruby, I'll always be your mother. I love you." She sobbed through the pain. Though her bloody neck wound was unnerving, it wasn't fatal. Not yet. "I was never any good at showing it. But I swear, Ruby, you're everything to me. I couldn't bear to burden you—"

"Lies, Jane," Martinez interrupted. "Even faced with your own death you continue to lie."

"I tried to tell her, but I couldn't. I never wanted to hurt her—"

"No, you lie for your own sake," he argued. "You lie to protect yourself. Through Jack's death, your *daughter's* misery, you deny the truth. The truth that you caused the death of Ruby's real mother."

My breath caught.

"No, that's not true!" Mom reared her head.

"The truth that you stole Ruby and pretended she was your own," he continued.

"It was all legal," she said through labored breaths.

Everything was going fuzzy around the edges. *I could see the bloody court papers in my mind.*

"The truth that you never even wanted her, but you thought you could save your failed marriage and repent for the sin of our affair if you adopted the perfect baby girl."

"That's a lie!" she seethed.

"The truth that when the baby's biological father learned he had a daughter and demanded to know his child, you denied him at every turn."

I was the baby from the petition.

A chill went through me as the "truth" froze me to the spot.

I could barely process the ramifications of his words, let alone the obvious pleasure he had in telling this twisted story.

"He abandoned her—"

"He didn't know she existed," he said icily. "I told you he'd come back for her!"

"Her mother was mentally unstable, she couldn't take care of her," Jane said. "As the appointed Guardian, I did what I had to do. Nothing more, nothing less. Ruby was in danger. The biological father was gone! It wasn't my fault that Kelly overdosed."

My lungs struggled for air. An invisible fog was suffocating me.

"You pressured her and lied in your reports. You wanted Ruby from day one, and you did what you had to do to get her," Martinez said.

"Ruby was found alone in a crib when the neighbors called the paramedics! That woman overdosed right in front of her own two-year-old child. What more evidence do you need that she was being neglected? I saved Ruby!"

"Oh, Jane," he said, "your argument would be so much more convincing if that wasn't the night you had Kelly Bracken served with the petition to terminate her rights."

The world started spinning. Their words kept flowing into my consciousness, but I was being taken back to the crib, to apartment 4E, to the sound of a woman's weak sobs just out of reach, to the feel of the bars, to being trapped and abandoned. The sketch at the fair, the picture on the wall of the burning apartment. It was her—my real mother. I could almost see her face in my mind. Not how it looked in the pictures, but in real life. Her long blonde hair, her soft skin, her smile.

Somewhere deep inside, I'd been holding on to her.

"I gave Ruby a good home," Jane Rose said. "An education, resources, things she never would have had in those seedy University apartments. Things I never had but fought to earn."

"That wasn't your call to make. She belonged with her mother— her *true* mother."

"No, she belonged with us! Jack and I tried for years to do it the right way. We paid thousands of dollars in fertility treatments for a baby of our own. That woman had a fling for a few months, and oop-sie, here was an unwanted pregnancy. Kelly didn't want a child. She wanted sorority parties, football games, and hot young military men to screw on the side."

"Do you really want to talk about women who like to screw on the side?" he warned.

"I'm not the only one at fault here! Kelly contributed to the prob-lem, and though I know postpartum depression must be truly hor-rendous," she said with all the sarcasm she could muster, "it didn't give her an excuse to neglect her own baby. I wasn't the one who called Child Protective Services on her. It was her neighbors, her friends."

"Odds are, she would have figured it out without your threats and sabotage. *You* backed her into a corner. *You* are responsible for her death. *You* are responsible for too many crimes to count. Not only in letting criminals walk free because of your incompetence, laziness, and selfish pursuit of political power, but in neglecting, abusing, and turning your back on everyone you've purported to love. You manipulated Kelly, just like you manipulate everyone else in your life. Like you manipulated Jack into marrying you, like you manipulated me into an affair that was going nowhere, like you manipulated the voters into electing you—and last, but certainly not least, like you *attempted* to manipulate Ruby's biological father to keep him away from her. So tell me, Jane, what did that get you?" His smirk widened as his voice rose. "Besides a dead husband?"

The world spun cobwebs of imaginary fog around me, cocooning me too tightly, constricting me too forcefully. I couldn't breathe. Was he saying that my father killed Jack—the man I'd always believed was my dad?

Suddenly, he put his hand to an ear-comm unit as if he was getting an urgent message.

"Speak of the devil," Martinez said with an evil edge. "It appears that the man of the hour, Commander Damon Silver, has returned to Grissom Island—and he is most eager to finish what he started the day he killed Sergeant Jack Rose."

D for devil.

D for D. S.

D for Damon Silver.

D for Dad . . .

CHAPTER 30

I felt him before I saw him.

He entered from the door behind Martinez, also wearing a bulletproof vest. I recognized his groomed salt-and-pepper-stubbled beard from the school surveillance photo. But unlike Martinez, he wasn't wearing a helmet or neck guard, and he didn't seem to be armed.

"Welcome, Commander Silver," Martinez said, his body turned midway between the door and us, his weapon firmly pointed at my heart. "You're a little behind schedule, but at least the introductions have already been made. All except for the formal father-daughter one, of course."

Silver said nothing. He just moved slowly to the edge of the scaffolding's cover where a dash of light spread across his face.

The way he looked at me didn't speak of anger or insanity. He was calm, steady, and maybe even—sad? His strikingly pale eyes creased around the edges, like he was trying to communicate something without words. He wasn't the raging lunatic I'd imagined him to be. Instead, his expression and body language spoke of submission and surrender. He even looked a little beat up.

Why did it feel like I knew him? Like his face, his manner, his eyes, were familiar to me. Not just because of that grainy surveillance picture, or because we were biologically connected—but because I'd seen him face-to-face. I couldn't find the exact memories, but I was sure they were there.

"I'm sorry, Ruby," he said quietly. "This isn't how I dreamed of meeting you." A heartbreaking grimace formed on his face. Why was he pretending to be decent? Where was his sadistic grin? If his strategy was to sedate me with his gentle approach—good cop/bad cop style with Martinez—it was working. I didn't know what to make of him.

"Very touching," Martinez mocked. "But we must be getting down to business. Despite the fact that Jane might *want* to kill herself after witnessing this little family reunion, I doubt she will. Mr. Violet will have to do it for her." Martinez shifted his weapon in Violet's direction. "Are you ready to make your choice, Mr. Violet?"

"Wait, no!" I raised my weapon, not knowing in which direction to point. "Don't do this." I looked at Martinez with his self-satisfied smirk. "Why? Because my mom chose my dad over you? Because he turned you in to Internal Affairs? Tell me why you're doing this!" The barrel of my gun settled on him.

"Oh, Ruby, do I really need to spell it out for you?"

"Martinez, no—" Silver started.

"If it weren't for *you*, Ruby," he said, "none of this would have *ever* happened. Jack would've walked away from the marriage, Jane and I could've been happy together, and Damon Silver never would have been involved. There would've been no need for all these lies, all these cover-ups, all these deaths!"

My jaw dropped. He blamed *me* for all of this?

"This is not her fault, James!" my mom shouted. It was the first time I'd heard her, or anyone, use his first name. He flinched.

"I warned you about her, Jane!" he shouted back. "That she'd grow up to be just like her father."

What was that supposed to mean? What did he know about my real father?

"I told you she was damaged goods," Martinez continued. "That one day she'd snap!"

"But you made her do it," my mom said, coming to my defense. "You set her up! You entrapped her!"

"Are you serious? I didn't make her follow those five criminals." He was incensed that she was standing up for me. "She did that all on her own. I watched her go out several times a week to stalk one of her Filthy Five." *He followed me?* "I've seen the thick criminal profiles she spent weeks and months accumulating." *He broke into my house and went through my things?* "Do you think that's normal behavior for a seventeen-year-old girl, Jane? No, she happily killed all those men. Don't be deceived by her innocent act. Jack knew exactly what she was, and he did his best with her—to rein her in and teach her about his holier-than-thou 'shoreline' crap." *That's what the training was about?* "But it didn't work with me when Jack and I were partners, and it didn't work with Ruby. As soon as Jack was gone, she became who she was always going to be—a sociopath. I told you that no amount of money or therapy would change that. And you still chose *this* over me!" Martinez was losing his mind, and control of his voice.

"Do me one last favor, Jane. Take a good look in Ruby's eyes when she pulls the trigger on you . . . or Violet. You'll see what she really is—the greatest mistake of your life!" He stopped waving his gun around to point it directly at my heart.

"Martinez, remember our agreement," Silver warned—except he held no weapon to back himself up.

"Of course, our agreement. How could I forget?" Martinez dialed it back a notch, suddenly amused by something. "Tell me, Ruby, did you know the blood of an assassin runs through your veins? Did you know your little hobby of taking out bad guys is a shared pastime of dear-old biological dad here?"

Silver pursed his lips as if he thought about defending himself but decided not to.

"Of course you didn't," Martinez continued. "But now that you do, I bet it comes as very little surprise. Sure, Silver's kills have always been sanctioned by clandestine government agencies, but he certainly knows how to get the job done. Which was shocking and troublesome information to the young Jack and Jane, who so quickly fell in love with you—or fell in love with the *idea* of you saving their marriage. But this information is probably a little less shocking to *you* at this point. Especially since Silver was your accomplice, in terms of cleanup and concealment detail."

I thought back to what cleanup Martinez could be referring to.

Target 2—Taking out the two human traffickers at the warehouse to save my friends and me.

Target 3—Cleaning up the boat and removing Father Michael's body from the water so I couldn't go to the police.

Target 4—The fire. A memory came to me, and I almost gasped when I realized that Silver had carried me out. My eyes strained to see his eyes once more. For a moment, I swore I could still see the flames in them.

"Tell us, Silver, have you kept track of how many dozens of lives you've taken in your career in special ops? I mean sure, Jack and I both had our share of forced shootings, but you—"

"This has gone far enough." Silver cut off Martinez.

"OK, I get it. You won't accept the trophy for the most accomplished killer of us all. But perhaps the District Attorney will." Martinez's eyes roamed all over her. "No, she's never actually pulled a trigger or set a fire. But as Ruby now knows, all it takes is a choice. And Jane Rose's choices have led to more deaths than we can even estimate. Make no mistake, Jane Rose will lie and cheat to get what she wants, no matter how many people are destroyed in the process."

Mom sat in her defendant's chair in the center of the room, while Martinez stood to prosecute her with the facts. Violet was the bailiff keeping her in place. Silver was a coconspirator—though I wasn't sure about that. They seemed to be at odds, and yet they shared some kind of agreement.

Which left me to be what?

The judge?

The jury?

The defense?

Or the victim.

"You have a choice, Ruby," Martinez said, his voice low, watching me. "Either you kill her, or Mr. Violet does. Who deserves to die more? A man who rapes and murders innocent women? Or a woman who destroys the lives of those she purports to love and protect?"

Really? Did he honestly believe I would shoot my own mother? Even if she wasn't my biological mother?

I would never do that.

He had to know it just as well as I did.

No, he didn't expect me to kill her. I had to remind myself that what he was truly trying to do was get me to kill Violet. Just like one through four. He started with me saving a stranger, then my best friend and boyfriend, then myself, then Dr. T, and now my mom— each time raising the stakes to ensure that I made the kill. He wanted to prove to my mom that I was the coldhearted murderer he thought I was—the psycho he'd predicted I'd be.

I turned back to her. Her tears were flowing freely.

"You can't do this," she said to me. "It's murder. It's wrong."

"Mr. Violet!" Martinez barked. "This is your last chance!"

Violet jumped, looked down at the knife in his hand and then up at me, as if asking for my help. This was it. I had to make my decision.

I raised my gun in the general direction of Violet, aiming somewhere to the right of him, when an echoing noise from above caught my attention.

It started out as a single clank of metal against metal. Then it rose to a chorus of tappings all around the decks of scaffolding. Through my veil of shock and rising panic, I couldn't work out what was causing it.

Then it dawned on me—coins. I ran my fingers over the engraved metal of my dad's Challenge Coin in my pocket. His SWAT team had finally moved in. Sergeant Mathews, his unit, and maybe Sammy were up there somewhere with their sights set on me. They were challenging me to do the right thing. And perhaps warning Martinez.

But they didn't know what was going on! Did they think I was really going to kill my mom or Violet? They wouldn't let me. They'd shoot me first—a shot to disable me. Lowering my weapon, I looked over to Damon Silver. He'd retreated further into the shadows, along with Martinez. SWAT would have no shot on either of them. Hell, SWAT wouldn't even be able to confirm that they were ever here. They'd escape the same way Silver had the night he killed my . . . other dad.

Wait. Silver killed my dad? I didn't understand. Jack Rose didn't *deserve* to die. I was just starting to get the feeling that maybe Silver cared for me. That he was trying to protect me. Not only from Martinez's setups, but maybe even from Martinez himself. So why would he take away someone I loved?

I turned to him in a flash of anger. "You didn't have to kill him!" I yelled into the shadows where I could see Silver, but anyone above couldn't.

"You don't understand," Silver replied quietly. "It's complicated."

I pointed my gun at him. "*Un*complicate it, then!"

"OK, Ruby, OK." He paused as if waiting for Martinez to stop him. But he didn't. "I've wanted to meet you for a long time. I don't expect you to remember this, but when you were three I came for you. I knocked on the door and Jane . . . your mother . . . answered with you in her arms." His deep voice cracked.

My head swiveled to Jane to assess if he was telling the truth. She didn't deny it.

"She warned me to stay away and shut the door in my face," Silver continued. "I tried for years to change her mind—or Jack's mind. The last thing I wanted was to hurt you or disrupt your life. Especially considering my line of work. So I let it go. But I never let *you* go. I watched you grow up from a distance. There were times when I could've reached out to you. So many times. Especially after the LeMarq shooting when I started following you to try to figure out what was going on. Then when I saw that sketch the day of your high school art fair—that's when I knew that someone was trying to dig up the past."

Could this be true? Was this why I felt like I knew him already? He'd been so near for so long and I had no idea.

"So you're claiming that it wasn't *you* digging up the past?" I asked, not sure I could believe him. "Why would you have risked coming into my school?"

"I received a letter asking me to come. *Supposedly* from you."

"What?" I asked, utterly confused. "I didn't send you a letter. I didn't even know you existed!"

"I knew it wasn't from you, but I had to go anyway." He paused and rolled his neck as if hesitating in his explanation—or his lies. "Almost a year ago, I received a very similar letter—on the same exact stationery—from Jack Rose, saying that he wanted to talk. When I read the suggestion that we meet here on Grissom, I became suspicious but figured I could handle it. You had just turned sixteen, and I thought it was finally time for us to meet. But when I got here, it was a trap."

"So you blew him to pieces?" My furious voice bounced off the walls.

"No, Ruby, I thought Jack set the trap for *me*. That he chose Grissom Island because one of his ex-Marine buddies is head of security here. I figured that when he realized I wasn't going to fall into his ambush, he called in his SWAT team and told them that I'd set the explosives. I escaped, and I honestly didn't know what had happened. At the time, I thought he must've made a mistake or tried to disengage one of his own traps to protect his men and . . . something had gone wrong." Silver sounded miserable. And he could no longer yell his side of the story over the clamor of the tapping.

I didn't understand this guy.

Why would my dad have messed with something he wasn't experienced with? He didn't work with explosives. Something wasn't adding up. If only he had trusted me enough to tell me what was going on. If only he'd told me the truth.

And then I realized what Mathews was really trying to say with the tapping. It's what Jack himself would have said if he were here—to remember to stand for honor, courage, and commitment. Jack Rose taught me everything I knew. Whatever his flaws were, or whatever mistakes he made, he shouldn't have died because of this madness. He was only trying to keep his family together. Prevent all this from happening. And he couldn't. Despite how hard he tried to prepare me for it, even his worst fears couldn't have dreamed up this particular nightmare.

"That's it!" Martinez cut back in. "It's time to make your choice. You shoot Mr. Violet or your mother. Ten, nine . . ."

There had to be another choice. If I took a Hail Mary shot at Martinez, he'd stop me—either with a bullet at my mom or me. Plus he had a bulletproof vest on. Same with Silver.

If I took the shot on Violet, SWAT would stop me.

If I chose to do nothing, Violet would be forced to act, bullets would fly, and Jane could get hurt all the same.

The problem was that all these choices produced the same unacceptable results:

- Both Martinez and Silver would escape—just like Silver did the last time SWAT had the place surrounded. Neither of these guys would ever surrender with their hands in the air.

This entire thing had been meticulously planned. I had no confidence that SWAT or Mathews could stop them.

- Liam would go to prison for the rest of his life if Jane decided telling the truth was still a major inconvenience. I couldn't allow myself to put all my trust in her again. If there was one thing I knew for sure now, it was that the woman could justify anything.

"Eight, seven . . ."

I stood frozen when the answer came to me. There was only one choice left.

I chose Jack Rose, and what he stood for. He might have made mistakes, but he willingly put his life on the line to protect me.

And he had died trying.

"Six, five . . ."

I looked back to Violet, who was slowly making his move toward my mom.

"Four, three . . ."

"Remember what I told you?" I asked Violet in a voice loud enough for him to hear through the noise. "You need to protect yourself. You have to fight."

He shook his head, not understanding what I meant.

"Ruby, stay where you are," Silver called out. "Don't move any closer to him."

"You'll have to stop me!" I screamed and ran full speed into Violet's waiting blade.

Too many things happened at once. I felt a searing pain in my side, my mother screamed, several gunshots tore open Violet's arm, and I collapsed. I looked down to find Violet's knife sticking up from my torso, like one of those Halloween costumes with the rubber knife poking out. I fought for consciousness through the blurring pain and blood loss to make sure everyone was still alive.

Violet was hurt, whimpering in the fetal position, but conscious. He'd be OK. He'd been shot before.

Mom was screaming like she was on fire, but she'd live.

Martinez had either retreated farther into the shadows or was gone. I figured as much. He got the revenge that he came for—our family was destroyed. He didn't necessarily want me or Jane dead, but he wanted us ruined, and most of all, he wanted Jane to regret raising me.

But I was relying on the opposite to be true for Silver. The man who was my real father surely wouldn't turn his back on me now. I scanned the room for movement, for a shadow to tell me he was still here. When I realized that he was gone, the throbbing in my side doubled—like a self-inflicted punishment.

He was supposed to save me. Just as he had at the warehouse and the apartment fire. It was my last hope of forcing him into a weakened position so that SWAT could disarm him. Then they'd take him into custody, force him to account for his involvement in all the crimes, and testify that Martinez wasn't even dead. Maybe he'd even have a way to lure Martinez back to be held accountable as well. Liam would be released. I would be exonerated for my part in the deaths.

I was so delusional. Silver was long gone.

An explosion went off, but from what direction I had no idea. An alarm sounded soon after. Through the ringing in my ears and the swirling emergency lights all around me, I heard shouting and commotion.

I blinked over and over to fight the pain and fear washing me away. I'd managed to get stabbed in possibly the most excruciating (but safest) location on my core. So long as no one pulled this thing out and the paramedics got here in time, I'd probably be OK, too. As long as the whole island didn't explode.

But it was all for nothing since the two men behind all of this had fled once again—

Suddenly, someone had me by the shoulders and was pulling me under the protected cover of shadows and scaffolding—it was

Silver, using me as a cover, knowing SWAT wouldn't shoot me. Relief fought with misery for control of my emotions.

I had him. Even if it was for the briefest of moments.

He picked me up like a baby and carried me gently to a concealed corner near his escape door. I pinched my eyes shut in agony as he set me down, partially on the ground, partially on his lap.

I fought to steady my breathing before I dared reopen my eyes and look at him. A wave of shock overcame me when his pale-gray eyes met mine. The *same* pale-gray eyes as mine. He was suffering, too. Neither of us spoke for the seconds that stretched on like hours. And he held me like I once held little Riley Bentley after LeMarq sliced into her. In my delirious pain, my mind took me back to the bloody warehouse when Riley and I were the only two people in the world. Silver stared down at me—just like I'd done with Riley—and he silently willed me to hold on, to be brave, to know everything would be OK.

I no longer saw a man that I feared. I saw a man who cared about me and wanted me to live.

"You look so much like her." There were tears in his eyes. At first I thought he meant Riley Bentley, until he said, "Except for the eyes."

He meant my mother.

In the short distance between our beating hearts, I felt a connection. In another time, under another set of circumstances, I knew things could have been very different for us.

"I'm sorry, Ruby, but I have to go," he said. "You're going to be OK. The paramedics will be here any minute, and . . ." He looked up to see whether any SWAT units had made it down to this level yet. We both heard the boots coming, and he was already getting up. He could be out that door in seconds, never to be seen again.

I couldn't let him slip away now. "Wait," I whispered. "You can't go."

He had to be held accountable for my father Jack Rose's death. He had to provide testimony on Martinez to let Liam go.

"I'm sorry," he said, now crouching over me. "For Jack, for everything. But you have to understand, those SWAT men will kill me without blinking. Martinez set me up. I now realize that *he's* the explosives guy. The traps lining this place today are the same ones I saw the day I came here to talk to Jack. Martinez made me believe that Jack had set the traps for me, while making Jack think I set the traps for him. And it had to be Martinez who set up the meeting— not Jack. He wants this to end badly for me so I can't track him down and make him pay."

So Silver didn't kill Jack.

"If that's true," I said, "then I'll protect you. But you can't leave. Not again." Not like when I was a baby, and not like the nights when I killed those men and was left wondering why.

I steadied the gun still clutched in my hand and slid it into his lower abdomen. The same place where I'd been stabbed and where his bulletproof vest ended. I took a hard look into those eyes that tore me apart. If I had to, I'd hurt him, but this ended now.

"Please, Ruby, you don't understand," he begged. If he really wanted to, he could've overpowered me.

"You're right. I don't understand any of this," I said. "And I certainly don't understand what kind of agreement you had with a psychotic madman like Martinez."

"Ruby," he said calmly. "Our *agreement* was that if I promised to come alone and unarmed today, then he wouldn't kill you. I'd give my life for you. To keep you safe. You have no idea how long I've wanted to be a part of your life. In my mind, you've always been that little girl at the door. The one I could see, but never hold. And it kills me to be holding you like this. Everything I did was to protect you—from pain, from prosecution, from Martinez. And I'm sorry that I failed."

Could he be telling the truth? He wasn't working *with* Martinez but *against* him? Was he lying?

"Then don't make me shoot you," I whispered through the pain.

And as SWAT rushed in and tore Silver away from me, I screamed at them not to hurt him. But as they violently forced him to the ground with his hands behind his back, I realized—

We'd all lost.

CHAPTER 31

"Are you sure this is OK?" I asked Dr. T as she pulled into her garage.

"Stop asking that," she said, smiling.

"I've never been homeless before." I took my seatbelt off and grimaced at the pain. The eleven stitches in my left side were still tender, and the Ibuprofen wasn't helping like I'd hoped. I'd told myself I was only allowed to take the good stuff for a week. When they discharged me, I wanted to be "clean." I wanted to see the world with fresh eyes. The holiday season had come and gone, a new year had begun, and I needed a fresh start.

"You are *not* homeless," Dr. T responded, unclicking her seatbelt. "Just having a little vacation until you and your mom find a way to"—she paused—"figure things out."

Her gentle eyes told me it was OK if it took a while.

She got out of her sports car and ran around to help me out.

"I'll get your bags out of the car later," she said, taking me by the elbow to walk me into her place. "I want you to see the view first."

"I never knew you lived on the beach, Dr. T. How come you never told me?"

"You never asked," she said.

She led me up a flight of stairs into the living room of her modest-sized beach house with an anything-but-modest view. The sun was setting on the Pacific Coast. Her large panoramic windows looked like murals hung on the wall. Either there were still drugs in my veins or this was the most beautiful sunset ever. The horizon was lit up with pumpkin oranges, electric pinks, and, of course, ruby reds. Like it was created just for me. Like someone was saying, "Isn't it good to still be alive?"

"Yes," I said out loud.

"What?" Dr. T said.

"Nothing," I said, a little embarrassed that she'd heard me talking to myself. "I'm just glad to be here."

She put one arm around me, and we watched the seagulls fly past the deck outside. In the distance I could see the surfers lining up near the Pier. I wondered if Liam had been out there since his release. They'd let him go two days after the Grissom Island Showdown, as Sammy called it. Turned out, Sammy got several shots and even a little grainy footage of me getting myself stabbed as SWAT moved in. It had looped endlessly on every news channel for a week. Which was why I had sworn off television forever.

Sammy sent me a nice card at the hospital, thanking me for the tip-off and the millions he'd make on the images. He even promised to cut me in on the deal, but I didn't want his money. What I really wanted was for him to take it and bribe all the other paparazzi to leave me alone.

Just to get here, we had to sneak out using the hospital's private drive. No one knew about Dr. T, where she lived, or what had happened to her. But there was no going home for me—at least not for a while. Partly because the cameras had permanently camped out there, and also because my mother and I weren't feeling especially close at the moment. She didn't love my unwillingness to come home, and I didn't love the time it had taken to drop all charges against Liam for Detective Martinez's murder. The dude wasn't even dead! Martinez was probably living off my dad's money on some Caribbean island. But the public didn't know that. Not yet, anyway.

It appeared that the current news cycle's headlining theory for the ever-growing list of murders was "revenge against the high-profile Rose Family." And if it wasn't for my "self-sacrifice," the District Attorney would've been the last and ultimate victim of "Viktor Gulav's rage against justice." The authorities would neither confirm nor deny the media's speculation that I'd killed the notorious criminal in order to save my mother. There was no mention of Silver or Martinez.

Once the CIA moved in and took over the case, they threatened us all with prosecution if we revealed any facts about the ongoing investigation, including details concerning Martinez's involvement. A cruel twist, considering how badly I wanted the world to know that it was James Martinez who killed my father, put my loved ones in danger, tortured my mother, and destroyed my soul. All in the name of exacting his vengeance—on his old partner who was going to expose his corruption, his ex-lover who'd jilted him, and a child whose very existence had supposedly ruined his chance at happiness.

When the Special Agent assigned to my case came to see me, he curtly told me not to worry, assuring me that he'd personally see Martinez face justice. I might have been able to overlook his 1960s-style slicked-back hair, outdated male condescension, and habitual use of the term *sweetie*—but only if in the very same breath he hadn't used a line right out of my mom's old playbook: "Sometimes you have to let a smaller fish go in order to catch the bigger fish." I wanted to tell him exactly where to go with his fish analogies.

As long as we cooperated and kept our guppy mouths shut, we could earn our immunity. Which sealed the deal for me. That's when I learned the real truth about Damon Silver. Special Agent Fishy opened up about Commander Silver—Medal of Honor recipient in the United States Army, Green Beret Special Forces Commander, and inactive operative in an elite Special Operations Group of the CIA. A real hero. "One of our bravest."

Who still hadn't come to talk to me, even though he'd been released almost immediately after his arrest.

Whatever. It was complicated—I got that. And somehow I knew I'd see Silver again.

As for Jane, after she was discharged from the hospital, her points in the polls skyrocketed. Her campaign managers knew exactly how to swing it—"Jane Rose the Survivor." But the media turned on her when their questions continued to go unanswered. Bill Brandon took advantage of her weakened position and began accusing her of scandal and cover-ups.

There were still several months until Election Day, but Brandon was quickly becoming the favorite. And I was glad. Not just because he'd be tough on violent offenders and make his slain daughter proud, but because I still held on to a shred of hope that maybe I'd get my mom back. That maybe if the fight for her campaign and career were over, she'd start fighting for me.

"Ruby, I need to apologize to you." Dr. T's voice pulled me back to the present. Her arm still held me close to her side, her eyes still centered on the bright horizon before us. She swallowed hard. "I needed some space after the fire. I had nothing to give, and I was scared that if I didn't distance myself from you, I'd be in more danger. I knew Martinez was trouble from the first moment you brought him up in our post-LeMarq sessions. I just didn't know it was leading to this—"

"What? You knew about Martinez?" I asked, pulling away.

"Ruby, let me finish. I'm sorry for keeping the truth from you all these years."

"What truth have you hidden?" I flinched at the pain in my side. It felt like one sentence had just reopened the wound.

"Ruby, please, give me a chance to explain—"

"So that's why he wrote the word 'SECRETS' over your mouth? Because you were in on it all along?" I backed away from her.

"Don't do that," she cautioned, using The Tone. "Don't spin away. Ruby, I was only trying to protect you."

I rubbed my forehead. "Why does everyone keep using that excuse? They didn't tell me squat because they were only trying to *protect* me. Does this gash in my side look like I've been protected?"

She closed the gap between us. "I always felt it wasn't my place to tell you the truth, or at least what little truth I knew. Your parents—Jack and Jane that is—were my clients before you came into their lives. I was their marital counselor. Your mother had been trying for years to get pregnant, and it was causing problems in the marriage. I knew about the affair. Your dad was hurt, but patient. He coped with alcohol. She coped by throwing herself into her work in the Family Court."

She stopped to gauge my distress barometer, like she knew I needed to take a breath before hearing more.

"She talked about you a lot in our sessions. She told me how neglected you were by your real mother. Unchanged diapers, left in your crib for hours. But most of all, how special you were despite it all. How you reached out to her. How you hugged her tight and wouldn't let go."

I'd never stopped reaching out to her. I still didn't want to let go.

"You had her heart, Ruby. Whatever she did to get you, I have no idea. I knew it was suspicious. I knew it was questionable. But I never doubted the way she felt about you. She may not have shown it well with her career taking up so much of her time, but I know she loves you."

I wanted to believe her. The memories of that special bond Jane and I used to share still lingered. The way she held me, the way she sang to me, the way we used to be a family. But after all she had done, part of me just wanted to hate her.

"I don't want to talk about her anymore." I shook my head and wiped my eyes. I couldn't hear any more of this. Maybe one day I'd forgive her, but not today. "I need some rest. No more truth for now."

"Ah, so you remember what I told you? God offers to every soul the choice between truth and repose. I tried to warn you."

It was true. She had tried to warn me. I hugged her, and she tightened in surprise, but I didn't let go. I wasn't sure words could convey my gratitude for what she'd gone through for me. But as she softened and squeezed me back, it seemed like she felt it.

"Well, I have just one more bit of truth to tell you before we rest," she said, pulling away with a mischievous smile.

"I don't know if I can handle one more bit, Dr. T." I slumped into a love seat and clenched my teeth at the pain in my side. "I'm exhausted. Can't you just bring whatever it is to me?" I made those wide kitty-cat eyes.

"Nope." She gently raised me by my elbow. "Just trust me."

"Fine, but this had better be good," I said, following her outside to the deck stairs leading to the roof. "And there'd better not be any dead bodies."

Looking sad, she shook her head at me.

The salty sea air replaced the tinge of black oil from Grissom Island lingering inside me. The crashing waves drowned out the residue of noise in my mind. It was like Dr. T was using her voodoo powers to heal me.

I reached the top, and she finally let go. Behind the licking flames of the rooftop fire pit, two familiar faces lit up, and my heart skipped a beat.

The boppy curls of my best friend, Alana, and the shaggy locks of the only guy who'd ever broken into my heart, Liam. My eyes fluttered between the two. I couldn't decide who I wanted to run to first—if I could run without my side tearing open.

"It's cool," Liam said, sliding his hand behind Alana's back. As though chivalry wasn't dead, he nudged her forward. "I can wait."

Alana came toward me with her arms outstretched. But now that I was looking, she had a small box in her hands—chocolate.

"Thought you might need some of this," she said grinning. "It's not your fancy European stuff, just some of my mom's chocolate-covered macadamias from her stash."

"It's perfect," I said. And it was.

Both of us took a deep breath, bracing ourselves for the lame girlie cry about being happy it was over. Instead, our eyes seemed to have a whole conversation on their own. She said she was proud of me. I said I couldn't have done it without her. She said she missed me. I said I missed her more.

"Thanks for coming—you have no idea how much this means to me." I squeezed her. "You guys are all I've got now." I didn't even know if I'd ever see Big Black or Gladys and the Pips again. Which I told myself was OK since I had the three of them. *People* not *things*. Dr. T would be so proud.

"That's not true." Alana pulled away. "You have millions of supporters."

"What are you talking about?" I asked.

"Rubik's Cube, the whole nation is on your side. Sure, you have your share of critics, those far-right fanatics and the hard-left lunatics . . . but you're kind of the Taylor Swift of justice. At least that's what this week's issue of *Teen People* is calling you. You should see the Santa Claus–sized bag of your fan mail downstairs."

"Fan mail?" That didn't sound right.

"Yeah, I'm thinking about dropping out of school and becoming your publicist or manager or something. So far, every single major news channel has contacted me to get an interview with you. I don't know why they called me, exactly. Maybe because they found out we were besties . . . but, Ruby, you wouldn't believe how much money they're offering."

I glanced at Liam. He'd crossed his arms over his chest and was smiling at Alana's energy. I honestly didn't want to hear what the nation thought of me. Or how much money they'd give me to continue keeping the truth from them. I just wanted to go to him.

"Come on, Alana," Dr. T said, suddenly at her side. "Let's go get that bag of fan mail sorted and let Liam and Ruby have a minute, shall we?"

Alana's excitement bubble popped. "Sure, of course," she said, taking in the way Liam and I were looking at each other. "Awkward," she chimed to Dr. T.

"We'll be downstairs when you're ready to come down," Dr. T said, leading the way.

As soon as Alana's head dipped out of sight, I turned back to Liam, and suddenly he was holding me, pulling me in, like we couldn't get close enough.

I nestled my head in his chest and let his heartbeat tell me what I wanted to know as I breathed in his minty-fresh smell. I hoped I didn't smell like hospitals or death.

"Ruby Rose, I missed you," he whispered in my ear. The goose bumps fired across my neck, with every hair standing at attention under his warm breath.

"I don't even know what to say." I pulled away to look up into his eyes. "I'm so sorry for dragging you into all of this . . . and for what my mom did to you . . . and the media—"

"Stop," he said. "I don't want to talk about any of that right now. All I want to do is be with you." He held my face in his hands.

"Does your mom know you're here? Tug and Christian must hate my guts."

"She knows I'm here," he said with a wide smile. "And no, they think you're amazing. They don't know the whole story, of course, but they know enough to understand how brave you were."

"The whole story, huh?" The thought of explaining the whole story made me tired. "Where do I start?" I asked.

"I already know everything," he replied. "I pried it out of Dr. Teresa. I hope you don't mind that she broke that doctor-patient confidentiality thing . . . and that whole CIA-sworn-to-secrecy thing. She thought I deserved to know that the guy I supposedly killed is the one who did all of this to you."

"No, of course I don't mind. I think sacrificing your life to save hers and mine earned you a pass to know what really happened," I assured him.

He smiled. "Anyway, she told me about your bio mom and bio dad. Man, I didn't see that coming."

"Me neither." Though my split-personality theory made a lot more sense now. Martinez set me up to hurt me, and Damon cleaned up behind us to protect me.

Talking about it drained me all over again. It must've shown all over my face, because Liam grabbed my hand and led me to a lounge chair by the fire.

"Come on, you need to rest," he said, helping me lie down. He grabbed a blanket, slid in behind me, and covered our bodies chin to toe. The ocean breeze swirled around us, making the fire bend.

The horizon was no longer brilliant shades of primary colors. Instead, it had faded to a navy blue, with wisps of silver outlining the clouds. Again, it felt like someone was creating this piece of art just for me. Here was *my* silver lining: Liam.

As we watched the last traces of light dip into the dark waters, I twisted to face him. The only thing that could have made Liam's lips any more tempting was if they were dipped in chocolate.

"Don't hurt yourself, Ruby, you just got here," he said, slipping one arm under my head for support and the other one around me. Was it me, or did the flames in the pit just kick their intensity up a notch? The heat between us burned just as strong, as if the anger, sadness, fear, and pain over the last year had culminated in one bonfire of emotion. Maybe the feel of his abs through his shirt had something to do with my rising temperature as well.

I wanted to say something to him. Express how grateful I was for him sticking by me, never turning on me when it might have gotten him out of jail earlier. The words weren't forming in my mouth.

Liam moved his face toward mine. Tingly anticipation tiptoed across every inch of my skin. I lingered in the moment, recalling all the times I'd fantasized about these breathless seconds. We were too close, and it was too dark to see his eyes, but I was pretty sure they were closed and waiting. Patiently hanging on for Ruby Rose's petals to bloom.

Whatever light was left in the twilit sky disappeared as I closed my eyes to give in to him. I clutched his shaggy hair and kissed him in a way I didn't know was possible. It felt like every time our lips moved against each other, a chunk of the wall I'd worked my whole life to build crumbled into the sea.

I grasped the back of his neck with my fingers and pressed my hips against his. My head arched backward when he moved his mouth down my neck and around my ear. Pulling my V-neck shirt off my shoulder slightly, he kissed my exposed skin. Every part of my body tingled—I'd never been touched like this before. I felt like my heart was going to burst out of my chest.

"I think I'm about to tear a stitch," I said breathlessly.

"Are you serious?" he asked.

"Maybe, if I could just keep my heart from beating a million times a minute, it wouldn't feel like my side is going to explode."

"Right," he said apologetically. "I should have thought of that. Sorry—"

"You don't have to apologize for anything." I took a few measured breaths. I unlocked my legs from his, and snuggled up to his side. I felt the Challenge Coin in my pocket. "Let's just lie here for a while. You can stay, right?"

"I'm not going anywhere," he said, brushing my cheek with his lips.

The moon was directly above us. The few stars brave enough to shine through the smog, cloud cover, and city lights of the Los Angeles coastline twinkled down on us. I glanced at the foaming whitewash on the beach and imagined my dad, Jack Rose, coming in from one of his twilight surfing sessions by the Pier. I could almost see him in his wet suit and with his longboard securely tucked under his arm.

I closed my eyes to better picture him. He stopped, shook out his wet hair, and smiled down at the little girl running up to his side— the little girl I used to be.

A few tears escaped from my shuttered eyes, and when I opened them again, the image was gone.

Dad had made it to his shoreline.

And he'd never stop guiding me toward mine.

The wind picked up a little, reminding me that Martinez and other dangers still loomed out there. But instead of baring myself to its power, I dipped under the covers and breathed in Liam's fresh scent until I fell asleep in his arms.

ACKNOWLEDGMENTS

I am especially grateful to the following people, who helped turn my dreams of publication into a reality:

To Courtney Miller and the entire team at Amazon Children's Publishing, whose brilliance has blown me away. To Marianna Baer, whose editorial guidance and knowledge of the cost of shoes has saved me much embarrassment. I am honored to work with such a supportive and innovative group of people.

To Sarah Davies, who let me persuade her to plant me—and Ruby Rose—in her Greenhouse, where we always belonged. She is, quite simply, my dream agent.

To Erin Summerill and Peggy Eddleman, my two writing partners and best friends, who've read all the crap I've ever written and still like me. Or at least pretend to really well.

To Sarah Donovan for being there from the start. To Emily King for keeping me from quitting. To Elana Johnson for guiding the way. To Angie Cothran, Chantele Sedgwick, Katie Dodge, Ruth Josse, Kim Krey, and Taffy Lovell for all the critiques, fun writing retreats, and never-ending support.

To my parents, who call me "spirited" when they really mean "sassy," and who are never surprised by my success. To my siblings,

John, Michelle, Julie, Chris, and Jeff, who have put up with me all these years . . . and hardly ever call me a B-word to my face.

To my Mr. Humphries, my best friend and leading man, for letting me be "yellow" and reminding me not to let "my dreams be dreams." Je t'aime. Finally, to my kids, who are Brave, Brilliant, Bigtime, and Beautiful. In that order. You are my favorite B-words.

ABOUT THE AUTHOR

Jessie Humphries was born and raised in Las Vegas, Nevada. She received a BA from San Diego State University, where she cultivated her love of the beach, then lived in France, where she cultivated her weakness for shoes, and finally earned a law degree from University of Nevada, Las Vegas, where she cultivated her interest in justice. Appropriately, her debut novel, *Killing Ruby Rose*, is a thriller about vigilante justice set in sunny Southern California with a shoe-obsessed protagonist. Jessie currently writes and practices law in Las Vegas, where she lives with her husband and children.